THE WEIGHT OF GOODBYE

ELIZA GRAHAM

Storm
PUBLISHING

Ebook ISBN: 978-1-80508-592-8
Paperback ISBN: 978-1-80508-593-5

Cover design: Arcangel, Shutterstock
Cover images: Sarah Whittaker

Published by Storm Publishing.
For further information, visit:
www.stormpublishing.co

ALSO BY ELIZA GRAHAM

Jeanette Day
1938–2024

PROLOGUE

JULY, 1940

Nervousness and anticipation rippled through the streets as Lucia cycled east from Chelsea to Westminster, passing the Houses of Parliament and turning right onto the bridge. Pedestrians laughed with one another, but jerkily, hands clenched. The German invasion could happen any day. Lucia felt the now-familiar taste of bile in her mouth. How was it possible that tanks might roll through these streets, that marching invaders might shoot at people as they had in France? Invasion was the stuff of nightmares and Pathé news reels at the cinema. Now it was threatening London as it had Warsaw at the beginning of the war, then Oslo and Brussels and Paris.

Lucia half expected Westminster Bridge to be blocked off – perhaps to prevent the Germans crossing the Thames from the south and capturing Parliament? It was open and the policeman directing traffic didn't give her a second glance as she signalled right. He didn't have much to do, as private vehicles were vanishing from the roads and there weren't as many military trucks around as she'd imagined. Maybe they'd all headed to the coast to repel the invaders. War was such a peculiar mixture of the terrifying and – to be frank – the dull.

She'd also wondered whether Big Ben would be silenced as it had been during the last war, but it seemed nobody thought the chimes would help the German planes orientate themselves if they came. *When* they came? What would happen then? Images of her mother and Della screaming, as soldiers burst into the house, made Lucia's stomach turn over. She forced the pictures out of her mind. Her mother and sister weren't under threat today. It was a sunny July day in London and people were buying ice creams and strolling across parks, just like they always did.

Towards her came a mother pushing a baby in a perambulator, saying something to the child, her face taut. Life was unpredictable, the woman was justified in worrying.

Lucia told herself to look away and propped the bicycle up against the parapet just as the clock started to chime. Twelve noon. Her eyes scanned each end of the bridge, examining each pedestrian. Nobody coming – it was just as it had been last Tuesday. She bowed her head, contemplating the murky water below. Her mind was hundreds of miles and another lifetime away from Westminster, London, the torpedo-shaped silver barrage balloons floating serenely above, the sandbags piled against key buildings, and the country awaiting invasion.

She turned towards the clockface and waited the fifteen minutes. When Big Ben struck the quarter hour, she looked around to be sure nobody was coming. Not today, not this Tuesday. No surprise, really. She'd come back next week and wait again. She wasn't going to let the spinning feeling inside her overwhelm her, not now.

Lucia mounted her bicycle and headed back to the Westminster side. The nervous anticipation had been replaced by dull acceptance. She was here in London for the duration now, cut off from her old life. The current would take her where it willed. Someone fired a gun outside the boarded-up front of the Palace of Westminster. A middle-aged woman gasped and clutched at the girl walking with her. 'Just a car backfiring,' the girl said. 'Keep your knickers on, Ma.'

Lucia smiled, but the perspiration trickled down her neck. A newspaper boy was pushing papers into the hands of those walking past.

GERMANS LAND IN CHANNEL ISLES.

The Channel Islands were where you went for seaside holidays, shrimping and bicycle rides. How could it be possible for them to be the new front line in the war? The sense of calm she'd felt briefly looking down at the Thames had vanished. She pushed down harder on the pedals. The exertion dampened down the emotion inside her but couldn't completely exorcise it.

It was her birthday tomorrow. She'd be twenty-one. An adult. She had a new name prepared to adopt officially. The change would be made by deed poll and she had the form ready to sign. Once she was officially Lucie Black, she'd find war work of some kind, she didn't care what. Those she'd hidden from wouldn't find her. Not unless she wanted to find them herself.

She felt a shiver run up her spine and couldn't tell if it was excitement or fear or both.

PART ONE

ONE

By some fluke Lucia, Della and Effie were all free for tea on the afternoon of Millennium Day: 1st January, 2000. Husbands and partners were invited too, but in such a manner Effie hoped it was clear they weren't required at her house in Barnes, in west London. Her own husband was planning a long dog walk, followed by a visit to the pub.

Sometimes Effie wished she could revert to being uncomplicatedly German and say the occasion was for the three women only, though perhaps it would make it easier for Lucia and Della to meet again with a male buffer? Of course the two Blake sisters saw one another at family gatherings, happy and sad, but the three of them hadn't been alone together for so long. It was time. Apart from anything, Effie really did need the Blakes to decide what to do with the box of their family possessions she'd recently discovered again up in the attic. Effie wasn't a Blake, wasn't a blood relation at all, even though it was easy to forget this most of the time.

Effie had only found herself custodian to these possessions because, when Claybourne Manor, the Blakes' country house,

had been sold and she'd helped Lucia and Della clear it, she'd
been the one who'd gone down into the cellar one last time, just
to check nothing had been left behind. She'd found the small
dark wooden chest, resting in a shadowy corner behind some
old wine crates. She'd run upstairs and out into the drive, only
to see Lucia and Della already driving away from the old family
house in their separate cars. She'd taken the chest home and for
decades it had sat in Effie's attic, hidden behind suitcases and
boxes.

Millennium Day felt a very particular date on which to ask
them to look at the contents, but it was hard to juggle family
engagements and the fact that Della now lived in Oxford. Effie's
house sale completion was coming up fast. The Blake sisters
needed time away from family with no distractions, otherwise
the chest would still not be emptied and decisions made on its
contents. It would have to follow Effie to the far smaller house
she was moving to. She'd carried the chest downstairs, but had
only had a cursory glance inside it, feeling it wasn't really for
her to empty it without the other two.

Anyway, it would be good to mark the first day of the new
millennium together, just the three of them. Effie mightn't be a
blood relation to the Blake women, but she was a sister in all
other ways. Their sisterhood had been forged at a time of fire
and destruction, so it was iron-clad.

She paced up and down the spacious sitting room, rearranging the tea table, taking off the Christmas cactus and then
replacing it. It was still technically Christmas, and anyway, the
millennium should be marked. At times during the war, it had
seemed too impossible to imagine being alive at this future date.
Besides, you couldn't rely on people going on in good health,
even though the three of them seemed to have been fortunate so
far. Lucia was eighty now, Della seventy-six, Effie the baby of
the trio at sixty-five. She might be the youngest, but she'd

become the intermediary between the sisters, who rarely seemed to see one another without Effie. Strange, when you looked at the old Blake family photographs and saw a proud four-year-old Lucia in a white linen smock holding newborn Della in her lap and beaming at the camera.

'Della can be tricky with Lucia, can't she?' Effie's daughter had observed this morning on a New Year's Day telephone call.

'Not tricky as much as, well... withdrawn. She's always fine with me.'

'Still? That's a long grudge she's held against Lucia.'

'Not a grudge, not exactly.' Effie's sigh had lasted a long time. Explaining the relationship between the Blake sisters was never simple. 'They just don't seem able to get beyond the past.'

'Yet you did,' her daughter said. 'And yours was arguably harder.'

It was true. Her childhood had been hard. Loving, most of it, but also terrifying and full of loss. Effie had made her peace with it. Did it come down to personality? Early family experience? Plain good luck? Or not having a sister to fall out with in the first place? 'I owe Lucia such a lot. She's eighty. She should be spending more time with her sister. I know Lucia would like that. They were very close as children.'

'And opening up this chest will bring them together?'

'I've only seen the top contents. But perhaps they'll be a talking point, if that's the right expression.'

'What was in it?'

'A few old books and toys. Pieces of what looks like their father's uniform, from the First World War.'

Yet again, Effie eyed the furniture in the sitting room and wondered how it would all fit into the new house. Their downsizing meant clearing the loft and selling or passing on children's toys, old tents and toboggans. She had few handed-down family possessions to assess. Sometimes this fact made her feel rootless. But having no need to make hard choices was perhaps a blessing.

Effie heard footsteps coming carefully up the frosty path. Lucia. As always, she felt the rush of warmth and security Lucia's arrival always generated. Della's company was always a tonic, invigorating, fun, but Effie couldn't help this instinctive pull towards the elder sister.

She opened the door to find Lucia as elegantly dressed as ever, even though her clothes were deceptively unexceptional for a woman of eighty on a January afternoon. When you looked more closely, you noted the way her outfits were cut or made from fabrics elevating them into something finer. 'Della's not here yet?'

'You're the first.' She took Lucia's cashmere coat and hung it up, musing on the words she'd just spoken. Hadn't Lucia always been the first? For all her gentleness and quick smile, there was a gravitas to Lucia, a dignity. Effie's children had secretly nick-named her The Queen when they were younger.

Lucia looked around at the Christmas decorations in the sitting room, her eye for good design probably noting lapses in taste or symmetry that Effie would have missed, but she smiled as she sat down on the sofa. 'It's just perfect, Eff. You must have had a lovely Christmas here.' They chatted briefly about family reunions over the season, children and grandchildren. 'You'll miss this house, won't you?'

'It holds fond memories, but we don't need all the bedrooms now and we aren't moving far.' The smaller house was only a few streets away, closer to both the river and the common.

The front garden gate creaked. 'Della.' Lucia's face lost some of its composure.

'It will all be fine.' As she went out to welcome Della, Effie found herself mentally crossing her fingers. Della could only have been Lucia's sister. She was taller than Lucia, her face more classically beautiful, if less striking, but you could tell from the way she dressed that appearances had never mattered as much to Della. Her clothes were flattering, well cut and good quality, but those of a woman who forced herself to go shopping two or three times a year to refresh her professional wardrobe and then forgot about it.

Lucia stood up when her little sister came into the room. 'Della.' They embraced briefly, kissing cheeks. 'Happy New Millennium, darling.'

She looked nervous. People often did in Della's company, given she was the recently retired principal of an Oxford college and, before that, a renowned economics editor on the *Financial Times* at a time when a position like this wasn't often given to a woman.

Yet for Lucia, Della would probably always be the little sister she'd abandoned for years and had never completely found her way back to.

As Effie boiled the kettle, she heard the sisters chatting about Christmas celebrations and Millennium Eve parties and expressing relief about the non-collapse of western civilisation as digital clocks across the planet reset themselves. As she brought in the teapot, both sisters sat up straight.

'It's good to spend a few hours together at a time when we're not calming brides' nerves or preoccupied with catering for large gatherings,' Lucia said, passing cups around. 'Just enjoying one another's company on a special day.'

'The millennium was a bit of an excuse to get you both here,' Effie said. 'Actually, more than an excuse as we can't really take it with us when we move.'

'What do you mean?' Della gave her the same piercing stare she might once have given a junior reporter. 'Can't take what?'

Effie reached forward and slid the dark wooden chest out from beside the sofa. 'This.'

'What is it?' Lucia asked.

'It came from Claybourne Manor. I found it when we did a last look around before we sold.'

'You've had it for twenty years?' Della must have realised she sounded accusatory. 'Sorry, Eff, I don't mean to sound as if I think you've secreted it here.'

'No, it's fine. It's been up in our attic, forgotten about. I just didn't know what you'd want to do with the contents.'

'What are they?'

'Old books and toys, a uniform tunic that must have been your father's. I didn't look much further.' Effie opened the lid. She pushed back the tea things on the coffee table to make room for what was inside the chest.

'I remember these books.' Lucia pulled them out. 'Look, Della. Mama read them to us.' She gave her sister a sidelong look. 'You actually wanted to give them away during the war and I objected.'

Della laughed, kneeling down on the carpet beside the trunk with a flexibility that was testament to decades of yoga. 'An old doll. Not sure what we'll do with her, but we'll take it all home and sort it out, Eff.'

'Oh.' Lucia stopped.

'What is it?' Effie hoped it wasn't signs of damage, moths, or, worse, mice. Mice still generated complicated and irrational feelings inside her, even so long after the war. Anyway, the chest showed no signs of rodent damage.

Della looked at the dark tunic her sister was pulling out. 'I hoped we'd never have to see that particular garment again,' she said.

'It's part of his uniform, isn't it? From the First World War?' It was what Effie had assumed, but from Della's expression it seemed it was something else.

'No,' Lucia said slowly. 'It's not from his time in the trenches. It's from a less honourable episode altogether.'

Now she was looking at the tunic more closely too, Effie

knew exactly what it was. The past seeped through into the new millennium. The Blake sisters sat rigid, the cheer gone from the room, the Christmas cactus mocking them with its bright colour. They could never escape. Effie should never have brought down this old chest for them to empty. She should have left it out in the street for someone to steal.

TWO

OCTOBER, 1936

Lucia could always tell when her father came into the room, even without looking. It was as though the atoms in the air rearranged themselves, fizzing from the energy he emitted.

She turned round to look at him. Her father had never looked as dazzling as he was this afternoon in his uniform – he was like someone from a film in his belted military-style tunic, breeches and riding boots. The puppy jumped off her lap and ran up to him to lick his boots and try again to chew the toes. 'No you don't, little fellow.' Very gently Papa lifted Jacko up and placed him back in his basket. 'No toothmarks on the leather, if you don't mind.'

'Jacko has Papa smitten,' Lucia said. She'd been away for the best part of a year, doing a few terms at a Swiss finishing school and then travelling in France and Italy. The puppy was new. Her little sister, Della, got up to sit by the basket, stroking Jacko and looking up at their father, eyes slightly narrowed, as if she was still worried about toothmarks on his boots.

He was looking at his Longines watch. 'We should be going.' He gave an apologetic smile at his younger daughter.

'Sorry, Della, sweetheart, but you are a little on the young side for this afternoon's outing.'

'Lucia's only seventeen and you're letting her go.' Della pouted.

'And Lucia's too young, really,' Mama said. 'It's a political rally, not an outing to the seaside.' Lucia blinked. It was unlike their mother to offer an opposing view to Papa.

'Lucia's just about old enough to hear our arguments and form her own opinions.' Papa was examining his reflection in the mirror, making sure his breeches had no dog hairs on them and straightening his belt. 'And there'll be plenty of policemen and our own protection, of course.' They'd had to bring in their own men, often veterans of the trenches, to protect their speakers from hooligans. Papa said it was ridiculous, a sign of how far their political opponents would go to stop free expression. And Britain was supposed to be a democracy.

'I would liked to have seen the police horses,' Della said sadly. She was crazy about all kinds of animals, especially dogs and horses.

'Next time, darling.' He swept her and Mama into his arms. He was so openly affectionate compared with most men of his class. Papa turned to Lucia. 'You've got a coat, Lucia? It's an open car and it will be chilly by late afternoon.'

She took her jacket and beret – the latter black, of course – from the maid, Harding, who looked almost as excited as she was. 'Good luck, Sir Cassian, sir. We'll be looking forward to seeing you on the news films.'

'The cameras won't be terribly interested in me, but thank you, Harding.' He twinkled at her and she blushed. Papa was the kind of person who made people turn pink and look down at the floor. This always tickled Lucia's sense of humour – her father, having this effect on people.

'Should I bring my camera?' she asked. He looked at her now and shook his head gently.

'You're on show, darling. Not in the audience. People will be photographing you, not the other way around. My beautiful daughter, who's such a credit to me.'

On show. It made her feel almost anxious. Oh well, the Leica camera would have to stay at home today. Shame. The large crowds would have been exciting to film, and the black uniforms and boots in stark contrast to the paler stone of the buildings would have made great photos.

The sports car had pulled up outside the house, its sleek black outline catching the attention of passers-by, even though this was a fashionable Belgravia address and people were used to fine cars and smartly dressed neighbours. The chauffeur, appropriately dressed, opened the rear passenger door for Lucia with a smile. She waved at Mama and Della. Della was still sulking but managed a wave in return. She'd have come round by tonight, and there'd be other rallies. At least they both had Saturday night at home together, Della having been granted an exeat from boarding school.

Papa got into the front passenger seat, beside the driver. They drove east, past Victoria and St James's and into Westminster. Outside the Houses of Parliament, people of all sorts were already waving placards and shouting. Papa shook his head. 'Some of those poor people are so misguided. We still have work to do on our communications and messages.'

'You often say you blame the schools for not teaching people the basics, Papa.'

He smiled at her fondly. 'What's the use of algebra and composition lessons if you can't see that you're being gulled by those in power?'

'People are definitely deceived and whipped up by the usual crew, sir,' the chauffeur said. 'And those who should know better but don't. University folk. Left-wing intelligentsia. They'll have us at war again if they can.'

'Isn't that always the way?' Papa said. 'Those with the

greatest advantages in life, often the most educated by tradi-
tional standards, are the ones who throw the less unfortunate to
the dogs.'

'But not you, sir.' The man spoke in low, reverential tones.

Papa had grown up in privilege: the only son of doting and
wealthy landowners who'd left him their country house and the
house in Belgravia. But years in the trenches in the Great War
had opened his eyes to what life was like for those who didn't
share his advantages. He'd come home a changed man, he said.
He wanted to improve the lives of working people. And he
never wanted to see young men sent to war again. Lucia usually
switched off when Papa talked politics, and she'd been abroad
for almost a year, out of touch with the arguments. Not that she
was terribly interested, truth be told. But a rally like this was
something else.

By the Tower of London, the driver was slowing to avoid
crowds of people marching. Some of the marchers had started as
far away as Hyde Park. Their feet must be aching by now. They
were heading for the first rally point. So many people wanting a
better future, wanting things to be different for them and their
children. It was inspiring. Her father seemed to read her mind.

'Think what Britain could be, Lucia. Think of what those
men and women could do, if we unleashed the power inside
them.'

'You should be speaking this afternoon too, Papa.'

He laughed. 'Not me, darling, I'm no orator. I'm just an old
infantryman.'

'You're definitely not old!'

He could have passed for ten years younger.

He smiled. 'I just want something better for ordinary British
people.'

Yet again Lucia wondered why anyone could find anything
wrong in this aspiration, which was so reasonable. At first Papa
had been drawn to the new Labour party, but it hadn't had the

answers, he said. Socialism just didn't have the passion to push through the apathy, its followers tied themselves up in attempts to show how democratic they were. Communism had the passion, but look at the Soviet Union and you saw oppression and despair, Papa said. He drew inspiration elsewhere.

At the rally point the column of Blackshirts, one of four marching this afternoon, would stop to hear an address from Sir Oswald himself. Lucia's heart beat harder just thinking about the leader. Papa was handsome, everyone said so, but Sir Oswald was something else. He was mesmerising. And his wife, Lady Mosley, was supposed to be the most beautiful woman in England, with her classical features, luminous blue eyes and golden hair. Perhaps she'd be here this afternoon too. Sir Oswald and Lady Mosley were like a Hollywood couple, but with more substance because they weren't just acting: they were intelligent, passionate about their politics, really caring about those working people who'd been ignored by the state despite fighting and toiling for it. Papa had explained it all to Lucia.

It was frivolous to judge a movement just on the physical grace of its leaders, Lucia reminded herself. Of course fascism had its glamourous side, nobody could doubt that when they saw the film footage of the rallies in Germany. The shirts and tunics of the fascists in Britain, in part inspired by those of Mussolini, the Italian dictator, did add to the drama of their rallies. There was so much more to them than cinematic appeal, though. Sir Oswald and Papa and all the others wanted to take back control of their country, Papa said. Move it back into serving its own people, instead of those who had a financial interest in war-mongering. Parliamentary democracy meant weak, watered-down pledges. Britain needed a strong, centralised state that prioritised full employment.

Mussolini was an inspiration. But it was far more than just uniforms he'd inspired. Look at the transformation of Italy from being a messy, disordered country. At Lucia's Swiss finishing school there'd been a girl from Florence who'd praised *Il Duce,* as the Italian called him.

Someone threw something onto the pavement, where it smashed. A pot, from an upper window. A *chamber* pot, with contents, fortunately mainly liquid. Lucia felt her nose wrinkle. Just when she'd been thinking about beautiful people and good public order. How ironic. And disgusting.

'And that,' Papa said, 'tells you all you need to know about what we're dealing with. Who it is we're confronting.'

The driver muttered something.

'Brinks.' Papa's voice was stern. 'I won't have language like that used in front of women.'

'Sorry, sir. Sorry, Miss Blake. I got carried away.'

'Entirely understandable, old man.' Papa patted the chauffeur's arm. 'You're doing a grand job, driving us through this rabble.' He sounded his usual genial self, but there was a note of something harder in his voice that Lucia hadn't heard before.

On either side of the road people chanted and shouted at them. Lucia hadn't expected to experience so much aggression from the crowds. She knew that the British Union of Fascists, as the Blackshirts were more formally called, wasn't warmly regarded by left-wingers and people like the Jews, who Papa said were internationalists, not totally committed to Britain. Even so, witnessing such passion, such anger, among the protestors made her cross her arms on her lap, as though she was holding on to herself.

The first tranche of mounted police trotted in from the north as they reached Fleet Street. The horses were large and handsome, but ridden with force, used as weapons to keep the crowds on the pavements, their riders' faces like slabs of stone. She felt herself shrink into the leather seats. 'Don't let them bother you, sweetheart,' Papa told her, turning towards her as if he knew how she'd be feeling. 'It's all just sound and fury.' He waved at those who were jeering at them.

But it looked and felt like more than empty threats and noise. The car was driving more slowly now. 'We were supposed to pick up the end of Sir Oswald's cavalcade here, sir,' Brinks said. 'Not like him to run late.'

'Traffic must have been sticky with all this commotion,' Papa said.

'The timing'll go to pot, sir.'

'Sir Oswald will be here on time, don't worry, Brinks.' Papa was always good at reassuring people. 'You can rely on him.'

'Yes sir, of course we can, thank you, sir.'

'Where'd you serve?' Papa asked him. As Brinks told him where he'd been during the Great War and how he'd been the only one of his group of four friends to return, Papa nodded. He never spoke much about his own personal experience in the trenches as a young lieutenant, where he'd received a shoulder wound that still caused him pain to this very day. Sometimes his eyes would fill with tears as he recalled the terrible injuries and deaths of his men and fellow young officers. The sorrow would turn to anger at the way the servicemen had been left to find their own way in a hostile world when the war was over and everyone just wanted to forget about them. Even when they'd found work in mining and steel-making, these brave fighting-men had been terribly treated and often lost their jobs at the whim of the mine-owners, he'd told Lucia and Della. Brinks was telling Papa about his little boys, whom he'd found it hard to provide for because he'd lost his job. Men like him had been all at sea, Brinks said, desperate, before Sir Oswald had come along and given him work in the Party as a driver and security officer at rallies and meetings. And, just as importantly, given him a sense of belonging, a reason to go on.

'You're so right, Brinks. A man needs purpose,' Papa said. 'Work isn't just about earning, it's about dignity. Providing his family with food and a home. Feeling part of something greater than himself.'

If the angry people in the crowd could have heard the conversation, they'd have changed their opinions about Papa. This wasn't about hating people, it was about justice. Papa would never stand for persecuting people, he was always considerate. On one occasion, coming out of the theatre where they'd seen the pantomime after Christmas, he'd actually unwound his cashmere scarf – a present from Mama – and, together with his gloves and hat, given it to a crippled veteran of the trenches, along with a ten-shilling note.

Another missile struck the car, this time on the boot, just behind Lucia, denting the bodywork. 'I think we should turn round, sir,' Brinks said, his voice becoming less deferential. 'This isn't safe for Miss Lucia.'

'Inclined to agree.' Papa sounded resigned. 'Let's double back towards Cheapside, see if we can fan into the cavalcade along there. At least we'll still be part of the afternoon in some way, even if we miss Sir Oswald.' She could tell by the way his shoulders stiffened that he was angry about being blocked, but he wouldn't show the anger in front of the jeering crowd. She felt even tenser as she observed this.

Some of the protestors on the south side burst past the police officers trying to hold them back and swarmed towards the car. Brinks put it into reverse so quickly that Lucia's head whipped back, hurting her neck. She gasped. 'All right, darling,' Papa said calmly.

The police horses were turning towards them, riders holding batons in their hands now. People were falling back. A rider on a huge grey pulled his horse into a rear, hooves flung towards the crowd. Della might have been impressed, but these were not horses like the ones at home who liked having their noses stroked and blew gently into your hair, their breath sweet and warm. The horses fanned around the car, forming a cordon. Lucia shivered, imagining how it would feel if they were charging directly at you, prepared to crush you. Della always claimed horses wouldn't purposely knock a human over, that it was only fear or training that made them do it. Had someone trained these horses as weapons? Lucia felt dizzy thinking about it.

'Lucia.' Papa turned around to her, his voice calm. 'You see that police van over there opposite the tailors? I'm going to ask you to get out of the car now and walk towards the officers there.'

'But I can't.' She felt paralysed.

'You'll be all right, darling. Look, they're sending a constable towards us to collect you. Go with them. They'll take you home. This car is, sadly, a magnet for these scum.'

'I don't want—'

'Do as you're told.' He was already reaching back to the door handle on her side, opening the door. 'Now, Lucia.'

Mechanically, she got out of the car. The constable had already reached her. 'Come with me, miss, don't you worry, we'll look after you.'

'The little darling's running away,' a woman taunted from the crowd. 'What's wrong? Can't Papa protect you, sweetheart?'

'Don't waste time on that little poodle,' someone else yelled. 'Watch out for the police.'

The policeman on the grey horse was lashing out at someone with his baton, an older man, thin, wearing a little black cap on his head with a placard, knocking him down. The man fell into the gutter, placard falling from his hands. Lucia watched him sit up, slowly, and put a hand to his head. Blood was running down his brow, and something white dropped from his mouth. She turned back to look at her father, to ask whether this was supposed to be happening.

In the car Papa and Brinks were watching. 'He's lost his dentures,' Papa said, clearly enough for her to hear over the shouts. 'Look, they've fallen into the gutter. Wonder if he'll put them back in.' He laughed.

'He can stuff them back into his Jewish gob, excuse me, sir.'

'One of ours will be delighted to do the honours for him,' Papa said.

Brinks pointed. 'That woman over there is about to get a truncheon up her ar—'

Papa turned slightly, noticing Lucia was still in earshot. For a second, they stared at one another. She'd misheard the exchange, hadn't she? She must have done. Her father pinkened slightly and looked away. She knew she hadn't misheard. He didn't see anything wrong in what was unfolding in front of them. Perhaps Lucia was seeing it in the wrong way? She'd heard him say things before about Jewish people, that they were sharp in business, unpatriotic, didn't care about British working people. She hadn't known enough to know whether he was right or wrong. But this, his delight in the aggression, this was new to her...

'This way, miss,' the constable said. She let him take her arm and direct her across the street to the police van, still feeling as if the world had shifted on its axis. Was it ever right to be violent to people whose politics you despised? If someone you loved did something that seemed... awful, did it mean the deed itself became less awful? Perhaps her father was shaken, not thinking carefully.

Reaching the police van, she shook her head. 'Thank you, but I'm going to walk now.' She couldn't be with anyone else, she had to think this over by herself. Her heart was pounding, and she kept rewinding the image in her head because she still couldn't believe she'd seen and heard it.

'Miss, your father said—'

She waved a hand dismissively. 'I'll just head away from trouble.'

A shriek and the crash of glass from further down the street caught the attention of her escorts. 'We've got to go, something's brewing over there.' The constable's face was kindly. 'Head back west, miss, towards the City. I don't think a single young lady is in any danger if she's not carrying any banners or chanting.' He moved away.

She mumbled a thanks. Papa always liked his girls to be polite to those who helped them. Why was she still thinking about what *he* liked them to do? Papa hadn't exactly been considerate or polite about the old man and the woman with the placard, had he?

The street opening up this side was quieter, still full of people marching and chanting, with a few fistfights, but the huge police horses weren't working along here and the atmosphere was less tense. People, mostly ordinary working men and women who seemed to be a mixture of those opposing and supporting the march, glanced at her, looking puzzled when they noted her clothes. Perhaps she should have worn something less fashionable. She'd dressed to look her best for her father. The black beret probably didn't help her.

The road curved. As she rounded it, she saw it was barricaded ahead of her. She turned around. Behind her a column of people with anti-fascist banners marched in the same direction. On the other side of the barricade she spotted another group carrying placards coming towards them. *Fascism Needs YOU. King and Empire.* As they spotted the barricade they broke into a run.

'Break it down,' they shouted. 'Kick the Commies! Kick the Jews!' Lucia was trapped between the opposing sides. She couldn't squeeze around the barricade. Both groups looked furious. They weren't just men, some of them were women, some barely older than Lucia, just as fired up as their brothers. The insults were becoming more vicious. A brick flew across the barricade. A window smashed.

She tried to push herself against the wall of the shop beside her. The group ahead of her had reached the barricade and started throwing pieces of wood and metal across. Lucia ducked to avoid a brick.

Someone tugged at her arm. 'Come in here, idiot.' A young woman, roughly her age, with dark auburn hair curling out from under a red beret, pulled her inside a door, which was slammed closed behind them. Her eyes blinked in the darkness of the shuttered interior. 'You're safe in our shop,' a second, older, female voice told her from deeper inside the premises.

'It's turned violent out there. Someone like you shouldn't be out on the streets alone,' the auburn-haired girl said.

Lucia made out the shapes of counters and cupboards. Against the side wall a row of tall canvas backdrops was stacked. As her eyes adjusted to the dark, she made out a Newfoundland dog on a lawn with a spreading chestnut tree, with what looked like a Scottish Highland scene partly visible behind. Lighting rigs stood in a corner. 'This is a photography shop – I mean studio?' She and Della had been taken to a studio in Mayfair to have their portraits taken.

'Well done, Sherlock,' the girl said. 'We've been here for years, doing quite nicely, thank you, and we don't want our windows smashed.'

The girl was about her own age, slight, with dark, curious eyes. Behind her an older couple stood up from the chairs where they'd been sitting. The girl's parents? 'You're...?'

'Jewish? Yes. I should still be out there,' the girl said. 'Protecting our streets. Alongside the others.'

She'd been protecting the streets against people like Papa? Yet Papa had said they were the ones who needed protecting.

'Then I saw you in front of me, ambling your way into trouble, you complete idiot.'

'Wanda—'

'No, she needs to know, Mum. What did you think you were doing, taking a stroll on an afternoon like this?'

'I thought...' She stopped. What she'd thought didn't seem to make sense anymore. 'I was with my father.'

'Oh. What happened to him? Was it the police?' Wanda sounded sympathetic now. 'We can go out later and see if we can find out where they've taken him in. I know a few lawyers who are good at getting people out. Usually there's no charge that will stick.'

'The police won't have taken my father.'

'Was he hurt?'

'I don't... don't think so.'

'People get lost.' The older woman said. 'When the violence starts, they take a wrong turn. It happens.' She reached out and patted Lucia's arm. 'You'll find him, don't worry, my dear.'

'He's...' She swallowed. She should stay quiet from now on, wait for the turmoil to die down. If they knew who Papa was, that he was on the opposite side, these people would throw her out of the shop to take her chances on the street, from where shouts and crashes continued. Hooves skittered.

'The horses,' Wanda said. 'They throw marbles down to make them slip.'

'Oh, poor things.' The words slipped out before she could stop herself. 'Sorry.' She smiled apologetically. 'I just like animals.'

Wanda's father, she assumed he was the man sitting quietly in the corner, gave a deep laugh. 'You're not much of a political activist, are you, miss?'

'I'm trying to learn.' She mustered as much dignity as she could. It was true. She really did want to know more. From both sides. So she could see if her father's response this afternoon had been appropriate, if what he'd told them about politics was accurate. It must be. This was her father, after all. Papa didn't lie. But then she'd seen with her own eyes how he had behaved.

'Do you live above the shop?' she asked. Trying to take her mind off things. 'Are you usually safe here?

The man motioned her to one of the chairs set out in front of the counter. The four of them sat down. 'I came here as a young man, from Tsarist Russia, where there were many pogroms against Jewish people.' She noticed the slight foreign intonation beneath the East-End accent.

'We met here in London,' his wife said, with a little smile. 'Raised Wanda and Olly.'

'Olly's our son,' the husband said proudly. 'He's at Cambridge University, a very bright mathematician,' he replied. Wanda rolled her eyes.

'I grew up here,' she said. 'Helping out in the shop when I wasn't at school.'

'A good life.' Her father nodded. 'Never much money, but a community around us.'

'And we felt safe,' Wanda's mother said. 'Most of the time. Not like people in Poland and Germany. So we thought.'

'Bloody Mosley stirred it all up.'

'Wanda!' Her mother's voice made Lucia jump. 'I will not have you using language like that, in front of a guest, as well.'

Wanda shrugged and stood up, walking to pull up the blind. 'A fancy girl like her, you mean?' She was peeping out of the window. 'They've all moved on now. The barricade's still up, but you can probably climb over the top.'

'I'll go with her,' her father said. 'She doesn't know the streets like we do. If the Tube's still closed, we might need to find a cab, if there are any on the streets.'

'There is no way you're climbing over barricades, Sidney,' Wanda's mother said.

'Oh, I couldn't possibly let you do that.' Guilt was burning in Lucia's heart. 'I have to tell you something before I go. Please...' Please don't hate me, she wanted to say. They looked at her, eyebrows raised. 'My father, he's one of... well, one of them.'

Wanda's father laughed. 'A Mosleyite? As if we hadn't

guessed.' He waved at her. 'Your clothes. That beret. The cut of that jacket. My sister is a seamstress, I can recognise expensive tailoring. You're obviously not a Socialist, their women dress like dishrags.'

'I certainly do *not* dress like a dishrag,' Wanda said.

'And you're not Jewish, either, young lady, I'd have said.'

'You've been kind to me.'

'Kindness is all very well. More importantly, we've talked.' Sidney's eyes took on a sharper expression. 'But chitchat isn't enough. Not these days. Do you read the foreign news, miss?'

Lucia nodded.

'And what do you think about Herr Hitler?' He was watching her intently.

'My father says—'

'No, what do *you* think?'

'Sidney,' Wanda's mother began, 'we—'

'It's all right. You took me in, you've a right to ask me. I don't know what I think about him.'

'You don't know what you think about him.' He repeated her words back at Lucia.

'He wants to stop Bolshevism and that seems sensible. The Russian communists are brutal.'

'And anyone who can do that, or claims they can, is acceptable? No matter how extreme they are?'

'No. But my fa—' She checked herself. 'Who else will do it?'

'There's a failure of western democracies, it's true,' he said. 'But what do you think would happen if this country adopted a similar political system to Germany's?'

'They'd stand up for the ordinary man and his family. The returning soldier who's been out of work or has a terrible handicap and can't find a job.' She was parroting what she'd heard Papa saying, she knew.

'But only if the ordinary man is Anglo-Saxon.' Wanda's father folded his arms. 'We pay our taxes. We are law-abiding.

We take care of our neighbours. Why are we less deserving, miss?'

'I don't think you are less deserving.' Lucia's mouth felt dry. 'I don't think... Oh, I just don't know what to think.'

'Leave the child alone,' Wanda's mother said. 'Get her a glass of water, Wanda.' When the glass was placed in front of Lucia, she drank gratefully.

'You admit you don't know what to think. That's a start,' he said, more gently.

'Yes. Perhaps. I don't know.'

'Ah. *Perhaps.*' He folded his arms. 'The English response. *We'll need to be cautious, consider all the arguments fairly.*'

'Perhaps if people out there had been more cautious, there wouldn't have been the violence this afternoon.' The words snapped out of Lucia. She blinked, surprised at herself.

Wanda laughed. *'Touché,* Dad.' Her father laughed too.

Lucia was looking around the shop, at the backdrops and light rigs. 'May I ask... I mean you mightn't want me to, but perhaps...'

'Come to the point, child,' Wanda's mother said.

'I have a Leica camera. May I come back and buy film and other bits of equipment from you?'

He blinked. 'You want to come back to Whitechapel?'

'I'd understand if you didn't want me in your shop.'

'We're more of a studio than a supplier.' He looked amused.

'But you do sell equipment too? And film?'

'Usually to other professional photographers.' From the way he looked at her, she could see he didn't think she fell into this category.

'You don't need to put on the Lady Bountiful act,' Wanda said. 'We can survive without your patronage.'

Her father scowled at her. 'A customer's a customer. Even if she does need to read more widely.'

'Just don't bring darling daddy with you,' Wanda said.

'Come on. I'm not going to let my father escort you, he needs to rest, he was up at dawn barricading the shop against your lot.'

'They're not my...' She'd been about to distance herself from the Blackshirts but couldn't in honesty say she hadn't been keen to come to the rally. Well, things had changed a lot today. 'Thank you.'

'I'll take you to the nearest Tube station,' Wanda offered. 'They've probably reopened it now things are dying down.'

Lucia thanked the parents, shaking their hands. 'I don't know what I'd have done if it wasn't for you.'

'I don't either,' the mother said. 'What's your name, child?'

'I'm Lucia Blake,' she said.

'Sir Cassian Blake's daughter?' The three of them looked at one another.

'What?' Wanda said. 'Really?' She looked incredulous.

Lucia nodded. Were they going to start shouting at her? Express regret they'd helped her?

'Well, well, well. Certainly explains some of the gaps in your knowledge,' Sidney said, frowning. 'Miss Lucia Blake, who'd have thought you'd end up in our shop, talking to us.' He looked sharply at her. 'You didn't plan this?'

'I'm sorry, I don't understand?'

'Innocent Anglo-Saxon maiden falls into the lair of the Hebrew? Some kind of stunt?' He folded his arms in front of his chest.

His wife was making tutting noises. 'Leave the girl alone, Sidney.'

'No. I didn't plan this.'

He was still looking her over. 'No, you're not a liar, are you?'

'Certainly not.' She very much disliked being thought one. She met his gaze and after a while he nodded at her.

'Come back when you want to buy your supplies or need your Leica servicing. You won't find better prices than at Silberstein's.' He opened the shop door and looked up and down the street. 'All quiet enough now. If trains aren't running, walk her west to find a cab, Wanda.'

'Do you really like photography?' Wanda asked, as they clambered over the barricade. 'Or were you just trying to ingratiate yourself with us? I wouldn't blame you if so. My father can be a fierce debater. He used to box and sometimes he still seems to think he's in the ring.'

Lucia climbed carefully over an iron bedstead, relieved her new skirt had a generous pleat in the front. Wanda was wearing slacks, she noticed. 'I do like photography. I'm very new to it and my sister says a lot of my pictures look as if they've been taken under water.'

Wanda grabbed her as the wooden plank she was clambering over wobbled.

'Thanks.'

The Tube station was a block further on. They joined the stream of people heading in the same direction. Judging by their placards, they'd protested against the Blackshirts. They passed rows of terraced houses, punctuated with what looked like workshops and schools and shops selling battered fish. Many of the signs were written in what must be Hebrew. Lucia wanted to stop and examine them more closely, but Wanda was going out of her way to escort her, so it didn't seem polite to delay her.

Lucia found herself on Whitechapel Road, trams clanking past. 'The station's just over there. People are going in, so they must have opened the Tube up again.' Wanda pointed. Never in her life had Lucia been this far east. She prayed there'd be a clear map of the Underground. A few people milled around the entrance. 'They won't harm you.' Wanda sounded confident. 'I know some of them.' She exchanged nods and brief greetings with two of the protestors, a young man and woman, both spectacled, holding banners, probably students. 'You've got cash? You don't seem to have a bag with you.'

She'd left it in the car. Wanda saw her face.

'Here.' She reached into her jacket pocket and pulled out coins. 'My mother hates it when I carry money in my pocket, says it spoils the line of the clothes, but I don't always do what I'm told.'

Lucia could believe this. 'I'll definitely have to come back to the shop now, to pay you back.'

Wanda shrugged. 'As you like. Have you actually been on the Tube before?'

'I've been down to Kew Gardens or Richmond on the District Line. And sometimes up to Green Park on the Piccadilly Line.'

Wanda seemed to find this funny. Lucia didn't like to ask why. 'But where do you actually live, Lady Fancy?' she asked.

Lucia bristled at the name. 'I think the nearest stations are Sloane Square or Victoria.'

'That's good. You won't have to change. Just make sure you catch a westbound District Line train.'

Westbound. Lucia repeated the word to herself. God knows where she'd end up if she went eastwards by mistake. In the docks, perhaps.

'Will you be here if I come to the shop?' she asked.

'Depends when you come. I'm at school still, studying for my Upper School Certificate. Saturday's Sabbath, usually we keep it quietly at home. Except for when Mosley puts on one of his rallies. But if you come on a Thursday afternoon, I'm home earlier and I usually help out for a few hours so my mother can have a rest. I'm guessing that you're not at school, Lucia Blake?'

Clearly her ignorance earlier had betrayed the fact she'd left academic education as soon as she could. 'Just completed a few terms at finishing school in Switzerland.' She gave Wanda a sideways look. 'I expect that amuses you too.'

'It does rather. But lots of things make me laugh and you're certainly not one of the funniest I've come across.'

Lucia couldn't work out if this was positive, but Wanda's

face was friendly. 'Thursday night it is, then.' She put out a hand. Wanda shook it.

'Travel safely, Fancy.' The name wasn't used unkindly now – more with a kind of droll amusement. 'And don't tell your father where you've just been.'

At home, Mama greeted her, her normal impassivity quite dissolved with concern. 'We thought you'd been kidnapped, darling.' She clutched Lucia's arm. 'Why didn't you telephone?'

She hadn't really considered doing that, so caught up by the Silbersteins and their shop. There'd probably been a call box by the station, but she'd felt the need to scuttle underground as quickly as possible once Wanda had left her. 'By the time I found a telephone, I just wanted to get home. And I left my bag in the car when Papa told me to go with the police.'

'The police?' Della came in, wide-eyed. 'What happened? Were you roughed up by the Commies, Loo? Were the protestors awful? Did you hear, Mosley had to turn round at Tower Hill, the police said it was because of all the demonstrators.'

'I was kindly treated. By a family on... the other side.' She remembered Wanda's warning, but decided to carry on. 'A Jewish family. In Whitechapel. They were very decent and took me into their shop when there was fighting outside.' She wondered whether the Silbersteins had heard about Mosley being turned round. Wanda would be delighted.

'Goodness.' Mama's eyes opened wide. 'They took you into their shop? A Jewish family?' She made it sound like Lucia had entered the lions' enclosure at Whipsnade.

The front door opened. Papa came through into the drawing-room. 'Lucia? Thank God you're all right.' His face was white. 'I couldn't find a single policeman who could tell me where you were. What happened, darling?'

'The police had to go and deal with a disturbance, and I tried to walk away. The street grew... busy so I sheltered in a shop until it blew over.' She looked at her father, still in his black tunic. She could end the story here, miss out the parts she'd told her sister and mother. Something inside her warned her that this would be sensible, and it was what Wanda had suggested. But she went on. 'They were Jewish. They knew which side I... where I'd come from, but they helped me.'

'They'd have known that if a hair on your head was harmed, there'd be consequences.' Papa looked at her quizzically. 'Do I sense the encounter with the Jewish shopkeepers was particularly significant for you, darling?' He sounded jovial but his eyes were cool.

She wasn't going to tell her father just how it had shaken her. She shrugged. 'They were just nice people. Interesting.'

'Oh, Lucia darling. You do have such a kind heart. This would all have been a feint.'

'That's what they wondered too, whether I had set the whole thing up. They believed me, though, when I said I was just lost.'

'They were probably laughing at you.' His face darkened. 'And at me.'

Wanda had found Lucia's lack of knowledge amusing. She'd teased Lucia, but there'd been no malice.

'Mosley had to turn round.' Papa's jaw was set. 'That was bad enough. But then I lose my daughter and she has to be rescued by Jews? The newspapers would love that, wouldn't they?' A small vein tightened on the side of his face. Too late Lucia regretted not taking Wanda's advice. 'They probably passed the happy news on to their chums in the left-wing press as soon as you left.'

The mood seemed to have moved from his concern and relief at her being safe to something else. Anger that the *wrong* people had helped her?

'It'll be all over the socialist rags. You didn't think about what this would mean to me, did you, darling?' He sounded sorrowful.

'Next time I feel threatened by men throwing bricks, I'll consider your reputation before I let someone help me.' As soon as the words left her mouth, she wished them unsaid. He turned white. She had never, ever spoken to her father like that before.

His mouth tightened. 'I think you should go to your room, Lucia. You must be tired after your afternoon.'

She was the opposite of tired, feeling as though she had just woken up, no longer regretting what she'd said to him. 'I'm not a child to send upstairs.'

'In actual fact, Lucia darling, you *are* still a child. A minor. Subject to my regulation until you come of age.'

'Can't we just talk about what happened this afternoon? I'd really like to understand—'

'This isn't some kind of psycho-therapeutic session. We aren't New York or Viennese Jews indulging in endless examination of their childhoods. You clearly need to rest, Lucia.'

'But Lucia and I were going to go to the cinema this evening,' Della said. 'Mama said I could—'

Their father spun round, his face white. 'I won't have insolence from you or your sister, Della.' He looked at his watch. 'Lucia is obviously a bad influence on you. Too late for you to be sent back to school tonight. You can catch the first train from Paddington tomorrow morning. Your mother will telephone them now.'

'Don't punish Della.' This was all taking such a strange turn, his rage seemed to be spiralling. 'Papa, please, Della hasn't done anything wrong, she was just sticking up for me, don't—'

The back of his fist caught Lucia on the cheek. She fell back, almost toppling into the fireplace. Mama gasped. She caught her balance, rubbing her cheek where he'd hit it. Her body was firing messages at her that her brain couldn't understand. This really couldn't have happened. Her father hadn't just hit her. She blinked.

Papa moved towards her, arms out. 'Darling, I didn't mean that to happen. I'm so sorry.'

She flinched away from him.

Della crept into Lucia's room much later, when their parents were sleeping. 'You shouldn't have stood up for me,' she whispered. 'He was already livid, couldn't you see? And he's been so nice to you, giving you the camera and everything.'

'It just wasn't fair to send you back to school early for no reason. Punishing you because of me. Has he ever hit you, Dell?' Even asking the question made Lucia feel sick.

'No.' Della got into the bed, pulled up the sheet and blanket and curled up next to her. 'He's never laid a finger on me. I only care because I wanted to spend time with you. Soon they'll marry you off and it won't be like this anymore.'

'I don't want to be married off.'

'It might be better for you.' Della sounded sorrowful. She propped herself up on an elbow and considered her sister.

'What do you mean, Dell? You just said he doesn't hit you. Does he strike Mama?'

'Not that I've seen. But she wouldn't say, anyway.'

This was probably true. Mama would think it desperately disloyal to say anything less than positive about her husband. 'He sometimes has these... rages,' Della went on.

'I can't remember them happening before.'

'You were still at finishing school in Switzerland. It started when the puppy arrived and chewed his new riding gloves. I thought he might actually kick Jacko across the room. I picked him up just in case.'

'What?' Lucia sat up. That was why Della had got up to sit by the basket this afternoon after Jacko had chewed the boots.

She'd been guarding the dog. 'But he seems... I thought he was always so gentle with animals.'

'It's as if someone pushes a button in his head.' Della sounded as though she was going to cry. 'Ever since he became more politically active.' Lucia pulled her sister in towards her. 'He's changed. I actually want to go back to school early, Loo. Away from here. If only you were still there too, and we could be together.'

'Once you've finished your education, we will be. We'll rent a flat together, just you and me, and go to the cinema whenever we want.'

'And eat toast in our dressing gowns.'

She'd find a way of getting Della away from their father. No matter what it took, her sister should be freed from his influence.

'But it probably won't happen again,' Della said. 'He knows it scares us. He's a good person. He's just... caught up in something.'

Her father's behaviour hadn't just scared Lucia, though. Seeing him like this today had shifted something deep inside her. The whole world looked different now. The future she'd accepted as hers: the London Season, the comfortable life split between the city and Claybourne Manor, it all seemed less solid now.

'I never really considered his views very carefully,' she said. 'I suppose I've been away for a while. Politics was just something people had an interest in, like rare orchids or collecting stamps. Papa said what he believed in and because it was him, I thought it must be right. The country would be better with a strong leader, socialists were weak, internationalists didn't have our interests at heart. The British Fascists were the only ones with the backbone to say what needed doing. I just didn't think about it very much.'

Della was silent. But she hadn't fallen asleep. 'You don't have to think, Loo.'

'What do you mean?' She shifted to look at her sister. 'Of course I think.'

'You've always been the one that just... does things. Always moving around, dashing off. If you were an animal, you'd be something like... a gazelle.'

'A deer?'

'Yes. People say you're vivacious, lively. They always want to play tennis with you or ask you to dance.'

'I like doing those things. I never liked sitting still with books. That's why I didn't do as well at school as I could have done. But you, you're like a wise owl, Dell. You're always sitting there, watching us, noticing things.'

'Perhaps you need to sit and watch too.'

For the second time since lunchtime, Lucia had been rebuked for not thinking enough, not knowing enough. She felt half-ruffled and half-piqued.

'You like taking photographs. It shows you can think about... what you're seeing.' Della's voice was fading. 'Just think... more.'

PART TWO

THREE

JANUARY, 2000

'That tunic is definitely not from Papa's time in the First World War.' Della leant forward to examine the garment they'd just taken from the chest. 'That's...'

'It's Papa's Blackshirt tunic. From the rally in 1936,' Lucia said.

'I'm so sorry, I really had no idea, I—'

'This isn't your fault, Eff,' Lucia said. 'How could you possibly have known?' She touched the tunic. 'Our father was handsome in this, I have to admit. Better looking than Sir Oswald himself, I thought back then.'

'*Every woman adores a Fascist,*' Della quoted. 'Sylvia Plath,' she said, in answer to Effie's puzzled expression.

'You're not quoting the next line, though,' Lucia said. '*The boot in the face.*' She looked amused at Della's surprise. 'Yes, even I read the occasional line of poetry.' She leant forward, rifling through the chest like a child going through a Christmas stocking. 'Oh.' She pulled out a handful of pamphlets. *Yes! Fascism Fights!... Blackshirts are Working for Fascism Next Time... Blackshirts Back Mosley Because Mosley Backs Britain.*

'Blackshirts were the British fascists?' Effie asked. 'I've never really liked to ask for clarification.' Of course, she knew about the family connection, but Sir Cassian's affiliation had been something talked about in whispers. The Blakes hadn't been the only ones shunning the subject. After the war, there'd been little public appetite for discussing the home-grown variety of fascism.

'Yup. They took Mussolini as their inspiration and adopted the black shirts from his mob, I seem to remember.'

'And people took them seriously? People like your father?'

'Oh yes. Some of them were very highly connected too. Sir Oswald's wife, Diana, was a society girl, a Mitford sister. And many of their supporters were educated people.'

'You must have been too young to remember us talking about it, Effie,' Lucia said.

'Actually, I don't remember us talking about the Blackshirts very often after the war.' Della gave a little smile. 'We adopted the usual British habit of pretending difficult things were best ignored.' She pulled out a little velvet pouch and tipped out the contents – small gold pins with lightning bolts enclosed in circles on the ends fell out onto the table, glinting as the light caught them.

'Poor Mama,' Lucia said. 'I imagine she couldn't think what to do with all of this. She'd have packed it all up in the chest to deal with another time. Can you blame her?'

The sisters' eyes met. There was only sadness and understanding between them now. The Blakes had really hoped they could shut away all the sadness and regret, just as they had the artefacts and memorabilia, and it would disappear for good. Effie loved them but sometimes despaired at their tendency to swerve difficult memories and conversations.

'And this.' Della was rummaging in the chest again. She removed an armband with the same lightning-bolt insignia on it. 'At least he didn't make you wear this to that rally, Loo.'

'I'd like to say I wouldn't have worn it, but I probably didn't know any better.'

'You were Papa's girl up until that day, remember.' Della said it without malice, as though it were indisputable. 'You hadn't seen what he was like because you'd been away most of the previous year, when his... well, disease, I suppose I'd call it, had built up in him.'

'Disease?' Effie asked.

'Not necessarily a physical illness. More a kind of obsession. It was such a shock for you, Loo, seeing him like that at the rally. And then he struck you.'

'Everything I believed about our father was challenged when I saw him laughing and sneering at those people who were being beaten up.' Lucia gave a little laugh that didn't sound very amused. 'I thought of him as being, I don't know, almost knightly. The kind of man who'd protect weaker and older people.'

'And then you met Wanda, and she explained it all to you.' Della really did sound amused now.

Lucia hung her head. 'It was her father who laid into me a bit verbally. Justifiably. But Wanda thought I was a naïve little fool too. And I was.'

'You weren't a fool, though. You were my big sister and you stood up to Papa for me that evening.'

Lucia looked moved by Della's words. Effie got up to draw the curtains against the January dusk. The room felt warmer, enclosed and safe. 'How was it with you all after the rally?' she asked. 'It must have been very difficult for you as a family.'

'For the rest of the autumn and winter I just kept my head down at home,' Lucia said. 'I paid visits to Whitechapel, obviously keeping quiet about them.'

'I knew,' Della said. 'You started talking about foreign affairs and history to Mama and me. You didn't pick any of that up at finishing school.'

Lucia laughed. 'Of course you knew, Dell. Nothing ever gets past you. Anyway, Wanda and I became friends,' she explained to Effie. 'We used to meet on afternoons when Mama was having her hair done. She thought I was having my nails manicured. Often it was just Wanda lecturing me, but she was funny too. She thought I was hilarious. Even when I didn't mean to be. We argued but there was something, some connection between us.'

FOUR

JANUARY, 1937

'Try from this angle, Fancy,' Wanda said. 'Move to your left a few feet. See? You'll catch the sun trying to break through the mist on the pond.'

They were on Hampstead Heath, Lucia with her Leica. It was too cold to stand around trying to catch the ethereal light over the pond on film, so after one more attempt, they walked on. 'You know quite a bit about photography, don't you?'

'Growing up in the apartment over the studio, it was part of our childhood. My brother was keener with a camera than I am, though.'

'Still at Cambridge?'

'Thriving,' Wanda said the word with pride. 'He still takes occasional photographs and he does a lot of the design and painting of scenery for student productions.'

'Highland scenes and faithful dogs like the ones in the studio?'

Wanda's laugh broke through the mist. 'I keep telling Dad we need something new but he swears those old-fashioned scenes are the most popular backdrops.'

'My sister would certainly back him on the dog. That's what

she'd choose.' They'd had a photographic portrait taken only last summer, the two Blake daughters in white summer frocks. But they'd been pictured in the orangery at Claybourne Manor: no need for an artificial backdrop. Mama had been very pleased with it.

'Della loves animals, doesn't she?'

'I wish you could meet her. She's much cleverer than I am. She'd be better with all those essays and books you keep making me read.'

Wanda looked at her sharply. 'Is this a way of telling me you haven't finished the article I gave you on the New Deal?'

'I actually did finish it. Some of it reminded me of Papa's lot, though.'

'What?' Wanda came to a halt. 'How could you possibly think that? Roosevelt bases his ideas on democracy and debate, rather than the cult of personality. There's no exclusionary nationalism...' She looked at Lucia and sighed. 'Very well, Fancy. You tell me why the New Deal reminds you of the Blackshirts.'

Lucia swallowed. 'Another big idea to deal with a big problem? A vision to solve everything?'

They walked on. 'All right,' Wanda said grudgingly. 'I can see where you're approaching this from. You think that applying a grand plan to complex, multi-factorial, systemic issues is a poor substitute for empirical, ad-hoc—'

Lucia put up a hand. 'I haven't a clue what you're on about. I just meant that all successful politicians need to inspire, whether they're keen on flags and rallies or not. But often human beings' problems aren't solvable with a single big idea.'

Wanda was nodding. 'And have you debated this view with your father?'

'Good grief, no. Over Christmas, we kept the talk to whether the cook's new plum pudding recipe was an improvement on the previous year's and whether Della's pony needed a molasses supplement. It helped that we weren't in London.'

Since the rally last autumn, the very sight of his elder daughter had seemed to put Papa on edge, although he'd not lost his temper with her again and certainly hadn't struck her.

'And you went on the Boxing Day Hunt with Sir Cassian?'

'I knew you wouldn't approve. It was partly for Mama's sake. She was so unhappy when there was an atmosphere between us. It cheered her up when I said I wanted to go out with him. Della doesn't hunt.'

Wanda gave an approving sniff.

Lucia had risen early on Boxing Day to help prepare the horses. Grooming the hunters, oiling their hooves and plaiting manes had been comforting, a reminder of more innocent days. She'd always loved the stables, the smell of horse, hay and tack, the warmth of the animals.

Her horse had fallen lame only an hour into the meet. With some relief, she'd dismounted to lead him slowly home down frosty lanes, with a farewell wave to her father, who'd commiserated with her before trotting off. Lucia wasn't sorry to miss the kill, though the blood hadn't worried her when she'd hunted in the past.

'I can't imagine why you want to condone a blood sport,' Wanda said.

'Foxes are vermin. You should see the mess in the field when they get in among the lambs. It's horrific.'

Ahead of them two small children were running along the footpath, skidding over a patch of ice, laughing as they shot across it, turning round to take another run-up at it.

'That doesn't mean you have to enjoy killing them, Fancy,' Wanda observed.

'I don't. It's more the sense of freedom as you gallop over open fields. I know it's a degenerate exercise of capitalist, imperialistic privilege and inequity, or whatever it was you said when I read the George Orwell essay about shooting the elephant. Poor elephant. I told Della and she almost cried.'

Wanda sighed again. 'Orwell's "Shooting an Elephant" isn't really about cruelty to animals.'

'But my going hunting is? I can't keep up with you, Wanda.' Lucia was watching the smaller child as she ran up to the ice, jammed her feet down and started her slide. Lucia broke into a sprint, reaching the girl and grabbing her by the hood of her coat, as she started flailing about, just about to topple over.

The child's mother smiled at her. 'What do you say to this young lady?' she told the child, who thanked Lucia shyly.

'How did you know she was going to fall?' Wanda asked.

Lucia shrugged. 'She just looked off balance, leaning too far back, I suppose. I didn't really think, I just started running.'

Wanda was observing her.

'What?'

'You've got a good instinct, haven't you? You notice things about people.'

It was rare for Wanda to praise her. Lucia felt herself swell up inside with pleasure.

'So you endured Christmas with your father and now you're back in town and he's still there and you and your mother are spending time planning your Coming Out?'

'I love clothes, I really do. But all the measuring and looking at samples of taffeta and satin, it's making my head spin. But my mother is in her element.'

'She must be proud of you, looking forward to presenting you.' Wanda's tone was gentle, though ordinarily she scoffed at mention of the London Season as outdated. She was very attached to her own mother, although she admitted to frequent squabbles with her.

'It won't be Mama's fault if I don't nab a baronet at least. Her sights are probably set higher.'

'An earl? A duke?'

Lucia groaned. 'Though it would get me out of the house.'

'And provide you with plenty of horses and all the cameras you desire.' Wanda looked more thoughtful. 'Seriously, though, don't just agree to marriage to escape your father. I mean, the British Union of Fascism is an abomination but you don't need to go the lengths of tripping down the aisle with a toff you don't love.'

Lucia swallowed. Wanda stopped. 'What is it?'

She hadn't known Lucia very long at all but always seemed to know when Lucia was keeping something from her.

'It's nothing, not really to do with the Season.'

'What then?'

'You aren't going to like it.'

'Your father's been made viceroy of some distant colony and you're all going with him to set a good family example to the grateful subjects?'

'Nothing like that. Papa wants us all to go on a trip. In May. Della has time away from school then.'

'Where to?'

'We'd start in France, by rail to Paris. And then we'd travel on to... to Germany.'

'Germany?'

'He wants us to go to a rally.'

Wanda's mouth opened. 'A Nazi rally? Nuremberg? But it's the wrong time of the year, isn't it?'

'Munich, actually. Some kind of alternative to the May Day workers' celebration. Just a small procession and address, apparently, to Papa's disappointment. Not the full experience like the September Nuremberg rally. But the timing is good, coming as it does before the Season starts.'

'Oh my.' Wanda shook her head. 'That takes the biscuit, that really does.'

'I was thinking I could go along with it but duck out at the last moment. Suspected appendicitis? An unmentionable female complaint the evening of the rally? I don't actually mind going to Munich. Apparently the city itself is beautiful if you ignore the flags and uniforms.'

'Probably hard to ignore those.' Wanda was shaking her head. 'I don't know what to say, Fancy.'

'You think I should just say I won't go? Brave the atmosphere at home between now and then?'

Wanda was frowning. They walked on for a while before she spoke again. 'You should go.'

'Really?'

'You should see with your own eyes what's going on, the way the whole thing is stage-managed, how the Nazis use psychology to manipulate people: the torches, the singing, the oratory. And you should watch the people in the crowds, how they respond. It will probably be utterly chilling. But you'll see what people like my family have been warning you about, especially when Hitler starts on international Jewry as the root of all evil.'

'I'm not sure I can face it. Before the Mosley rally last autumn, I would have been really excited. But then you and I started meeting up and talking.'

'I know I've been an insufferable prig, Fancy. And even calling you that name.' Wanda made a face.

'I quite like being Fancy. Like the hens.' Wanda looked puzzled. 'They have pretty fluffy feathers. Probably like my brain, you'd say.'

'There's nothing wrong with your brain, stop talking yourself down. I can come across like a schoolmistress, my mother says. But I hope...'

Lucia looked at her inquiringly. Wanda was blushing.

'Well, I know you'll be moving in circles I could never hope to enter, especially once the Season starts and you're married off to someone from the top drawer.'

'If I get any offers.'

'You will. Men just take to you. Even my grumpy dad.' Wanda swallowed. 'I wish I had your way with males. Anyway, I'd understand if you can't see me when it all kicks off for you later in the year.'

'Of course you'll see me.' Lucia tucked her arm into Wanda's. She usually walked like this with Della, but it was the first time with Wanda. 'I can't imagine my life without you. It would be so terribly boring and I wouldn't know half the things you've told me about.'

'You're not dim, Fancy. You understand more than you allow yourself to admit.'

It was true, Lucia reflected. She'd always gone along with the persona her old school had assigned her: the girl who liked tennis and playing the piano and was kind to younger pupils, but was far from being a scholar.

Make people laugh, partner them well in doubles and make witty but non-threatening dinner-table conversation, be half-way decent-looking and you'd be popular.

Adopting this role was sufficient for so many women of her class, but no longer enough for Lucia.

In the meantime, she'd do as Wanda advised and go on the family trip to Munich, as an observer. They were stopping in France first, and that part at least would be less complicated.

In the meantime, she'd enjoy these meetings with Wanda. It seemed hard to believe she hadn't even known her until October. 'I love our chats,' she said. 'Even if you do make me read stuff that makes my brain ache.'

'You're quite up to reading those articles and books. But when you come home again from France and Germany you'll have seen things I haven't and you can enlighten me. Anyway, this freezing fog isn't getting any better. Let's find somewhere to have tea.'

'And you can tell me about your love life.'

The girls walked on briskly, Wanda telling her about a boy she'd met at a Young Socialists meeting.

FIVE

MAY, 1937

The champagne felt like crisp snow on a winter morning. Lucia felt her pupils dilate as she took a sip. She took another one and felt a frisson through her body. Della looked at her, mouth pursed.

'When you're older, you can have a glass, Della, sweetheart,' Papa said, smiling at her. very much the indulgent paterfamilias this evening. The first leg of the rail journey to Munich via Paris had gone smoothly. They'd crossed the Channel on the night ferry and spent a few days in northern France before travelling on to the capital. Today they'd visited the Louvre and strolled around the Tuileries gardens. The sun had shone, tulips had swayed in flower beds. Tonight his womenfolk were dressed up for dinner at the Ritz in a manner that drew approving looks from the perfectionist Parisians: Martha in an emerald silk gown, Lucia in a softer aqua, and Della in a pearl-grey, mid-calf dress as befitting her being still at school.

'But I'll always be nearly four years younger than Lucia,' Della said. 'And I won't be toasting our arrival in Paris.'

'I'm sure there'll be many other trips to Paris for you,

darling.' Mama hadn't said much since they'd arrived here. Perhaps, like Lucia, she was dazzled by the city and especially the Ritz. The conflicting sentiments Lucia held about her father jostled in her head, setting her on edge. How could he be two such different people – the kindly father, pointing out paintings in the Louvre she might like to look at, and the man she'd witnessed in the East End last autumn?

She distracted herself by looking around the Ritz's dining room, wondering whether she could spot Coco Chanel or Noël Coward beneath the crystal chandeliers. The light rippled from lamps to mirrors and down onto the glassware and silver cutlery. Weaving through the white-linen clothed tables, the waiters danced like a corps de ballet.

Even her father seemed to relax into his velvet-upholstered chair, at ease with the world.

Lucia had carefully limited her remarks in front of her father to comments on the landscape or history as they toured northern France. Three years to go until her twenty-first birthday and her legal adulthood. Three years was nothing; it would go quickly, especially this summer, with all the fuss around her approaching London Season. Not that the prospect of being a debutante exactly filled her with joy. Presentation to the King and Queen. Balls. Dinners. The expectation that she would hook an eligible bridegroom from the men she danced and rode with on Rotten Row. Well, it was what she'd been brought up to expect, wasn't it? Wanda would remind her. And perhaps, if she married someone intelligent and cultured, it would give her the freedom to live a life most women could only dream of? Marriage would mean her father's authority over her would be weakened or completely cut. The right husband might encourage her to expand her mind, might enjoy talking to her about the things she and Wanda discussed. She made a point of sighing at Wanda's explanations – sermons, she called them – but her mind was engaged when she was with her friend.

'...by night, Lucia?' Her father was asking her a question. Lucia felt herself jump. He was enquiring whether she had enjoyed the sights of Paris by night when she visited the city on her way home from finishing school.

'The companion they sent us home with wasn't keen on nighttime sightseeing,' she said. 'So I've never seen the Seine by moonlight or gone up to Montmartre when the stars are out.'

'I remember it being terribly romantic,' Mama said. 'Perhaps we could wander down to the river, Cassian?'

'It's a bit of a walk from here if you want to see Notre Dame, but let's see how we feel when we've finished dinner.'

'Oh, please let's do it.' Della clasped her hands together. Cassian smiled at her.

'Well, you deserve a treat to make up for the absence of champagne, so what say we limit ourselves to three courses at the table, no coffee, and use the time for the walk instead?'

Mama put a hand on her lower abdomen. 'Just as well if I'm going to squeeze into the clothes I'm having fitted tomorrow.'

'Don't want the couturiers scolding you, Martha, darling. Not that there's an inch of spare flesh on you. You're a sylph.'

Mama blushed at his words. He was like an old Ottoman pasha with his women round him, dropping little words of kindness on them. But Lucia hadn't forgotten how his mood could swing.

The *Babas au Rhum* arrived. Lucia wasn't sure she really liked the taste of the rum, but it amused her to realise her father had forgotten that rum was alcohol. 'Ooh, it's a strong taste,' Della said, as she swallowed her first mouthful. 'It makes me feel warm inside. Surprised you didn't stop me from having this, Papa.'

Lucia said nothing, but perhaps some of her amusement

showed on her face. Her father glared at her and she felt the colour rise to her cheeks.

When they'd finished, he sent them upstairs to change into shoes they could walk in. Della rummaged through the clothes the maid had unpacked, searching for a wrap, before putting on her flattest shoes, lamenting that they were schoolgirl's style. Lucia herself found a pair of pumps that probably didn't do much for her satin evening dress. She pulled the gown off and put on her light wool crepe day dress, with its long sleeves. 'Easier to walk in this.'

'How can you bear to take off that lovely gown,' Della lamented. 'I can't wait to wear long dresses.'

'I'm far more comfortable in this day dress, but, yes, the gown is lovely.' They were generous, her parents, sparing nothing to provide her with clothes. Tomorrow they'd be collecting some of the gowns ordered for her Season, sending them back home along with Mama's Parisian purchases, while they continued on to Munich. There wouldn't be too much time for visiting galleries and museums, but the afternoon was free. She picked up her Leica. Shame she hadn't really mastered nighttime flash photography yet. It would have been good to practise on the banks of the Seine, with the moon's reflection over the river and the outline of Notre Dame to add drama. But Papa would be tapping his foot if she held them up riffling through her suitcase for the extra equipment she needed. Reluctantly she put the camera away into a bedside table drawer.

The four of them headed out onto the Place Vendôme. Papa pointed at the statue of Napoleon. 'Another one of history's great men.'

'Like Herr Hitler, you mean?' Della asked.

Lucia tried to control her features so she looked interested but non-committal.

'The schoolbooks will surely mention them together,' Papa said. 'Along with Frederick the Great, perhaps.' He didn't look at Lucia as he spoke, but she knew the comment was directed towards her.

'Or Mussolini?' Della asked.

'Mussolini's corporatism appeals to the British Union of Fascism,' Lucia said, without thinking. 'And he's less anti-semitic, more concerned with national rejuvenation, so less controversial.' Not that the Blackshirts didn't enjoy a bit of anti-semitism. She recalled the afternoon of the rally, when her father had laughed at the old man the mounted policeman had knocked over.

Mama looked at her as if worrying she was coming down with something.

'Well,' Papa said. 'It's good to know you've been paying attention after all, Lucia.'

I have been paying attention, she wanted to say. *But not to you.* Wanda had some choice things to say about the Fascists in Italy. Lucia wished she could forget them. Suppose she accidentally let slip Wanda's observations about Mussolini being an ape and clown?

It was a relief to leave the statue behind and walk along the Rue St-Honoré, with its boutiques and restaurants and old Parisian townhouses, to pull the conversation away from history's great dictators. Lucia felt a longing for Wanda, even as she tried to forget her utterances about Papa's idol. She and Wanda should come to Paris, spend time both here in the fashionable arrondissements, with their windows full of glittering, expensive objects, their impeccably clad women, but also down on the Left Bank in cafés Wanda had told her about, where people like Papa would never venture. They could go to theatres where ideas were expressed that would leave him apoplectic. Wanda hadn't been to any of these places herself, she'd admitted, having never actually left Britain, but related stories she'd read about them in novels. Wanda was always reading. Lucia had brought books with her on this trip but they were mainly detective novels. Della was reading *Pride and Prejudice.* Perhaps she'd borrow it from her when she'd finished. It apparently wasn't a heavy read.

Lucia paused to admire the ornamental façade of a shop and to let the others catch up with her. Papa had Mama on one arm and Della on the other. She was the outlier, as usual. Once again, Lucia arranged her features into a bland smile. 'Aren't the shops just full of beautiful things?' she exclaimed.

'Can't wait to go shopping tomorrow,' Della said. 'Some of the stationery is divine. The writing pads and notebooks. So useful for revision notes.'

Lucia touched her sister's arm. 'Even on holiday you are ever the scholar. You're going to do so well in the end-of-year exams.'

A noise ahead of them made Lucia turn around. Running up towards them came two young men, pursued by a crowd, some carrying sticks and bottles, most shouting and jeering.

'Stand back in this doorway, everyone.' Papa said it calmly, walking out to the kerb, looking for a taxi. How strange to see such an upheaval in a boulevard as calmly elegant as this. The two being pursued were close now. Lucia made out smooth, boyish, features. Brothers, perhaps? The men chasing them weren't gaining on them: these two were athletic figures.

From a doorway ahead of Lucia a foot came out, tripping up one of the two. He nearly lost his footing, but managed to recover his balance with a graceful little bound. His brother turned briefly, long enough for a hand to grab him. 'Let him go.' The first brother wrestled with the figure in the doorway, a well-dressed man in his thirties. The two of them freed themselves and inched towards the doorway where the three Blake women stood, but the group pursuing them had almost reached them.

Whistles shrilled behind the men. The police. 'About time too,' Papa said.

The group muttered to one another, obviously wanting to

rough up the young men but constrained by the arrival of the police. Papa still hadn't managed to find a taxi. He was beckoning them back the way they'd come from the Place Vendôme. The walk by the Seine wouldn't be happening tonight.

'Criminals... paint... provocation.' Shouted accusations rained down from the crowd. It all seemed out of keeping with their surroundings.

The two boys looked at one another and then towards the open pavement beyond Lucia, who moved backwards, further into the doorway, to give them more space to get away. One of them muttered a thanks. He didn't look like a thug. A tress of hair fell out from under the trilby hat. He was a she: a girl in trousers, hair pinned back and up. 'Quick,' Lucia muttered to her, nodding up the boulevard.

Papa frowned at Lucia. 'Just one moment.' He moved in front of the young pair, stopping them so the police could catch up. 'I don't know where you think you're going. Officer,' he addressed one of the police officers in French. 'I think you need these two.'

The young man and girl tried to weave around Papa, but he was deft on his feet, his boxing training showing, blocking their escape with his larger body. Behind him, in the doorway, Mama and Della cowered. Lucia tried to make more space for the two captives to squeeze past her. Papa frowned at her. 'What are you doing, Lucia?'

'Merci.' One of the police officers came towards them. 'We will take these two, monsieur.'

The young woman cast Lucia an imploring look. There was just enough room for her to escape if Lucia squeezed back even further against the front of the boutique behind her. She did this quietly and slowly, not daring to make a sound to alert the girl.

Her brother had no such exit route. He was surrounded. 'What did they do?' Lucia asked the officers.

The two policemen couldn't have looked more stunned. 'Mademoiselle, do not be frightened, we will take these hooligans away.'

'I'm not frightened. And one of them's a girl, anyway.'

'We have received serious accounts of vandalism.'

'Accounts from them?' She nodded at the crowd of sneering men standing behind the police. Some of them wore pale blue shirts. Another carried a banner with what looked like a Celtic cross on it – some kind of French fascist or nationalist symbol?

'Defaced a wall,' one of the men growled. 'With Socialist lies.'

'We just wrote "*Non*" on your posters,' the girl said. 'There was no vandalism.'

'Only because you saw us coming,' he shouted back. 'We got there in time to stop you.'

In the second that the officers had glanced towards the accuser, the young man managed to slip out of their grasp. In a flash, he'd grabbed his female companion's arm and the two of them were squeezing past Lucia and haring away. Three of the crowd tore after them, but the accused pair had a head start and were quick on their feet. They vanished up a side street, heading north, roughly in the direction of the Opéra, Lucia thought. If they could keep that pace up, perhaps jump onto a tram or down into the Metro, they might escape.

The policemen left, shrugging their shoulders. Papa addressed the remaining group of men, who eyed Lucia contemptuously. Whatever he was saying seemed to pacify them. If they were some group of internationally minded pro-fascists, they might be impressed with having Sir Cassian Blake in their midst.

The men shuffled away, still casting looks over their shoulders towards Lucia, not completely mollified. 'What on earth were you playing at?' Papa asked Lucia. 'You seemed to be aiding them in escaping?'

'Those men looked like thugs.'

'Ever since last October your head has been turned by that girl you befriended. You see things that aren't there.'

She stared at him.

'Victimhood. Oppression.' He spat the words out.

'Better that than letting those men beat up a girl and her brother. They were harmless.'

'You don't know that. You should let the authorities decide.' He almost shouted the words. Passers-by raised eyebrows. A young man in a dinner jacket shrugged sympathetically at Lucia. Papa noticed and turned pale. He'd think he had been made to look foolish in public.

He took Lucia's arm. 'You and I are going to have a little talk when we get back to the Ritz, Lucia. Tonight's excursion is at an end. A pity for your mother and sister.' His grip on her arm was tight. She bit her lip.

He didn't release her the whole way back to the porticoed entrance to the Ritz, retaining his hold even as they walked through the hotel reception, guiding her into the lift with a cheerful *merci* to the bellboy. His fingers weren't actually hurting her skin, but she sensed that if she tried to pull away, the grip would tighten. In the mirrored walls of the lift she saw Mama's and Della's reflections, their faces tense, concerned. Della looked as though she might actually cry. Lucia looked into her own reflected eyes and saw defiance and foreboding mixed together. She'd provoked her father and all this was her fault.

They reached their floor. Papa marched her to the main door of their suite, ordering Mama to unlock it, only letting go of Lucia when they were standing in the sitting room. 'Della, go to your room.' He poured himself a glass of brandy at the small drinks cabinet, his hand trembling.

'Cassian,' Mama started, 'perhaps we should—'

He raised a hand to interrupt her. 'She was trying to help criminals get away. And she was disrespectful.'

'They'd only painted words on a poster,' Lucia said.

'And you aided them in escaping the police.'

'The police didn't even bother running after them when they ran off. So it wasn't too serious.' She knew immediately that she shouldn't have said this. Her father's jaw tightened.

'No apology, then, Lucia, for showing us up in public?'

She could say she was sorry, end this now. Della was standing in the doorway to their room. Lucia hesitated too long. 'Go inside your room and shut the door, Della,' Cassian shouted at her. 'And you, Martha, go into our bedroom.'

'I really need to use the lavatory,' Lucia said. 'I'll be quick.' He was going to forbid her to leave the room, but Mama must have made some kind of mute protest.

She only had moments to do what she needed to do. Following Della into the bedroom, she pulled her sister to the furthest corner, out of their father's earshot. 'I'm going,' she said. 'Tonight. I don't have to stay with him.'

'What on earth do you mean, Loo? You can't leave.'

'I have to. I just... I can't live with him anymore, Della.' She cast a look back towards the sitting room. 'I'm going to be punished for what happened out there tonight.'

'You think he'll hit you again? Mama won't let him.'

'She daren't say a word to stop him.' She kept her grip on Della's shoulders. 'I have money. I can go back to England.'

'He's waiting for you out there.' Della nodded in the direction of the sitting-room.

'We have our own door onto the corridor.' Until now they had only used the main door out of the suite. Papa might not have noticed or remembered this one.

'You're mad, Lucia. Where would you go? He'd be even more furious when he found you at home.'

Della was right. A wilder thought struck Lucia. 'We don't have to go back to Newton Terrace or Claybourne. We can stay away until we come of age.'

'We?'

'You could come too.'

Della's eyes opened wide. 'That's almost seven years for me. I'm only fourteen, I can't run away from home. How would I go to school, Loo?'

Of course Della couldn't run away with her. She was too young. 'I understand.' The wistfulness dripped from Lucia's voice. 'You can't go off with me. But I have to go, Della. It's just not possible for me to stay here.'

Della was shaking her head, hands clasped. 'In a few weeks you'll be coming out, Loo. Just a few months of your Season and you could be engaged to be married.' She took a breath in. 'After you leave home on your wedding day, Papa'll never be able to make you do anything again.'

Lucia could almost smell the flowers in the church, hear the rustle of silk and taffeta, the murmured congratulations and admiration. Lucia Blake would marry well, everyone said. Pretty figure, well brought up, not over educated, but with an engaging manner. Good hands on a horse and skied like an angel. She'd overheard one of Mama's friends, an elderly society figure, listing Lucia's attributes as she would a thoroughbred horse she'd seen in a Tattersall's sale catalogue. Yes, she could probably find herself a bridegroom who'd take her away from her father and allow her, if she managed him well, to organise her life as she wished. But the risk... 'I could be swapping one tyrant for another.' She looked towards the sitting-room. Any moment now, her father would tell her to hurry up. 'I have to go.'

'Don't leave me, Lucia, please.' Della's voice was rising. Lucia put a finger to her lips.

'I'm going. Listen, you have to help me, Dell. Can you go into the bathroom, flush the lavatory, run the taps while I get away? Make it sound as if I'm still in here?' Della's mouth was opening and closing.

'Don't go, Loo, you can't. You're mad.'

Lucia released her, scanning the room. Her smaller suitcase was on the rack by the wardrobe. She opened it up. They were only here a night and she'd asked the Ritz's maid to leave it unpacked. She threw in a jumper from her larger case, two pairs of stockings, a pair of socks, extra underwear and a few changes of shirt. In the bathroom, her toiletries and toothbrush were already lined up. She ran in and swept them up, returning to cram them into her suitcase. What else? Her money was in the little handbag she'd been carrying on their promenade. She took it out and put the purse in the larger bag she'd used on the train. 'Not a word,' she hissed at her sister.

The jewellery pouch in which her pearls were wrapped would be in the safe in her parents' bedroom, damn, but what she'd been wearing tonight for dinner, the gold bangles and the pendant with the little single pearl, they would do. Her passport. Where was that?

The receptionist had handed it back to her after a cursory examination, because the daughter of Sir Cassian Blake was hardly a subject of scrutiny. It was still in her day bag. Della was watching her, mouth open. Any moment now, her sister would call out for help.

'Please don't go,' Della whispered. 'I'm begging you, Lucia.'

She put down the suitcase and took her sister's hands. 'It's only until I know he can't make me live with him. I'll let you know where I am, Dell.' A sudden thought struck her. 'Do you have any French coins?' She had some bank notes, but coins would be more useful for Metro tickets and telephone calls. Della frowned and opened her lips. For a moment it seemed as if she might call out. She went to the little satchel she'd worn on the train. Papa had given her some francs for buying sweets and postcards. She handed them over, her fingers seeming to resist at the last moment, before the coins landed in Lucia's palm. Lucia put them quickly into her jacket pocket.

'Where will you go?' Della asked. 'By yourself, in a strange city?' She wiped her eyes on the back of her wrist.

'I was here before, remember, on the way home from finishing school. I know some quiet places to stay.' Let her parents believe she was going to some respectable small hotel or *pension*. From the sitting room came the sound of Mama's voice, low and imploring. Begging her father for mercy for Lucia? Too late now. The time for Mama's intervention had long since passed.

She wanted to put her arms around Della, kiss her, promise her she'd be in touch, but there wasn't time. Blowing Della a last kiss, Lucia opened the door into the corridor. She closed it without a sound, heading towards the door to the staircase, rather than the lift. Two floors to descend, she could make reception before her father could reach it. Her ears strained for the sound of his footsteps pounding down behind her.

She took a breath and walked through the lobby with the calmest smile she could force. The man behind the reception desk looked at her, puzzled. He was going to ask if he could help her. She increased her pace. 'Mademoiselle?'

Any moment now a concierge or bellboy would appear at her side, asking if she needed assistance. There'd be a fuss. A call might be made to her father upstairs. Lucia walked out into the cool evening air. The taxis outside were a temptation: already a uniformed young man was trying to escort her towards one of them. Tempting, for the speed a taxi would provide, but too easy for her father to trace her. With a murmured thanks, Lucia turned left, heading vaguely north, she thought, in the direction of the Gard du Nord, where they'd arrived today. She could catch the ferry train back to Victoria tonight, even if she had to buy a replacement ticket, and be in London for breakfast.

Wouldn't that be what her father would expect her to do? Return to the familiar? Her pace slowed as she tried to think it through. Papa had connections in the Metropolitan Police; she'd heard him on the telephone after the rally, asking them why on earth they hadn't allowed Mosley to continue as planned that afternoon. If he put a telephone call through, they'd keep an eye on the major London railway stations for her.

No, if she returned to England, it would have to be by a less obvious route. Her mind was whirring. As children, they'd spent a holiday in Brittany, crossing by ferry to St Malo. That was a long detour to the west, it would take ages. But between Brittany and Calais, there were other Channel ports, weren't there? She tried to remember. Dieppe. Le Havre – they connected with Portsmouth, a big enough port to lose herself in. Which railway station in Paris connected to Dieppe and Le Havre?

St Lazare. From somewhere in her memory, the name of the station popped into her mind. It was late now, perhaps too late for a train to the coast. Would there be some kind of waiting room at St Lazare station where she could hide in the meantime? She needed to reach the station quickly. Lucia looked around. Coming towards her was a taxi, which stopped when she hailed it. She managed to bat off the driver's curious inquiries with a smile.

It took some time to get there, and her heart beat faster the closer to the station they got. Finally, the driver deposited her at the station entrance and she ran inside.

The information desk was closed and she had to read the impenetrable timetable on the board before she discovered she was indeed too late to reach Dieppe or anywhere else that provided a ferry link to England tonight. A last train to Rouen would leave in five minutes. Rouen had a cathedral, didn't it? It was the kind of town where respectable hotels might exist, where she could safely spend a night out of the capital, considering what to do next. She bought a ticket, second- not first-class, because first class was what they'd expect her to buy if she'd been tracked to St Lazare station.

To her relief, nobody else seemed to be heading for Rouen at this hour and she sat shivering in the carriage, even though it wasn't cold. As Paris was left behind, her sense of panic built to a crescendo. She eyed the carriage door, wondering if she could jump out and run back towards St Lazare station. *What have you done, what have you done, what have you done?* the train asked as it built up speed.

By the time Lucia arrived in Rouen, many of the hotels had already closed their doors. On her fifth attempt, the night porter opened up to her ring of the bell. 'Mademoiselle?' He eyed her with suspicion. 'You are alone?' She had only the one small suitcase and probably looked dishevelled, although she had attempted to tidy herself up on the train, remembering all the while their nanny's indictments of women who vulgarly groomed themselves in public.

'*C'est très tard*, mademoiselle.' He was about to shut the door.

'I know it's late. A rail connection failed,' she said, thankful for her fluent French. 'This establishment looks respectable, so I knew I would be safe here.' She met his eye as confidently as she could. 'I hope I'm not mistaken, monsieur?'

He opened the door and led her across a shabby but reasonably clean tiled lobby to the desk. 'Passport?'

She pushed it across the chipped wooden counter. He looked through it, lifting his head to examine her. 'And you are alone, mademoiselle?' he asked again. Was he imagining some disreputable male was hanging around outside, waiting to slip into the room with her?

'Because my rail connection failed, and I could not join my aunt. I am expected in Dieppe, for a ferry home to England.' She regretted the words immediately.

But the mention of the aunt and ferry seemed to soften his

suspicion. She'd become a virtuous English girl who simply wanted to go home. He returned her passport and found a key. 'It's not our best room, but it is clean. Come with me, please.'

The man who examined the gold bangles and pearl pendant she pushed across the jewellery shop counter the following morning frowned at her. 'These are good pieces, mademoiselle.' His eyes were questioning.

She nodded, trying not to give anything away, trying not to think of her grandmother, her mother's mother, who was dead now and who'd left the pendant to Lucia in her will.

'Three hundred francs.'

She had no idea how much the jewellery was worth, but thought it would be more. 'Six hundred.'

'Four hundred and fifty.'

Lucia looked down at the small gold ring on her right hand. It had been a sixteenth birthday present from her parents. He saw where she was looking

'Six hundred francs for the bangles, pendant and ring.'

Instinct told her he was driving a very hard bargain on her jewellery, but then she'd come in off the street with pieces she couldn't prove she owned. Anyway, she didn't have much of a choice.

'I must be going soft, mademoiselle.' He took out a key and opened a money box, counting out notes briskly.

Lucia felt a pang as she took the ring off. But it was like a kind of shackle, keeping her tied to her old life. She took the notes, thanking the man.

Time to make some decisions. She needed someone to tell her what to do, where to go. Automatically, she thought of Wanda. Wanda would probably lecture her to at least send a telegram to the Ritz to tell her family she was safe before she did anything else. Well, she couldn't do that – it would give away her hiding place. She'd find a way to contact Wanda, however, swear her to secrecy. Wanda would help her launch her new life.

Lucia found herself wandering the streets of Rouen, which at any other time would have enchanted her with their half-timbered buildings. Ascending to an esplanade by a basilica, she found a memorial to the town's most famous resident, Joan of Arc, who'd been burnt at the stake for heresy when not much older than Lucia was now. Lucia was exasperated by her own feebleness. She wasn't threatened by flames, she simply had to find a way of existing by herself. Or return to the family home.

'It's simple,' she told herself, pausing to sit on a bench. 'Either go home and face them, face *him*, live with what he is, hope you can get through the next few months, marry someone easy and kind. Or find a way of living without any of them. Including Mama and Della. Either way, stop being pathetic.'

The thought of home, especially Claybourne Manor, was like a tug. Perhaps she could manage to live there, away from him? She'd have her horse to ride. But her parents would never agree. They'd make her stay up in town, preparing for the Season. And Papa would be there too, as he always spent the late spring and early summer in town. Could she apologise, keep her head down and avoid her father? Surely she could just tolerate his rages and his political extremism? He'd only hit her once, and might not actually have raised a fist to her last night in the Ritz. Wanda had told her of families in Whitechapel where the man of the house would regularly beat up his wife and any children within striking distance. 'They have no choice but to stay, Fancy,' she said. 'They have no money of their own, their earnings are taken for rent, food and beer money, leaving them nothing.'

Well, Lucia wasn't without the power to choose. She would have her own money when she was twenty-one, before if she married, as a trust fund was settled on her – an inheritance from her mother's family, which nobody on the Blake side, not even Sir Cassian, could take from her.

Just three years to go. In the meantime, how on earth was she to support herself?

She found herself standing up and returning to stare at Joan of Arc's statue, as though the stone girl could advise her. Nothing on the martyr's face gave her an indication of what to do. Hers was hardly a martyrdom situation, was it? She had enough money for now. Nobody was going to be lighting a pyre under her.

Lucia walked around the memorial. Beyond Rouen, France sparkled in the light of a spring morning, hills blue in the distance. She worked her way around to the northern side, to look in the direction of Dieppe and the Channel ferry home to the known and familiar: the silk gowns in the wardrobe, the hair appointments and discussions of dinner-table placements and ball attendances. It was a life that had been laid out for her since the day of her birth. With apologies and regret, she could still reclaim it. Her father would treat her harshly, but if she returned promptly, without scandal, she could slot back into her old existence. Girls were allowed to be briefly flighty, as long as it didn't look like a sign of deep-rooted instability.

Lucia circled around again to look vaguely south-east, in the direction of Paris. She could telegram the Ritz. There was still time to retrace last night's rail journey to return to the hotel, where Della would be waiting for her.

And where Papa would still want to punish her because she'd humiliated him on the Rue St-Honoré.

Lucia turned her back on Paris and walked around the monument to face south. 'That's where I'll go,' she said to herself. 'I'll head towards Spain and stop somewhere on the way.'

Where exactly somewhere on the way might be, she wasn't sure. That part of Southern France wasn't the Riviera or the

Alps, or the chateau-rich Loire. It was unchartered territory for her. Nobody would know Lucia Blake down there. Going south would place even more space between her and Papa. But that meant being further away from Della too. She almost felt a pain in her heart.

One day she would reclaim her sister. This running away was only temporary. Perhaps Papa's infatuation with the fascists would weaken.

'I'll be back,' she promised Della silently.

SIX

JUNE, 1937

Sainte-Claire, Cévennes

'Mademoiselle?' Lucia turned to see a young man observing her.

She blushed, holding out the small trowel she'd picked up off the ground. 'This is yours?'

'I heard something drop off my pack. I should have stopped but they were serving lunch at the camp and I was late.' He took it from her with a smile. 'Merci. They're always telling me off for not tying things on securely.'

'You're with the archaeology team?' The group of young men had been working away on a ridge a kilometre or so out of town. Something to do with the Romans, Lucia had heard from her landlady.

'I am.' He looked at her solemnly. 'And you live in the town, don't you? I think I've seen you at the baker's.'

'That's right.' She was still shy of saying too much about herself. She hoped he hadn't noticed the times she'd been hanging around the baker's at the end of the day when the older bread was given away.

'Sebastien Durand.' He held out a hand.

'Lucie.' She didn't give a surname.

'*Enchanté*, Mademoiselle Lucie.' A well-mannered young Frenchman, not quite like those she'd met during her Swiss finishing-school days, the brothers of some of her friends. This one was more intellectual, she thought. Less of a socialite, a little more earnest. 'You're walking back to town now?'

'I have a session starting soon.'

'A session?' he asked.

'I provide English conversation lessons.' It sounded rather grand for what she did: conversing with a couple of Spanish families fleeing the Civil War, who were trying to improve the odds of their children obtaining visas for America – England, if this wasn't possible. 'You're camping up there, aren't you?' she nodded up the hillside. 'I've seen your woodsmoke.'

'Close to the dig so we can keep an eye on it. And so we don't waste time trooping up and down every day.' He grimaced. 'I do miss proper beds, though. And the dips in the river aren't quite like the bathroom at home.'

'I know what you mean.' She said it with feeling. 'Not that I'm bathing in rivers, but the arrangements at my lodgings are... basic.' A rusty tin bath that the landlady filled with warm water once a week; otherwise, whatever she could manage using the basin in her room.

'Where is home for you, mademoiselle?'

She stopped. 'I go this way. *Bonne journée*.' She cursed herself as she walked on briskly. She was obviously English, alone, out of place in this historic but remote town. Easily identifiable, she already knew this. Time to move on again? She couldn't bear the thought.

When she'd left Rouen, Lucia had taken a roundabout rail journey south, avoiding Paris and sticking to routes between provincial towns and cities. She'd found herself in Sainte-Claire, a small fortified town in the Cévennes, chosen only because a friendly librarian in a larger town to the north had mentioned the refugees in Sainte-Claire who were looking for an English tutor. She'd hurried south, almost as keen to form a connection with human beings as to earn the money she needed. Her lodgings were basic, but the landlady was kind and she felt safe here. The families she taught didn't ask questions, probably because she was undercharging them for her conversational classes. Damn that polite young Frenchman. She should have left the trowel on the ground to rust instead of picking it up to place on a boulder. And damn the fact that she felt so lonely at times that she had actually found herself on the verge of sending a telegram to Belgravia.

Yet again she asked herself what would happen if she went home now. Would her father lock her up? Beat her? Could she beg to be allowed to live away from the family, out of his orbit? The Season was underway. Her mother's plans were in ruins.

Perhaps her mother and father wouldn't let her come back to the family? The thought chilled her. She couldn't put it out of her mind, picturing herself on the doorstep of 6 Newton Terrace, being refused entry to her home. If she still felt like this next week, she'd write to Wanda, which she hadn't done yet because she was scared Wanda would be interrogated by Sir Cassian. Though if Sir Cassian had by now washed his hands of her, why would he do this? Lucia's mind oscillated between the two scenarios. She noted that she was now thinking of him with his title, rather than as Papa, her father. He'd become a personage distinct from her. Good. She'd be happier for distancing herself from him.

When she ordered her lunch in a small restaurant on the town square – a bowl of aromatic lamb stew with a piece of bread – she asked the waiter casually about the archaeologists, how much longer they'd be in the area. 'Those boys?' The waiter asked. 'Their summer away from university has just begun. They'll be up on the *garrigue* for weeks. Plenty to find up there.'

The garrigue was the scrubland characterising the slopes of the region, fragrant with marjoram, thyme and lavender. Lucia had been ignorant of the history of this part of France. In truth, she hadn't known much about most of the country. Afternoons spent in the library had introduced her to the stories of Romans, Crusaders, pilgrims and Cathars. And earlier peoples had lived up here too. With little else to read, she'd sat at the library desk with a dictionary. Wanda would be so proud of her, extending her knowledge like this. If only she was here too. She'd love the sunshine, the old buildings and wildflowers.

Lucia finished her lamb, thinking about the young archaeologist. 'Are they a big group?' she asked the waiter, as he brought Lucia a plate of cheese to finish her meal. If only she could eat like this every day. Tomorrow, she'd buy a cheap piece of cheese in the market, she promised herself. It was just good to eat in the restaurant with other people around sometimes, rather than alone in her bedroom, perched on the faded quilt and staring at the window that was shuttered to keep out the heat.

'About six of them youngsters. All young men of course.' He gave Lucia a knowing smile. Perhaps he felt sorry for her, always by herself. She was probably drawing attention and that was a bad thing. Maybe it really was time to move on, even though living here was affordable and she had fallen in love with the old stone buildings and the views across the hills to rocky peaks.

In the meantime, she would adapt her daily walk so that there was less chance of running into the archaeologists. It was a shame. Time with people her own age would have been refreshing. She slept as well as she always did up here in the hills, but aware of wind and rain hammering the shutters.

In the morning, the town was full of stories of the storm and the trees that had fallen and rivers that had flooded. On her way to the bakery, Lucie saw a raggle-taggle collection of muddy young men, rucksacks on backs, carrying boxes, rubbing their eyes, yawning. One of them was Sebastien. He stopped. 'The weather was too much for us, mademoiselle.'

'What will you do?'

'Find somewhere to store our work temporarily down here. Then we need to go back to the dig and assess the damage.'

'I hope your work hasn't been too badly affected.'

'We saved most of the artefacts we recovered, but there's a lot of damage to the site.' A quick smile covered his face. 'But that's archaeology – working against the elements, time, weather, terrain.' One of Sebastien's colleagues beckoned him on with a wave. 'Must go.'

'*Bon courage.*' Mixed with her sympathy for the compromised work was a prick of envy. What must it be like to have something in life that mattered so much, a mission? She enjoyed her English conversation sessions, but the work was no mission – it paid for her food and lodgings. Even Mama had transformed herself from languor into animation when it had come to organising Lucia's doomed London Season. She had really seemed to enjoy sitting at her writing desk with endless lists, telephoning dressmakers and florists, making appointments, conferring with other society mothers.

And then Lucia had run away before the work could come to fruition. Perhaps it wasn't what Wanda had meant by the dignity of labour, but Mama's efforts had meant something to her. And Sebastien's work obviously had meaning for him. What meaning did Lucia's work have for her?

She saw him again in the café at lunchtime. 'Our camping stoves didn't survive,' he said. 'Until we can replace them or rebuild a fire we'll eat our main meals down here. There are some compensations.' He nodded at the chicken joint on his plate. 'Would you like to join us? There's room at the table?'

How she longed to be part of a group, to laugh and joke and chat. 'I have a lesson shortly,' she said. 'Well, a conversational session, not really a lesson.'

His face fell. What harm could it do to join the group for a meal.

'But it would be good to find out more about your work.' She sat down at the table and Sebastien filled her glass with local red wine from a jug. At home, a group of young men like this would have been talking about horses or cricket. These students switched from philosophy to literature to politics as readily as they did the archaeology and history of the area around Sainte-Claire. Lucia found herself questioning them about Cathars and heretics.

'Mademoiselle Lucie, you should come to one of our seminars when term starts,' Sebastien said. 'You ask more interesting questions than most of us students.'

'Come up to the dig,' one of his colleagues said, a man a little older, though only in his late twenties, she estimated. 'Normally we don't encourage visitors, but we'll make an exception for you.'

'I'd really love that.'

She looked at her watch. 'If I don't go now, I'm going to be late for my afternoon session.' Placing coins on the table for her food, she promised to walk up to the dig in the early evening.

'If it's still flooded, we may ask you help us bail it out,' the leader said.

'Definitely.'

'Meet you where I dropped the trowel, at five,' Sebastien said.

As promised, he was waiting for her, the same shy smile on his face. The scrubland smelled fresh in the evening sun, the rain having brought out the aromas of mint and thyme. 'I'll miss this when I'm back studying in autumn,' Sebastien said. 'Sometimes, I fancy myself staying here.'

'Lonely in winter.' She was already dreading the thought of winter. But she would have moved on by then. He looked as though he was holding himself back from asking questions. Instead, he told her about himself, his family: a brother and sister. Their apartment in Paris and the house in the country near Tours. His father had intended him for a legal career, perhaps with a view to politics and had been disappointed when his firstborn had shown such a passion for history and archaeology. His brother was obsessed with learning to fly and his sister loved ponies so much she would probably sleep in the stables if she could.

'I have a sister like that too.' Lucia bit her lip. Again, he gave her a probing look, but fortunately, they had reached the dig. She'd been expecting something like the photographs that depicted the uncovering of Egyptian tombs. Sebastien laughed at her disappointed face.

'Often it does look like a random collection of ditches. The good thing is that they are all still intact. We feared it would look like a mud bath up here, but the water seems to have been kind to us, it's drained away.'

The next few hours were like being in a different world with its own language and tools. 'We think we've found part of a paved Roman road,' Sebastien told her. He showed her what they'd excavated so far and the maps and diagrams that had led them to believe there was something up here in the first place. Lucia marvelled at the delicacy with which the students brushed dirt from apparently ordinary rocks to reveal level paving stones and tried her hand at the work. He took her to the tents where they cleaned and labelled artefacts.

She stood on the hill and imagined roman legions marching through the scrubland, smelling the same scents, seeing the same rocky peaks and felt herself part of something very ancient. She was no longer the displaced English girl, Lucia Blake; she was just one part of a larger story linking the English and the French to ancient Rome. Perhaps some of the Romans trooping through these hills had eventually found themselves across the Channel? Her knowledge of ancient history was patchy, and she was almost embarrassed to ask.

Sebastien was smiling at her. 'You feel it too, don't you? The pull of the past.' His face fell. 'But we're so behind because of the storm. There's barely going to be time to photograph everything, and Guy, he's our photographer, is struggling to keep up because we all need to do the salvaging.'

'I could help.' She felt startled at hearing herself offer.

'You can use a camera?'

'I was quite keen at one stage.' She'd left her Leica in the Ritz. It had taken her a few days to realise this, and she'd felt a pang. 'I wish I could photograph this view. *Earth hath not anything to show more fair.*' Wanda would have been amazed that Fancy could recite as much as even a single line of poetry.

'Keats?'

'Wordsworth. It's about the only bit I know, and I think he was writing about dawn on Westminster Bridge rather than open country. But it's how I feel.'

'It makes me want to see Westminster Bridge and the view too,' Sebastien said.

'Probably not the same bridge as back in Wordsworth's time, and the city is a bit grubby with all the smoke. But it's beautiful too.' She felt a pang of homesickness, but it wasn't as strong as it had been a few days before.

'In the meantime, let's talk to Guy.'

He led her back to the camp and poured her an enamel mug of water. The tents had been retrieved, not too damaged by the storm, and re-erected, a new fire laid. The others drifted back and a jug of wine replaced the water.

'I have found you an angel,' Sebastien said. 'Lucia is a photographer.' Guy looked a little more sceptical, muttering about clarity of images and the importance of accurate representations. Lucia shrugged.

'What did you use at home?' he asked.

She told him about her Leica and the photographs she'd taken.

'We don't use a Leica. It's a Zeiss, but that's also a rangefinder camera too,' Guy admitted.

'Can't do any harm, can it?' Sebastien asked Guy. 'If it's a question of not having photographs at all?'

'No, we won't be any worse off.' Guy shrugged. 'Tomorrow, I'll show you where I got to before the storm and any help you can give will be gratefully received.'

Soup was heated up and bread and cheese cut. The sun dipped behind the hill, replaced by the moon. Lucia stayed by the fire with Sebastien, even when the other members of the team said their goodnights and went into their tents. 'Thank you for putting in a word for me.'

'I wish we could pay you for your work, but we're all volunteers here.'

'It's the work that matters.' She smiled to herself, hearing an echo of Wanda's voice, telling her she should always negotiate for fair pay.

To her relief, Lucia found the Zeiss camera straightforward to use. When she wasn't adjusting light meters and extension poles, or checking labels on objects and arranging them carefully to photograph them, she was still giving conversation classes. Life became busy.

She photographed the coins, vase fragments and pieces of metal that Sebastien and Guy told her were remnants of jewellery and weapons where they were uncovered on site, and then catalogued them carefully back at the camp, with further, more detailed photographs. As more of the road was excavated, Lucia tried to find the angles that would most clearly show what had been revealed, marking the position from where she'd taken her photographs and ensuring she took some pictures from the same spot each time more of the road was uncovered, so that perspective could be shown. She surprised herself with how absorbing the work was, how careful she was to be accurate. Sometimes days passed and she didn't think about home or her family. The only person she longed to communicate with was Wanda. She would have been so interested in the site and the team.

Guy and Sebastien discovered that she could drive a car and insisted on her having a go in the team's battered Citroen truck. 'Pierre is our driver, but we really need him up here onsite. If you had a few hours free from your own work and could drive it down to the station...' Guy, having been sceptical about her skills, gave her a sheepish grin. 'If this goes on, you'll have to attend lectures with us, Lucie. Sometimes there are a few women there.'

She smiled, not wanting to explain that her academic credentials would probably barely allow her to work in a post-office, let alone qualify for French university.

Pierre took her out for a test drive and she reassured herself and him that she could navigate the hairpin bends in the roads, along with the clunky gearbox. The task of driving crates of discoveries down to the railway station for transport back to the university was handed to her. Proving herself capable of operating cameras and trucks made her feel an emotion about herself she hadn't noticed before. Praise for looking pretty or well turned out wasn't as sweet as gruff thanks, or a pat on the back, for carrying out a task competently. The young men still eyed her curiously – she wasn't like their sisters at home in the breeches she'd taken to wearing when she was with them – but had accepted her. She half wondered if they'd make passes at her – men were men, after all – but it didn't happen. Perhaps her suntanned face and sun-bleached hair wasn't terribly attractive.

In their time off, Sebastien and Lucia went for long walks

into the hills, taking bread and cheese in rucksacks. In the evenings, they drank the red wine served in local bars and hostelries with the team, or, more frequently as the weeks passed, by themselves. By now, the project had absorbed her. Who'd have thought Lucia Blake would be interested in archaeology? Wanda and Della would be so amused when she told them about her job and this friendship with the earnest young man who'd walked into her life. Sebastien was such a serious fellow; sometimes he found it hard to tell if she was joking, he told her. He was the only son in a conservative Parisian family, who regarded his passion for archaeology with suspicion as most of the men in the wider family were civil servants, lawyers or priests.

'They think I'll grow out of it, so for now they indulge me. And fund me. What about you, Lucie? Aren't you ever going to tell me anything about your people?' he asked one Sunday afternoon when they were resting under the shade of an ancient chestnut tree. 'I know nothing about you.'

'I'm not proud of my father. He has difficult political views.'

'In what way?'

'He supports Oswald Mosley.'

Sebastien nodded. 'Ah yes. We have people like that in France too.'

'More than just supporting, though. He's high up in the Blackshirts. It's changed him.'

'How?'

'He was always interested in people from all levels of society and told us how important it was to treat workers with respect because they powered the economy. He hated what the Great War had done to some of the men he'd served with and wanted them to be treated better. But then, I don't know, he changed. Became bitter about the status quo. Said British politics was too lethargic to solve the big problems.'

He nodded. 'The economic crash at the beginning of the

decade pushed many like your father into more extreme views. But your sister and mother?'

'They aren't like Papa at all. My mother is very gentle, and my sister has an inquiring mind. But she's younger than I am.' She stopped abruptly. Guilt about leaving Della could still swamp her. What was Della doing now? Thinking about her was too painful.

'Perhaps you'll find your way back to them? You must miss them?'

'I'd like to see them. Maybe in the autumn, when I've had time to think it over. If they still...' She gulped. 'They mightn't want to see me now.'

'They will.' He placed an arm around her shoulders. It was the first time he'd made any real physical approach. The warmth of his body made her feel as if she belonged to the world in a way she hadn't for weeks and weeks.

He was so unlike the boys she knew at home, but that meant she could relax with him. It wasn't as if he was a suitor, so she could just enjoy his company.

PART THREE

SEVEN

JANUARY, 2000

'I always wondered if Wanda knew where you were,' Della said. 'I decided to go down to Whitechapel and talk to the Silbersteins. It was impossible during the school term, because of exams. But when I came back in the summer, I looked at the Tube map and saw it was a simple journey on the District Line.'

'By yourself?'

Della nodded. 'I chose a Saturday morning. Papa was out of town, at a rally in Birmingham. Mama was having her hair done. I found the studio, but it was shuttered. Then I remembered they were Jewish. So silly of me. I was going to knock anyway, but I felt it wasn't right to disturb them. A neighbour came to the door and asked if he could help me. I said I was looking for Wanda but didn't want to disturb the family. He said she was in the Lake District, hiking.' Della looked awkward. 'I didn't like to ask if he'd heard anything about my sister. It felt so... desperate. Though of course, that's how I felt.' She grimaced. 'He asked if he could take my name and address and he'd ask Wanda to be in touch. I couldn't bear the thought of him seeing my surname, so I murmured something and left.'

'Oh, Della.' Lucia blinked hard. 'If only...'

Della hadn't thought to pass on the idea of approaching the Silbersteins to her parents? Effie wondered whether she'd been concerned about exposing them to her father's aggression. Sir Cassian turning up at the studio and demanding they tell him everything they knew about his errant daughter?

'I thought Mama could go to see Mrs Silberstein, perhaps,' Della said, reading her mind. 'But she would never have agreed to do anything behind Papa's back. I assumed Wanda wouldn't tell us where you were anyway. And to be honest, it hurt to think you might have told her where you were, but not me.'

Lucia took her sister's hand. 'No. She knew no more than you.'

Della looked a little mollified but the two of them were still trying to break through the hurt caused so long ago.

The past was like that, Effie thought. You deluded yourself into thinking it had been processed, or at least tidily boxed away, like the objects in the chest in front of them. But all the old memories and emotions could tumble out.

Millennium Day should have been a day of new beginnings but it felt as if the old century wasn't going to let go of them without a fight.

EIGHT

SEPTEMBER, 1940

The mouse

Sundays used to be fun. People would come to the small house in Chelsea after lunch to play music: Papi on his violin and Mami on the small upright piano, with whichever other instruments turned up. She was going to be seven next birthday, and had started learning piano with Papi. One day she might be good enough to join in too.

The guests laughed as everyone squeezed in together, their faces turning more serious as they played Schubert or Brahms. Afterwards they'd take the chairs out into the small garden, really just a paved area with pots of flowers. The guests and Papi and Mami would talk and laugh some more, even when the news from home was sad. It was a shame none of the visitors had children to play with her, but just seeing fresh faces was fun, even if they were just grown-ups, longing for talk about the old country, the loved ones left behind, the war, letters received, bad news, sad news.

'Ulrich, you and Hanna and your little one made us forget

everything with her chatter for a few hours and that's a tonic,' they'd say as they left in the evening, patting her on the head.

Afternoons like this hadn't happened for weeks and weeks now. 'You're more like a *mäuschen*, a little mouse, than a chatterbox these days,' Papi said, sounding sad. She liked the idea of being a mouse, white, bright-eyed, with twitching whiskers, not making much noise but watching everything, everyone.

Sundays were quiet days now. Nobody visited. The family didn't go out very often. The mouse's parents didn't laugh as much and had conversations in low voices when they thought she couldn't hear. Some of the guests had been taken off somewhere and hadn't returned. Papi himself had vanished for two days earlier in the war, but had returned, looking relieved. 'I'm in the right group,' he said, ruffling her hair. 'Nobody's concerned about a man who makes false teeth.' Mami smiled at him, saying she'd always known things would work out, but her voice had quavered.

Before the war, Papi had worked for Siemens, but it had closed down. Now he went to work in a dental laboratory in Ealing. Each morning, when he left, it was as though it might be the last time Mami might see him.

This Sunday, when the breakfast dishes were barely washed up and Papi was talking about a quiet walk by the river as the sun had come out, there was a pounding on the front door. Mami and Papi looked at one another, just as they had last year, when the uniformed men had come to the house to take Papi away.

This morning the uniformed men didn't shout. One of them looked as if he didn't really want to be in the tiled hallway at all; he shuffled and half smiled at Mami, but perspiration still ran down her forehead.

'You are Ulrich Ketterer?'

'That's right.' Papi showed them his identity papers.

'And you formerly worked for Siemens?'

'Yes, until the job was terminated at the start of the war. I've been working in a dental laboratory since then.'

'A dental laboratory.' The two visitors looked at one another. Papi made false teeth, which was funny, but the men didn't laugh.

'I'm afraid I must ask you to come with us, sir. Please pack a small suitcase now.'

'I think there must be a mistake? Last time I was taken in, just after the war started, I was given paperwork showing that I am in Group B.'

'We have you down as Group A, sir.'

'Ulrich, don't let them take you.' The two strangers looked at one another as Mami spoke, as though her opening her mouth was a bad thing.

But Papi was already gently releasing himself from Mami's hands. 'Best to sort it out at the station,' he said.

'You'll be going straight to the camp, sir. They'll process you there.'

'The camp? Process?' Mami said, as though the words scared her. Papi headed for the stairs. As he passed the mouse, he bent down and stroked her hair. '*Mäuschen*, you'll have to write to me. Better still, send me some of your beautiful pictures.' She wanted to grab his hand and stop him from leaving, but knew she had to let him go. She and Mami followed him upstairs, each footstep heavy on the stair treads.

Perhaps Papi had guessed he might be taken away for a second time, because it didn't take him long to put the things in his suitcase: shirts, jumpers, underwear, his razor and toothbrush, soap. He came downstairs and hesitated by his violin case, sitting in its usual spot by the fireplace. 'I wonder if they'll let me take this too?'

'You need blankets, a thick coat, Ulrich,' Mami said. 'Those are far more important. Think of the damp.'

'It can't be as bad as the Baltic in winter.' He smiled, the strain showing on his face and immediately became more serious again. 'Hanna, we need to talk about you two. Without my pay you're going to find it hard to stay here. If I'm not back within the week, rent a few rooms locally. When they let me go, perhaps we can return here, or find something similar.'

Mami nodded.

'And perhaps, just keep yourselves to yourselves for now. You too, *mäuschen.*' He bent down to her. 'Can you keep on being as quiet as a little mouse when you're with other people?'

'They'll still know who we are,' Mami said. 'What we are. Everyone does.'

'That's why moving makes sense. There's nothing about the two of you that looks like... well, what they'd expect.'

Mami sniffed. 'No, we don't fit the stereotypes, do we?'

What were stereotypes? None of this made sense. She ran to Papi and wrapped her arms around his legs. 'You can't go, Papi.'

'*Mäuschen,* I have no choice.' He scooped her into his arms and kissed her. 'I want you to stay inside now while your mother and I go out with these gentlemen. Perhaps start on that first drawing you're going to do for me?'

His embrace was so fierce it almost hurt. Papi set her down gently and picked up the suitcase and violin. He and Mami went outside with the men in uniform. Papi turned back briefly, one hand out to stop the mouse. 'Stay indoors now.'

'I'm sure things will be sorted out soon.' Papi sounded confident as he kissed Mami. 'Look after yourself and the little one. There's money in the desk that will keep you going while you look for something cheaper to rent. Perhaps I'll be back in a day or two, anyway, before you've even had time to find somewhere. Could you telephone work for me? Let them know what's happened.'

The front door opened. When the mouse ran upstairs and looked out of her bedroom window a van was starting up its engine outside. One of the policemen opened the rear doors. Three other men and a woman sat inside. They shuffled up to make space for Papi. The mouse banged and banged on the window, no longer a small, shy creature, suddenly filled with anger. They had to let Papi out; this was wrong, a mistake. Tears burned down her cheeks.

Mami stood in the cobbled road watching the van drive to the end of the mews and head for the main road. Curtains in the houses opposite twitched – the neighbours, watching behind windows. In the street an elderly couple muttered to each other. The man spat at Mami, but the spittle didn't hit her. Spitting was a dirty habit, but nobody told the old man off. Another man, with a long, torn dark coat and matted hair down to his collar, yelled something incomprehensible while raising a fist at the van, before shuffling away.

Mami came back inside and slumped on the second-to-bottom step. She crept downstairs and onto her lap. Mami stroked her hair but didn't seem to notice that her cheeks were wet. 'We need to find somewhere else to live,' she said, distractedly. 'But where? Everyone will know who we are. Everyone will hate us.' They sat there in silence before Mama gently lowered her onto the floor. 'No good just sitting here like this. We're going for a walk. I'll look at the cards in the red shop window. Someone might have a room to rent.'

They called it the red shop because the awnings were the same colour as the buses and post-boxes. So bright and cheerful, Mami said. Sometimes it still stocked chocolate and the shopkeeper was friendly, occasionally handing out small, withered apples to children she liked.

'We will manage,' Mami said. 'Your father will be back with us soon.'

It was a struggle to believe her.

NINE

JANUARY, 1941

'Wakey-wakey, breakfast is served. By your la-di-da continental standards, Fancy, probably not much.'

Lucia woke to her flatmate's voice. Wanda had cooked her a fried egg on toast and brought it to her in bed on a tray with a cup of tea. The shift last night had been long. Images of burning buildings and motionless bodies, and worse, were still occupying Lucia's head. She pulled herself into the here and now. 'You've given me your egg?'

'I've gone off them.' Wanda pulled the blackout up. Dust motes floated in the light.

'Rubbish.' Lucia frowned at her.

'You gave me your cake last shift we were on together, remember? And you swapped shifts with me last week. And I've got the day off and I'm in a good mood.'

'I gave you the cake because it had sultanas in it. Not even total war can make me like those squashy things.' Lucia yawned, sat up and looked at her wristwatch. 'Can't believe it's this late already.'

'Tough last night?'

Lucia looked away, not wanting to bring the images of what

she'd seen in the night into this room. Wanda gave a nod of understanding, not asking more. They never dwelled on what happened when they were out in the ambulances, limiting conversation to stories that were darkly funny or banal. Once you started describing what you'd seen, what you'd had to do, who knows what it might open up. And it wasn't fair to the listener to dump it all on them when they'd face something similar too.

Sometimes Lucia and Wanda drank more than was sensible. Other times they took the Tube up to Piccadilly Circus and found a nightclub, dancing themselves almost to the point of collapse with any males who were halfway decent-looking. If you couldn't find an outlet, a distraction, you couldn't go out there on ambulance shifts again and again. 'It makes me forget,' Lucia had told her flatmate one night, as they pooled their remaining cash to take a taxi home in the early hours and the gin had loosened her tongue. Wanda looked at her questioningly, as if she wanted to ask what exactly Lucia wanted to forget: ambulance shifts, or something more?

Lucia's years in France lay between them, yet to be fully unravelled. The Blitz had started last autumn and four months on, still dominated life.

This Tuesday morning, Lucia had an egg. The day was looking promising. But days could trick you like that. She wasn't going to think any more about the house she'd been to last night, which had folded almost politely into itself when the walls finally collapsed. She'd run to get clear as it started to fall. When she'd turned round again she could almost see the atoms rearranging themselves in the empty space where the bricks, wood and tiles had stood. People had died in that house, the essence of what had made them suddenly gone. All these months into the Blitz and she wasn't yet used to it. The ambulance had taken a survivor, the elderly mother, to hospital. But it was the house that had lingered in Lucia's mind. How could the pile of rubble possibly be all that was left? It seemed to be too small to represent a family's home: their life and memories. Her mind was snagged on the moment of the house's collapse, because thinking about the family who had perished would have been intolerable.

Lucia finished her egg. Wanda was watching her, even though she tried hard not to make it obvious. Outside it was raining, drops pattering on the flat roof of next door's outhouse. Her room in this flat in Chelsea was small. With Wanda perched on the bed, there was hardly any floor space left. Luckily she was tidy. Lucia was either in an ambulance, at the station, waiting in a grocer's queue or out finding distraction on her nights off, all of which meant her room wasn't much more than somewhere to sleep and store her few clothes. Wanda must have been reading her mind.

'Still not tempted to go home to Belgravia to sleep in linen and silk in glorious space?'

Lucia shook her head, half-annoyed, half-amused by the persistence. 'This suits me. And they probably wouldn't have me back, anyway, assuming they aren't all down at Claybourne, away from the Luftwaffe.'

Wanda raised her eyebrows but looked as if she was pleased. 'You've got an afternoon shift, haven't you, Fancy?' They kept a small blackboard in the kitchen, where they noted their rosters. 'In the meantime, get some fresh air.'

'God, I'm living with my nanny again.' Lucia smiled at her flatmate to soften the words. 'Any post?' she asked.

'Nothing for you.'

Lucia tried to look unconcerned.

'Don't forget we're going out tonight. Gaumont. Eight o'clock. Comedy spy film set in the Blitz.' Wanda made a face. 'Might be better than it sounds.'

'I'm splitting my sides with laughter already, but it sounds better than Tommy Hadley on the wireless.'

'And parts of the Blitz are funny in a black sort of way.' Their eyes met. It was true that they had shared laughter at the bizarre episodes that sometimes came their way. Wanda took the tray out to the kitchenette.

When Lucia pulled open the blackout and curtains, the view was a reminder of how her life had changed. Claybourne Manor looked on to meadows and farmland. Her old bedroom in Newton Terrace, not so very far away from this flat, over-looked white stuccoed buildings mirroring their own elegant Belgravia house.

Now she overlooked stained, sooty walls and crumbling chimney pots. Sometimes a barrage balloon. It wasn't what she'd have imagined of the romantic haunt of artists and other Bohemians, but it had become home. Not that she was often in the flat to admire it. Shifts kept her busy. When she was off-duty, she went out to the cinema or, less often, to one of the less fashionable nightclubs where she wouldn't run into anyone she'd known at school. If she was off-duty during the day, there seemed to be endless domestic chores or shopping trips to carry out. It was no bad thing. If you kept moving, you didn't dwell on what you'd seen.

Last night, before the house had fallen, when she'd helped the woman out of the kitchen into the ambulance, there'd been parts of a second, possibly third, body on the wall: the tattered sleeves could have been male or female. She'd tried not to look at the bloodied remains, praying she wouldn't be on the recovery operation later. You could control how you felt, but you couldn't completely suppress it. She noticed she'd devel-oped a patch of inflamed skin on the back of her neck and on her wrists. She wondered whether it was her body's way of indi-cating distress.

Bad shifts always made her think of her sister more urgently. Della and Wanda were similar personalities, even though one had been born in Belgravia and the other in

Whitechapel. Living with Wanda couldn't compensate for the loss of Della, though. If anything, it made the void left in Lucia's life even more marked.

Anything could happen to people. You couldn't take their survival for granted. Della was seventeen now. Was she staying on for Higher School Certificate? A Swiss finishing school wouldn't be Della's plan. She was so much more intelligent than Lucia. Anyway, Switzerland was out of reach now.

Her sister still on her mind, Lucia washed and dressed, while Wanda took the ration-books and left for the shops. In a fit of energy, Lucia turned her attention to the kitchen and small bathroom. Scrubbing the hand basin with Vim, she wondered if wartime had meant Della also accustoming herself to domestic duties. Whether she was at school or not, her sister would be finding some way to do her bit. She wouldn't just sit back while people, some of them boys barely older than she was, were being maimed and killed.

Perhaps Della was thinking of continuing her education, like Wanda, who'd completed higher school certificate and gone to university, to St Hilda's in Oxford, no less, to study History. If Lucia had taken the ferry straight home after she'd fled the Ritz that night, perhaps she could have hidden herself in some suburb, finding a job and studying in the evenings. It wouldn't have been like university, but it would have made her better educated. 'You missed all my time at Oxford,' Wanda had remarked when she'd come looking for her back in May last year, days before Hitler invaded France. 'I could have taken you punting.'

'I would have loved that.' The thought of the two of them, drifting down the Cherwell, laughing and chatting, the innocence of it all, had brought a lump to her throat.

'You never wrote,' Wanda said 'Not after you sent me the postcard from Rouen. I worried you'd walked into trouble. I thought you were dead, Fancy.'

'I should have written. I... If my parents came looking for you in Whitechapel, I didn't want you to have to lie.'

She knew Wanda. Telling anything less than the truth seemed to physically hurt her friend.

'I'm sorry I put you through that. It wasn't that I didn't want you to know where I was. At times I...' She'd longed for Wanda. She shook her head, unable to express how she felt, how she had felt in the early weeks of her exile and in the months that had followed.

'I was hurt you didn't let me know you were all right for so long. But I'm sure you had your reasons.'

'I was living a quiet life, in the Cévennes.' A quiet life, but one that still reverberated through her heart. 'Then I went to Paris.'

Paris. Just saying the name of the city aloud took effort.

'I made ends meet by teaching English.' This much was perfectly true. Wanda had looked at her, eyes screwed up, as though waiting for more to be added. 'And my French improved massively.'

'And wherever you were, you learned some pretty advanced driving skills.'

'Certainly helped clinch the ambulance job.'

Lucia had picked up the rudiments on Claybourne Manor's long private drive. She'd honed the skills on the twisty Cévennes roads, driving a truck around bends that made her feel nauseous, knowing one slip would mean almost certain death.

She couldn't think of the memories, couldn't bear to lose herself in them just yet. Today was a Tuesday, so there'd be time later on, when she went to Westminster Bridge for the weekly ritual.

Out of the window, she saw the rain had reduced into a dreary but light drizzle. Wanda wasn't using the bicycle today and the pull of her old home was irresistible this morning. She'd go and stare at Number 6, Newton Terrace. Swinging her gas mask over her shoulders, she found mackintosh, gloves and hat.

The cycle from Chelsea to Belgravia was barely more than ten or fifteen minutes, but Lucia took a longer route, deviating to avoid the ambulance station. No point thinking about work until you had to. Coming through the backstreets kept her in off-duty mode, but it did little to cheer her up, as the drizzle seemed to turn icier as she cycled. She shivered, wishing she'd worn her thick navy work coat instead of her mac. She still hadn't worked out what she was going to do once she'd reached the family house. Hide behind the postbox like a spy all morning, waiting for someone to come out?

The house in Newton Terrace wasn't on the scale of some of the other Belgravia properties in the streets around Eaton Square, but spacious enough for her planned coming-out dinner. Lucia felt yet another pang of guilt at the thought of her mother returning to London, explaining to her friends that her elder daughter had run away into the night, her planned London Season aborted.

Lucia had never stopped yearning for Della, and to a lesser extent her mother. For the umpteenth time she reminded herself that contacting Della would have put her sister in an impossible situation. It would have been unfair to expect Della not to say anything to their parents, especially given the nature of what—

A grocer's delivery van pulled up beside Lucia, causing her to brake. A man jumped out and took boxes of food out of the back. Instead of oranges, grapes and pineapples from all over the world, the boxes contained parsnips and carrots, with the occasional limp cabbage or wrinkled apple. A delivery for a house across the road. The van shielded her and she could watch the front door of number 6. A light was on in a room on the first floor. Was that still Della's bedroom, next to hers? The voile curtains parted and she saw her sister's face. Lucia's heart

gave a huge thump and she heard herself gasp. Della's face had
grown thinner, her hair, now shorter, was pinned back instead
of plaited, but her expression, curious, questioning, was just the
same. Lucia's eyes watered as she stared at her. Her sister
looked down at the delivery van before letting the curtain drop
back. Just looking out to see what was happening in the street
below or checking the weather?

The rain became more persistent, trickling down Lucia's
neck. She was wearing a wool cloche, stylish, a present from her
time in France, but definitely not waterproof. The delivery man
returned to the van, gazing curiously at her before he replaced
the boxes and drove off.

She couldn't stay in plain sight like this. Suppose her father
came out of the house? She hadn't read anything about him in
the papers since her return. She shivered, recalling his fury with
her, the good-humoured mask slipping to reveal a cold anger
that only she seemed to attract.

Once again, she wondered whether she should have written
to Della on her return to London. She hadn't been sure she
could bear the thought of Della either ignoring her letter or
replying that she didn't want to see her. She'd been a coward,
thinking she could take her sister by surprise, force a meeting on
her when she wasn't expecting it. Della was still only seventeen.
Lucia herself had only been a year older when she'd run away
in Paris.

Her head full of conflicting emotion, Lucia turned,
mounting the bicycle. Being this close to Della had made the
loss even more marked. A lump formed in her throat and her
eyes filled. She could barely even see the road ahead of her.

A boy jumped off the pavement as she steered around a
corner, causing her to slam on the brakes and almost go over the
handlebars.

'What on earth did you think you were doing, you complete
idiot?'

'Sorry, miss.' He looked startled. She felt ashamed.

'No, I'm sorry. It was my fault.'

The near miss had jolted her out of her self-pity. Lucia turned the bicycle around and cycled back towards Newton Terrace. She'd ring the bell and ask to see Della, like a normal human being calling on a family member. If her father was there, she'd face him down. They couldn't stop her seeing her sister, could they? They weren't living in Victorian times. She'd caused grief, no doubt, but she hadn't broken any actual law.

As Lucia approached the house again, the front door opened. Della was coming out. She wore a navy school uniform coat that Lucia didn't recognise, but in place of a usual felt school hat or beret she wore a curiously adult hat that almost covered her face, its veil falling over most of her features. The hat jarred with her schoolgirl outer clothes. The three years that had passed had given Della more height – she'd obviously had a growth spurt, just as Lucia herself had done at the same age, and was now taller than her older sister. But so thin, so terribly thin, even allowing for the effects of rationing. Della carried a brown-paper parcel and a leather school satchel, her gas mask slung over her shoulder. Going back to boarding school? No, she didn't have enough luggage, unless this had just been a quick visit. And the coat wasn't right – in winter, girls at their school wore hated bottle-green capes.

Della looked down the street. Up went her arm. The taxi she'd hailed pulled in to pick her up. As the taxi drove past her, Lucia saw her sister lift the veil. Her heart gave a jolt. Della's face was set, serious. It didn't look as if she was paying a social call. Hospital appointment? Visiting a sick or injured friend? Was it Mama? Could it be that Mama had some awful sickness and Della was visiting her in a clinic?

Della's taxi took her south, into Ebury Street. Lucia pedalled after it. She hadn't a hope of keeping up with a motor vehicle, but a delay at the junction with Elizabeth Street meant she caught up briefly. Should she call out, shout at the driver to stop? What would Della think if she was reunited with her sister in the middle of the street?

Before she could come to a decision, the taxi turned right into Buckingham Palace Road, indicating left at the junction with Chelsea Bridge Road. Was Della crossing the Thames to Battersea where the power station puffed its black smoke into the atmosphere? The bombing that side of the Thames had been fierce, the power station acting as a target for the Luftwaffe. Who did Della know over there?

Perhaps the taxi driver was diverting across the river to avoid a road closed by bomb damage. Or perhaps Della was heading for St Thomas's hospital further east, opposite the Houses of Parliament. That would explain the brown-paper parcel. Fresh nightwear for a patient?

Lucia's imagination was working overtime. A clock struck on a church tower, rousing her from her thoughts. She'd lost track of the time and would have to cycle quickly to make it to Westminster Bridge by noon. She could have crossed the river like Della's taxi had, but instead she continued on the north side of the Thames, through Pimlico and past the Victoria Tower Gardens by the Palace of Westminster, staring at the clockface of Big Ben as it came into view, and picking up speed.

She made it on to Westminster Bridge and propped the bicycle against the parapet, heart beating fast, checking her watch as Big Ben's hands reached twelve. The ambulance roster meant it wasn't always possible to be here each Tuesday as she'd promised, but this week it had worked in her favour. Lucia waited until the quarter hour was struck, thinking of the past few years, looking up and down the bridge. The person she was thinking of still wasn't going to come, not this week. Probably not next week, either. Nothing had changed.

She cycled back to the north side of the bridge and headed home to Chelsea, but taking a different route, across St James's

Park, and over to the steps at the Duke of York column. The bicycle was heavy but she carried it up the steps, ignoring the gallant offers of some Canadian privates coming down. At the top, she headed left, making for Carlton Gardens, where the Free French government was based.

She braked and scrutinised the French officers coming and going for a moment until one of them noticed and raised an eyebrow, probably wondering if she was trying to pick him up. Girls did that. The Frenchmen were dashing and generous on nights out. Lucia blushed and cycled on.

When she reached the flat, Lucia lay down on her bed, looking at the cracks in the ceiling as though they were a map that might guide her, her mind no longer on Della's taxi but caught up in the past, back in France.

TEN

JANUARY, 1941

The mouse

'It's only for a little while,' Mami told her. 'Don't look so sad, *schatz*. Plenty have it worse than us.'

This new house smelled of cooking and clothes that were never properly clean. The other people here went quiet when the two of them entered the kitchen, where they were allowed to prepare meals three times a day. There was no sitting room or dining room downstairs as all the rooms were given over to lodgers, so Mami and the mouse brought their meals upstairs to eat, perching on the bed. At first this had been fun, like camping. The bedroom, with its peeling wallpaper and window that had been taped in case it shattered in a blast, felt like a prison. Suppose Papi couldn't find them when he was released? And there wouldn't be room for three of them in the narrow bed. Could they go back to the old home then? They'd had to leave boxes of possessions down in the cellar, including most of the toys, as there wasn't room for them here. Mami grew upset when she asked too many questions about a possible return home.

'We haven't got as much money now. We need to keep ourselves to ourselves. Don't talk when there are other people around,' Mami urged her. 'And never ever chat to people when I'm not there. I need to make sure we give the right answers. I don't want us to be taken away too.'

In the mornings children passed the house, holding hands, chatting, carrying skipping ropes. 'When can I go back to school again?' the mouse asked, looking out of the smeared and taped windows. 'I'm seven. I should be learning.'

'Not for a while,' Mami would say. 'It's too dangerous now.'

'I miss playing with other people.'

'Those children shouldn't still be here in the city. They should have stayed in the countryside when they were sent away last year.'

'Why did they come back?'

'Their parents missed them.'

'Does Papi miss me?' Perhaps he'd forgotten about her by now.

Mami knelt down and took her by the shoulders. 'Of course. He misses you so much.' She sounded fierce. 'You know he wrote to you.'

'He didn't say much.'

'I'm sure he'll write a longer letter soon. I know you're feeling confused. And bored. I'll teach you at home. You'll like that, *mäuschen*. We'll have fun.' Mami released her with a kiss.

It had been a long time since they'd been to the cinema. Perhaps they could go to see the Disney film about the mouse? Mickey wasn't a sad, grey kind of mouse, he was bright and did all kinds of magical things. 'Let me think about it,' Mami said, when asked.

In the meantime, they went to the swings when other children were at school. If anyone else came into the playground, Mami reminded her not to talk. 'Just smile and nod,' she'd say.

The mouse was becoming more and more like her nickname

– quieter, greyer and more timid each day. Mami even swapped the red-knitted cap sent by Oma, her grandmother, before the war started for a grey woollen hat, which Mami said was less eye-catching. She went through all their few clothes and removed labels too. Mami didn't speak to other people much either these days, barely saying a word to the woman in the grocery shop when she passed over the ration books. She'd always been quiet. Papi had done most of the talking outside the house.

'Hanna can't get out of her mind what happened to her brother,' he'd told one of the Sunday-afternoon musicians. Onkel Franz had been taken away. Something bad had happened to him, but Mami and Papi only ever talked about it when she wasn't in earshot.

Occasionally letters came from Papi, still on just a single side of paper, not really saying much. He seemed to be in a camp just outside the city. *Camp* sounded as if it ought to be fun, with games and singing, but Mami shook her head. 'They think people like us are dangerous and need locking up. That's what happened to—' Mami stopped herself. 'Don't look like that. I shouldn't tell you these things, *mäuschen*. Don't worry. I'll keep you safe.'

'I don't even know where Papi is.'

'I'd show you on a map if I had one but it's probably best we don't even have our old *London A to Z* with us now.' Her face tightened. 'They'd say we were spies. Papi's camp is to the west of London. If you were on a boat on the Thames, going downstream, past Hampton Court – remember, we took you to the maze? – it's down there. Cold and exposed this time of year. I hope he packed enough warm clothes.' She'd looked anxious. 'I must try to knit for him. It's so hard to get the wool.'

The shadow fell back across her face. 'Perhaps we made a mistake coming here in the first place,' Mami whispered. 'It wouldn't be so hard to bear if we were still with your Oma.'

Again she seemed to regret her words. 'No, no, that would have been far more dangerous. We are safe. This will pass. It's a case of mistaken identity.'

'What's mistaken identity?'

'There's probably another Ulrich Ketterer—'

Someone knocked on the bedroom door. Mami's face paled. When she opened it, her voice was high-pitched, shaky as she talked to the woman. 'Yes, I've registered myself and my daughter as required, I assure you.'

She closed the bedroom door. 'I think she'll leave us in peace. I hope so.' Mami sat down on the bed. 'She's not a bad sort. I wasn't quite truthful, though, I only registered at the grocer's, not with the local warden. I didn't want too many people knowing exactly where we live.' She put a hand to her brow. 'Sometimes I think I'm going mad.' Mami tried for a cheerful smile, but it didn't work. 'Even that elephant of yours would talk more sense, *mäuschen*.'

The plush toy elephant was one of the few toys taken to this new home, even though she was getting a bit old for soft toys. With the elephant on her lap, it was easy to pretend they were somewhere else – the house they'd just left or, even better, though harder to picture, the house they'd lived in with Oma. Christmas memories burned more brightly. She could still remember the huge tree in the entrance hall her grandmother decorated every year, with its scent of pine forests and oranges. Snow mantled the garden. They threw snowballs at one another. Mami came outside and Papi threw one at her, so Mami stuffed one down the back of his coat, laughing. Oma came out and told them they were worse than children. Then, when they turned their backs, Oma rolled up two huge snowballs and threw them at Mami and Papi, looking innocent as they turned round, all indignant, snow dripping down their collars.

Onkel Franz was there too, always busy, writing away in his study, his face tight as the words sprouted out of the typewriter.

Onkel Franz's face and even Oma's were hard to recall now, but that world of snow and Christmas scents felt more real than this room, with its peeling wallpaper, the taped window looking out at other houses and its smell that was like sadness itself.

When Papi had first given her her mouse nickname, she'd imagined herself as a pretty white mouse, like the ones magicians had, but she was really just a dull-coloured creature nobody would even notice, living in a mousehole.

Mami had found some scraps of paper and the colouring pencils taken with them from the other house. 'Draw something for me, *mäuschen*.'

'Tell me about the camp where Papi is again? I'll draw it.'

Mami's mouth tensed. 'They used to race horses there. It was a place to have fun.'

She sat the elephant up against the pillows on the bed and dropped down to the tatty rug on the floor. The colouring pencils in the wooden box felt comforting. The lost world recreated itself: the trees, the garden, the snow, even the dirty brown river with its barges. And then the horses, running round a track, Papi watching them.

ELEVEN

Lucia and the others on the afternoon shift were told to sweep the ambulance interiors and hose them out. They did this on their return from every call-out, but in the dark, it was hard to get into every nook and cranny and make sure that blood and other bodily fluids had been removed.

'It's remarkable how much can leak from an injured human being,' Gardner remarked, as they took down the curtains at the back of the van that replaced doors – easier to open in a hurry. Gardner was Lucia's usual partner on shifts. Her Christian name was Alice, but they always called one another by surname. The disinfectant they diluted in enamel buckets made Lucia cough, but was also somehow bracing, clearing her head.

The old Lucia Blake would have found the work a shock. But in the Cévennes she'd grown accustomed to physical labour under a warm sun. She glanced upward at the sky in the hope of glimpsing it now, that reminder of long, light days and laughter, wine in a stone jug, an arm around your waist, pulling you close... but the sun had evidently decided that wintery, dirty London wasn't its home. Lucia returned to her task. At least

returning ambulances to a pristine state took her mind off everything that was painful to recall.

Lucia was heading back to the tap to refill the bucket so she
could give the tyre hubs a final rinse when the siren sounded.
She and Gardner stopped, looking at one another. Overhead it
sounded as though the bombers would head further east into
the centre of London. They carried on rinsing the tyres. The
alert sounded. Under the station mess they had their own shelter. If they weren't called out, they'd usually go down there. 'No
point getting blown up for no good reason,' Potts, the station
supervisor, always said.

Something crumped nearby, answered by another crash.
The building shook. Before they could head into the shelter, the
telephone rang.

'That'll be control for us.' Gardner put down her bucket
and went to answer the telephone, reappearing with a piece of
paper with an address on it, followed by Potts, a small woman in
her forties who'd apparently been a florist before the war 'but
could have been a dictator,' Wanda had once muttered. Lucia
found it hard to imagine Potts gently twisting stems into dainty
shapes and tying satin ribbons round bouquets.

The crews had already gathered, but Potts blew the whistle,
as if concerned that they mightn't have noticed what was
happening. She pointed at Lucia. 'You'll be driver, Black, with
Gardner here accompanying you.'

Lucia still had to remind herself that she was Black now.
Lucie Black. She hoped the momentary lack of response wasn't
visible on her face.

'Explosive and incendiaries and at least one casualty to
remove by stretcher. Heavy rescue's been called to see if there's
anyone else there. Some reports of a child. James will take the
car for sitting cases.'

Sitting cases were casualties a doctor or nurse could treat at
the scene of the bomb, patching them up so they didn't need to

be taken to the hospital, reducing the pressure there. James, a quiet, former doctor in his early thirties, would carry out this role from the station's Wolseley car while Lucia and Gardner took the hospital cases in the ambulance.

Lucia and Gardner abandoned the buckets and cloths and got into the ambulance. Everything had been checked, their first aid supplies inspected and replaced, tyre pressures had been tested and the engine topped up with oil.

This Austin van was certainly clunkier than Mama's Morris Eight, which she'd learned to drive in, but not as temperamental as the truck she'd driven in France. When she changed gears as she slowed for the junction, the ambulance screeched a protest but obliged. In its former life it had been a wine merchant's delivery van and sometimes an aroma of claret and sherry seemed to underlie the tang of disinfectant. Perhaps the vehicle missed carrying out deliveries, resented driving into smoke and flames, retrieving the wounded and dying, and that was why it emitted its complaints. Sometimes Lucia felt an urge to reassure it that one day it would return to its more cheerful existence, conveying champagne and burgundy for celebrations.

Gardner would think she was mad if she talked to the ambulance, if she explained that driving it through an air-raid made her feel paradoxically stable, tethered to the world instead of drifting unconnected from everything and everyone.

Gardner already regarded Lucia with a similar wry amusement to Wanda. Lucie Black never talked about her upbringing, but something of Lucia Blake's former existence clung to her. She ought to expand Lucie Black into more of a person, but it felt dishonest.

The overhead percussion, as Wanda called it, grew to a roar. 'Not just a light lunchtime concert,' Gardner said darkly. Lucia felt a shiver and the almost electric jolt that passed through her each time they set off for an incident. Their eyes met briefly.

TWELVE

The mouse

'Not a word, *mäuschen,* and keep quiet. Remember what I said?' Mami was putting on her hat, picking up her basket. 'I won't be long. The queues at the grocer's shouldn't be too bad after the lunchtime rush.'

'Can't I come with you, Mama?' She sighed when she saw her mother's face.

'I don't like us being out on the streets. People stare at us. I wouldn't go out at all if we didn't badly need food. We can't eat that whale meat. It'll make us sick.' She shuddered at the memory of it.

'Don't leave the room,' Mami continued, picking up her gas mask and closing the door behind her. 'I'll be as quick as I can. 'Don't talk to anyone.'

Who to? Nobody disturbed them in the bedroom. And why couldn't she go shopping too? Was Mami still frightened that the men in uniform would snatch them on the street?

Being left alone was the worst of all things. She knew the few books they'd taken from the other house off by heart and longed for new ones. As the front door clicked open and then shut very quietly, she found the pencils and precious sheets of paper – only two left – and drew. Mountains in the background, the sun in the sky. In the foreground, a house with steep eaves and red shutters. She could barely remember it now, but sometimes the red awnings on the grocer's shops brought back the image of the faraway house, and Oma. The heaviness in her chest made her put down the pencil. Why were they being punished like this?

Something scratched at the door. The cat. She went to let him in. Mami wouldn't approve of her playing with Timmi, who belonged to their landlady in the bedroom next door, but he was so friendly, rubbing against her ankles.

'You're a cat and I'm a mouse, but we're friends.' He lay on his back, purring, letting her rub his stomach. If only she had something for him to eat. On the table in the kitchen, the piece of whale meat still sat on its enamel plate. 'Fit only for a dog or cat, that's all,' Mami had said. 'But if someone sees me throwing it away, who knows who they might report me to?'

Nobody was stirring in the house. The landlady worked nights in a factory and was sleeping. Who would know that Timmi had eaten the whale meat?

She stood up. 'Come on,' she told him. 'You're going to have a treat.' Picking up the toy elephant she opened the door quietly and went downstairs, Timmi jumping down the steps behind her silently. The elephant came with her everywhere she went nowadays.

The whale meat smell reached her before the kitchen door was opened. Screwing up her nose, she put the plate on the lino floor. The siren sounded. She froze. They were supposed to go down to the public shelter a block away. Unlike their last home, this house didn't have a cellar, nor did it have an Anderson shelter in what was called the garden – really just a grey patch of grass and an outhouse where the lavatory was. She'd never gone to the public shelter by herself. Mami was only going to be away for a short period. Perhaps she should just wait here until she returned.

The house shook to the vibration of the approaching bombers. Cups rattled on their hooks. When she'd still been going to school, a teacher had told them about a cupboard under the stairs being a safe place to go if you really couldn't make the shelter. Where was Timmi? He should go into the cupboard with her too.

The cat had already eaten the whale meat and vanished, perhaps hiding himself in some tiny safe space he knew. The planes really were very loud now. The house shook as though it was terrified. Guns fired. She clutched the table. *Time to move,* Papi's voice shouted in her head. *Get under cover.*

The understairs cupboard was full of bulky objects. A vacuum cleaner, an ironing board. A spider's web brushed her face. She squeezed into the small remaining space between the vacuum cleaner and board, just like a small mouse. It was dusty but warm. Mami would surely know to look for her here when she came back. Anyway, she knew the sound the all-clear made when the planes had gone. She'd get out of the cupboard then. Sometimes, you were forced into public shelters if they caught you outside. The wardens wouldn't listen to any excuses. That would be where Mami was now – safe, but clenching her hands tightly around the shopping bag because the two of them had been separated.

The rumbling overhead became a deeper thundering as the planes flew over and the guns responded with fire. The pilots didn't really know where she was, they weren't aiming their bombs at her, but it felt as though they were up there, pointing to where the Ketterer girl, the mouse, sheltered, and trying to hit the building. She clutched her knees to her chest and closed her eyes. Her plush elephant was on the kitchen table. If only he was in here with her now.

Bombs whistled above her. Very close now. It felt as if all the air had pushed itself out of the cupboard. Something crashed overhead. The cupboard shook. The ironing board rocked but didn't fall on her. Mice were safe in air-raids – so tiny, they could wriggle into spaces where bombs couldn't reach them. They scuttled out when the all-clear went, unharmed, even when larger creatures were hurt. She was safe in her mousehole.

She opened her eyes again. It was still dark.

Her scream wasn't a mouse squealing; it was a terrified child's cry, but the sound was lost in the roar of the bombers overhead and the guns firing.

THIRTEEN

Lucia steered sharply to the right to avoid a large chunk of burning metal. Overhead, Dorniers and Heinkels rumbled against the ack-ack from the ground and the crash of walls crumpling down. It was daylight. The raid shouldn't feel as apocalyptic as it did in the dark, but seeing the bombers above was like a slap in the face, a blatant display of aggression. Gardner was dabbing Vicks under her nose. 'Want some, Black?'

She nodded, extending a finger for Gardner to dab it on. The menthol blocked the smells of burning rubber, brick and fuel, and the more human smells they'd might encounter. It could be bad where the drains had burst or fire had incinerated an occupied building. When she and Della had been small, their nanny had rubbed Vicks on their chests in cold and flu season, telling them it would keep the germs out of their lungs. Nanny would have retired now. She wondered if Mama had pensioned her off in one of the cottages back in the country. If so, Nanny would be bored rigid... Lucia nudged herself mentally as her concentration slipped. Daydreaming was dangerous.

The road was littered with metal and brick, sometimes Lucia had to brake, reverse up and steer round fallen masonry and shrapnel. The side of one house had collapsed, leaving the rooms inside apparently intact. Exposed to curious gazes, it was like a giant dolls' house, with curtains still hanging in windows, a wardrobe and lamp standing sentinel in a bedroom. It made Lucia feel like a voyeur. *A slice of life in 1941 London.* Perhaps future archaeologists might uncover blitzed houses and photograph them, washing and labelling artefacts, pondering the destruction and asking what on earth humankind had been thinking.

Beside her, Gardner had fallen quiet. Sometimes, there was nothing to say. They were bracing themselves for what they were about to find. The constant crashing around them made it hard to have much of a conversation anyway. The smell of burning penetrated through the van's vents and even through the Vicks aroma. Lucia coughed. Incendiaries had fallen into smashed roofs and set off fires in houses that looked reasonably unscathed.

'Turn right here,' Gardner shouted, looking at the map. 'Number eight is the fourth house on the right.'

When they'd first started working together, Gardner had told her side streets like this one had been slums until well into the twentieth century. The terraces now housed tradesmen and shopkeepers' families, with a few operating as lodging houses. Not everyone in Chelsea was either a Bohemian aristocrat, an artist or utterly destitute, as Wanda liked to remark.

Number six, the house adjoining number eight, had taken a direct hit. Flames poured from its roof, the smoke thick and greasy. An engine pulled up outside, men working hard with hoses. Number eight itself had lost a large part of its roof. The first-floor bedrooms had probably gone too, and the ground-floor would be littered with fallen masonry and timbers. Sometimes, it was worse inside than it appeared externally. The warden, a woman, waved them down.

'Here we go,' Gardner said darkly.

Lucia braked, feeling a shiver and the almost electric jolt that passed through her each time they arrived at an incident. Their eyes met briefly before they opened the doors and jumped out.

'Two deceased, removed from number six,' the warden told Lucia. 'The stretcher party are bringing out a badly injured woman from number eight for you. We're still not sure whether there's a child in there too. No minors registered but a neighbour thought she saw her.'

In some streets people came and went like flotsam on the tide, bombed out, moving to new jobs, or sometimes with other reasons for not registering with the wardens.

The sitting-cases doctor, James, had arrived before them in the Wolseley. He tapped Lucia on the shoulder. 'I'm driving back to the station to see if they need me elsewhere.' He had to shout above the crashes of falling buildings and the glass splintering and crackling to the ground. 'I've looked at the female casualty from number eight. Definitely a hospital job. She might make it.'

'The heavy lifting squad are clearing a path through to the cupboard under the stairs,' the warden said, coming up to them. 'They may have put the child in there.'

'How do you know there's a child if the woman's not able to tell you?' Lucia asked. Some of the wardens had an almost supernatural ability to tell who'd been in the house when it was hit: a kettle still warm on the stove, shoes removed by the front door and coats hanging, plates of food on the table.

The warden reached into her deep jacket pockets and pulled out a plush toy elephant. 'It was on the kitchen table.' She frowned at Lucia. 'Are you all right?'

Lucia was staring at the elephant. A string was being pulled very deep inside her, tugging out something delicate into the blackened air and fury of the air-raid.

'Sometimes it's the kids' things that get you,' Gardiner said gruffly. 'Buck up, Black.'

'Sorry.' Lucia took a breath and blinked hard.

Emerging from the dust and smoke, the stretcher with the female casualty approached, the stretcher-bearers picking their way cautiously through the rubble. Lucia pulled open the curtains at the rear of the ambulance so the stretcher party could slide the casualty inside: a woman in her thirties, face blackened, lying very still. 'Just about alive,' one of the stretcher-bearers told Lucia. 'She caught the worst of the roof falling in.'

Lucia made herself pay attention. The woman had rings on her left index finger. The mother of the missing child? Gardner wrote out a label – X for internal injury – and tied it through the woman's pyjama jacket buttonhole. Above them, a harsh skirling-like sound meant more bombs: this time, explosives. A splattering incendiary fell beside them in a flash of white light.

'Stand clear,' the warden called out, running for the stirrup pump to extinguish it. Firemen shouted and redirected hoses as fires broke out up the street.

As she backed up the ambulance, Lucia heard a cry behind her. One of the stretcher bearers banged on the windscreen. 'Stop, miss, there's another casualty.'

A rescuer was carrying out a bundle of what looked like old clothes. Except that a small white arm dangled down. It moved. 'The child.' Lucia pulled on the brake, heart pounding. 'Still alive.'

'Our adult casualty looks pretty desperate,' Gardner shouted at the rescuer. She looked at Lucia. 'Has James left?' Lucia spun round to see James's car just turning into the main road. Too late.

'Can you squeeze the child in with you?' the warden asked,

running up to the window. 'No obvious injury but she's not talk-ing, probably in shock. Or a head injury.'

Gardner got out to help. The child was loaded in, the warden handing her the toy elephant. Obviously hers, she clutched at it, her face relaxing briefly as she was reunited with it. 'She was in the cupboard under the stairs,' the warden said. Lucia stared at the child and the elephant, mind spinning. Gardner shouted that she was going to sit in the back of the ambulance with the kid. Once the two of them were safely inside, Gardner banged on the internal partition, rousing Lucia from her thoughts. She was here, in Chelsea, in a raid, with patients to take to safety, people who needed her to concentrate. She put the ambulance into gear and let it roll forward.

The daytime raid was brief and seemingly isolated, the all-clear sounding as they approached the hospital. The afternoon returned to being another grey, late-winter London day, locals emerging from shelters, brushing off earth and dust from clothes, looking at watches, trying to recall what they'd been doing when their afternoons had been broken up. Yet again Lucia thanked her stars she was driving in daylight. At night, she feared crashing into another poorly lit vehicle, or even running over a pedestrian who'd missed the edge of the pave-ment. The ambulance was painted grey, with only a white A on the nearside, its lights taped according to blackout regulations. Easy to miss at night and to walk out into the road in front of it.

At St Stephen's they waited in a queue for the porters to come and empty the ambulance. Sometimes, it felt like being on a conveyor belt in a factory. Was the child the daughter of the woman on the stretcher? How awful it must be for her, seeing her mother like that. Perhaps they should have taken her into the front with them so she didn't have to look at the motionless body, but it was strictly against the rules. At night you might get away with it, but not in daylight.

Gardner got out and spoke to a porter, nodding and running

up to the driver-side window. 'They're sending a stretcher to take in the woman, but it's bedlam in there. They want us to take the kid somewhere else.'

'Shouldn't she be in the same hospital as her mother?'

'If that's who she is.' Gardner shrugged. 'The girl can sit up now and looks brighter, but she's still not saying a word. Don't know what we're to do with her. I've begged a doctor to assess her quickly.'

A doctor in a white coat came outside. Lucia jumped out. 'We can check your child patient over quickly for you inside, but there's no bed if she needs admitting. You'll have to take her on to the Fulham or Chelsea.' He scooped up the child, who looked about six or seven, into his arms. 'Come on, little missy, let's have a look at you in the warm.' He looked over his shoulder. 'One of you will have to come in with her too. We haven't got time to bring her back out to you. Sorry.'

'We haven't got time, either,' Gardner muttered. 'We're not their lackeys. We need to go back to the station, Potts will be fretting.'

'All-clear's sounded. Might as well just go with it.' So many males, either doctors, orderlies or other auxiliaries, seemed to regard them as domestic subordinates. At first, it had riled Lucia, but not this afternoon. Something about the child, her silence, her smallness, had caught at her. And the doctor had only been curt because he had so many people to see, had probably been working without rest for longer than she could imagine. 'I'll go in with her.'

She followed the doctor's white coat into the hospital. He swept the child into a cubicle in what had once been the reception hall. Lucia waited outside. A WVS, volunteer service woman, wheeled a trolley and offered her an enamel mug of tea. 'I've got a friend out there,' Lucia said guiltily as she took the mug. 'She'd love something to drink too.' She'd only been exposed to the bombed house for minutes, but the dust had settled in the back of her throat. Gardner's throat would feel just as gritty.

'Your colleague in the ambulance will be my very next customer.' The woman pulled a cover off a dish, revealing a plate of biscuits. 'I save these for the people I think need them most.'

Lucia felt guilty, but took a digestive biscuit gratefully. 'Why's it so busy in the hospital? This raid wasn't as bad as some?'

'We can't clear the casualties as quickly as we'd like.' She nodded in the direction of the ceiling. 'The wards upstairs are jam-packed. We took in a lot from the East End too. They were overwhelmed over there last night.' The WVS woman looked guilty. 'But you didn't hear that from me, I'm not supposed to comment on the hospital or its admissions.'

Anything that might be considered bad for morale was not to be spoken of. It was a rule the ambulance crew quietly broke among themselves, snorting with derision at official newspaper accounts of raids, which often came days after the bombers had flown away and were sparse in detail, for fear of giving away useful information to the Luftwaffe.

'That little girl you brought in looked very pale.'

'I don't think she's actually physically harmed—'

Lucia broke off as the cubicle curtain opened. The doctor beckoned her inside. She handed the half-empty mug back to the WVS woman with a quick thanks.

'Nothing wrong with the lass,' he said. 'No bones broken, barely a scratch. No concussion, but she's very shaken, aren't you, little one?' He stroked her head, looking more tenderly at her than the terse voice suggested. 'Won't let go of her elephant. Find a social worker to take her somewhere for the night.'

A nurse bustled in. 'Doctor, the woman with the head injury...'

He nodded at Lucia. 'Back to you, find the social worker,

good luck.' He glanced back at the child and his face was still tender.

Lucia watched him scurry out. The girl was still lying on the bed, the elephant beside her. 'Are you hungry?' In her pocket she had a small, precious bar of chocolate that Wanda must have given her at some point. The girl took it, looking pleased, but still silent. At least she had some appetite, that was promising.

Lucia scanned the ground floor, finding the back offices where the administrators worked. Nobody seemed to know where the social worker was. Her temporary office was empty. Lucia found the WVS lady again and explained the situation.

'Miss Goodley has probably gone to the rest centre,' she told Lucia. 'The welfare adviser there was overwhelmed with East End children needing beds for the night. She's probably lending a hand. Perhaps take your misplaced child down to her there?'

'We should really go back to the station with the ambulance.' Gardner would be growing restless.

'I'll take her to the rest centre, if you want. My shift's nearly up and I can walk home that way.' The woman had a frank and cheerful face – she'd be kind to the girl. Logically, this was the best course of action to take. But Lucia knew she couldn't walk away.

'She hasn't been labelled and we don't even have a first name for her. She'll be lost in the system. We brought her in with a woman who wasn't looking so good.'

'Have a quick word with the nurse, see if there's any information about the mother, if that's who she is. I'll write it on a label for her.'

Lucia forced herself to nod. She dashed outside to tell Gardner what was happening. 'Sorry for keeping you waiting.'

'Raid's over,' Gardner said. 'If we go back now, we'll just be polishing hub caps.' She nodded at the seat beside her where a tattered copy of *Punch* sat. 'I begged this off one of the orderlies. Another ten minutes won't matter.'

Stopping housemen, nurses and a few cleaners to ask directions, Lucia eventually tracked down the ward where the adult female casualty was being assessed. The nurses scurrying from bed to bed were too busy to talk to her, shaking their heads as she approached, but she caught the eye of a doctor, an older man behind a desk, who came over to ask her what she wanted. He frowned when she described the woman. 'I'm afraid there's only one female who fits that bill and I don't think she made it.'

'I've got her young daughter, we presume that's who she is, downstairs.'

'Social worker.' He stood up from the desk, looking over her shoulder. 'Miss Goodley. That's who you want. I need to press on, sorry.'

'Was there a name for the female casualty?' she called after his back, but he was already preoccupied with what a nurse was telling him about another patient and didn't respond. Someone shouted at her to stand to the side. Another party of stretcher-bearers came carrying an elderly woman.

Everything seemed to lead back to this Miss Goodley who couldn't be found. Downstairs, the WVS lady was tidying up her trolley, replacing cups and mugs and counting teaspoons. 'No luck?' she said. 'I can tell by your face. Let me take the little girl with me to the rest centre.'

Again, something stopped Lucia from doing this. She didn't want to be burdened with tracking down missing family, it wasn't her job and the ambulance needed to be returned to the station, tidied up, and her shift completed. Yet the image of the girl clutching her toy caught at her. 'You've been really helpful, thank you, but we'll drive her to the centre.'

The girl seemed happy enough to return to the ambulance with Lucia. 'Squeeze in here between us, kiddo,' Gardner said. 'It's a bit lonely for you and your elephant rattling around in the back.' She winked at Lucia. 'This little one can duck down if we see anyone who might have a problem.'

Lucia's heart sank as they pulled up outside the rest centre. People were spilling in and out of the doors, carrying bundles of bedding and crying babies, shaking their heads, looking baffled, sometimes angry, mostly resigned. 'I heard they were taking in some of the East End families to relieve the pressure over there.' Gardner shook her head. 'There might be a social worker or someone from Welfare in there, but we haven't a hope of finding them before our shift finishes.'

Lucia looked down at the child. If they left her alone in that centre, she'd be swallowed up in the morass of humanity. Nobody would know her, or where she'd come from. They could write her address on a label and fix it to her clothing somehow, but she was a child and children pulled labels off or removed outer layers. She exchanged glances with Gardner.

'We could leave her here and then make some telephone inquiries when we're back at the station?' Gardner said. 'Tell the social worker we dropped her off here? I know we're not supposed to use the telephone, but I can distract Potts while you make a call.'

'I just don't think I can leave her in there.' Lucia pointed at another large group emerging from the front door of the rest centre, quickly replaced by a group alighting from a charabanc. 'Look at that coach-load of people getting out. It'll be a scrum inside. I just...' She felt as if something was blocking her throat. 'I can't... She...'

She couldn't leave this child alone with strangers, a small being surrounded by the noise and crush. Every cell in her body rebelled against it. Gardner looked at her. Lucia thought she was going to tell her that the child had to be left here. 'Please,' she said. 'It just feels wrong.'

Gardner was still staring at her, a look of puzzlement on her face.

'I know, I'm being sentimental. She just reminds me of...' She stopped. This wasn't the time.

'She reminds you of someone in your family?'

'My... little sister. We're estranged.' She couldn't go into details about Della and it felt wrong to even refer to her. 'We were close when she was small.'

Gardner sighed and put the ambulance into gear again. 'Let's get you into the station, Little Miss Whatever-Your-Name-Is. You can have some cocoa and we'll do some telephoning. Perhaps you'll start talking, which will make everything easier.' The child remained silent, but something in her features made her look less wary.

'Absolutely irregular.' Gardner had not been successful in keeping Potts away from the telephone. 'This station is not an extension of a welfare office, Black. Or a nursery.' Her face softened as she looked at the child, sitting at the table in the mess and eating Lucia's ham sandwich. 'I see you've fed her, but what now? She's not a stray cat who can camp out here in a cardboard box.'

Lucia tried again to explain about the chaotic hospital, the bursting rest centre, the elusive social worker. Potts cut her short, looking at her watch. 'Your shift ends in half an hour, Black. You have that much time to resolve the situation. Less, if there's another alert.' Potts threw a leather-bound address book at her. 'I keep useful telephone numbers in there. Good luck.'

Luck did seem to be on her side as Lucia managed to find someone in the hospital's administrative office who gave her another telephone number for the social worker's office. Luck ran out as the telephone rang unanswered. No surprises there – it was half-seven now.

Gardner brought in the bucket and sponge she'd been using to clean out the dirt and blood that the child and her mother, if she was her mother, had brought into the back of the ambulance. She looked at the clock on the wall. 'Time's running out, Black.'

'I know.' She was supposed to be meeting a group for the cinema tonight. Wanda was going to meet her there. The child sat on the bench, cocoa mug in her hands, her eyes on her. Lucia tried to look away, but found herself turning back. This girl was now completely reliant on strangers and couldn't even tell them her name.

Potts was coming in, her heavy boots pounding across the yard. Lucia held out a hand. 'Come on, kid, let's take you home for the night.'

Gardner was saying something, but Lucia cut across her. 'I just can't think of anything else, can you?'

'No. But—'

'But what?'

Gardner shrugged. 'We could have taken in other kids who didn't have anywhere to go, but we haven't before. What is it about this girl?'

'I ... don't know.' The child had pulled at something inside her that she didn't want to explain. She'd disinterred emotions that had been buried deep inside Lucia, taking her back to the time before bombs and destruction. Gardner looked at her, the puzzled frown back on her face.

'Hope you know what you're doing, Black,' she said.

So did Lucia.

Wanda would be looking at her watch by now, sighing at Lucia's lateness though probably imagining it was work-related. Lucia was supposed to go straight to the Gaumont to meet her for the film. There were a crowd of them going out, she told herself, so Wanda's night wouldn't be spoiled if she didn't appear. Wanda would have heard the alert. She'd be worried.

Lucia couldn't bring herself to leave without using the decontamination shower. The warm water – far more reliable than that at the flat – would help her sort herself out, clear her head. 'I'll only be a few minutes,' she told the girl.

She stood under the hot water for as long as she felt she could justify. When she had towelled herself off, she dressed in the spare clothes she kept here, rolling up the trousers she'd worn to take to the laundry, the child watching her inscrutably from the wooden stool in the shower room.

'All clean,' Lucia told her brightly. 'Come on.' She sat the child on the bicycle seat. 'Let's put your elephant in the basket.' The girl grew rigid. 'I'll be very careful.'

Reluctantly, she let Lucia take the toy. Lucia held the elephant for a moment and stroked it, noting that the plush fur was wearing a bit in places. The girl must have had it since babyhood. Images of an infant with the elephant sitting at the bottom of the crib flashed through Lucia's mind, unbidden, unwelcome. Seven was old to be carrying a soft toy around, but she'd seen plenty of children the same age who'd been bombed out or evacuated who clung to reminders of earlier, more secure times.

She placed the toy carefully in the basket with her rolled-up trousers. 'Hold on to my arm.' The girl looked around at the houses as Lucia pushed her along, silent, seemingly unalarmed that a stranger was taking her somewhere unknown. Lucia's mind raced ahead. Did they even have food in the kitchen to feed their guest?

When she and the child arrived upstairs, the blackout was pulled down and the light switched on, Lucia saw that a film of dust coated her small body. 'Let's see if I can heat up some water for a bath for you.'

It was Wanda's turn for a bath so there wouldn't be much hot water. Lucia put the kettle on as well. The gas flame burned weakly. Gas pressure was so variable after raids, when mains had been blown or the supply turned off. Sometimes it wasn't switched on until the following day, or even longer. Clean clothes were going to be a problem too, a quick look at the girl's skirt and jumper told Lucia. She'd wash them, but in the meantime, other garments would be needed.

'Bath first and then I'll cook you some supper.' The girl barely seemed to blink. 'You know, I need a name to call you by.' A flicker of understanding passed over her small face but she didn't speak. 'You're not going to tell me, are you?' Lucia sighed. It had been a long day. 'I hope you'll trust me soon.' She smiled. 'Hope? That's what I'm going to call you for now. There are so many things I hope for.' She faltered, thinking of them.

The girl smiled very slightly.

'Hope it is then. You sit down here at the table while I sort your bath out. Wanda has a bottle of Floris bath essence. James at the station gave it to her, said he'd found it in a friend's bombed-out bathroom.' She wondered why she was prattling on to the silent child. 'I think James likes Wanda, although he's a bit old for her and she has a host of male admirers. She won't mind if we use a little. It will make you smell of geraniums and you'll feel all clean and ready for sleep.'

Sleep. Where on earth were they to put the little guest? If Hope slept on the sofa, she'd be disturbed by Wanda on her way home. She'd have to take the cushions and make Hope a bed on the floor of her own room. If she had nightmares, Lucia'd be on hand to comfort her.

For the first month of her exile, Lucia had suffered from terrible dreams that her father, dressed in his black shirt, burst through the bedroom door, henchmen behind him, to pull her out of her bed and drag her back to Newton Terrace. The nightmares had faded away under the clear starry skies of southern France and had never returned. London nights with the Luftwaffe overhead provided enough bad dreams.

Yet Lucia still had dreams that caused her to wake full of regret and longing. They weren't nightmares, more unbearable windows into the past.

FOURTEEN

Lucia imagined her guest might wake in the night, but woke herself, with a start, at half-six. For a few seconds, she lay there, listening to Hope's even breathing. She had a morning shift, half-seven until half-three. Fifteen minutes to walk to the station, seven if she could take the bicycle. But what to do with Hope? Wanda must be home now and wondering what had happened to the sofa cushions.

'Are you awake, Hope?' she asked, sitting up. 'We need to get up now as I have to be back at work.' She hadn't got around to washing the girl's clothes last night. They'd have to give them a quick brush down. What on earth was she going to do with Hope when she went to work? Could Wanda be persuaded to keep an eye on her while Lucia was at work? Her next shift started in the afternoon as Lucia's ended.

Hope sat up in her improvised bed. Her face looked brighter this morning and she smiled tentatively at Lucia.

'Good, you're awake. Let's get you up. I'll sponge the worst of the dirt off your clothes.' She smiled at the girl. 'You can talk, you know. You're safe here.' The girl looked down at the floor. Lucia reproached herself silently. Best to let Hope be.

Scrubbing at the blouse and skirt with her flannel made them look a little more presentable. She gave them back to Hope, telling her to wash. 'There's a spare toothbrush in the cupboard by the basin, you should do your teeth too.'

No eggs this morning, so toast would have to do. Lucia found her weekly butter ration and scraped it on the toast. Some people predicted butter would be more severely rationed soon and they'd have to switch to loathsome, greasy margarine. Wanda, who'd eaten margarine since childhood, was always scathing about Lucia's dislike of it. 'Did the Blake family have their Jersey cow to produce their butter?' she'd mocked.

Wanda's bedroom door opened, and she emerged, rubbing her eyes. She stopped, blinked and looked from Hope to Lucia. 'We seem to have a guest?'

'Wanda, meet Hope. Hope, meet Wanda.' Hope examined Wanda expressionlessly, before returning to her toast. She seemed hungry this morning. Shame there wasn't more food for her. 'I'll explain in there,' Lucia added, nodding at her bedroom. 'Eat up, Hope.'

In the bedroom, Wanda closed the door behind them, eying the sofa cushions on the floor. 'I just thought you'd spilled cocoa on them again.'

'She was pulled out of a house we were sent to. No injuries, and the hospital was full and we couldn't track down anyone from Welfare. Chelsea's still flooded with East-End bombed-out as well as our own.' She was babbling away.

Wanda groaned and sat down on the bed. 'Lucky you could give her a bed for the night.' She frowned. 'Fancy? You're finding somewhere for her to go tonight?'

'Absolutely. Just a one-night stopgap.' She looked at her watch. 'Thing is...'

'You're on the morning roster and Pottsie'll blow her top if you bring Hope back to the station.'

Lucia nodded. 'She might just let me make telephone calls to sort something out for Hope.'

'On the station telephone? The one we keep open for control to ring us on?'

'Yes, I'll be chancing my arm.'

Wanda made a slight face. 'I planned on cycling down to Wimbledon Common as it's not actually raining or freezing today.'

'Sorry.' It wasn't fair to ask Wanda to give up her exercise. 'Of course. I'll take her with me. Potts will have to bear it.' She lowered her voice even more. 'If she's that incensed, she can tell me what exactly I'm supposed to do with a child nobody seems to want and...' She checked the door was properly closed. 'Whose mother has probably died. Apart from leaving her alone in a heaving rest centre.'

'Her mother was a casualty?' Wanda let out a sigh. 'Poor kid.'

Lucia shrugged. 'If she actually was the mother. They pulled her out unconscious.'

'And you haven't even got a full name for this kid?'

'I haven't got a name at all. She won't talk, so I called her Hope.'

Wanda frowned. 'Didn't the warden know the family?'

'She didn't think they were registered with her. I had to call the girl something and that's what I came up with, because, well...'

'Because it would be good to have something to hope for.' Wanda nodded.

'I should go.' She was running late. No, it was more that she didn't want Wanda to see the longing on her face that talk of hope had brought to the surface.

'Leave Hope here, Lucia. I'll try and find your warden for you.' Wanda's voice was gentle. 'Write down the address and I'll walk down there with Hope. She might have found out more. Someone might even recognise her.'

'I don't know why I didn't think of that.'

'By the time we've finished a tough shift we barely know our own names.'

They looked at one another in silent understanding for a moment, before Lucia made a dash for the bathroom to clean her teeth and pin up her hair. Potts was going through one of her pushes on neatness at the moment. Lucia's dark blond hair had always been thick and she kept it tidy, but Potts would pounce if a single lock fell out from the side, even under a helmet at the end of a long and difficult shift. They weren't in the forces, and they didn't have proper uniforms yet, just wearing warm, dark and practical clothes they cobbled together. Potts was right to insist they looked well presented, Lucia conceded. If you were pulled out of a bombed house, you needed to believe that the people looking after you were trained and competent.

Lucia and Wanda had been taken off shifts together. For once, Lucia was grateful for this or else she would have to have left Hope alone in the flat, which would have been traumatic for the girl, given what had happened yesterday when her mother had gone out shopping without her.

Potts had thought Wanda and Lucia disruptive when they were on the roster together. They'd probably laughed too much. Gardner was quieter, older, kept her thoughts to herself. Lucia barely knew anything about her other than that she lived with her elderly father.

Gardner was a decent sort, with an acerbic sense of humour. She was a good partner, quick and precise with directions, sharp at calling out a warning if she spotted a hazard in the road or a pedestrian about to spring out. Probably, if Wanda had been on shifts with Lucia, they'd have argued in the same way they did in the flat, about silly things that seemed to take on more importance than they merited. Wanda could be so bossy, and Lucia didn't like taking orders, or advice, as Wanda preferred to call it. Spending more time together might have meant Wanda's curiosity about France would have broken through. She might have asked questions Lucia wasn't ready to answer. Potts might actually be like a half-decent games' mistress, pulling together the right teams.

Lucia said goodbye to the other two, telling Hope that Wanda would look after her. Hope looked down at the crumbs on the kitchen table, her shoulders slumping. Poor kid, she must think everyone just handed her around like a parcel. Wanda sat down next to her. 'Do you like drawing? We have some coloured crayons somewhere. I found a roll of old wallpaper in a cupboard here. You can draw on the back of it.' Hope looked up, seeming interested.

At the station, Potts eyed Lucia as though she might be secreting a child under her navy coat, but didn't ask about Hope. Lucia decided it was best to say nothing. The ambulances were clean, but Potts, of course, requested that the exteriors and tyres should be hosed down and polished yet again. The blankets also needed changing, she decreed, and Lucia should carry them all down to the laundry. No need to drive, she could roll them up and carry them over her shoulder. She was being punished for yesterday. Gardner offered to come with her and share the load.

'I need you to check the batteries in all the vehicles,' Potts told her. 'We can't afford to have a vehicle that won't start for a call-out.'

Clement, a middle-aged man who was apparently a well-known Chelsea artist, offered to help Lucia. 'Those blankets weigh a ton and Black's no carthorse.'

'Black's a strong girl for all her slightness. Anyway, I want you to whiten the As on the ambulances.' Perhaps Potts thought that Clement's talent as a portrait painter made him skilled at signage work. He and Lucia exchanged raised eyebrows. His were very finely groomed, she noticed, better maintained than her own. Wanda said Clement was a regular in some of the bars and nightclubs in Fitzrovia, to the north of Covent Garden, where men went for entertainment and company that wasn't conventional. Shouldering the bulky duffle bag of blankets, Lucia wondered why the laundry van couldn't have collected them, but it wasn't worth asking and receiving another reprimand.

To be fair, the laundry was only a few blocks away. A faint wintery sunshine was even trying its best to brighten the day. Without Hope on her mind, Lucia might even have enjoyed the errand. Work like this left your mind free while you took some exercise. She was paid two pounds a week, her rent was negligible because the flat belonged to a naval friend of Wanda's who didn't want the place left unoccupied. So, they paid one pound a week between them in return for keeping the flat well maintained. In the laundry, she chatted briefly to the girl behind the counter about the previous afternoon's raid. 'We found a kid yesterday,' Lucia told her. 'Six or seven. Light-brown hair. About this high.' She indicated Hope's height.

The girl shook her head. 'Sorry. Can't she tell you who she is?'

'She won't talk. Or can't.'

'Sounds like she needs a speech therapist. My brother had one when he couldn't speak when he lost his hearing after the mumps.'

Lucia wasn't convinced there was a physical reason for Hope's silence. It was more that she wouldn't talk, that she was under some kind of constraint. But what did she know about a girl Hope's age? How on earth could she herself offer Hope the professional help the child needed?

'I'll put the word around,' the laundress told her. 'Someone'll know who she is.'

When Wanda came in for the start of her shift at lunchtime, Potts had gone into her small office to eat her sandwiches, so they could talk in the mess. 'Hope's in the yard, sitting on a bucket,' Wanda said quietly. 'Your warden wasn't on duty again. I knocked on doors but nobody was around. They mightn't have been allowed back until the houses are checked for structural damage. Those were heavy explosives dropped yesterday.'

'I'll take her to the rest centre this afternoon, see if we can find the welfare officer or social worker. Thanks for helping.'

Wanda shrugged. 'She's no trouble. Just wish she'd say something. I feel strange burbling away without a single word back. Most kids that age chatter on like mad. Walk past an infants' school when they're outside in the playground and you'll be deafened. Anyway, Hope's had a decent lunch and I picked up some fresh clothes and underwear for her from the garment exchange.'

Hope had changed into a bottle-green corduroy pinafore dress and a smart navy wool coat. Her hair was pulled back with a hairband. Some of the families who donated clothes could be friends of Mama's. Lucia wondered whether any of Della's and her childhood clothes had found their way to a clothes exchange. Nanny had kept some of their lawn cotton nightdresses, smocks and cashmere cardigans laundered and wrapped in tissue paper, in the hope of a future generation of Blakes to dress them in.

'You look very smart,' Lucia told Hope. 'I'll have to change into my best things too, so I don't let you down.' The same quick smile came to Hope's face. Lucia looked at her more closely. She gave the impression of being a bright child who'd been well looked after, her hair thick and glossy, her skin and teeth excellent. She was going to say this, but Wanda would only scoff at Lucia knowing anything about child welfare.

'Ask Hope to draw some pictures of her family,' Gardner

called after them. 'It might help.' Lucia hadn't seen her watching them.

'Good idea,' Wanda said.

Wanda's trip to the garment exchange had yielded more than just clothes. She and Hope had picked up a jigsaw puzzle, a game of Snap, and a box of coloured pencils, which sat on the kitchen table. Wanda was so good at knowing what people needed, Lucia reflected.

Lucia made tea for them both. 'We'll go over to the rest centre when we've drunk this. In the meantime, draw some pictures for me, Hope. Show me the people you like the most.' It was important not to stare while Hope drew. Instead, while she drank her tea, Lucia concentrated on the crossword that Wanda had started over her breakfast. Pencils scribbled on the sheet of paper. When she looked up, she saw Hope had drawn a picture of three people: a man, woman and girl. Behind them stood a house with flowers in the window boxes. 'You and your mother and father?'

The girl looked down.

'Where's your daddy now, Hope?'

Her answer was to pull the sheet of paper back towards her and draw some kind of vehicle. A van? So the father had left home. Lucia wanted to ask about the mother, but hesitated. If the female casualty had been Hope's mother, what kind of turmoil might she cause by asking about her? Lucia looked again at the house Hope had drawn. It didn't look like the house she'd seen last night. Were those cobbles on the road? The house was small, with a brick arched lintel, as though it had been converted from some other use. It seemed too small to have been a factory or brewery. Hope put aside the sheet and started on a new creation. Barges on what looked like a river. The Thames, just a quarter of a mile away from the street where they'd found Hope?

Time to visit the rest centre and make more official

enquiries. Hope couldn't go on like this, separated from her family and under an adopted name. Looking at her, head bowed over the drawing, Lucia felt the same emotions she'd experienced the previous day. She couldn't let herself be unsettled again. 'Let's go.' She helped the child into her coat. 'We'll catch the bus, save those legs of yours. Someone must know who you are.' She kept repeating this, as though it was a fact that someone would recognise Hope.

Some of the chaotic atmosphere had left the rest centre. It was still crowded, people sitting on mattresses on the ground with possessions piled up around them. Although the air remained thick with the smell of jammed-together bodies, over-stretched lavatories and damp clothes, attempts were underway to freshen the hall. Women in overalls with buckets and mops moved around the space, shooing children outside to play in the asphalted back yard while they cleaned the floors and opened windows.

Lucia and Hope were directed towards the social worker, who was sitting in what must have been a windowless storage cupboard. A woman in middle-age, she looked up from the form she was filling in, brow furrowed, as they came inside. 'If you're needing beds, I'll have to send you on to Fulham, but you've more chance if you are prepared to travel further out. Kingston still had capacity, last I heard.'

'It's about missing family.' Quickly Lucia explained how she'd found Hope. The social worker frowned.

'You left the casualty site without tying a name tag on the child?'

'She was taken in with an unconscious casualty we believed was her mother.'

'And where is the patient now?'

Lucia glanced down at Hope and shook her head quickly.

'I see. Can the child not tell us more about herself?'

Hope blinked slowly at her.

'Hope doesn't, can't, talk.'

'But she has a name?'

'I just called her Hope because we needed something. I don't know what to do.' The last words came out more despairingly than Lucia intended. How was it she could act calmly and methodically when the bombs were falling and she was driving the ambulance, but feel so upside down now? The social worker looked fleetingly impatient and then more sympathetic. 'I took Hope home with me last night because there was nowhere else she could go. But there'll be people looking for her. I just don't know how we find them.'

The social worker proffered a hand. 'Jane Goodley. Miss, not Mrs. Tell me exactly what happened.'

Lucia introduced herself and ran through the previous day's events.

'A brief but fairly deadly air-raid, I heard, with a last serving of incendiaries to follow the explosives.' Miss Goodley glanced at Hope. 'All right, we need the address where you collected her and... the other person.'

She opened a buff cardboard file and took out a form, completing it with address, time, casualties collected, ambulance number, the hospital the female casualty had been taken to, anything Lucia could think of. 'Meanwhile, young lady, it looks as though we may have to put you into one of our children's homes for a few nights.' She put the cap back on her fountain pen. 'Until we can find your family.'

Perhaps Hope didn't understand what a children's home was. She turned to Lucia, eyes wide, just looking at her.

'You'll have other youngsters to play with.' She turned back to Lucia.

'Does she have any possessions with her? You can always drop them off later if not.'

'Just a few things my flatmate found for her at the clothes exchange.'

Miss Goodley sighed. 'Yet another one who's lost everything.'

'I can't leave her here.' Lucia's heart was thumping. Inside her, emotions fought.

Miss Goodley put down her pen and gazed at her. 'But I thought that was why you were here? To drop her off? You have a job, Miss Black, after all. An important one.'

'Yes. But there's always school. And I can probably find someone to sit in with her the rest of the time. Other women manage childcare with shifts. And my flatmate is an ambulance driver too. We don't usually work the same shifts.'

'Taking on a small child is a very, very serious undertaking, Miss Black. Even temporarily at a time like this, when safe homes for evacuees are like gold dust.'

Lucia struggled to explain just how much she understood the seriousness of the undertaking. 'I might not seem ideal. But I think Hope likes living with me.' As if to add her agreement, Hope gave a broad smile. 'And you were just saying how busy you were, Miss Goodley.'

'I know what I said.' Miss Goodley gave a wry smile.

'You could visit us in the flat, see for yourself.'

'I could do all manner of things if I didn't have all those families out there in the hall to find beds for tonight. Does your flatmate know what she's been signed up to?' Jane Goodley raised her eyebrows at Lucia's silence. 'I didn't think so, Miss Black.'

Hope let out a long sigh and folded her arms. Jane Goodley regarded her solemnly. After a pause, she sighed too. 'Hope can stay with you for two more nights. Then I want you both back here, on Friday, nine o'clock sharp, so I can make other arrangements.' She frowned at Lucia. 'What's the matter, Miss Black?'

'I have a night shift on Thursday. It would be hard to get

home in time to collect Hope and bring her over here. And I'll be...' She'd not be in the best state, possibly covered in grime if there was a raid and no time to shower after.

'Yet you think you could commit to getting Hope to school and back if the arrangement went on longer?'

'I just know she'll do better with Wanda and me, in our little flat, even if it's not perfect, than she will if she's sent miles away. We live close to her home. There's more chance someone will recognise her.'

Miss Goodley's brow was furrowed. She was going to insist on Hope being taken to some orphanage, where children slept in cold dormitories and ate their meals at long tables, without laughter or affection.

'She needs care and attention.' The last words came out more fiercely than she'd intended. She'd probably blown it now, implying Miss Goodley's team wouldn't be up to the task. 'You have to keep your eye on children,' she muttered. 'Things change quickly.' She must sound like an idiot.

'We'll make it Friday afternoon, then, so you have more time to get yourself over here. Two o'clock. I'll look for a place for her in a home in the meantime, in case family can't be found.' Miss Goodley scribbled a note to herself. 'We'll need a photograph of her and I can make inquiries of the local infants' schools.' She paused and then added another note. 'I'll ask the hospital if more is known about the female casualty you brought in with Hope.'

Lucia remembered something. 'Hope drew a picture for us. I don't think there are brothers and sisters, just her and her parents. And some kind of black van.'

'Van?' Miss Goodley frowned. 'A delivery van?'

'More like an army truck.'

'The father could well be serving in the forces. Perhaps there are aunts or grandmothers, though.' Miss Goodley looked curiously at Lucia. 'Usually, it's the middle-aged couples or the women with their own children who offer voluntarily. But a girl like you?'

Lucia shrugged. 'She's just so small.' Did Miss Goodley hear the tremble in her voice? 'It's tough to be alone at that age. When the stretcher party brought her out, there was something that just seemed...' She couldn't describe what it was about Hope that had tugged at her. She forced herself to sit up straight again, to meet Miss Goodley's eyes. 'I was once close to my sister,' she said. 'She's younger than me. We're not close now and it makes me feel... a need to help someone else.' This much was true.

'I'll reserve judgement until Friday.' The older woman's smile was kind. She opened the file again, removing yet another form. 'I'll need some details before I let the two of you go.'

'Just until Friday, Miss Goodley agreed,' Lucia said jauntily. Wanda let out a half sigh. 'She doesn't really understand why I want to keep her anyway. I'm sure she'll find somewhere more suitable.'

'I know some people adopt dogs and cats they've found in the rubble, Fancy. But taking in human waifs and strays is something else.'

'We'll need to find that warden,' Lucia explained, to head her off.

'Perhaps she's on leave or off sick.' Wanda looked at her watch. 'Must fly. I'm off to the pub with the gang.'

Usually Lucia would join in on the night out if they were both free. Tonight she'd have to stay in with Hope. Wanda would walk out to the Cross Keys and the others would come in and there'd be a buzz of chatter and laughter as they drank. If there was a raid, she and Wanda would run over to the station to help out, off-duty or not. It was just what they did.

If you had small children, everything revolved around

looking after them. Unless you had staff to carry out childcare. Her mother had played with them, though. Lucia remembered picnics out on the lawn, a dolls' tea party spread out on the rug in front of the nursery fire. In London, she'd taken them to Hamley's store to look at toys and the decorations in Regent's Street.

Yet if her father told Mama not to pass the time with her daughters but to spend it with him, helping his political ambitions, Mama would limit her time in the nursery, turning instead to planning dinners or tea parties. She mightn't have put on the Blackshirt woman's long grey skirt and black shirt and attended rallies, but Sir Cassian always came first. His word governed them all. Papa's every wish had been law in the family, even when a flash of something in Mama's eyes showed she didn't agree. And she'd entertained those friends of Papa's who thought that people like Wanda were the cause of everything that was wrong with the world, just because they were Jewish.

Yet Lucia missed her mother, her softness, the scent of her, the expression in her eyes when she was ill or scared, the way she laughed. There'd been times in the last year in Paris when she had wanted to send a telegram home, begging Mama to come to her. But she'd resisted. And now she was back in London, she couldn't have her mother without her father. Della, though... she *could* perhaps still have a relationship with her sister? If she could just see Della again everything else would be bearable.

She thought again of Della's grim-faced taxi drive. Where had her sister been going? She had to find out.

Hope was watching her curiously. She had the feeling that the child was almost on the point of saying something and smiled at her, trying to encourage the words. When Hope remained mute, Lucia sighed.

Lucia cleared the supper dishes and did her best to tidy the living room. Wanda flourished in tidiness and Wanda needed to be kept sweet. When everything was back in place except the sofa cushions acting as Hope's bed, Lucia switched on the radio. Dance music, Tommy Dorsey. It would be better in a dance hall with flesh-and-blood men to dance with, so she could forget everything outside in the dark and damaged streets, the threats the next morning would bring. Often the men she danced with wanted more than just dances, but she was good at rebuffing them gently but firmly.

No alert tonight. It would be a quiet shift at the station. Somewhere to the east, she heard bombers rumble to the accompaniment of ack-ack. Other ambulance stations would be preparing for whatever the night brought them.

They had camp beds to sleep in when the bombers didn't come, the pillows and blankets smelling of men's hair oil and stale bodies. She and Wanda had occasionally spent nights there together and it had reminded her of boarding school, though she didn't share that observation with Wanda. Good friend as she was, she would make some quip about Fancy's upbringing.

Wanda had been such a support, helping her with her name change last summer, lending her money for the first few months to tide her over and persuading an acquaintance to rent them the flat for such a reasonable amount.

Wanda's patience with having Hope here would be finite. At some point, a choice would have to be made. Keep Hope, if Miss Goodley agreed to extend the arrangement, or carry on living in the flat with Wanda. But where on earth would she go, with a child in tow?

If she explained the muddle of memories and emotions inside her that finding Hope had generated, perhaps Wanda would understand. Lucia was reaching the point of knowing she had to tell her about Sebastien. And the rest. She promised herself she'd pluck up courage to do it.

FIFTEEN

Thursday night. Lucia was getting ready to cycle down to her shift. Wanda was playing Snap with Hope at the kitchen table, wondering whether the thrill of snapping down a paired card might provoke her into calling out. Once or twice, the child's lips opened as if she was going to shout snap before she checked herself.

In between card games, her jigsaw, and drawing on the back of the old wallpaper, Hope still looked on edge. Understandable. She'd be worrying about her mother. For better or worse, Lucia prayed they'd find out soon what had happened to her. If the clearance teams found paperwork in the rubble, it would help to identify the woman they'd pulled out, but it might be days yet before they finished, as they'd always prioritize bomb-sites that were blocking busy roads or where, conceivably, someone might yet be alive under the bricks and timbers.

When Lucia had pulled down the blackout blinds, the streets outside had felt watchful. 'See you in the morning.' Wanda's eyes locked on hers as she said goodbye. 'Break a leg,' she added, smiling but her eyes betraying her. Lucia knew it wasn't Hope on Wanda's mind making her fidget with a loose

button on her cardigan sleeve. It was a shared gut instinct that
something was on the way tonight. They wouldn't admit it, not
even to one another, but the understanding was there between
them.

At first it was quiet for those on the roster at the station.
Lucia won tuppence at cards and someone had brought in a bar
of milk chocolate. It melted on Lucia's tongue like a kiss and she
closed her eyes. 'Steady,' Clement muttered. 'More exciting
things to put in that pretty mouth of yours, Black.'

Gardner tutted but only half-heartedly. Potts, red-cheeked,
muttered about them checking all the first-aid boxes, but they'd
only done it at the end of the previous shift, so the idea was
allowed to fizzle out like a dud incendiary. They heard bombers
rumbling to the east, towards the city or docks, but it was quiet
in the streets around them. Clement told them a story about a
bishop's wife and an actor at a West End opening night that
made James clear his throat and brought tears of horrified
laughter to Lucia's eyes. Potts looked as though she wanted to
tick Clement off but didn't know how. Smoothly changing tack,
Clement told them about a Moira Hess lunchtime concert at
the National Gallery he'd been to. 'Schumann. Divine. But so
freezing, she had to wear her fur coat. Even so, we were all
utterly transported.'

'I must go along to a lunchtime concert when I'm not on the
roster,' Lucia said. 'They sound magical.'

He frowned. 'I've seen you haring along on that bike of
yours through Westminster, Black, looking as though you had to
be somewhere on time. I assumed you were trying to make a
concert.' He looked at her face and looked down at the cards in
his hand. 'But perhaps it was just an appointment or
something.'

The alert went off, sparing Lucia a reply.

Instantly, chitchat, smutty jokes and gossip were laid
aside. Lucia thought of Wanda and Hope. Wanda was

scrupulous about going to the shelter. She'd take good care of Hope.

Bombs crumped to the north, not that close to the station or the flat. The telephone rang. Potts went to answer it. She returned with the address written out. 'Large explosive. Heavy rescue are on their way. Black, you and Gardner can take your usual ambulance. James will accompany you in the sitting-case car, as there are casualties we can probably manage at the scene.'

Lucia put on her rubber one-piece, waders, helmet and gloves automatically now. Gardner picked up their first-aid case and they were off.

Gardner directed her north. 'Another block further along and it wouldn't have been our call. We'd still be listening to Clement's filthy stories.'

'Probably just as well for our morals. Sometimes, I think it's better to be out on the streets in the ambulance in a heavy raid, anyway.'

'Waiting at the station, just sitting there, hearing the carnage but doing nothing? Yes, that's harder.'

The thumping racket seemed to be amplifying by the minute. Searchlights cut the night sky, revealing the black outlines of the bombers. Pattering down onto the road came pieces of shrapnel, incendiaries whistling in accompaniment. The symphony of the night, Gardner called it. None of the buildings they passed had been struck yet. Lucia marvelled yet again at how localised damage could be: one street stricken, the next almost untouched, barring a few tiles on a roof. Nobody seemed to know just how accurate the Luftwaffe were. Did they strike residential streets on purpose or because they were aiming at something else they viewed as strategic, and kept missing? Potts said the Germans were learning all the time. If the war ran on into years, they'd have refined their tactics and accuracy. Would this mean fewer human beings to pull out of wrecked buildings? She felt sick contemplating that it might mean the opposite.

Gardner handed her the little pot of Vicks to rub under her nose. 'Not far now,' she shouted.

They were approaching the turning. Lucia slowed, peering hard to see the road, the taped headlights barely illuminating the yard or so ahead of the ambulance, making out the outline of a stray dog, thin and shaking, slinking back into the gloom for refuge. The dog made her think of Della, who loved them so much. When she braked at the junction, Lucia saw James through the rearview mirror, coming up right behind them in the Austin, nearly crashing into them. Her brake lights were so dim he couldn't have seen her. She made a note to herself to apologise to him. 'Here we are,' Gardner said, as if she was a taxi driver dropping off a passenger. The worse it was in a raid, the more calmly Gardner would react.

As they turned, the fire in the house blazed in front of them, yellow, red and gold flames bursting into the sky. Timbers crashed down. The warden ran towards them, directing them through the piles of debris. 'A woman and a man. She's bleeding from a head injury but mobile, he's unconscious.'

Behind them, James was getting out of the Austin. 'Nearly had you back there when you slowed, Black,' he called to her, cheerfully. James was quiet at work and when they were waiting around at the station, but when he was working you could feel his presence like an arm around a shoulder, his every movement controlled and efficient, making you feel more in control yourself. Gardner had once muttered something about Dunkirk, a tragedy on a naval ship. He walked with them towards the house, pulling a handkerchief over his mouth. Potts had told him he should stay with the car at call-outs, rather than entering a bombed house, but he quietly disobeyed her when he thought it appropriate and usually didn't bother putting on a helmet.

As they approached the house, the air felt like an oven. Lucia stumbled, even though the path had already been cleared. She gasped as she recovered her balance. Gardner frowned at her. 'All right, Black?'

'Caught my boot on something.'

The heavy rescue team had cleared a path so they could take the stretcher inside what must have once been the kitchen to the casualty sitting slumped over the table, unconscious but bleeding. Lucia thought of the statues on tombstones when she saw the man, his face white from the dust or perhaps from his injuries. James was already examining him, his hands quick as he ran them over the body and shone a light into the eyes. 'Airways open, just as well he fell forward not back. Internal bleeding, probably. No head injury I can see. But mind his neck as we get him onto the stretcher.'

He moved the torch beam from the man's face, illuminating the wall. Lucia spotted something red and hanging. A beef steak pinned to the wall? Even now, her brain would try to protect her from what she saw. Gardner had seen it too, she could tell by the way she blinked and looked away. Gardner had been the one on the scene when a heavy explosive had hit a dairy, confronted by the remains of the milk-cart horses sprayed on the walls. When she'd returned to the station, she'd wept, saying the innocence of animals meant they should be spared the horror. Lucia had thought of the horses at Claybourne Manor and how they would trot to the paddock fence to blow into your face, ears flicking forward and back, the smell of their breath and coats.

Potts might send them back to this house with the lidded bucket to recover what they could of what had been living human beings to the morgue. For now, the living were the priority. Was it even right to pray transferring the casualty to a hospital might delay them enough to spare them the recovery of body parts? But if Gardner and Lucia weren't given the task, some other team would have to do it.

'I'll take an end,' James said, looking at the stretcher. Gardner started to tell him they could manage, he could go back to the car, but he shook off the suggestion and took the opposite end. Together, they moved the man onto the stretcher. Lucia studied his face, looking for some sign that he was still inside himself.

'He blinked,' she told James as they raised the stretcher. James gave her his gentle smile.

'They can always surprise you, can't they.' He bent down a little towards the man. 'Hang in there, old chap.'

She backed out of the kitchen, step by step, cautious. James, facing the other way, directed her left and right around obstacles, his voice steady. One of the heavy rescue team wanted to take her side of the stretcher, but she thanked him and continued, trusting James to steer them out.

Gardner had taken the woman with the bleeding head wound to the ambulance and sat with her, the curtains at the back open, bandaging her head. 'This will need stitching.' A flash of searchlight showed Gardner's intent face. The woman looked up as the stretcher party approached. 'He's not dead then?' She sounded politely enquiring rather than distraught. Shock would do that to you.

James told her gently that the man – her husband – was suffering internal injury from the blast. The situation was grave. When they'd manoeuvred the stretcher in, Gardner finished the bandaging and wrote the labels for the two patients.

'Don't treat me like a parcel. I don't need a label,' the woman said.

'Yes, you do.' Lucia was remembering how Hope had come out of that other house without any identification, and tied the label firmly round through the woman's jacket buttonhole. 'Just in case.' Sometimes people lost consciousness even as they'd been sitting up and talking to you.

The oxygen from the air around them was sucked away. Lucia knew the bomb was falling before she saw or heard it. She sprang across the woman, pushing her down onto the ambulance floor, hearing her shriek in protest a split second before the world crashed down around them, the vehicle rocking on its wheelbase. Something pushed hard against her chest. The sound had been cut off. When she lifted her head, it was curiously quiet. Particles of brick and mortar floated around her, light as feathers, in a world turned to white dust. Something grabbed her shoulder. Gardner, her mouth opening and closing. Lucia blinked hard, trying to remove the grit from her eyes. Gardner was saying something she couldn't hear. The ground still trembled, but that was her own confused senses.

Incendiaries dropped beside them, like huge malicious hailstones.

She managed to stand, shaking her head as Gardner tried to help her up. The woman with the head injury was complaining about being thrown around like a sack of potatoes. The bandage around her head was intact, no fresh bleeding. 'I'll report you all,' she told Lucia. 'No respect.'

Lucia climbed down from the ambulance. 'Just need a breath of air.' She caught her foot on something that felt like a log. When she looked down, she saw a leg, dismembered, but still trousered, male. A neat pinstripe because he never put on rubber waders when he came out. James. The rest of him was under a heap of brick, what was left of the front wall of the house. Automatically, she stooped down again, pulling bricks off him so she could reach his neck. She placed her fingers there and then on his wrists and pulled out the little mirror she kept in her pocket for checking for breath. No moisture misted the surface of the mirror, nor was there a pulse to feel. His head was undamaged, the eyes open and his expression peaceful, as if reassuring her that she was carrying out all her checks correctly.

Her ears still crackling, she heard her own cry. Gardner was behind her now, tapping her shoulder, saying something. '... need another ambulance here... more casualties... warden's gone to ring for one. We need to take in our two patients, Lucia, there'll be more for us to do.'

'We can't leave James here like this.'

'We can't do anything for him.'

'Let me close his eyes.' His eyelids were still warm under her fingers. She brushed the dust and dirt off his face. Gardner pulled her towards the ambulance.

That was James lying there, gazing up at the clearing smoke so peacefully, James who liked card games and music and whose gentle gaze sometimes fell on Wanda. She didn't even know his Christian name, she realised. How many hours had she spent talking to him at the station without knowing this?

'You fit to drive?' Gardner asked, shouting against the roar of flames and hiss of the firemen's hoses. When had the fire-engine arrived? 'Black? Pull yourself together.'

No Christian names, just surnames. It was how they operated, that mixture of distance and intimacy you needed for this work. Lucia nodded. James had given Wanda the bath essence but had never called her by her first name.

She brushed the dirt off her clothes, checked that the two patients were secure in the back, drew the curtains and climbed into the driver's seat, moving stiffly. The woman was still complaining about being labelled, her voice shrill above the gunfire and explosions.

As they approached the hospital, some of the shock was already gone. She wouldn't think about James. If they were held up here, there wouldn't be time for them to return to the bomb-site for his remains. Her stomach lurched, but even though she hadn't wanted to be the one who cleared up the kitchen, she wanted to be the one who made sure that James was looked after properly.

It was the same hospital doctor as when she'd brought Hope in. A flash of recognition passed over his face. He nodded at her. 'Not so rammed full tonight. We can keep these two for you.' He was walking away, directing the auxiliaries who had run up to take the stretchers in, but turned. 'What happened to the youngster you brought in the other night?'

'Still not talking. She's staying with me until we can trace family or relatives.'

His eyes widened. 'You do take duty to the very limits.' He nodded at her with something that was almost approval. With a wave of his hand, he was gone. She wasn't sure that duty was motivating her to look after Hope.

'Let's go back and see if we can do anything for James,' she begged Gardner when she returned to the ambulance. Gardner shook her head. 'It's not right just leaving him there like that,' she pleaded. In pieces, among scorched bricks and twisted metal.

'Potts will kill us if we don't return to the station for our next instructions. You know the rules, Black.'

'But James…'

'Put him out of your mind for the rest of the shift.' Something flashed ahead of them. A building rumbled. 'The recovery team and warden will watch over him until he can be collected by another crew.'

Lucia slumped back in the seat, driving mechanically, careless of pavement kerbs and lights. 'Buck up, Black,' Gardner said. She put a hand on the driving wheel. 'Want me to take over?'

Lucia sat up again. 'No. Sorry. It was just… I just…'

'I know. Ask Potts for a few days off. None of us can go on

day after day. We don't talk about what we see, but it's always there, inside us. Sometimes there's just one thing that we can't move on from. For you, tonight, it's James.'

Lucia thought about the things she couldn't move on from and countered with her own question. 'Who was it for you? The horses at the dairy?'

She thought Gardner wasn't going to reply. She waited for Lucia to change down the gears to take a corner. 'That was an obscenity, but it was actually a dog that first... caught at me. Everyone had been crushed in the building, but the dog got out. A Labrador. He just sat there, looking at the house, what was left of it, waiting for someone to tell him where to go. He was so good. He wasn't going to run away or be a nuisance, he just trusted that someone would be along.' She was speaking loudly over the racket outside, but her voice suddenly sounded raspy. 'I couldn't take him with me, of course. But that dog just haunted me. And he wasn't even human and he wasn't even injured.' She shrugged. 'He just symbolised the futility.' She glanced at Lucia. 'That kid last shift pulled something similar in you, didn't she?'

'Maybe.' Lucia kept her gaze on the blackness ahead of her, as if she was concentrating hard on her driving again.

'You just look at them, a child or an innocent animal. And it haunts you.'

Haunt was the right word. As if to underline the idea, a screamer bomb shrieked its way down somewhere to the east of them, followed by another and another, like threatening ghouls.

'Hope still doesn't talk,' Lucia said when the racket died down and the thought of the dead was becoming too unbearable. 'What will happen to her if she goes off to some home and they don't know who she is, and nobody ever claims her?'

'Unlikely. Someone will find out. This is still a nation of form-fillers. I should know.' When the war had first started, Gardner had been working in a council office in a south London suburb. 'Hope's not talking now, but she will do eventually,' Gardner went on. 'How many adults do you actually know who haven't spoken since they were six?'

Lucia smiled, remembering something. 'I was probably around that age when my nanny said she'd give me a penny if I could stay silent until teatime. I lasted about an hour.' Ordinarily she never talked about nannies and other servants, her pony in the paddock, because she didn't want to underline the difference between herself and Gardner and Wanda. She wanted to be like them. But Gardner was just smiling, eyes warm.

'I didn't have you down as a chatterbox, Black.'

'I had to learn to be less talkative, to not always say what was on my mind.' It had taken until her father had struck her in the drawing room at Newton Terrace for the lesson to sink in completely. The lesson had been usefully deployed when she'd run away from him in Paris and spent those months eating at *pension* tables with strangers looking curiously at her. She'd learned to smile and pass the time of day briefly, without saying much about herself or her plans. Within a few months she'd felt less like the spoiled daughter of a baronet and more like a fugitive making a new life in a foreign country, without the paperwork she ought to have. As her French improved, she'd made transitory friendships with the people she taught English, but there'd always been that need to keep quiet about her family. Until she'd met Sebastien. But she wasn't going to think about Sebastien now, not tonight. What had happened to James had just shaken her up, that was all. She was fine.

They were approaching the station when the all-clear sounded. 'In five minutes, Black,' Gardner said, dreamily, 'we'll be sitting in the mess with mugs of cocoa, if there's enough milk. Some of those buns might be left over from earlier on. Then we might have a bit of kip before the shift ends. Forget everything else.'

But at the mess table there'd be an empty chair where James ought to sit.

Returning to the flat just after eight in the morning, Lucia slept for an hour. Her dreams took her back into the past. She was a small child again, standing in a huge crowd, somewhere abroad, attending a rally, listening to what the speaker said but not understanding the words. Someone asked her a question in German, quite urgently, tugging at her shoulder.

'Lucia doesn't know where her mother is, don't ask her,' her father said. He leant down to comfort her and Lucia woke up, knowing it really was just a dream because her father wouldn't do that.

She was just conscious enough to remember that this wasn't completely true. She'd once fallen off her pony and he'd jumped off his hunter and scooped her up, pulling her into an embrace, telling her she was all right, he was always watching over her. Then he'd put her straight back onto the pony. For the seconds she'd clung to him, as he'd spoken to her softly, he'd been her whole world. In her dream, she gazed up at her father's face, but it turned into Sebastien's. He was stroking her hair, telling her everything was all right. Half knowing her mind was deceiving her, half longing for it to be true, she lay silent.

Reality crept in. Wanda was rattling plates and cutlery in the kitchen. She was on morning shift, Lucia remembered. Hope had already got up and made up her bed, the elephant sitting on the pillow. Wrapping her dressing gown around her, Lucia went into the kitchen. Wanda was frying sausages and Hope was laying the table.

'There you are.' Wanda had her head down over the frying pan.

Lucia started to say something, but Wanda shook her head. 'I heard. We went to the grocer's and Clement was in the queue. It would be him, wouldn't it? It's always the good people.' Wanda banged the frying pan down on the cooker top. Hope looked at her. 'Sorry, sweetheart, don't mind me. I just feel sad because our friend died, and he was decent and kind, and we'll miss him terribly.' She looked at the door. 'Go down and see if the post's arrived for me?'

Hope trotted off obediently. They heard her undo the front door and go down the stairs to the ground floor where post for each flat was stacked on a table.

'Hope spoke last night,' Wanda said quietly.

'What? What did she say?'

'It was...' Wanda checked Hope was still well out of earshot. 'It wasn't English.'

'What do you mean?'

'I couldn't hear, the bedroom door was closed...' Wanda dropped her voice. 'I just had this sense it wasn't English, that's all.'

Hope had come upstairs, standing there, looking wary, as if she could sense what was going on in Lucia's mind. Was Hope Dutch? Or even Norwegian or Danish? People from these countries had fled here when Hitler had turned his sights on western Europe. And there were many Poles in London.

'She certainly understands English, don't you, Hope?' Hope's head seemed to nod very slightly. 'So we've moved on a bit communication-wise,' Wanda said heartily. 'Just in time for this afternoon's deadline.' She looked meaningfully at Lucia. 'Perhaps there'll be news of Hope's relatives?'

Oh God, the meeting with Miss Goodley was this afternoon. This week's shift pattern and the loss of James had destroyed Lucia's sense of time. 'In the meantime, there are sausages,' Wanda said. 'Allegedly. Mostly bread. Even if I was fastidious about keeping kosher, I wouldn't worry, as pigs haven't done more than oink in the direction of these beauties. I'll do you one too, Lucia. I managed to get an egg for Hope.'

They didn't have a ration book registered for Hope at the grocer's. Sausages weren't rationed, but Wanda must have used her own vouchers for the egg.

'Don't worry.' Wanda must be reading her mind. 'It's a temporary situation, after all.'

Hope wouldn't be eating breakfast with them again, she meant. She'd be with another set of strangers. Separation from her family must be bewildering for Hope. Lucia remembered Della that evening in the Ritz when she'd run off, paying no heed to Della's pleas. Della had looked devastated and confused. Her face had haunted Lucia. And Lucia hadn't written a single word to reassure her sister in those years that followed.

A longing for Della so profound she could feel it like a pain in her chest swept through Lucia. It could be the loss of James last night that had brought on this longing, but she had to see her sister. It was the only thing that could make her life bearable, as bearable as it could be when so much else had gone. She had to know why Della was seemingly at school in the city now, instead of in their old country boarding school, with its dull, safe rituals. She needed to know about Mama too.

'Penny for them?' Wanda was looking at her. 'Or perhaps not. They don't look happy thoughts, Fancy.'

'Could I talk to you,' Lucia started to say. 'There's something—'

'If it's what I think it is, we talked about this before,' Wanda said. 'You know my views.' She shot a meaningful glance at Hope.

'No, that's not what...' She couldn't find the way of explaining that she didn't want to talk about Hope, it was something else, something that would make sense of all she'd done or failed to do since she'd run away. 'I really need to tell you something.'

'You're fretting over Della again? Of course, let's talk later,'

Wanda said. 'I'm off to Whitechapel to see my parents, just a quick visit to make sure they're managing. The air-raids have been fierce their way.' Something seemed to catch her in the throat.

'Wanda?'

'You know, James asked me to go to the theatre with him next week.'

Lucia leant forward. 'What?'

'Noël Coward.'

'I didn't know this. Did you, what did you say...?'

'I said yes. I know he was probably too old for me, and it would have been off, working with him and going out with him too, but I really liked him. His name was Harry, you know. Harry James.' Wanda had been holding the egg slice while she spoke. She looked down at it as if she wasn't sure what it was doing in her hand.

'I'm so, so sorry, Wanda.' They stared at one another over the tatty lino floor.

'He read a lot, books I hadn't even heard of, and I thought I'd spent enough time with my head in a book.' Wanda came to a halt, looking dazed.

'I really liked Harry too,' Lucia said. 'He taught me a lot and when he was around, I always felt I'd be all right. There aren't many people you can say that about.' She put her arms around Wanda.

Wanda surrendered briefly to the embrace, before pulling back, rubbing a hand across her eyes briefly.

Was this the moment for Lucia to talk about her own loss? No, Wanda looked crushed. She needed to feel the fullness of this blow before she could take on anyone else's. 'I do understand,' she managed. Wanda nodded slowly.

'Let's talk more about Della later, when I'm back from Whitechapel.'

'It's not...' Lucia forced herself to look composed again. 'But as you say, for later.'

Wanda returned her attention to the frying pan. 'What are you going to do this morning?'

'I'll take Hope out for a walk.' It wasn't that far to walk up to Belgravia. What would they do when they got to the house in Newton Terrace?

'You're on the roster again tonight?' Wanda asked.

'Yes.'

What would happen if she told Miss Goodley she wanted Hope to come back with her this afternoon and Miss Goodley agreed? The girl in the laundry might know of someone who'd sit with her tonight, take her into the shelter if the sirens went. Women who worked factory shifts while their husbands served away from home must face this every single day. The complexity of juggling work and children was why so many families had sent them out of London. Yet it was possible for a woman to care for a child alone.

Hope seemed happy to brush her teeth and put on her outdoor clothes. She walked beside Lucia, looking around at the shops with the people queueing outside them, the assessors and recovery teams working on the bombsites. She seemed a curious, alert kind of person. On the pavement outside a wrecked terraced house, a woman and her children were pulling out possessions. A boy pounced on a small piece of blackened metal, claiming it as a toy soldier. How he could have spotted it in the jumble of stone and singed wood, Lucia couldn't tell. His mother had found a saucepan and clutched it to her chest. Her youngest child, a girl of about two, sat on a pile of bricks, banged pieces of broken crockery together, singing to herself, as though this was all normal – entertaining, almost. Lucia glanced at Hope, worrying that the sight of this devastation might remind her of what had happened to her own home. But Hope was looking across the road at the milkman's horse and cart. They cut north through side streets until they reached the King's Road. It was another twenty minutes' walk on to Newton Terrace.

At Peter Jones in Sloane Square, miraculously undamaged by bombs, women were still bustling in to buy fabric and buttons. Rumours of clothing rationing coming in were sweeping the city, but it hadn't happened yet. Clothes were becoming harder to buy, though, as so much production was given over to what the armed services needed. Lucia was wearing the dresses and skirts she'd had made in France, but frays at the cuffs and thinning material at the seats and knees warned they'd soon need replacing.

She remembered coming to Peter Jones at Hope's age with her nanny and a tiny Della to try on shoes. They'd each been measured for summer sandals and then they'd bought sunhats and swimming costumes for the annual holiday on the South Coast. Nanny had taken them into the café afterwards. Lucia had wanted a sundae and then Della had insisted too, because she always had to have what her elder sister had. Nanny had fussed, saying they'd upset their stomachs and spoil their appetite for proper wholesome lunches, but her eyes were soft as she nibbled on her own shortbread biscuit.

Lucia realised with a pang that when she'd vanished into the night, Nanny would have feared for her safety and had probably worried about her ever since. But she had thought about Nanny frequently, sometimes hearing her voice in her head. *A good routine never hurt a soul... Fresh air works wonders. Simple food, cooked well, is the best medicine.*

Hope spotted a large teddy bear in the Peter Jones window, probably not for sale, just for display purposes. She came to a halt, smiling at it. Her own elephant had been left at home. 'I wish I could buy that for you,' Lucia told her. 'Though I don't know where he'd sleep. We're a bit tight on space.' On impulse she added, 'What's his name, do you think?'

Hope's lips seemed to open to form a B. Then she stopped. Perhaps Miss Goodley could look into a speech therapist for her.

A layette for a baby was spread out across a cot in the same window display. Most of the tiny garments would be out of stock. Those on display had a faded appearance, as if they'd been in the window for too long.

Ten minutes later they stood in Newton Terrace outside the Blake family house. Foolish, because anyone looking out of the front door would have clearly seen Lucia. But what did it matter now? Lucia was too old to be imprisoned by her father, even if he was here and not at Claybourne Manor. He probably wouldn't want her in his household, anyway. She clasped Hope's hand more tightly, feeling a sense of comfort in the smallness of the hand in its woollen mitt. Lucia knocked on the door. The first knock sounded hesitant so she rapped again, more confidently, like a daughter of the house, except a daughter of the house would have her own key.

'Perhaps everyone's out.' It almost came as a relief. Hope looked at her gravely. 'At least we had some fresh air.'

Just as they were turning away from the door, the sound of footsteps came from deep inside the house. A woman's, judging by the lightness. It was a thin-faced middle-aged woman she didn't recognise, who looked doubtfully at the two of them before noting the quality of Lucia's shoes, still apparent despite the scuffs.

'Good morning, I'd like to see Miss Della Blake, please.' She met the woman's inquisitive gaze.

'And you are?' This was not the way a servant should address a caller. Lucia's cheeks burned.

'Miss Blake, Lucia Blake.' She hadn't used her old name for eight months and the words seemed to choke her. Perhaps the woman thought she was a fraud; she pursed her lips.

'Lucia Blake?' The woman folded her arms. 'Miss Blake hasn't been seen by the family since May 1937.'

'I... that's right.'

'We have no way of knowing if she is still alive.'

'My sister will recognise me.' She emphasised the second word.

'I see.' She opened the door a little wider. 'Wait here in the hall, miss, while I see if anyone's home.'

'I don't want to see anyone other than Miss Della Blake.' If Mama were here, Lucia wasn't ready to see her, not yet. The thought of her mother brought up feelings so powerful and complicated she couldn't find the strength to untangle them.

'Very well.' The woman motioned them inside.

The entrance hall hadn't changed at all. The black and white checkerboard tiles were just the same. The large white marble console table still sat just inside, leatherbound visitors' book on top, fountain pen ready. Many of the society names in that book would be regarded as suspicious these days. Beside the visitors' book sat a brown-paper parcel tied neatly with string, gas mask on top of it.

The other incongruous detail was a box of old toys and books at the bottom of the sweeping staircase. Lucia felt Hope pull her hand. 'Oh, it's our old things,' Lucia said, letting the child lead her towards them. 'Oh, look at this doll, I think she was mine.' She knelt down beside the box, taking out the doll, with her worn painted face and faded blue eyes, her pink gingham pinafore dress still well-laundered and pressed. 'I adored her when I was your age. The wooden horse was Della's. I remember her playing with it when she was only just walking.' Her voice shook. 'And they read these books to us at night.'

Hansel and Gretel. The witch had always made her feel so scared. But Hope was pulling the book out of the box, sitting down on the bottom step, opening the pages. The woman who'd let them in came back and sighed. 'Miss Della put that box together for refugees, don't let that child undo all the work, please.'

'Sorry.' Lucia replaced the doll in the box. She could have said that these were her old possessions too, but restrained herself. She stood up. Hope was still clutching the copy of *Hansel and Gretel*. 'I'll find you a copy of that book somewhere else, Hope, we can't take it.' But Hope had already opened it. Lucia saw the inscription in the front, *Darling Lucia, With lots of love from Granny*. A present from her mother's mother, a woman she'd adored. 'Actually, this book is mine, I think we might take it after all.'

The maid, or housekeeper, or whoever she was, folded her arms. 'As I said, we don't know who you are, miss. I'm not going to let you help yourself to goods put aside for needy children.'

'I told you, I'm Lucia Blake.'

'Crosby, let the little girl have the book, for God's sake.'

A voice, from above them. Lucia stood up. Della. Ice ran down Lucia's spine. Her sister was coming down the stairs, very slowly. As she approached, the colour seemed to leach from her face. She stopped. 'I can't...' Della shivered, clutching the banister as if she might topple. 'Is it really you, Lucia?' She looked as if she was on a ship, pitching and rolling in a storm. Her face was still ashen. Lucia felt the old urge to run up to her, to hold her little sister steady, but she knew she had to go slowly, let Della take in what was before her eyes. 'Lucia?' Della said again.

Hearing her sister call her by her name brought back a sweep of emotion. She needed to cling on to something too. Hope had stood up as well. Lucia clutched the child's shoulder. The years fell away. She was eighteen, pleading with Della in that Ritz hotel suite in Paris, imploring her to run away with her. The black-and-white-tiled floor was swaying.

'Yes. It's me, Della.'

She might actually be sick. She'd waited for this moment for so long but now she wasn't strong enough.

Della descended the steps, one by one, very slowly, her eyes never leaving Lucia's face. Her skin was still as pale as the marble console table, as though all the blood had left it. Her sister was very beautiful, Lucia thought dispassionately, maturity having refined her schoolgirl roundedness and leaving her with a face that was high-cheeked with a fine, straight nose and eyes so blue it seemed impossible. She was like a softer version of Sir Oswald's wife, Diana. Like her, Della might have been cast as a classical statue. She seemed older than her years, even though she was wearing a uniform, not their old school uniform, one that Lucia didn't recognise. Was she now a day pupil in one of the remaining suburban schools?

Della put out a slender hand. Lucia gasped. The ring on her middle right finger was the gold one she had sold to the jeweller in Rouen. She took the hand, staring down at the ring. Della smiled. 'Papa questioned pretty well every jeweller and dealer in second-hand gold in every single town along the railway line out of St Lazare.'

'He found the taxi driver who took me to the station?'

Della nodded. 'Money always buys answers.' She sounded older than her years. 'Once Papa worked out which trains had departed St Lazare after you left the Ritz, it wasn't hard to track you to Rouen, Lucia. I was so upset when they found your ring that Papa bought it for me.' Della shrugged. 'I wanted to hold on to a little bit of you. It was a comfort, anyway.' Her eyes were narrowed, as though she no longer believed this to be the case. 'I'm not supposed to wear it at school, so I hide it when I get there.'

'You tracked down the jeweller, but that didn't lead you to me?'

'Papa found the hotel where you'd stayed a night. A man who worked there said he thought he'd seen you the next day, wandering around the Joan of Arc memorial.' Della gave a little smile. 'Did you fancy yourself a martyr, Lucia?'

'No.' But her cheeks flushed.

'By then the trail had run cold. The woman in the ticket office thought she might have remembered you buying a ticket south to Orleans, but already days had passed.'

Yes, she'd passed through Orleans, tempted, as soon as she arrived, to find a telegraph office and beg her family to bring her home. She'd tried to forget these first weeks, the terror that had eventually become energy, propelling her southwards.

'For months, that was all we knew. Although we still had a notification from the French authorities whenever they found a female body in a river or off a coast.'

Lucia put a hand to her throat.

'We never knew whether to feel relieved or... exhausted when it was never you, and we knew we'd have to go through it all over again, the next time they found some other poor girl.'

A noise was coming from Lucia's mouth. Not words, more of a cry. Hope looked up at her, eyes narrowed.

'Where have you been all this time, Lucia? How long have you been in London?' Della was looking at Hope, puzzlement on her face. 'And who is this?'

'This is Hope, I'm looking after her temporarily. And I came back in spring last year, just before Hitler invaded the Low Countries.'

Della's eyes opened wide. 'What? That long? And you didn't tell us, you didn't let me know?' Her puzzlement had turned to bewilderment. 'I don't understand. Why wouldn't you get in touch with me, Lucia? Even if you couldn't face Mama and Papa? You must have known how desperate we were about you, especially after war broke out and we didn't know where you were. When France fell, we thought you were still over there and we were beside ourselves. We thought you might have been strafed, fleeing the Wehrmacht.'

'I didn't want Papa to know.' It sounded such a bald, pathetic excuse.

'Why? In case he dragged you screaming back here?' Della's upper lip curled. 'He was worried, Loo. Distraught. He thought you were suffering from a nervous breakdown. For years he read police reports in French newspapers in case you'd been found suffering from amnesia.' Small spots of colour appeared in Della's cheeks. 'He talked about men from the trenches who'd forgotten their names because they'd had head injuries.' She put a hand to her mouth for a moment, her eyes wide, as though reliving it. 'All the guilt would fall on me again.'

'On you? Did they blame you for me running away?'

'They never made me feel guilty. I did it to myself.'

'Why would you feel guilty?'

'I couldn't stop you running off from the Ritz. Nobody blamed me but I blamed myself. It was just me and you in the hotel room that night. I should have persuaded you to stay.'

'You tried to stop me.' She remembered how Della had begged her not to leave.

'Yes, like a fool, I thought you really cared about me, Loo.' Her sister's cheeks had little red patches on them. 'I cared so much about you. But I wasn't enough for you, was I?'

'I...' She was finding it hard to describe her state of mind after she'd fled the Ritz, the sense of liberation and terror. And after, the freedom of living her new life. 'It will take some time to explain.'

Della ignored the hand Lucia extended back towards her. 'Time I don't have. I'm on my way out.'

'May I call again?'

Della didn't answer, but walked towards the cupboard by the front door where coats and hats were stored. She put on a beret with a school badge Lucia didn't recognise.

'Last time you wore a hat with a veil.'

Della swung back to her. 'You've been watching me? Spying on me?'

'Just once, a few days ago. You were in a taxi. I didn't...'

Didn't have the courage to approach her sister. Della slung her satchel around her shoulder, looking younger. She was still only seventeen, Lucia remembered, not eighteen until the summer.

'I got into trouble for turning up at school without the correct uniform on.' She looked sharply at Lucia as though expecting another question.

'May I see you again? Please?'

She frowned at Lucia. 'I'd have to tell them you're back.'

'Can't we keep it to ourselves?'

Della turned, her face scornful. 'You may be able to keep secrets like that, Lucia, but I can't. You broke their hearts.'

'Did Papa have one to break where I was concerned?'

'You have no idea what you're talking about.' The blue eyes burned cold and the cheeks were definitely red now. 'How could you? Staying away for years? Not even letting us know you were back in England when France was invaded? Waiting all this time to let us know you were safe?' Della's accusations felt like missiles.

'Let me think about it before you tell them. Please.'

Della shrugged. 'If you want to see me again, you've got to let me tell them you're alive and well. In the meantime, I need to be going. I have a... an appointment.' She stopped. Another appointment? Like the one she'd had a few days ago, when the taxi had taken her somewhere? 'Then I'm going on to school in Wimbledon.'

Lucia extended a hand towards Hope. 'We're leaving now, put the book back.'

'Oh, let her take it, whoever she is, that stuff was only going to bombed-out children.' Della's tone was dismissive. 'It's just old junk.' She looked at Lucia as though she was really saying that the relics of their shared childhood were nothing to her.

A noise distracted Lucia. Hope? Yes, she'd spoken, said something, and Lucia had missed it. She spun around, the emotions of the last five minutes receding. 'What was that?' She looked back at Della. 'Did you hear that?'

Della frowned. 'What?'

'Did you hear her speak? She doesn't talk, not since the bomb, we've been listening out... Hope, what was that you said?'

Hope looked stricken, clutching the book to her chest, head lowered. 'Obviously not worth repeating.' Della picked up the paper parcel and her gas mask and opened the front door. 'After you.' Her voice was icily polite.

'I'll come back, Dell. Tell me a good time. My shifts are a little erratic, but they'll settle down eventually, the Luftwaffe can't go on like this for ever.'

On the pavement, Della's back went rigid. 'Thinking about it, there is no good time for you to come back here, Lucia. Not unless you're going to be open about being back in London. I don't want you causing more pain. Mama's well. You didn't ask but you might like to know. But she found your running away extremely distressing, as you can imagine.'

'She's living here?'

'Mama offered up Claybourne Manor to evacuees and a midwifery unit. She spends a lot of her time up here so she can...' She stopped again, swallowing.

'Please, Della. I have to see you again. And Mama, you're right, I should see her.'

'You have absolutely no idea, Lucia.' The tone was contemptuous. 'You don't know what it's been like for us.'

'I'm sorry.' The full damage she'd done Della by walking out hit her, cold and overwhelming. And her mother. She'd harmed her too, more than she could admit to herself. 'I'd love to see Mama again. It's just ... *him* I can't see.'

'Oh, I can promise if you come here, you won't be seeing Papa.' Della spotted a taxi and put out a hand.

'He's working away somewhere?' Lucia frowned. 'Some kind of war work?' Sir Cassian was too old to serve in the forces, wasn't he?

Della laughed. It wasn't a cheerful sound. 'Not exactly. Although he is indeed away and sometimes he does work.' The taxi pulled over. 'Of a kind.'

'Where to, miss?'

'Wandsworth Prison, please.' The look she gave Lucia was a mixture of resentment and defiance.

SIXTEEN

'Can't imagine you'd want to visit Papa in prison, would you?' Della said, lip curled. 'Perhaps you won't even feel the need to come back to this house and sully yourself again. It's not fun, I admit, going to visit someone who's regarded as a traitor, a Quisling. Last time, I hid behind that veil. But why pretend I'm not the daughter of the man holed up with criminals?' Della's lips quivered and her eyes welled. She wiped her hand across her eyes and her face reset itself so rigidly, she looked ten years older. Lucia's heart broke for her. She put a hand out.

'Della...'

Della pulled back, out of reach. Without another word, she opened the passenger door and got in, the taxi pulling away before Lucia could say another word.

Lucia stood on the pavement, feeling a chunk of her heart vanish with the taxi as it turned a corner. She waited for a moment, as if hoping it would double back. The front door of the house closed behind them. Hope looked up at her inquisitively.

· · ·

'Your father's in prison? They took him in with the rest of Mosley's gang?' Wanda's eyes looked as though they were going to pop when Lucia told her what she'd learned. She flopped down in a chair before going to change for her shift. 'I didn't think they banged them up unless they were a security risk. I must have missed the newspaper coverage. I'm sorry, Fancy. It must have been a shock.'

'Why should you have realised? I probably should have worked it out myself. Well, if his great idol, Mosley, is imprisoned too, at least Papa has some congenial company.' The sarcasm in Lucia's voice was so marked that Hope looked up at her, eyes wide. She smiled at the child to reassure her.

'Nothing about Wandsworth Prison is very congenial, Fancy. It's a harsh, filthy place. Before the war, I visited a friend who'd wound up there – obviously not for being a fascist, he was a communist. Mosley himself is in Brixton, but neither would be what your father is used to.'

Lucia poured her a cup of tea.

'Mustn't forget, I've got these.' Wanda removed a tin from her string bag. 'Lemon and almond cakes from my mother.'

Apparently, the photography shop was still operating, though subject to all kinds of stock shortages and restrictions. 'And some idiots think we must be spies,' Wanda said, wearily, standing up to fetch plates as Lucia boiled the kettle.

'Spies?'

'Silberstein sounds German. Try explaining to people that my grandparents actually came from eastern Poland.'

'Why would a Jewish family be spying for Hitler?'

'You tell me. Apparently they're taking photographs for Goering so he can tell the Luftwaffe where to aim their bombs.' Wanda caught Lucia's eye and laughed. 'I know, it makes no sense.'

Lucia would have to leave shortly with Hope to see Miss Goodley at the rescue centre. She cupped her hands around the teacup, which felt warm and comforting, and tried not to think about the separation. The cake tasted sweet and citrus on her lips. Hope ate the one Wanda had given her, looking appreciative.

'I dread to think what my mother did to buy the lemons and almonds for these cakes,' Wanda said. 'I can't even remember the last time I saw a lemon.' She licked her fingers. 'What will you do now, Fancy?'

'I don't know. Try to see Della again. But I—' She shrugged. 'I'm not sure how keen she was to see me again, anyway.' Lucia remembered something. 'Oh, something else happened.' Wanda raised an eyebrow. 'Hope spoke again. Just a single word, I couldn't make it out.'

Wanda's face lit up. 'That's wonderful. What did you say, Hope?'

The girl looked down at the cake she was eating.

Lucia sighed. 'I wish I'd heard more clearly. It was while I was trying to persuade Della to let me come back. I missed it.'

'You know how to snatch the happy punchline from a story, Fancy.' Wanda made a face. 'It's something, though. Miss Goodley will be relieved that some progress has been made.'

'Wanda?' Lucia looked at her meaningfully. 'Hope, could you take your cake into the bedroom please?' The girl did as she was asked.

Wanda twirled the fringe on her scarf around in her fingers. 'I know what's coming, Fancy. We agreed Hope was to stay here only until today.'

'Which is fine if Miss Goodley's office has tracked down family or friends. But if not...'

'If Hope stays here, it means we can never both go out together and have fun when we're off-duty.' She looked directly at Lucia. 'Some of the shifts... Well, you know. One of us would have to stay in to look after Hope. I sound selfish. But I'm being realistic.'

'We could find someone to mind Hope at night so we can do those things. And she'll be at school. In the holidays, there are state-run camps.'

Wanda looked at her quizzically. 'Never had you pegged as the broody type, Fancy.'

She couldn't explain her emotional reaction to seeing Hope pulled out like that, the girl's smallness in the arms of her rescuer, her silence, the way she clung to the toy elephant. She shrugged. 'War changes people.'

'Some people. Others just become even more themselves. More selfish. Or more selfless.' Wanda was staring at her. 'You've got a good heart, Fancy. You care about people. But we mightn't be the best ones for the task, you know? Our rosters can change at the last minute. We live in a tiny flat somewhere the Luftwaffe enjoy visiting.'

Lucia nodded.

'Honestly. It wouldn't work to have Hope here.' Wanda's voice was kind. 'And I think you know that too, in your heart. You've done a good thing, but now it's time for someone else to take over.'

'Her parents... If only we could find out where they were.'

'No reason why you can't keep on making enquiries.'

'If they're alive, they'll be beside themselves. They'll be...' She thought of her own parents, how she'd left them like that. A mixture of shame and something even more corrosive washed through Lucia. 'Losing a child, it's just the worst thing, it...' She couldn't speak any more.

'I've got to go. I've let you know how I feel. I know you'll make the right decision. See you later.' Wanda stopped. 'And, Fancy, don't give up on your sister. It was bound to be difficult first time you saw Della again. You were prepared for it. Della wasn't.'

'I really think she hates me.'

'She doesn't.' Wanda smiled her quick little smile that you

could almost miss. 'We didn't have that other conversation, did we? The one we planned this morning? But perhaps it was about Della anyway?'

She could tell Wanda now, she had it in her to explain about France, about Sebastien, all of it. Hope was out of earshot and Lucia felt warm and safe here in the flat with her closest friend, who never judged.

'Oh no!' Wanda looked at her watch and jumped up. 'Next time.' She popped her head around the bedroom door and waved at the child. 'Bye, Hope, and good luck, sweetheart.' Lucia could just about make out Hope's blonde head as she sat on the floor with her elephant, reading *Hansel and Gretel*.

Lucia turned to more practical matters to quell the storm inside her. She needed to get Hope ready. And show Miss Goodley she'd looked after the girl well, and could find somewhere else for them to live – and quickly, if Wanda really was unhappy about this arrangement continuing.

How likely was it? New lodgings would have to be close to the ambulance station and ideally Hope's school, assuming that was local. With so many people bombed-out, so many homes smashed up by bombs, the search would take weeks. It wasn't realistic. And she'd be abandoning Wanda. How could she choose between the two of them? She looked through the door at Hope reading her book and had to look away again, eyes prickling.

Lucia supplemented Mrs Silberstein's cakes with a late lunch for them both: a tiny piece of bacon fried up with a few cold boiled potatoes and bread and butter. Feeling almost too anxious to eat anything herself, she forced her lunch down. She needed fuelling for her night shift.

The clock rolled round to half-one. 'Come on.' Lucia stood up and put on her coat. She wrapped up clothes, pencils, puzzle and *Hansel and Gretel* in brown paper. Hope held her elephant tight. 'You know I'll do all I can for you, Hope. With luck, they've found out something about your family,' she told her.

Hope blinked. Lucia put the parcel down again. 'I'll come back for these later.' Removing Hope's few possessions along with Hope was just too final for now. 'We'll sort things out,' she promised, hearing confidence in her voice she was far from feeling.

SEVENTEEN

Hope

Lucia took her hand. 'Come on, Hope.' Hope was a much better name than her old Mouse nickname. Lucia's hands were hardly bigger than Hope's and very slim. Mami had had larger hands. Papi joked that they were a horsewoman's hands, designed for holding reins. Where was Mami now? Sometimes Hope felt an overwhelming urge to break her promise and talk to Lucia, begging her to find her. Mami had only popped out to the shops. She couldn't have been far away from the house when the siren started wailing.

Hope shrank into Lucia's side as they entered the rest centre. So many people. So loud. And the smell of boiled vegetables and unwashed people made her stomach feel peculiar. Would Lucia really leave her here? If she did, she'd escape, run back to the house. It was smashed up, but it was where Mami would look for her, not in this hall full of people, bedding and noise.

And yet there were other children here, bouncing a ball, chanting nursery rhymes as they played skipping games. It might be fun to join in with them after spending so long without playmates. Hope couldn't resist smiling as they walked through to the cupboard where Miss Goodley was waiting. Some of the children grinned back.

'Now then, young lady,' Miss Goodley started. 'We haven't had any luck finding your family. It's very hard without your real name.'

Hope shuffled in the chair.

'And you didn't live in the house where we found you long enough for people to know you, apart from the woman... the lady who was in the house when it was bombed. Who we now know wasn't your mother.'

Of course the landlady wasn't Mami! She bit her lip. Miss Goodley leaned forward. She had a kind face. Hope was nearly tempted to tell her everything, but she might be put on a train and sent to a camp. And it wouldn't be the same one as Papi's, as in his letters, Papi said it was only for men. She'd be completely alone. And she had to keep her promise to Mami. Mami had been acting strangely before she'd vanished, but she was still a grown-up and knew what was right.

'For now, we feel Hope would be better off in a children's home, with other youngsters and access to people who can help her. Or better still, a good foster home.' Miss Goodley was looking at Lucia. 'With someone who isn't already doing their bit working long, dangerous shifts as an ambulance driver.'

'No,' Lucia was saying. 'I don't mind. I love having Hope. I'll do anything so she can stay with us.'

The conversation couldn't be going well, otherwise Lucia wouldn't be raising her voice, flushing. Lucia really cared about Hope, it was clear in her voice. This woman, Miss Goodley, wasn't as kind as she seemed. Hope wouldn't be going back to the flat with Lucia, spending another night on the bedroom floor, where she felt safe from the men in uniform. She knew what happened when children were taken away from their families to orphanages – she'd heard Mami and Papi whispering about it. Sometimes the people who took them changed the boys' and girls' names so their parents couldn't find them. Lucia had given Hope a new name, but for a kind reason. Even so, would her parents know that Hope was the mouse?

Lucia was still arguing with Miss Goodley, more quietly now, as if she knew she wasn't going to win, her hands knotting themselves together, reminding Hope of Mami's. Neither of them were looking at Hope or at the door, which was only partly closed. She sprang out of the chair, elephant in hand, and through the door. Miss Goodley shouted. Chairs scraped on the floor as the two of them jumped up after her.

Hope was glad for the throng of people in the hall now. Instinct told her to hide among the huddle of children waiting their turn on the ping-pong table and edge herself towards the door on the side of the hall. Glancing over her shoulder, she spotted Miss Goodley and Lucia rushing in after her. She broke into a run, dodging a woman carrying a tray of enamel mugs, who gasped as she nearly collided with her. Some of the tea slopped to the floor, mugs crashing together.

'Steady now, young lady,' the woman called after her. She bolted through the door and into a narrow passageway opening into a road. Miss Goodley was shouting at Hope to come back. A row of dustbins was lined up on the opposite side of the road. Hope crouched behind them, pulling her knees up to her chest so she was in a ball. The wet and muddy pavement would dirty the back of the coat Wanda had found for her, which made her feel bad. *Quiet now*, she warned the elephant.

The women's feet ran up the passageway and along the road past her, Miss Goodley's heavy in her solid black shoes, Lucia light-footed and quicker. They'd be back in a moment to check in the other direction. Should she stay here? Would they think to look behind the bins? This was like a game, except it was serious. She wouldn't be laughing if she was discovered. Peeping round, she spotted a bus pulling up at a stop. She hadn't been on a bus alone before and had no money for the fare, but she could jump on and off the platform before the conductor approached her, couldn't she? Miss Goodley was still looking in the other direction. Lucia had vanished.

Hope emerged from behind the bins and ran quietly to the bus, springing on to the platform just as it pulled away. The conductress had already started walking up between the seats to collect fares, her back to Hope. No passengers sat near the platform and nobody seemed to notice her. She climbed halfway up the stairs to make herself invisible from the pavement.

She counted slowly to ten before descending again, peering down the street. Miss Goodley had been left behind, her back turned to the bus. Lucia wasn't in sight. The conductress was still busy collecting fares on the lower level. Hope returned to her position halfway up the stairs until the bus slowed at a junction and the conductress's footsteps thumped towards the rear of the bus. She crept down, leaping off the platform while the bus was crawling along, heard the conductress shouting 'Oi' but didn't look back. Mami had tutted at children jumping on and off moving buses, but Papi laughed, talking about a game of tag he and his friends had played on Berlin trams as children.

She ran into a side street and stood behind a postbox, turning to make sure nobody was coming after her. Not a single person was looking in her direction. Again it felt like a game of hide and seek. Her fear about the children's home had almost faded in all the excitement. She was out on the streets again, free.

Hope didn't know where she was, but when she walked up the side street it led into a bigger road. A familiar set of red shop awnings appeared in front of her. Her heart thumped. She knew this street. This was the grocer's where they shopped, not far from their old home.

The memory of how it had been there in that little house,

when there'd still been three of them, washed over Hope so strongly that she came to a halt, no longer exhilarated. She bent over, hugging herself to stop the sad feelings. When the three of them had lived in that house, she'd been able to talk as much as she wanted. They hadn't been cooped up in one bedroom.

'We'll just have a quick look,' Hope silently told the elephant she was still clutching. 'To remind us of what it was like. Then we'll go back to that horrible house. Mami will know to look for us in the outhouse.'

Yet something inside her felt strange as she remembered how Lucia had run after her. Giving her the slip felt wrong and rude. When Mami found her again, she'd surely let her see Lucia to explain?

A darker thought came to her. Lucia didn't yet know she was a German girl. That warm look on her face might turn cold. Lucia might agree that the men in uniform had been right to take Papi away to a camp. Germans were the baddies here. German bombs smashed up houses and killed people like their landlady.

Hope made her way to the red-shuttered grocer's. She knew to turn right when she came to the next junction.

In a few minutes, she'd be in the little mews: that was what the small, cobbled street was called. She couldn't stay there, she'd have to go back to the other place again and wait for her mother, just as she'd promised. But she'd just peep through the windows downstairs and see if it still looked like it had before Papi had been taken.

EIGHTEEN

'Please,' Lucia said. Wanda was in the kitchen, back early from her afternoon shift because Potts was training recruits and needed one of the ambulances. The ironing board was up, and she was pressing the dress she was obviously intending to wear out tonight. 'I really need you to swap shifts with me. I have to look for Hope.' She was still out of breath from running back to the flat.

'You said Miss Goodley contacted the police. And surely they'll alert the local ARPs on duty this evening?'

'Yes, but Hope trusts me. I think she's scared of people in authority. She'll come to me if I keep looking and calling.'

Wanda turned her dress over on the ironing board. 'She's not a dog, Fancy. She's not your responsibility, either.'

Lucia slumped onto a chair, exhaustion washing her. 'It feels like my fault.'

'How'd you work that one out?'

'I took my eyes off her.'

'You can't keep her permanently in your line of sight.'

'She grew scared when we started talking about children's homes.'

Wanda's sigh was a long one. 'I was going dancing at the Palais. It would be a...' She shook her head. A distraction, she probably meant. From James's death. Guilt flooded Lucia but still she couldn't stop herself.

'I'll change the roster so I do two shifts for this one. Please, Wanda? I can't let her be lost.'

Wanda sighed. 'All right. I'll do it. On two conditions.'

Lucia looked at her.

'You drink a cup of tea before you go out, take ten minutes to draw breath. You look dreadful. Then I'll go out to the telephone and tell them I won't be at the Palais tonight.'

Ten minutes when the winter afternoon was already closing in. But Wanda's set expression made it clear she wouldn't accept any argument.

'And I want to know what happened in France.'

Lucia's heart thumped hard. 'I... I don't know... I...' Earlier on today she'd wanted to talk about France, but now she'd lost Hope and the prospect was overwhelming.

'Those are my conditions.' Wanda folded her arms. 'France is like this big dark vacuum between us. I thought I didn't mind. But I do. You're my closest friend but I don't feel I know you. I thought it was all guilt about leaving Della. But I'm not sure. Those mysterious Tuesday lunchtime excursions.' She gave a half laugh at Lucia's expression. 'Oh, I noticed. I thought perhaps you'd taken on religion and were going to a regular service.'

In a way it was a kind of religious ritual, Westminster Bridge at noon.

Wanda was peering at her more closely. 'But the more I think about it, the more certain I am it's a man. It is, isn't it?

Lucia nodded.

'All those fellows desperate to take you out for dinner and you just brush them off. I've been wondering why.'

Unravelling all that had happened in France was a task so

huge she barely knew where to start. Wanda deserved the truth, not as part of a deal but because she was a friend.

'That's part of it, yes. I'd tell you now, but there's not time.'

'So it is a man. Thought so. Tomorrow will do.'

'Tomorrow.' Their eyes locked, making the solemn promise. Lucia filled her cup from the teapot and added milk.

'Hope can't have gone far.' Wanda folded up the ironing board and hung up the dress.

She gulped down tea and stood up. 'See you tomorrow,' she said to Wanda as she pulled on her outdoor things. 'And thank you. Again.'

'You take care out there if the alert goes,' Wanda called from the kitchen. 'I can't afford to lose anyone else, Fancy.' Her voice shook. Lucia's conscience pricked her. Wanda needed the solace of a night out with her friends, which Lucia had now denied her.

'I'm going to be causing you trouble for a while longer yet.'

She heard Wanda's answering laugh as she closed the front door.

Which way to go first? Lucia had already woven her way back from the rest centre to the flat, taking detours around side streets and alleyways, calling out to Hope, asking passers-by if they'd seen her. Surely Hope couldn't travel far on foot at her age? She didn't have any money. Thank God she had on the warm coat Wanda had obtained from the garment exchange. Frost would soon glisten on pavements and jagged ruined walls.

She reached the smashed-up house where she'd first encountered Hope. A tape and sign warned her that entering the site was subject to punishment, but the warden was nowhere near. A woman outside a house across the road stared as she stepped over the tape and pointed at Lucia. 'You nick a single thing from there and I'll have the coppers on you.' Lucia wondered what was possibly lying in the rubble that could still have any value, but people felt strongly about thieves who took advantage of other people's misfortunes to steal what little remained of their old lives.

'I'm looking for a little girl?' Lucia shouted back. 'About six or seven? She was living here at the time of the air-raid.'

The woman crossed the street, her suspicious expression fading. 'Light-brown hair in plaits? They've already come around asking about her and her mother. I barely seen the little mite. The mother would take her out sometimes, but they'd scuttle along, heads down and you wouldn't get a word out of either of them.'

'We thought she might come back here.'

The woman sniffed. 'No chance of that now. Poor Jenny met her maker when the bomb hit.'

'Jenny was the woman we took to the hospital that night?'

The woman's face softened. 'You were ambulance crew, weren't you? You look familiar now I think of it. Yes, that was Jenny. She took in lodgers as her wages didn't cover the rent after her husband died.'

'Jenny didn't tell you anything about the girl and her mother?'

Suspicion had returned to the woman's face. 'You working with welfare as well as driving ambulances, miss?'

Lucia shook her head. 'My flatmate and I took the girl in as nobody seemed to know anything about her. Now she's taken fright and run off because they want to send her to a children's home.'

'Not surprised, poor mite.'

'I won't let that happen if I can help it. I'm desperate to find her before night falls.'

The woman examined her for a moment before nodding. 'The doors are boarded up. She can't have got inside that house.'

'What's at the back?'

'Outhouse with the privy in it. There's no shelter.'

'It didn't sound like the kind of place a child would choose: dark and malodorous.

'I'll help you have a root around the back. Just mind your step and watch out for falling masonry. I heard them saying how unstable it is when they came to rope it off. Shame you haven't got your helmet with you.'

The two of them picked their way round the side of the house, the rubble unsteady beneath their feet. 'Why didn't the kid's mother take her to the shelter when the alert sounded?'

'It seems she'd left the house when the raid started,' Lucia said. 'Probably got pushed into a shelter.'

'Some of those wardens are little Hitlers. Strange she hasn't come back to look for the kid, though.' They looked at one another, both reading the same thought in one another's faces.

They called out and shone Lucia's torch into each shadow and pit, moving into the backyard. Something shot out between Lucia's legs as she opened the outhouse door. She gasped.

'It's just Timmi,' her helper said. 'Poor Jenny's cat. I'll put out a saucer of whatever I can find for him later.'

There was no way Hope could have entered the house, the doors and windows of which were boarded up. 'She's not here,' Lucia said, hearing despair in her voice. 'I'll have to keep walking around.'

The woman gave her a friendly pat on the arm. 'I'll keep my eyes open and remind the warden to look out for her.'

Lucia thanked her and walked on. She'd head up to the hospital. Hope might manage to find her way to see if her mother was in a ward, but it wasn't a straightforward walk from the rest centre. As she walked, Lucia tried to imagine herself at the same age, small and frightened? She'd run away herself, but not in a blind panic like a young child.

She stopped and turned round. A young child would probably seek out a familiar place. The woman had vanished into her house, but she banged on the door. 'Where did the little girl and woman live before they came to Jenny's house?' she asked, when the door opened.

'Somewhere else in the borough. Nicer than this, but not exactly Cheyne Walk, by the sounds of it. Jenny said they'd walked here with their things when they moved in. Not that they brought much with them.'

Lucia raised a hand in thanks and set off, heading blindly towards the rest centre again. Perhaps Miss Goodley had found Hope in the interim and she was safely back at the hall, playing with the other children or tucking into a hot meal. She speeded up her walk, stopping now and then to peer up the side passages between houses. At a public shelter, she saw the door was unlocked, and ran down the steps to check it. 'The siren hasn't gone yet, sweetheart,' a passing soldier in Canadian uniform jeered as she re-emerged. 'Want to go down there with me so I can take your mind off the Luftwaffe?' She shot him a look of contempt and he muttered and walked away.

There was no shelter in the back garden of Hope's home, so she and her mother must have used a public shelter. Pinned to a map on the wall of the ambulance station was a list of all the public shelters in the borough. But that would mean confronting Potts, who'd be unhappy about the changing of this evening's roster. Time would be wasted while she scolded Lucia for swapping with Wanda.

Another public building that was reasonably warm might be worth trying first. Would Hope's mother have taken her to the public library in Manresa Road, just north of the King's Road? Judging by the way she'd responded to *Hansel and Gretel*, she loved books.

Time was running out. Had Hope left any kind of clue at all? She'd drawn and painted on the back of the roll of wallpaper. What was it she'd depicted? Boats – barges on the river. Had she lived closer to the Thames before she'd moved? Instead of heading north, Lucia turned towards the river.

She reached Chelsea Embankment and stopped, oppressed by the approaching nightfall. She hadn't a clue where to go. This was all her fault. If she'd left Hope at the rest centre when they'd first found her, she would be safe, not out on the cold, dark streets when an air-raid was a strong possibility.

A single policeman on a horse clomped past her, nodding. Lucia thought of the afternoon of the Mosley rally, of the horses charging the protestors, the marbles rolled onto the road to send the horses tumbling. This policeman on his horse was a friendly presence. 'Excuse me,' she called.

He pulled up the horse. 'Yes, miss?'

She gave him a description of Hope.

'Your little sister, is she?'

She shook her head. 'I was just looking after her. Not very well.' Her voice trembled. She blinked hard.

'Littl'uns wander off all the time, especially now.' He removed a notepad from his upper pocket, clicking at the horse to steady it while he wrote down a description of Hope.

When she'd passed on the information, he trotted off, telling her he'd sweep along the Embankment as far as Albert Bridge and head north.

But the chances of them finding the girl anywhere in the open streets started to feel remote. Most people were decent, Lucia reminded herself. If someone else found Hope, they'd take her to the police or find a warden. And yet she couldn't help reminding herself of stories she'd heard about strange men snatching children displaced from their homes to do unspeakable things to them. More realistically, wandering around in unlit streets, without a torch, could result in Hope tumbling into the road to be hit by a poorly lit vehicle.

The siren wailed. Strictly speaking, as she was close at

hand, Lucia should report to the station too, even though she was off-duty. But unless it was a heavy local raid, Potts would have her doing extra bandage-folding or checking tyre pressures.

Lucia increased her pace, heading away from the river, out of ideas now and reliant only on blind instinct.

NINETEEN

Hope

The flowers in their front window boxes had died from the cold. Hope peered through the windows but couldn't see anything. Perhaps the blackout blinds had been pulled down inside. Footsteps behind her on the cobbles made her turn round. A man. Long black coat, straggly unbrushed hair falling beneath his collar, swaying. He stopped, blinking. 'Little girl, you shouldn't be out alone. They'll be back tonight, I can feel it. The alert will sound any minute now.'

She shrank back into the wall of the house.

'Cat got your tongue?' He came closer. He smelled of mothballs and damp clothes. His eyes widened and narrowed as if he was trying to wake himself up. 'You know where the air-raid shelter is?'

She nodded.

'Get yourself down there as soon as the siren goes. These streets aren't safe for people your age.' For a moment, the features of his face seemed more like a normal person's. 'Some of the people out at night... I used to see you with your parents,' he said. 'They kept you safe. I saw them take your father away.' His eyes were full of understanding. 'Do you know what happened to him?'

Her lips were opening to reply. She remembered just in time that she shouldn't speak.

'Ah, you don't know either, do you, poppet? What a world we live in.' He swept off his black hat and bowed, winking as she laughed, before ambling away. When he'd turned the corner into the street and out of sight she moved on.

You reached the back yard, or garden, as Mami had liked to call it, through the house as there was no side passage between the houses. During games of hide and seek she'd found out that there was a tiny gap between the last house in the row and the wall separating them from the main road beyond. From there, she could wriggle through to the garden of the end house, really just a paved-over yard. Old furniture was stacked up there against the fence dividing it from their yard and she'd climbed into the garden, delighted to surprise her parents by knocking on the back windows. Mami told her not to do this again because the junk had sharp metal edges, but the need to get inside their old home was even stronger now. It was where she belonged.

Just like a mouse, she climbed the fence, elephant stuffed into the front of her coat, and dropped silently into the garden. There was a chance Mami might have forgotten to lock the back door. Hope tugged at the handle, but it refused to budge.

The grey evening was turning to black. She shivered, her legs feeling heavy now. Hiding from Miss Goodley had sapped all the energy from her. If only she could get inside this house, she could go down to the cellar, where Papi had prepared the little room for them to shelter safely in during air-raids.

Hope gave the back door a last futile tug. Coming here had been the wrong thing to do, even if being taken to a children's home was terrifying. Maybe if she could find her way back to

Lucia's flat, she could ask to stay with her a little longer. Papi had said she sounded like an English girl now, after English nursery school and then reception class. But Hope had accidentally spoken in German twice in front of Wanda and Lucia. She'd got away with it, but what would happen if she forgot again?

The siren sounded. Hope looked skywards. Already lights were scoring the greyness above, looking for the planes that came from her old homeland. In a moment the guns would start firing. Heavy bombers would rumble overhead. She was already shaking. Time to go to the public shelter.

She remembered something. She'd left her gas mask in the office at the large hall. If she went to a shelter, they'd tell her off for not having it with her.

Shivering, Hope lowered herself to the ground, back to the door, arms shielding her head. 'We have to be brave,' she told the elephant clasped between her knees, who observed her with his shiny blank eyes. Yet Hope herself was nothing more than a timid mouse.

TWENTY

Incendiaries crashed into the streets and onto rooftops, the Luftwaffe lighting up the dark streets so they could aim their bombs at god-knows-what below. The Lots Road power station, perhaps? The hated whistler bombs with their mocking shrieks joined in.

A warden shouted at Lucia to take shelter immediately. She darted around the middle-aged man, his eyes narrowed with irritation. She stopped. 'A girl, six or seven, blonde hair. She's lost.'

Instantly the anger left him. 'I'll keep an eye out for her, miss, don't you worry. Now you should—'

But she shook her head and broke into a run. 'Her name is Hope,' she called over her shoulder. 'Please tell her Lucia is looking for her.' His shouts followed her down the street as she cut against the current of people making for the shelter.

Usually in a raid she had her helmet on, ambulance waiting for her, Gardner's quiet presence bolstering her nerves. Tonight, she was by herself, not sure what do to, where to go. Panic was curling its fingers out to clutch her.

A figure, dark, waving its arms, jumped out in front of her. 'They took her father and they'll see her die.'

She took a step back to avoid him. 'Excuse me.' Lucia wove around him. A hand reached out, grabbing her sleeve, halting her.

'They'll see her die. The little 'un. The father's taken, so nobody will know what name to put on the shroud.'

Behind Lucia, incendiaries pattered down. 'Whose father?'

'The child. The one with the elephant.' A screamer bomb wailed its way down behind them, making it impossible to speak for seconds. 'And the mother never came back from the shops.'

She stared at him. 'You've seen her, Hope?'

His face, filthy, seemed to crumple. 'No. I saw Effie.'

'Effie?'

He said something rapidly in what sounded like German. '*Nichts auf Deutsch... nur Englisch.* Don't say anything, that's what they were saying in German. But I learned a bit, see, in the last war, when the Hun took me prisoner.'

'So her real name is Effie? That's why she didn't speak, because she'd been warned not to give away that she was German.' Lucia said it aloud, slowly. Her companion put a hand to his ear.

'Her mother got scared. I saw her on her way to the shops, hunched over like this.' He raised his shoulders up and leant forward. 'Effie, the little mouse, wasn't with her.'

The noise above them was building its way up to another crescendo. 'So where is Effie now? Do you know?'

He pointed down a side street. 'Last but one on the left.' She ran past him into the street, shouting a thanks. A flash above her illuminated the cobbles. Nobody was outside the house. 'She'll be round the back,' a voice said in her ear. He'd followed her, footsteps drowned out by the crashes around them. 'In the yard. I've seen her climb in over the wall at the end.'

She muttered another thanks, running to the end of the mews, which must once have been a service street for the larger houses close by. Grooms and other servants had lived here, horses beneath the premises, carriages cleaned, standing ready at a master's whim. Newton Terrace had its own mews behind it too. The wall at the end of the row was easy for Lucia to leap over. Hope – she corrected herself, *Effie* – could easily have done it too, she calculated. She found herself in a yard behind the end mews house, old furniture piled up against the fence bordering the neighbouring property. She clambered over it. 'Hope,' she called, before correcting herself again. 'Effie?'

Someone gasped and moved. Her eyes blinked. The beam of a searchlight cut across the sky and for a moment, Lucia saw a small figure huddled up by the back door. 'Effie,' she called. 'It's all right, I'm your friend. *Ich bin deine Freundin. Hab' kein Angst.*'

Was this even comprehensible German? It had been some years since her term in Switzerland and the finishing school had been in the French-speaking part. But Effie was moving towards her. Her arms went round Lucia's lower body. '*Hilf mir bitte,* Lucia,' she said. '*Hilf meinem Vater und meiner Mutter.*'

'I will,' Lucia said, also in German, the words coming back to her somehow. 'We need to take shelter now, then we'll make a plan.' Effie said something about the *keller*. Lucia stared at her blankly for a moment before understanding. This house had a cellar. They'd be safe down there if they could just break inside.

The rumble of an exploding bomb very close shook the ground. Lucia detached herself, took her torch from her pocket and struck the nearest window with the metal barrel. The blind wasn't down, presumably because the electricity had been cut off and there was no risk of showing a light. She wriggled her hand inside and found the window catch, pulling it open. The windowsill was low enough to the ground for her to lift Effie into the room inside. 'Go and open the door,' she said, 'let me in.'

Effie vanished into the gloom. Seconds later, in a momentary lull in the explosions, Lucia heard a bolt the other side of the door screeching, sounding too stiff for the child to open. She was about to tell Effie not to wait, to go on down to the cellar, she'd squeeze through the window somehow, when the door creaked open.

Lucia darted through. 'Where's the cellar door, Effie?' A flash of light above illuminated a small interior.

Effie opened a door on the left side. 'Down here.' Lucia turned on her torch.

'We'll be fine,' she said, aiming the torch down the stone steps. The beam caught on something spherical and glass. 'Look, there's a lamp on the table we can light.' Someone – Effie's parents, presumably – had done a good job in turning the cellar into a shelter. There was a small camp bed with a sleeping bag laid out on it, presumably where Effie had slept during nighttime raids, and a couple of chairs. The cellar was damp, but not as cold as it was outside. For a few hours, it would keep them as safe as anywhere could be, unless a bomb landed directly on top of the house. Yet again, Lucia reminded herself of how statistically unlikely this was, even though she knew plenty of occasions when this had happened. She found a box of matches beside the lamp and lit it. The glow revealed the small space. Someone had hung a picture up on the wall, a painting of a little house with steep eaves and shutters, surrounded by pine trees, snow-tipped, alone.

Alone like Lucia and Effie. Nobody knew where they were. No warden would have their names on a list to rescue. If the house took a direct hit, it might only be the stink of their bodies under the fallen masonry that alerted a recovery team to their whereabouts. The thought chilled her. But she couldn't let Effie see her concern. 'Why didn't you speak?' she said, sitting down on one of the chairs. 'Were you scared?' She'd switched to English, which Effie could clearly understand well.

'They took my Papi. Mami said we should be careful not to let people see we were German or they would take us too.' Effie's English was so slightly accented as to be barely noticeable.

'Took him? Who took your father? The police?'

Effie looked blank. 'Some men in uniforms. With a van. There were other people in it. They didn't take Mami and me but we had to move from this house because we didn't have enough money after Papi went.'

'Where is your mother now, Effie? Do you know?'

Effie's face seemed to close in on itself. 'Mami went shopping and the bombers came and she didn't come back. And then the bomb landed and you took me out of the house. You shouldn't have done that, Lucia. If she comes back, she won't find me. She will think the bad men came for me too.'

'You couldn't stay in a bombed-out house, Effie.'

Effie frowned at her. 'How do you know that's my name, anyway? I didn't tell you.'

'The tramp told me – the man with the beard and long black coat.'

Effie nodded, looking placated. 'He's a bit scary but he's kind, really. When the people were laughing at Papi being taken, he looked sad and cross.'

'Those others shouldn't have laughed either. I'm sorry, Effie. I'm sure your father is a good man.'

Overhead, a group of heavy bombers shook the house. Another screamer bomb wailed its way to its crashing finale. Lucia had always hated the sensation of bricks and mortar trembling around her. She did her best to put out of her mind the image of dirt blocking their airways, collapsed walls crushing the air out of their lungs. 'Do you remember much about living in Germany?'

'I was just little then. But my Oma, my grandmother, lived there, in a house with woods around it and snow in the winter. I liked that house.'

'Like the one in the painting on the wall down here?'

Effie nodded. 'We haven't heard from her for a long time now,' she went on. 'When we left Germany for the very last time, Oma cried but she said it was for the best. My uncle had already been taken away.'

'Why did they take him?'

'They said he wrote bad things.'

Was the uncle some kind of political enemy of the Nazis? Her eyes went to a small crucifix on top of a crate. Clearly the family wasn't Jewish, but other groups in Germany had been targeted as state enemies.

Lucia wondered how the family had managed to stay on in England. Were they naturalised British subjects now? If they'd been allowed to live freely after the original panic round-up of Germans and Austrians in the autumn of 1939, why had the father been re-arrested now? Probably questions Effie herself couldn't answer. The girl had unwound her arms and was sitting more upright now, though she shivered, her elephant still clasped in her arms. Lucia spotted a blanket on a shelf and stood up to fetch it, wrapping it around Effie and the toy. A memory like a sliver of ice cut through her and she shivered.

'Tell me what your mother looks like,' she said, to distract herself. 'What she was wearing when she went out shopping just before the bombing started. And which shop she was going to.'

Effie described her mother's shoulder-length hair. 'Same colour as yours, but not wavy. She wore it pinned under a grey hat. She wore her dark navy coat and brown leather boots. She is a bit taller than you. Thin. Her eyes are blue like mine. She

was going to the shop with the red... what do you call them?'
She made curved shapes in the air. 'Over the windows. The
grocer's shop.'

Lucia reached inside her jacket pocket for the notebook she
carried with her for her shifts and made notes. She thought she
knew of a red-awninged grocer's, a bit of a walk from Effie's new
home. They mightn't have reregistered their ration books at a
more convenient store. Effie's mother might have worried at
undertaking a new registration process now that her husband
had been arrested. The tramp had described the woman's
anxious appearance. She must have felt desperate, alone with a
young child, her husband behind internment camp wire.

Her eyes went to the crates beside the walls. 'Are these your
family's things, Effie?'

Effie nodded. 'We couldn't take everything when we
moved, but they let Mami keep the boxes down here.'

'Would there be photographs of your parents here?'

Effie jumped up, looking pleased at having something active
to do. It was always better to distract yourself during raids. The
crates weren't nailed down, just fastened with catches that
opened easily. China, books, music scores, a couple of jigsaw
puzzles, all wrapped up in newspaper and straw. A doll. 'That's
mine.' Effie pounced on the latter. 'I don't need her, she can stay
here. My elephant's enough.'

Lucia opened another crate. A leather album. Old
photographs of the same house painted in the picture hanging
on the wall. A wedding photograph. Effie's parents – a handsome couple, radiant on the day of their marriage. Lucia carried
on flicking through the album, finding a photograph of the
three family members, now including a smaller Effie. They
were on a toboggan at the top of a slope. Effie's mother wore
corduroy trousers, tucked into laced-up boots, a warm coat and
cap, and beamed into the camera. Like her husband she seemed
carefree.

'We had to leave the toboggan at my grandmother's house.' Effie sounded regretful.

Lucia was peering at Effie's father. He looked like a kindly, decent man, not that you could tell by looking at people whether they were Nazi sympathisers. Take her own father; he had those handsome, warm-eyed features that attracted people to him. She wasn't going to think about him now. 'I'm going to take this photograph,' she told Effie. 'Only because it may help us find out what happened to your parents.' She removed it from the frame and tucked it into her inside pocket. 'I'll take care of it, and I'll give it back when we've found them. Are there any of your clothes down here, do you think?'

Effie shook her head. 'We took the ones that still fitted me to the new house.'

And they'd been destroyed in the explosion.

Lucia repacked the crates and they sat down again.

'Papi said there used to be horses where he was now.'

She turned to the girl. 'Horses?'

'He wrote to Mami and said they'd used it for horses.'

Lucia tucked the information away in her head. A cavalry barracks, perhaps? An old stables?

The all-clear wailed. She stood up, wincing as she moved cold legs. 'Let's take you back to the flat.'

Effie looked mutinous. 'This is where I live.'

'There's no electricity here, probably no gas. We need to be somewhere warm.' Effie's face was still set in opposition.

'Will that mean I go to a children's home?'

Lucia hesitated. 'I don't know. But Miss Goodley is a kind person and wants to help you, Effie.' She put an arm on the girl's shoulders.

'Perhaps the photograph will help find Mami and Papi.'

'Maybe.' Or the photograph could be taken to the local morgue to see if it helped identify any female casualties. She was glad for the darkness hiding her face from Effie. She realised too late that she should have looked for papers giving the parents' full names, but couldn't remember seeing paperwork in the crates.

They walked past the ambulance station. Automatically, she counted the ambulances. All back.

Lucia's conscience pricked her. 'Wait here,' she told Effie, leaving her in the yard. If Potts was in the office, she might make a comment about Lucia's failure to report as an extra hand during the raid. She could at least offer to do some of the tiresome routine jobs, tidy up the first aid kits, fold the blankets, spare those on shift some of the load after a heavy raid. Effie could sit quietly in the corner. Surely Potts wouldn't object if she explained that it was the last night Effie would stay?

Before they reached the station, Lucia found a public telephone box. She needed to leave a message for Miss Goodley, telling her Effie was safe. She'd have left work for the night long ago. Instead, Lucia eventually found the number for the police station and told the on-duty officer the girl was with her.

Potts and the others were sitting in the mess with mugs of cocoa, mostly untouched. They looked up as she came in, but glanced away again. Lucia's eyes went from one of them to the other and then up to the pegs on the wall, where they hung their helmets on their return. One of the pegs had nothing hanging from it. Lucia blinked hard, looked away and looked back. The peg was still empty.

'What happened to her?' The words came out with a heavy dullness.

'Incendiary caught the sacks in the warehouse they were called to. The heavy rescue team had assessed it, but someone had been hiding black-market sugar in there. It ignited very quickly while the crew was loading an injured person onto the stretcher. A rafter came down.' Potts said it mechanically, as if she was reading a report. 'Wanda was right underneath. Gardner managed to jump clear. The injured man rolled away from the rafter as it fell.'

'We took Wanda to St Stephen's,' Gardner said. 'The doctors and nurses tried very hard to save her. But she was bleeding so much.'

'But I—' Lucia's throat was constricted. The room was spinning. Someone was pushing her onto a chair before she fell. 'I was supposed... Wanda swapped shifts with me because I... I had to... I thought...'

'Always something more important than a shift, eh, Black?' Potts' smile was ghastly, as if she was a living skull, the lips pulled up into a rictus grin. 'Girls like you, it's just a hobby, work. If something better comes up, you just flit away to do it.'

Gardner was saying something, but Lucia couldn't make out the words, only that Potts was batting them away as though they were irritating flies. 'Wanda Silberstein was one of the best. Rigorous. Thorough. Knew every protocol.' She looked at Lucia. 'What were you doing on your night off, Black? Dancing? Cinema? Perhaps an exciting West End production that one of your admirers found tickets for?'

'I... I was looking for Effie. That's her real name, not Hope. She ran away and I found her.'

'That's good,' Gardner was saying, raising her voice against Potts. 'I'm pleased you found Effie and she's safe. Take the child home, Lucia. I'll find someone to take on your shift tomorrow.'

'No, no, no!' Potts banged the table beside her. The mugs slopped tea onto the surface. 'From now on, no more swapping shifts. I set the roster, and you will keep to it, Black and Gardner. There are children's homes for abandoned minors. Drop off the child somewhere appropriate in the morning and come in for your shift at one-thirty. On the dot. You won't be driving the ambulance. You'll be on cleaning duties, Black. Time you learned to be a member of the crew, not some kind of dilettante.'

Lucia nodded, her mind not on the next day's penance – Potts could set her whatever tasks she wanted, she didn't care – but on Wanda, Wanda who'd been supposed to go dancing, Wanda who'd agreed to swap shifts because that's what she always did: bend to Lucia's wishes, Lucia's needs. 'Wanda's parents...?'

'The hospital telephoned them,' Gardner said. 'I had to leave before Mr and Mrs Silberstein arrived.'

Lucia still found she couldn't speak. She was shaking, head to toe, even though the electric heater was throwing out a good heat into the room and she could feel perspiration on her brow.

'Go home,' Potts said. 'You're no good to us here, Black.' Her voice had lost some of its hard edge.

Again, she nodded. Potts was right. It would have been better if Lucia had been crushed by the falling rafter and Wanda spared. Wanda, who was going to do something wonderful and useful with her life with all her education and her ideals. Wanda's parents would be planning the funeral of their daughter. Their clever, kind Wanda. Jewish families buried their dead quickly, she recalled. Could she attend? How would she even know where to go? Mr and Mrs Silberstein wouldn't want her there anyway, if they knew Wanda oughtn't to have been there in that warehouse, that it should have been Lucia on duty.

Outside in the yard, Effie stood up, shivering as Lucia came towards her. The child was cold. She needed to be indoors, fed and watered and put in a warm bed. She could have Wanda's room now. The realisation seemed so cold, so heartless, that for the first time, tears prickled in Lucia's eyes. She pushed them back. Not in front of the girl. 'Come on,' she told Effie. 'Let's get back to the flat.'

'Where's Wanda?' Effie asked. 'Why are you looking like that, Lucia?'

'Wanda's dead.' How flat her voice sounded, as though she

was giving a football score. Inside, a chasm was opening, filled with cold nothingness. *Wanda is dead*, she told herself, trying to make sense of it. *You will never see her again. She will never make sure you have your gas mask and torch before you leave the flat. And it is all your fault.*

Effie looked sidelong at her, and said nothing.

TWENTY-ONE

'We'll have to see Miss Goodley again,' Lucia told Effie. They'd both slept until nine, to Lucia's surprise. Grief did this, knocked you out because there was no more hope, only darkness to wake to. 'We will tell her your parents' full names. Nobody's going to put you in a camp, Effie.'

Effie looked down at the toast on her plate.

The authorities wouldn't harm Effie. Not by intent, but they would place her in a home. Could an orphaned, abandoned or otherwise unaccompanied enemy alien minor like Effie be expatriated to Germany via Switzerland. It would take a huge amount of bureaucracy, money and time. Was the grandmother even still alive?

'Miss Goodley will do all she can to track your mother down.' There was a sliver of hope. If Effie's mother had been knocked out, lost consciousness, she might come to and the two of them could be reunited. In all the darkness, a mother and child would be together again. That mattered to Lucia. It mattered in a way she hadn't explained to Wanda because there'd never been time. She'd left it too late, should have told her everything long before now. She'd tucked her past away and fooled herself that it would never need unfolding again. Wanda had been no fool, though. She'd simply been patient, waiting for Lucia to open up.

'Mami won't tell anyone who she is,' Effie said. 'She doesn't want them to take her off to a camp in one of those vans. Once you're there, you don't get out. Only if you're very ill. Or dying.'

Lucia looked at her sharply. 'They let someone out because they were ill? Was this here or in Germany?'

'Germany. My grandmother wrote and said they let my uncle out of the camp, but he died because he was sick. Perhaps that is what'll happen to Papi now too.' Effie put her hands over her eyes. Lucia hugged her, feeling the child's sobs go right through her own heart.

'It's not like that here, Effie. They don't beat people up and starve them in the internment camps.' All the same, she'd heard rumours of harsh treatment on the ships that transported male internees to Canada and Australia. 'If your father has been locked up, we can find him. There are people who will help get him released.' She'd read about MPs intervening to release Germans and Italians of good character, sometimes refugees themselves from the Nazis. If Effie's father had still been allowed to work, he must have been considered a valued employee.

'Papi wrote to us and said they didn't believe him when he said he was a good person.'

'I'm sure he is. He brought you up well. Tell me your mother's and father's full names?'

Effie released herself from the embrace and looked away from Lucia. 'Mami said not to tell people because we are German.'

'You do trust me, don't you, Effie?'

Effie nodded.

'I promise I won't give their names to anyone who will harm them. I only want to help you.' Effie observed her, her expression briefly reminding Lucia of Della's wariness when they'd met again.

She felt a longing to see Della again. The loss of Wanda made her crave her sister. The craving was an acute, physical one, running through her veins. She wanted to plead for a second chance. She couldn't lose them both. The black-shirted figure of their father seemed to throw a shadow from his cell between the sisters. She still hadn't seen their mother yet, she remembered.

Lucia stood up. 'Hand me that plate, Effie. I'll wash up and then I'll ring Miss Goodley on the way.' Effie's shoulders slumped at the mention of the social worker. 'She won't take you anywhere where people are unkind. I won't let that happen, either.' What was Lucia actually going to do to stop it, though? She had no control over child placements.

'Ketterer,' Effie said. 'That's my *familienname*.'

'Effie Ketterer? And your parents? What were they called?'

'Hanna and Ulrich.' Effie gave their names with a little gasp, as if she'd given too much away. Lucia understood this more than she could explain.

When she telephoned, Lucia's stash of coppers was almost depleted before she found a secretary in an unspecified office somewhere in the borough who could take a message for her. 'The child called Hope is really Effie Ketterer. She's safe with me.' Lucia promised to bring Effie to the rest centre later on, when Miss Goodley would be in her office. Effie watched her inscrutably as she delivered the message.

'Now Wanda's not here I can't work and look after you, Effie,' Lucia told her. 'I can't leave you in the flat while I'm at the station overnight.'

Effie nodded. 'Wanda was kind.'

'She was.' A pain shot through Lucia's heart.

'When my mother left me to go shopping and there was a raid, I...' She put a hand to her throat. 'I was so scared when the bombers came and I was alone,' she whispered. Lucia pulled her into her arms again and held her, feeling Effie's heartbeat against her chest.

'I don't like being alone during air-raids, either.' It was one reason why she hadn't minded being on the roster during air-raids. Dangerous and deadly it might be, but you were always with other people, part of a team.

'Where are we going now?'

'I want to see my sister again.'

'She was cross last time.'

'Yes.'

As they passed a church, Lucia felt a compulsion to go inside and light a candle or pray. What would she be praying for? To go back in time and not persuade Wanda to change shifts with her? Wanda herself hadn't even believed in God. Though if her consciousness lived on somewhere, maybe she'd be angry her life had been lost when it needn't have been, when she had so many things she wanted to do, so many ideas for making the world better.

Yet if Lucia hadn't swapped shift with Wanda, she wouldn't have found Effie. Effie would have remained outside in the back yard during that air-raid. She might have met the all-clear physically unscathed, albeit terrified and cold, to be found by a warden or someone else who'd have taken her back to Miss Goodley. And Wanda would still be alive.

You could never know what might have happened, or turn back the clock to try for another version of life. If she hadn't run away from Paris she and Della might have fallen out for some other reason. But she knew this wouldn't have happened. She had caused the rift because of her own selfish action all those years ago. The impulse to run away had been understandable, she could forgive herself that. Yet she could have returned to the Ritz. She could have written or telegrammed from Sainte-Claire. Every month she'd stayed away had enmeshed her further, keeping her from returning to Della and Wanda. Every Tuesday at noon she stood on Westminster Bridge and now Wanda would never know why, or that her heart was still in France. The one person in the world who understood why the ritual was important was so far away.

Perhaps her hand around Effie's had tensed as these thoughts passed through her mind, because the girl squeezed her fingers and looked up at her. Lucia smiled in what she hoped was a reassuring way at Effie. 'Nearly there.' They passed a group of children with their nanny who looked as if they were off for a walk, chatting and skipping. Most of the schools in this part of London had been evacuated, but some children still remained. Effie turned to smile at them.

'Where was your school, Effie?' Lucia asked.

'Near our old house.'

'Not too far to walk?'

'I came home for lunch. But most of the children were vactuated.'

'Vactuated? Oh, evacuated.'

'Mami said, even if the school came back to Chelsea I couldn't go, because the teachers might tell the police about us.'

The kid's mother seemed to have lived in near-terror of the British state. No surprise if she'd seen her husband arrested twice.

They reached Newton Terrace. She stopped outside number six. It was roughly the same time of day they'd appeared on the doorstep last time. Della would probably be at school. Lucia's mind was too splintered to think clearly.

The door opened to her ring of the bell.

Lucia stepped back when she saw her mother in front of her. 'Lucia?' Mama clutched the door. She was wearing a day dress made of bottle-green corduroy and thick lisle stockings. Her face was more lined than Lucia remembered, but seemed more alert, alive. 'Della said... I almost thought she must have dreamed you, it seemed so extraordinary. Come in.' She reached out and touched Lucia's shoulder lightly, as if she wanted to pull her inside but didn't dare.

She and Effie stepped inside. No maid this morning.

'We tried and tried to find you when the war started and then again after Dunkirk, when they thought the Germans would invade. How did we miss you?'

'I'm actually called Lucie Black now. I changed my name by deed poll.'

Mama's eyes widened. 'I wanted to call you Lucie when you were born,' she said. 'But your father thought Lucia had more gravitas.' She stopped. 'May I give you a hug? Just quickly?' Her voice shook a little. Women like Mama were brought up to control emotion, but Lucia could see how much this was costing her.

Without Lucia knowing how it happened, she found herself in an embrace with her mother, who smelled of the same scent she'd always used. They held one another for a long beat, until Lucia pulled herself gently free.

Her mother blinked hard and smiled at Effie. 'I don't think we've met, have we, sweetheart?'

'How do you do. I am Effie Ketterer,' Effie said politely.

Lucia's eyes were taken up with her mother. Mama had been twenty-one when Lucia was born. Her early forties were suiting her, wartime austerity or not. She wore fewer cosmetics, just a rosy-pink dab of lipstick and something on her eyes, but her skin, despite the new faint lines, was clear. She looked fit and toned, her posture was upright. The corduroy dress was simple but well-cut. 'Old things,' she said, seeing Lucia's eyes on her clothes. 'Because we turned part of the garden into a vegetable patch and digging makes everything so muddy.' She beckoned them through the hall. 'During the day, if it's cold, I keep the stove going in what used to be your father's study. It's small and cosy.'

Her father's sanctum, now used by his wife? Mama opened the door. 'Shame you missed your sister.'

Papa's desk had been pushed over into a corner and a small sofa and armchair brought downstairs from one of the bedrooms, bright cushions arranged on them. A vase of early narcissi gave off the scent of spring. A dark wooden chest sat by the window, lid open. Lucia recognised the books, wooden horse and doll from the collection Della had put out for donation to a charity. Had her sister changed her mind about giving them away?

'I'm sorting things out to take down to Claybourne,' Mama said, following her gaze. 'They'll be safe in the cellars there.' She smiled wistfully. 'Easier to keep objects safe than it is human beings, it seems.'

Did she mean Papa? Her mother's eyes were soft on Lucia. Her mother meant her. She dropped her head, feeling overcome and ashamed.

'For so long I wondered if we'd ever be together again,' Mama said. 'I was ecstatic when Della told me you'd come here. I wanted to employ a private detective to track down your address.' She shook her head at herself as she indicated that they should sit down. 'But Della was furious.' She gave Lucia a sidelong glance. 'I'm afraid she's still very angry with you.'

'I can understand why.'

Effie was looking at the doll and books.

'Would it be all right if Effie took out some of those things to play with?' Lucia asked. 'I'm looking after her temporarily,' she added.

'Of course she can.'

Effie placed her elephant on the fender in front of the fireplace and knelt beside the chest. Mama was observing the interactions between Lucia and the girl. 'You were always good with children. I always thought you'd be a wonderful mother in time.'

Lucia swallowed and looked down.

'You doted on Della when she was a baby and she always worshipped you.'

'Did you hate me too when I caused you so much worry?'

Her mother's eyes widened. 'Hate you? How could I hate you? I just feared for your safety.' She slumped onto the armchair. 'After you ran off in Paris, we searched and searched for you. Months later, we found someone who'd spotted you in the Cévennes area. But by the time I got to the town where they thought you'd been living, you'd vanished again.'

'You went to Sainte-Claire?'

'Of course I did.' For a moment her mother's eyes blazed. 'But it was too late. I found your landlady but she said you'd gone to Paris and hadn't left an address.'

Too late indeed. If her mother had found her in Sainte-Claire, would everything have turned out differently? Probably not. Regret for what she'd done burned through her like acid. She'd been so naïve, so self-absorbed.

Wanda had told her that she'd changed during her silent, self-imposed banishment, and yet again she regretted that Wanda would never know why that was. Her eyes filled with tears. Her mother stood up and went to her on the sofa, placing an arm on her shoulder.

'You don't have to be upset, darling. I know you had your reasons.'

'No.' She wasn't ready to tell her mother everything, but she could tell her about Wanda. 'It's something else too, something that's only just happened. My friend, Wanda, she... It was only yesterday.' Now the tears were running down her cheeks. 'She swapped shifts with me last night. She died. I feel... I...'

'You feel it was your fault?'

Lucia nodded.

'Life doesn't punish us in that way. Even if we sometimes think it does.'

She looked at her mother. 'You blamed yourself when I ran off?'

'Of course I did. I was your mother. You were my child. I should have looked after you.'

Lucia felt herself collapse internally and struggled to regain control. She needed to tell Mama that she understood that sentiment. But how could she have the conversation with Effie sitting in the room?

'I shouldn't have let your father behave like that to you.' Mama swallowed. 'I was weak.'

'We... you can't always control what happens,' she managed. 'Della told me about Papa, where he is.' She changed the subject with relief, although her father's imprisonment was hardly a light distraction.

'Who'd have thought Cassian would end up in a cell?' But she didn't look surprised.

'Do you visit him?'

'Yes.' Mama returned to her armchair. 'But Della insists on going in too, when she can. The school isn't happy, as you can imagine.'

'How long did they sentence him to?'

'There was no trial and no official sentencing. It's just... internment.'

'So there wasn't any actual offence committed?' Surely if there had been, Wanda would have known and told Lucia?

'It's all based on what he said before the war. His refusal to accept that Hitler was a threat.' Mama shrugged. 'He wasn't alone. Plenty of our friends who weren't even Blackshirts didn't wake up to what was happening. But unlike your father, they hadn't been photographed attending rallies and giving speeches. They hadn't written articles. They hadn't held dinners in honour of Sir Oswald and Lady Mosley.'

'I'm surprised there was nothing in the papers about his arrest.'

Mama gave a half laugh. 'Mosley and eight others were arrested in May last year at the British Union of Fascist headquarters. Your father happened to be at Claybourne Manor that day and so he was taken in the next morning. There was a brief line about it in the newspapers, but the battle at Dunkirk started the same day.'

Everyone had been preoccupied with the fate of the British troops stranded in northern France, with the Germans approaching.

'All the same, as long as your father's considered an enemy of the state, he'll remain in Wandsworth Prison.'

'With no appeal granted?'

'There's a tribunal next week and perhaps they will decide it is safe to let him out.' She sounded neutral. Perhaps she didn't want him back. But of course she would. Mama was a loyal, dutiful wife, wasn't she? 'The lawyers think he has a reasonable chance, as he held his tongue as soon as the war started.'

'Is he...? Was he...?' She was struggling for words to ask her mother about Papa's temper, whether he was still as prone to those explosions. The clock above the fireplace struck. Time had run out. 'We have to go. I'm on duty this afternoon. Put the books and dolls back, Effie.' Her voice sounded clipped. If her mother noticed her change of tone, she covered up well.

'She can keep them.'

'Thank you,' Effie said. 'But I have more toys in my real home.'

Mama smiled at her. 'What does Effie do while you work, Lucia?'

'She's been living with Wanda and me, but now...' Her voice wobbled. 'It won't be possible to continue."

'She can stay here with me if that helps. I'd enjoy her company.'

It was so tempting to say yes, leave Effie here, ask her mother to sort things out with Miss Goodley. But Effie was her responsibility. Lucia stood up, signalling to Effie that they needed to go. 'I really do appreciate that offer. I'll think about it.'

A glimmer of approval passed over her mother's face. Did she think her elder daughter was showing herself to be more reliable now? How little Mama really knew about Lucia. But her mind had gone back to her sister.

'I must see Della again.' How wistful her voice sounded.

'Give her time. Your sister's loyalties are divided. She thinks she has to protect me. But all I want is to be with both my girls again.'

'That's what I want too,' Lucia said, choking a little.

They walked past the door into the drawing room where her father had struck her that evening after the rally. Lucia put a hand to her cheek. She could almost feel the blow on the skin. Her mother was watching her.

'I find it hard to forgive him for what he did to you. I don't think it's for me to forgive, though. That's for you.'

'And the rest? His politics? The Blackshirts?'

Mama sighed. 'I think the scales long since fell from his eyes where the Blackshirts were concerned. You going, that did make him think. He was truly shocked.'

Lucia's lips tightened. She wasn't yet ready to consider her father's change as being connected to her departure. 'He really wouldn't have helped a German invasion?'

Her mother shook her head. 'After Hitler moved into Czechoslovakia and then Poland, your father saw the reality. He supported the British war effort from the start, but he could have done it more publicly. And denounced his former heroes or distanced himself from them. But it was painful for him.'

Lucia struggled to feel sympathy for her father but experienced a measure of relief that his conduct hadn't been what she'd feared. 'And the two of you will live here when he gets out?'

'He owns the house, darling. And he's still my husband. We would probably spend more time at Claybourne Manor, though.'

Out of the public gaze.

'I spent most of the summer there, and will go back this spring.'

A pang of homesickness swept Lucia. 'How is it down there?' How long had it been since she'd spent time in the ancient house, with its fields and woods? There'd been an Easter at Claybourne, just before their family trip to Paris and Munich, she remembered. Daffodils waving on the newly green lawns. Lambs in the fields.

'Not as changed as you'd imagine, which is comforting. Nanny lives in the house again and keeps an eye on the refugees and midwives plus mothers and babies.'

'Refugees?'

'Czechs and Poles, mainly. And some evacuees from the East End.'

'Where Wanda came from.' Her voice shook.

'I'm so sorry about Wanda.' Her mother kissed her, holding on to her upper arms. 'Please come back again soon. You didn't tell me what your work is?' She sighed in exasperation. 'How could I not even have asked you until the very moment you're leaving?'

'Auxiliary ambulance driver.'

Her mother's eyes widened. 'Going out in the worst of it, when everyone else is sheltering underground? I'm proud of you. But not surprised.'

'I'm glad you think it's useful work.' She paused. 'I always felt so terrible about all that work you did for my Season. And then I just ran off.'

Mama shrugged. 'Gowns and dinner table plans, that's all. All that mattered was that you were safe. That you came back. And now you have.'

But Mama's work on her behalf had been more than that. Her Season had been planned with such love and attention. Mama released Lucia and knelt down to Effie. 'And remember I can always keep an eye on this one here for you, if it's needed. We'd have fun, sweetheart. There's still a swing in the garden and these toys.' Effie smiled at her, a genuine, open smile.

When her mother opened the door to let them out, their embrace felt natural. It had been a long time since anyone had held her like that. The contact made her feel shaky. Again, she longed to tell her about Sebastien and the momentous, terrifying and wonderful thing that had happened to them, but not now, not with Effie around.

She'd forgiven Mama for standing by, for saying nothing, when her father had hit her. They would form a new, more honest relationship. More than that, she and her mother would be friends, she knew. But Della... Della would be a harder nut to crack. Yearning for her sister overcame her so strongly she wanted to crumple onto the pavement and howl. Some of that overwhelming sorrow and regret was for Wanda, as well. She'd have to go back to the flat again and live with Wanda's abandoned possessions. It would be unbearable. She'd take them over to Whitechapel to the Silbersteins and explain that it was her fault that their daughter was gone.

But first, she had to see Miss Goodley.

'You were right. I can't carry on looking after Hope – Effie Ketterer, her real name is. My flatmate isn't... She can't... Wanda...' Lucia still couldn't say the words. 'She died during an air-raid.' She placed the brown-paper parcel containing Effie's possessions on the desk.

Miss Goodley didn't look surprised.

'My sincere condolences. But you did well to find the child, Miss Black.'

The words were kind, but Lucia burned with guilt hearing them.

'To track down a child in an air-raid takes some courageous detective work.'

Compliments were unbearable. 'I found out more from Effie about her father and mother.' She told Jane Goodley what Effie had admitted to. 'There seems to have been some persecution of Effie's uncle in Germany, which is perhaps why Effie's parents brought her here. And I took this photograph of the family in their old house.' Lucia slid it across the desk.

'So now we know your proper name.' She smiled at Effie. 'The right name is important, isn't it, Effie.'

'I'm German,' Effie said.

'I know.' Miss Goodley's expression was unchanged.

'What will happen now?' Effie asked.

Miss Goodley was looking at the photograph of Effie's family. 'I will circulate this among police stations and hospitals.'

'And until then?'

' Knowing Effie's German has given me an idea, someone I have known for years. It might take a day or two, so in the meantime, I'll place her in a home.'

'Where is the home?'

'Richmond-upon-Thames. So not far from here. And now,' Miss Goodley stood up, 'the ladies in the hall will introduce Effie to the other children. As it's dry outside, games are being organised. You might wish to say goodbye quickly now.'

This was always how it was done: avoid emotion because it was too exhausting, too weakening. If you let a chink of grief, fear or anxiety show, you might collapse like a fatally wounded building. She couldn't let that happen to her today. There'd be no Wanda at home to talk sense into her. Her friend was lying cold in a coffin, never to mock her or make her laugh again. Never – finally – to be confided in.

'Come on, Fancy,' Wanda's voice said in her ear. 'Buck up. Do what's best for Effie. Be the grown-up now.'

'I will see you again, Effie,' she said, in German to the child, putting her arms around her. 'I promise.'

'Will you make sure they find my parents?'

She met Effie's eyes. 'Yes.' Gently, she released herself. Whatever it cost her, she would do this for Effie.

She didn't look back at the pair of them as she walked out of the tiny, stuffy office.

PART FOUR

TWENTY-TWO

JANUARY, 2000

'I remember you leaving me there with that brown paper parcel, Lucia,' Effie said quietly. 'I watched you walk out of the office and through the hall packed out with all those families.'

Effie might be well past middle-aged now, but she had become a girl of seven again, silently screaming at Lucia to turn around and come back, to bring her home to the flat, because that was what the flat had become in the few days she'd been there. 'I knew you couldn't keep me with Wanda having died. I also realised, as you left, that I hadn't even thanked you for looking after me.'

Lucia put out a hand and clenched Effie's. 'You were a child. You deserved everyone's help.'

'And yet, with you, it felt like more than duty.' Effie frowned. 'It was so many years ago now, but I can still remember how I felt when I was with you. Safe.'

Della cleared her throat. 'You invited us here for a quick look through that chest and a quiet celebration. But you're having to live through painful memories, Effie. I'm so sorry.'

'So am I,' Lucia said. 'It's my fault. We've been diverted by my past, and that's pulled you in too.'

'I've talked about it before.' Effie hadn't believed in secrets. 'Just not all the details. Facing the past is a good thing to do, a brave thing.' Looking at Lucia's strained face now she wished the older woman had confided more years ago too.

Della was nodding.

'Miss Goodley was right. You needed more than I could offer.' Lucia seemed to be struggling with her memories, her hand tightening on Effie's. Effie had left the sitting room, the Christmas decorations, the Blackshirt memorabilia spilled across the coffee table. She was back in 1941 too. She could smell that rest centre, the packed-in bodies, the disinfectant tang, the soup heating up on the improvised cooking stove.

'You've never told us what happened to you when Miss Goodley took you away,' Lucia said gently. 'Was it awful? I have felt too guilty to ask.'

'You had nothing to feel guilty about. And it wasn't awful. It was bearable.' She saw herself arriving in the large house in Richmond, with the three other resident children staring at her over through the banister. She couldn't remember much after that. Perhaps she'd been numb. The children had been friendly, she remembered. They'd played ping-pong in a large room over-looking the garden and shared a bar of milk chocolate one evening. None of them would stay in the house for long; all were to be fostered.

'Then they sent me on to Hertfordshire a few days later.' Miss Goodley herself had collected her and taken her on the complicated train journey. 'That was fine too.'

'Really?' Lucia asked.

'Nothing could be as bad as finding myself alone outside the house in the air-raid. You rescued me. For the second time. You'd told me you'd find my parents. I trusted you.' Effie looked Lucia square in the eyes. 'You've always been trustworthy, Lucia. You say you'll do something, and you do.'

Della nodded too. She'd hardly spoken all the time that

Lucia been relating her story. Once or twice, a spasm had passed over her face when Lucia had mentioned her. Effie knew her well enough not to ask her questions. 'Isn't it strange that you chose a career that meant using your voice, Effie? Or perhaps not.'

It was perhaps no coincidence that, after she'd had children, Effie had found herself working as a radio continuity announcer, moving into narrating novels for cassettes and audios. She'd been making up for that quiet time in her early life when she'd lived alone with her mother, experiencing her mother's growing paranoia and an increasingly claustrophobic life in a rented room. The silence in public places, the whispering even when they were at home, the fear that they would be picked up and taken away. Her mother must have known that, however harsh, Papi's imprisonment wouldn't be like Onkel Franz's. But she'd been beyond reason by then, so scared that a single word would condemn the two of them.

With a final squeeze, Lucia let go of Effie's hand and reached forward into the chest to extract a heavy object from the bottom. She took out an old camera. 'My Leica. I always wondered where this had gone.'

'There's probably still the roll of film inside it from our trip in 1937,' Della said. 'With photos of Paris on it.'

An old film probably couldn't be developed after a certain time, Effie thought. What a shame. Yet the images stored in their memories were all retrievable. And the three of them were sharing them fully for the first time.

'I left you with Miss Goodley and went back to the flat,' Lucia said. 'I was the grown-up, the ambulance driver, but I was all at sea.'

'It must have been tough returning for duty at the station,' Della said. 'After the way Potts had treated you the night Wanda died.'

'I dreaded it but felt it was all I deserved,' her sister told her.

TWENTY-THREE

Lucia had returned to an empty flat before, of course, when Wanda had been on shifts, out with friends or visiting her family in Whitechapel. But knowing Wanda would never return here, the flat seemed empty in a way it had never been before, as though the atoms in it had already settled into a heavier mass.

Every trace of Effie had gone. The cushions had been returned to the sofa. All Effie's possessions had gone into the parcel left with her at the rest centre.

Lucia changed into her work clothes and checked she had everything she needed for the shift. From now on, it would be up to her to remind herself before she left the flat – no Wanda to tease her about forgetting her torch. Although she'd probably only need her waders and overalls today, if she was on cleaning duties. No doubt Potts would find tasks even worse than sluicing out the ambulances or cleaning the staff lavatory.

Good. It was what she deserved. Any punishment handed out to her would be welcome.

'And here you are, Black,' Potts said breezily when she arrived at the station. 'Hope you've had something to eat?'

She'd barely even thought about eating.

'There's fruitcake,' Gardner said. 'I saved you a slice.'

Lucia waited for Potts to tell her that she didn't deserve cake, but Potts was silent. Gardner motioned her to sit at the mess table and brought her the cake and a mug of tea. 'I thought you'd want to know that Mr Silberstein rang the station first thing,' she said under her breath. 'He said they were holding Wanda's funeral today. They wanted to adhere to the Jewish tradition of doing it within a day. She's to be buried in the cemetery in Brady Street in Whitechapel.' Her hand squeezed Lucia's shoulder. Lucia could only nod her thanks.

'Now then, Black, eat up.' Potts frowned at her. 'Something about you looks different? Ah, your hair. Very neatly arranged today.' She nodded and walked off.

'Her ultimate compliment,' Gardner said. Her smile was warm. Lucia remembered how distant she'd found Gardner at first, but perhaps she'd just been shy, or wary of someone like Lucia, with her fancy ways. Lucia finished her refreshments and stood up to take the plate and mug to rinse out. Gardner looked across the mess to check Potts was out of earshot. 'You're still on the roster for call-outs with me.' She nodded at the blackboard. 'When you came in last night, Potts was in shock, lashing out because she was so upset about Wanda. Don't take it to heart.'

'Potts was right to be angry. It was my fault Wanda was out last night.'

'No, Wanda's luck was up last night. Could have happened when she was dancing in a nightclub or sitting on the Tube, like those people at Sloane Square.'

A bomb had crashed into the underground station as a train was pulling out and blasted it almost into the next station.

'Wanda didn't want to swap with me last night. I persuaded her.'

'Before we got the call-out, Wanda told me you'd utterly surprised her.'

'For the worse, perhaps.'

'She meant you were unselfish, Black. She admired you.' Gardner took her plate and mug to wash. 'Now buck up. You need to check the first aid box again. None of us were concentrating well when we got back last night. The tyres need checking too.'

Potts gave her another nod as she passed her on the way to inspect the ambulance. It looked clean inside, but Lucia filled a bucket with diluted disinfectant and scrubbed it out again. She counted and listed every item in the first aid box and polished every metal fixture and fitting she could see. The tyre hubs were scratched from nighttime collisions with rubble, metal and pavement edges, but she worked hard on them.

The only bombers they heard were way over to the east and they weren't called out. By the time they finished, Lucia felt part of the station crew again. New faces would appear to replace James and Wanda. If the station had a bad night, they'd be struggling to manage with their current numbers, Potts said, when they sat with tea mugs on their break. New people would be joining within days. Meantime they'd have to call on other stations to assist with call-outs.

Lucia had almost forgotten that James was dead too and felt a pang for his dry laugh. Sometimes, she'd seen him looking at Wanda as she lectured them on class war and the need for a new socialised health system and his eyes had been soft. She hadn't noticed Wanda's reciprocal interest in James, caught up in herself and latterly her mission to care for Effie, unobservant about her closest friend.

'See you tomorrow evening, Black,' Gardner called as Lucia walked across the yard. Each step of the way home felt as if she was pushing against a mighty wind. She ought to have cycled. It was Wanda's bicycle, though. She should cycle over to

Whitechapel and hand it to her family. Decent bicycles were precious these days. And visit Wanda's grave. What had Wanda's favourite flowers been? How had she lived and worked with her but not known this about her? There might be anemones. Or if she was lucky, narcissi. When early blooming flowers appeared in the markets, people grabbed them up, craving scent and colour even more desperately this year.

When she reached the door of the flat, Lucia unlocked it as quietly and quickly as she could, flinging the door open as though she thought she might trick nature and glimpse Wanda at the kitchen table with some worthy book on Socialism or economics she'd ordered, blowing cigarette smoke out in concentrated puffs.

Almost ashamed of her ability to delude herself, Lucia made a point of taking off her outer garments and hanging them neatly on the pegs by the door. If she was going to exist without Wanda, she would make her friend's best attributes her own. Organisation, tidiness, clear-mindedness – these would become Lucia's traits too.

And tomorrow she would go back to Newton Terrace and see her mother again. Her sister too, if Della was at home and would tolerate another meeting.

TWENTY-FOUR

This time, Mama took her through into the servants' quarters, opening the door to the kitchen – a part of the house Lucia had rarely entered before the war – and made her tea in a slightly chipped, still-beautiful china pot that she recognised from childhood, smiling at Lucia as she poured the tea.

'Now, darling, I see the little one isn't with you today. Tell me everything. Did you find her parents?'

Lucia explained where Effie was now. Mama lit a cigarette and put it to her mouth, leaning back, waiting, alternating between sipping tea and smoking.

'My friend... Wanda, I told you that she'd died, I...'

'You felt responsible, although it wasn't clear why.'

'She... A warehouse was hit, with casualties, Wanda was on the crew dispatched.' Lucia put down her cup before she could drop it. The words wouldn't come out, they hurt too much. 'She swapped shifts with me. I should have been driving that ambulance, going into the warehouse.' Lucia could feel her breath coming fast and shallow. The room was blurring in front of her eyes. Something was throttling her.

Her mother was holding her hand, talking quietly but urgently to her. 'It's all right. I understand. Oh, darling.'

Sobs were trying to escape. Lucia hadn't cried properly for years and years, afraid of exactly what was happening now, her body betraying her, shaking, bleeding tears that ran like rivers. She tried to apologise, but her mother shook her head, saying nothing, making no attempt to placate or rationalise, just listening, holding her hand, not yet moving closer to embrace her, but waiting.

Lucia was seventeen again, feeling the sting of her father's blow, hearing the shocked intake of breath from Della and Mama. 'Why didn't you say something?' She looked up, surprised by her own words, to see her mother's puzzled expression. 'When he hit me?' Why on earth was she asking these questions now, when this grief was all about Wanda, wasn't it? Or was it all bound up together in some complex, tangled plait with France?

Mama's sigh filled the room. 'I've been waiting for you to ask me. And I have no excuse to give at all.' Her eyes were full of remorse. 'I was weak.'

The regret about running away, the half desire, half fear at coming to this house had been about her mother as much as Della. It was only now that Lucia realised the truth. Had her mother been physically intimidated by her husband?

Perhaps her mother could read her mind. She carried on. 'Your father held me completely spellbound then. I knew he was wrong about so many things, but it was as if he kept me in his orbit and I couldn't spin out of it.'

'Did he ill-treat you?'

She shook her head. 'Never. But once he was sucked up into the Blackshirts, it was impossible to reach the true Cassian I'd fallen in love with all those years ago when he was a young officer. Even when I started to... wonder... everyone told me how glamorous he was, how he stuck up for ordinary people, how proud I ought to be.'

She grimaced. 'You start to distrust yourself. If everyone else tells you how wonderful it – he – is, perhaps you're the one who's wrong? I didn't trust my own instinct.'

'You became very quiet.'

'Yes.' Mama was looking down at her hands. 'That started as a way of, I don't know, rebelling against what he believed. I didn't agree but I couldn't oppose him. So, I refused to comment, wouldn't go with him to rallies, hinted at some unspeakable woman's issue that made it impossible.'

They'd taken it for granted that Mama wouldn't attend the Mosley rally in the East End with Sir Cassian.

'It was only when you ran away I found I could speak up again. I was so angry.'

'With me?' Well, Lucia had probably deserved it, hadn't she?

'With him. With myself. But then as weeks passed, Della took up more of my focus.' Mama drew hard on the cigarette. 'She was so broken at first, it took all I had to persuade her back to school. She ran away twice, saying she wanted to be at home, so we found her the new day school in Wimbledon. She agreed to go if she could come home each afternoon and I was there. It was as though she was worried I'd leave as well.'

'I broke her.'

'At first, Lucia.' Her mother's look was honest. She wasn't going to soft-soap the effects Lucia had had on the family. 'But your sister is a fighter. For a few months I thought she'd never be able to think about anything else except what had happened that night in Paris. She was obsessed by the foreign press, spending all her allowance on buying newspapers from France, reading every inch. She pleaded with your father to employ private detectives.'

'Private detectives? The ones who almost found me in Sainte-Claire?'

'They made quite a bit of money from us, but after we'd missed you there, one of them, a decent man, told your father they were fairly certain you were alive. You didn't want us to find you and we should respect that. Your father was desperate to carry on, so was I. But as we reached the anniversary of your running away, the three of us agreed it was time to... to let you go. If something terrible had happened to you, the embassies and consulates across Europe knew all about Sir Cassian Blake's missing daughter.' She managed a wry smile. 'Mussolini's private office even told us he had offered his police a reward for tracking down Lucia Blake in the event she had crossed the Italian border.'

Papa had always been so full of admiration for Mussolini, now an enemy to be fought and defeated, alongside Hitler.

Something was on Lucia's mind, something to do with Wanda. 'Did you speak to my friends?'

Mama knew whom she was thinking of. 'I went to Whitechapel. I found the photographer's shop where you'd sheltered the previous autumn. The brother was there but the rest of the family were visiting family on the coast. He didn't know anything.' Mama looked thoughtful. 'I didn't think of going back to Whitechapel again after the war started and asking if there was any news of you.'

Had Wanda kept Lucia's secret reappearance in London from her own mother and father? That would have cost her. Wanda was so close to them. *Had been* close, Lucia felt another jolt remembering that Wanda wasn't just on a shift, to return later on with dust on her jacket and a raging appetite for tea and toast. Wanda had never told her that Mama had come asking about her at her family shop. Perhaps her brother hadn't told her about the visit.

She needed to put thoughts of Wanda to one side. 'I

suppose Della's at school?' Her own words sounded wistful. 'Not back until late afternoon?'

Mama shook her head. 'Della *ought* to be at school. She'll probably be in detention again because she's claimed tonsillitis for the second time this month. She's actually gone to Kempton Park.'

'The racecourse?' Why on earth would Della go there? Racing there had been suspended at the start of the war.

'They're interning people at the racecourse.'

Kempton Park was just on the western fringes of the city, on the railway line from Waterloo. A faint bell was ringing in Lucia's memory. Something someone had said...

'One or two of them know your father. I told you there's a tribunal coming up shortly? Evidence is being collected.'

'And you think he'll persuade them to let him go?' Even now, a doubtful tone couldn't help but insinuate itself into her voice. Her mother looked down at the quarry-tiled floor.

'I can see why you'd feel sceptical.' Mama stubbed out her cigarette with vigour. 'All I can say, is that I know he's sincere.'

'So who's Della seeing at Kempton Park?'

'An Austrian and a Czech. Your father says they've also been interned unfairly. And they can probably corroborate his story that he isn't a national security threat.'

'What have the Austrian and Czech got to do with Papa?'

'They are a barber and a pastry chef, respectively, accused of espionage. Your father was supposed to be their spy-master.' Even now, Mama couldn't resist a smile. 'It's one of the absurdities we're trying to shine a light on. Your father was occasionally shaved by the barber and we once had dinner in the restaurant where the Czech chef worked.'

It would all have sounded like complete nonsense if Lucia hadn't read of similarly hysterical stories in the newspapers, and if she hadn't come across Effie.

'Della wants to persuade them to give statements if we can send a lawyer to the camp.'

'Will they let her in?' Internment camps were grim, weren't they? Lucia had never believed the early propaganda in the papers that they were full of cosseted foreign enemies lounging around at the state's expense. How could a girl Della's age be admitted?

'Della wrote to our local MP and he has somehow managed to obtain an entry pass for her.'

'Goodness.' Della, her passive, sweet sister – writing to MPs, visiting prisons and internment camps? No longer quite so passive and sweet, she reminded herself. Capable of icy fury. Contempt, almost.

'When will she be back?'

'Fairly soon. She has a test she doesn't want to miss. She didn't want to wear her uniform to the racecourse and remind everyone she's a minor, so she'll come back to change and collect her schoolbooks. I don't know how she keeps her schoolwork going with all the time she's had off.'

'She was always the clever one.'

'And you were the glamorous older sister she worshipped, the one with the style and presence, the one who skied and rode like an angel.'

Lucia looked away. 'I should have taken more time to study. Wanda was always telling me I was woefully ignorant. She made me read all kinds of things.'

Mama smiled. Footsteps rang out in the hallway. 'That'll be your sister now,' Mama said.

Lucia's heart thumped hard. 'Perhaps I should go.'

'No.' Mama's tone was firm. 'I will not have this schism becoming permanent. This family belongs together, whatever we've done or failed to do. I'll go out to your sister and tell her you're here.'

Mama rose and left the room, back poker straight. She closed the door, but Lucia could hear her voice, urgent, low, and Della's, more strident. The door opened abruptly and they came in. Red spots sat on of Della's cheeks. She met Lucia's eyes defiantly. 'Back again?'

'I had to see you.'

'Della—'

'It's all right, Mama, I don't want a fight.' She shook her head at Mama and slumped into a chair. 'I have to get changed and get to school in time for the German prose test.'

'You're studying German?'

Della nodded. 'It was useful this morning, though most of them speak very good English as they've been in this country for years.'

'The prisoners at the camp?'

'I suppose that's what you'd call them, prisoners, though most of them haven't done anything wrong.'

'Do you think the men you saw will be able to help Papa?'

Mama nodded at Della. 'I told your sister about your mission.'

Della looked momentarily put out, then shrugged. 'The barber and the pastry chef Papa told me to talk swore they don't have links with fascist organisations or anyone linked to German secret services. They barely know Papa and they'll make statements saying all this. Would you telephone the lawyers this afternoon and ask them to go down to the race-course to take the affidavits?' Della addressed the last sentence to Mama.

'Of course, darling. That's good news.'

The bell rang again inside Lucia's memory. Hope – no, Effie – had mentioned horses, hadn't she, when she talked about her father? 'Do the internees at Kempton sleep in the stables?' she asked.

Della looked surprised. 'You never used bother your head about prisoners' rights, I seem to remember.'

'I've learned a lot since I left you in the Ritz.'

Della's lips formed a cool smile. 'Well, you're right to be worried. I believe some of them are housed in stables. It's cold and unhygienic. Inhumane. Most of them are moved on fairly quickly, but some are then shoved into ships and taken halfway round the world.'

Quickly, Lucia explained about Effie's father. 'I wondered whether perhaps he was at Kempton?'

'Easy to inquire. Internees have to be listed. We're not Occupied Europe, where people vanish at night.'

Lucia wondered how one might go about inquiring. She didn't like to ask her sister, whose face still showed resentment. A question to put to Wanda, she started to think, before reminding herself that she could never again rely on Wanda to help with problems in her complicated life. She stood up to quell the churning in her stomach. 'I have a shift. I should be going.'

'Come back again soon,' Mama urged. 'I can offer rather a good meal now from my garden produce here.'

'I'd like that.' She kissed her mother's smooth cheek and hesitated in front of her sister.

'Excuse me,' Della said, rising and side-stepping her. 'Must dash. District Line trains down to Wimbledon are a bit sparse in the middle of the day.'

Della left the room with a brief nod at Lucia.

'I will come back,' Lucia told her mother.

'Why not move back in here too, darling? You could have your old room and I could cook for you. I'll be here until spring, as I said.'

For a moment, Lucia was tempted. But Della wasn't ready for them to be reunited like this. She needed time to come to terms with Lucia's reappearance. 'We paid rent on the flat up to the end of the month,' she said. 'And it's close to the station.'

Her mother nodded, looking sad but accepting. 'Don't leave it too long, Lucia. Sorry, *Lucie*, darling,' she said.

'I don't mind you calling me Lucia.' Reclaiming her old name felt curiously natural.

'Our number is still the same, so you can always telephone if you want to be sure I'm home.'

Did Mama mean so Lucia wouldn't encounter Della?

Outside on the pavement, she examined her watch. If she hurried, there was just enough time make a piece of toast before her shift. As she passed the Peter Jones store in Sloane Square, a man in a long dark coat moved swiftly in front of her, striding down the King's Road and cutting north into a side street. The coat, shabby, torn in places, looked familiar, and so did something about his gait. She'd seen him before, recently.

It was the tramp from the night she'd found Effie and Wanda had died. He'd moved further north, to the borders of Kensington, where perhaps people who still had money would give him coins or food. Without him, she wouldn't have found Effie. He was too far ahead to catch now to thank, to hand some coins.

That was wartime for you. People drifted in from one area to another and then on to somewhere else. Sometimes she'd be on nodding terms with women queuing for rations and see them several times a week for weeks and weeks. Then they'd be gone.

She could write to Herr Ketterer at Kempton Racecourse. If he wasn't there, the Red Cross would surely forward the letter so he'd know his daughter was being looked after by Miss Goodley's team and that his wife seemed to be missing. And once they knew where he was, Lucia could send him a package, at least. Those internment camps were probably freezing and damp, nobody wanted to *cosset* possible enemy traitors.

Lucia came to a halt, a sudden realisation hitting her. How had she missed this? There was someone else who might be able help her find Herr Ketterer via the Red Cross or other another way. The original source of Della's information. Someone she hadn't yet seen, hadn't wanted to see. Her father.

TWENTY-FIVE

Lucia checked the enamel basin was wedged securely under the back of the driver's seat in the ambulance. She hadn't yet had time to do anything about visiting her father.

The afternoon shift was a quiet one, she and Gardner agreed when they took their break in the mess. 'Perhaps they're winding down their raids on London,' Gardner ventured, placing her fingers on the wooden table top as she said it. 'Sorry,' she added when those sitting around glared at her. 'I don't mean to jinx us.'

'Never presume anything about the Luftwaffe, Gardner,' Potts said. 'We're all the happier if we are pleasantly surprised.' But she was trying to twist her mouth into a smile to soften her words. Potts had been less strident for the last day or so, even to Lucia.

'If they pull back from London, it's because they're concentrating on other cities,' Clement said. 'I know bullies like that. They always have to have someone in their sights.'

Lucia almost wished for the alert to shriek, for the station telephone to summon them to a call-out. Sitting here, Wanda's and James's ghosts seemed to haunt her. Perhaps Potts felt the ghosts too. 'We're going to practise bandaging,' she announced. 'Black, take the spares out of the cupboard and bring them here.'

For the next hour they unrolled bandages and wound them round arms and legs and torsos. Potts was as fussy as she'd ever been. 'I know a club where men would pay to be bound up by her,' Clement whispered as Lucia practised a tourniquet on his leg. 'Don't look like that, darling Black, you should open your mind.'

When the night shift started and she faded away into the gloom, Lucia walked home via the telephone box to ring the house in Newton Terrace. Her mother answered, sounding pleased to hear from her, astonished when Lucia told her why she was telephoning.

'Visit your father? In Wandsworth Prison? I wasn't expecting that. You'd have to go through the lawyers, though they may need all the visitor times themselves to prepare for the tribunal. Let me give you the telephone number.'

When the call had finished, Lucia stared at the number she'd written down. Why was she really doing this? Was there a hope he'd be able to help her track down Effie's father? She hated her father, didn't she?

She wasn't on duty next morning, so made her way back to the telephone box on the street, with as many pennies as she could find. The law firm's receptionist sounded confused at her introducing herself as both Lucia Blake and Lucie Black, in an attempt to cover all bases. 'May I call on my father's solicitor?' Lucia asked. 'It might be easier to have the conversation in person?'

It was agreed that if Miss Black – or Blake – could make her way to Lincoln's Inn Fields, an appointment could be made for her at eleven with Mr Crosby, her father's lawyer in the matter of his detention, as it was delicately put. It was a Tuesday. She was going to ask if it could be made a little earlier, but stopped herself. Tuesdays, her day for going to Westminster Bridge at noon, she'd almost forgotten. Shame flooded Lucia. She wasn't working so of course she should stand over the Thames as the clock struck and think of those she'd left behind. The last few days had been such a whirl that the life in France and the Westminster Bridge ritual had slipped from the top of her mind. Effie appearing from the rubble with that toy elephant, a child nearly suffocated by dust but brought out, needing care, it had triggered memories and emotions, making the ritual obsolete.

Lucia took Wanda's bicycle, feeling guilty at benefiting from its convenience, not that sacrificing herself to lengthy bus and tube journeys would do Wanda's family any good. Mr Crosby was a man younger than Lucia expected. A limp as he stood up to greet her made her wonder if he'd suffered a war injury. 'Should I address you as Miss Blake or Miss Black?' he asked, eyes cool.

'Either will do.' Her name barely seemed to matter.

'Well, Miss Blake, I will use the form of address most likely to gain you access to your father. He can receive visitors, but as you know, we are in the middle of preparing for his tribunal.'

'I wouldn't want to get in the way of important meetings.'

He nodded. The eyes lost some of their coolness. 'As it happens, I was due to visit him myself tomorrow. The appointment was for ten. Would that suit?'

She was on the roster at the station. 'I couldn't make ten tomorrow.' She explained about her job. She stood up. 'I shouldn't have come. I'm sorry. Thank you for your time, Mr Crosby.'

How could she possibly ask Potts to change the roster now? As she reached the door, Mr Crosby was saying something else. She looked back. 'Very short notice, this afternoon?'

This afternoon. She was on duty again at eight, so that would work. She must have looked puzzled. He gave her an approximation of a smile. 'If you don't mind acting as a messenger for the firm? I have a package for your father: newspaper articles mainly, nothing contentious, nothing sensitive.' The smile dropped. 'But, Miss Blake, I should warn you that a prison visit will not be pleasant. Conditions are squalid, and although you will see your father outside his cell, you will experience the... discomfort.'

'I've taken casualties out of bombed buildings where sewage pipes have burst and discharged their contents. Sometimes, the people are not even... entire, when we extract them.' What was she saying? She was breaking the code, unspoken if nothing else, that meant that ambulance crews did not discuss what they witnessed with those outside the service. 'Mr Crosby, excuse me. I shouldn't have said—'

He raised a hand. 'I too saw things I shan't be able to forget when my ship went down last year.' He swallowed. 'You're telling me the squalor of Wandsworth won't shock you as perhaps it might have before the war?'

A flicker of understanding passed between them.

'I'm so glad finally to have the chance to meet you, Miss Blake. For years, we thought you lost to the family.'

'I thought that too.'

'And now?'

'I'm hoping to rebuild the relationship with my mother and sister. To be honest, I don't know about my father.'

'I understand. Sir Cassian's political history has been... at times, challenging for his family. I'm sure I'm not being indiscreet to my client in saying so.' He rang the bell on his desk.

'May I ask... Did you, do you... My father's political views...?'

'Was I a supporter of Mosley Is that what you wondered?' He shook his head and smiled. 'My father was your grandfather's lawyer. His father handled the Blake family's affairs too.' He looked thoughtful. 'I only came into the firm when I was invalided out of the navy. By then, Sir Cassian was already in prison.'

'Do you think he's a threat to the nation?'

'My client will robustly argue that his imprisonment under the 1940 Treachery Act is unnecessary.' He said the words mechanically.

'Is that what you think too?'

He gave a wry smile. 'You're very like Sir Cassian, Miss Blake, if you'll allow me to say so. You won't put up with evasion. I think your father genuinely changed his mind, but I'm speaking personally here, not in my professional capacity. Some say he left it very late. But I suspect he had growing doubts in his mind before Hitler marched into Poland. The fact he stopped writing articles and attending rallies a year or so before this happened suggests as much. As a lawyer, this is the evidence I shall put forward.'

When his middle-aged secretary appeared, Mr Crosby asked her to give Lucia the parcel for Sir Cassian Blake. 'It will save us sending a clerk,' he said.

As she left the office, Lucia checked her watch. She could still cycle to Westminster Bridge in just under twenty minutes. Better to do it in a little less, if she could. The streets around the Houses of Parliament were quiet this morning. She reached the bridge, dismounting halfway along just as twelve noon was struck.

She waited the full fifteen minutes, feeling it was a waste of time. He never came, he never would. Lucia closed her eyes and willed herself across the Channel to France, or wherever Sebastien now was. When she'd last seen him, she'd barely been capable of taking in what he was telling her about his posting. And, of course, that had been before the Germans had overrun France. *Where are you?* she asked, silently. *Will I ever see you again?*

PART FIVE

TWENTY-SIX

JANUARY, 2000

The midwinter afternoon was already taking on an evening greyness. Effie, Della and Lucia sat over the collection of objects on the coffee table, feeling the world of more than fifty years ago in the fold of the military tunic, the shouting capital letters on the political flyers, the lightning-bolt insignia. So much anger in the thirties, Effie thought. Bubbling up and pushing the world into armed conflict. Bombs and death. Her own mother and father, forced out of Germany because Mami's brother had been a lawyer who'd written articles the Nazis hadn't liked.

She'd brought the memory of all this anger into this sitting room, with its earthy-yellow walls and bright rugs. The Blake sisters were so still that they might have been frozen in place. When she looked at them, for all the lines on their faces, Effie could see the girls they'd been during the war. For Lucia had still been just a girl too, only twenty-one when she'd rescued Effie from the ruined house.

Lucia had talked about her decision to visit her father in prison, but Effie wasn't certain yet as to whether that was just to ask for help in finding Ulrich Ketterer, or whether Lucia had actually been yearning for her own father.

'I'm sorry,' Effie said. 'I've encouraged you to talk but perhaps Wandsworth Prison isn't what you want to recall about on Millennium Day.'

Della was frowning slightly. 'Never mind Wandsworth Prison, I don't understand about Westminster Bridge,' she said. 'You've mentioned in passing that you used to go and stand on there in some kind of act of memory. For a man called Sebastien? But it seems more complicated, something bound up with Effie too? And you never got round to telling Wanda about it?'

'I...' Lucia put a hand to her throat. 'Sorry.'

'Let her tell the story as it comes out,' Effie said softly, hoping Della wouldn't be offended by the interjection. She too sensed that she and Lucia had a connection that hadn't yet been explained. Perhaps she'd known it for years and years.

Lucia gave her a grateful look, before turning to Della. 'You've every right to ask me questions. But yes, let me finish telling you about seeing Papa in prison.' She gave a rueful laugh. 'If I rewind to 1937 now, I might distract myself and we'll be here until 2001.'

'All right.' Della looked at Lucia more softly, more like a sister and less like someone interviewing a subject for an article. 'Go on to when you finally went to see Papa in Wandsworth Prison,' Della spoke. 'That meant a lot to him, Loo. He told me as much.'

Effie could see it cost Della to admit this. Lucia swallowed and nodded. 'To an extent, though, I was using Papa to find Effie's father. And I only went the once. You'd been to Wandsworth several times.' The sisters' eyes met.

'Grim, wasn't it?' Della shivered, as though the prison's damp, oozing walls had reclaimed her.

Lucia closed her eyes momentarily. 'The stench of the place. I told the lawyer I'd manage, that it wouldn't upset me, that I was used to... filth. Pulling people out of bombsites with effluent flowing around us. Wandsworth smelled the same way. I saw rodent droppings in the corridors. He was thinner, smaller.'

'You would have seen a big difference,' Della said. 'A bit of shock, I imagine.'

'Yes. But he was dressed in clean clothes. Clean shaven. Fingernails immaculate.'

God knows how he'd managed this, Effie thought. Surely life in a wartime London prison must have been grim for someone like Sir Cassian, if not the brutal experience Onkel Franz had had in Dachau. From the sounds of it, Cassian hadn't been given special treatment. 'Didn't the other prisoners and guards resent him?' she asked.

'He told me the guards treated him well in the main,' Della said. 'In the beginning, they'd placed men in cells in random pairings. A German Jew might be placed with a hard-line Fascist. Communists and Blackshirts were cellmates. He'd had a Jewish refugee from Silesia in with him for the first few weeks.' Della sighed. 'They'd got along quite well. Papa genuinely seemed to like the man. They played chess.'

'It seems a big reversal of his previous views about Jewish people,' Lucia said, fingering the gold pins with the lightning bolts on them.

'What did Papa really know about them? I doubt he'd ever met people like your friend Wanda. He just listened to the men in his club and around his dinner table who passed on their old prejudices. He'd have disagreed with Wanda on many political matters, but he mightn't have seen her as a threat if he'd got to know her.'

Lucia shot a grateful look at her sister. It was rare for Della to speak warmly like this about Wanda, the old vestiges of jealousy still hanging on through the decades.

'I didn't know what to think. Sometimes I still don't. I remember how he was back in the pre-war years, the rallies, the sneering at Jewish people, anyone whose political views he disagreed with, the preening confidence.' Lucia put a hand to her throat. 'The aggression.'

'That aggression towards you was unforgiveable,' Della said. 'Every time I was inclined to feel angry towards you for running away, I'd remember the way he hauled you along the boulevard back to the Ritz. Or before, when he hit you in the drawing room in Newton Terrace.'

'It wasn't that uncommon then, physical punishment of women and children,' Lucia said. 'And it wasn't just men in poor slums, lashing out in frustration or because they'd taken to drink. But it did shock me. Because it was Papa, who'd always been so loving towards me.' She picked up the Blackshirt armband and stared at it. 'But then I went to Wandsworth Prison and I saw this man in front of me and he was just... my father. And I could see...' She took a breath. 'I could see he loved me.' She put the armband back on the table. 'And what really shook me up, I could see I still loved him too.'

TWENTY-SEVEN

JANUARY, 1941

'Lucia.' Her father shook his head. 'Forgive me, your mother said in her letter that it's Lucie, now. Spelled the French way, I gather. Lucie Black.'

'It doesn't matter. Mama's been calling me Lucia too.' Lucia took the hand he passed across the table and for a moment they touched. The guard muttered something and left the room, locking the door behind him. It clanked as it shut. Lucia gave a start and let go of his hand, unable not to suppress the fleeting panic at being confined. Even signing in at reception and finding herself in the prison's central rotunda, wings of cells rotating out like spokes on this floor and on levels above her, had made her shiver.

Now she was with her father her body was sending her contradictory signals: half anxiety, half relief at seeing him. He seemed calm, pleased to see her, none of the anger there'd been almost four years ago in the Ritz.

'It takes some getting used to, hearing that lock turn,' Papa said. 'But it's better than having someone in with us all the time, listening in. When your mother first visited it was more public, a group of us at tables in an open room, guards walking up and down. Impossible to talk about anything that really mattered.'

What really did matter to him now, Lucia wondered, looking at the brick walls, gleaming with moisture. A single small window – high up, barred – revealed a grey patch of sky if she cranked her neck back. The light was switched on overhead, but the bulb seemed only to emit the faintest, sickly beam.

'Della has insisted on visiting me, you know. Of course, I love seeing her, but I hate her coming to a place like this. I'm almost relieved that the lawyers need to take up most of my visiting hours now. She's been a warrior, traipsing down to Kempton Park Racecourse too, which is probably almost as bad.' He let out a breath. 'Not what a girl her age should be doing. Sorry, I'm talking too much. It's a peril of this place. I want to know about you, darling.' He used the endearment as naturally as he always had in the past. It felt strange hearing it. Did he still love her?

'What are you doing? Are you well? Do you need anything?' He sat back to take her in. Lines wrinkled around his eyes and there were hollows that hadn't been there before. He'd lost weight and he had never had weight to lose.

'I'm an auxiliary ambulance driver in Chelsea. It pays enough to cover the rent.' Her words came out as a squeaky rasp.

'The bombing's been bad down there. You're very brave.'

'Plenty of others facing worse.' Hearing his praise jarred. Yet, if she were honest, she felt a stab of pleasure.

'The lawyers told us you hadn't claimed your trust money.'

She shrugged. 'Not much to spend it on.'

'When the war started, we enquired of all the services we could think of: the Wrens, the WAAF, even the Land Girls. We knew you'd want to come back and do something useful, and we thought we might find you.' He frowned. 'We didn't think of ambulance drivers. When I say 'we', I mean Crosby and your mother. I couldn't do much from here.'

'What exactly do you do with yourself?'

'Read. All kinds of things. Mainly nineteenth-century novels, but also George Orwell, would you believe? My education wasn't as broad as it should have been. I see that now.' He looked at her directly. 'I thought I knew the answer to the economic and social problems this country had, Lucia. I thought it was simple. A strong leader, like Mosley, a centralised economy. It seemed to work in Italy and Germany.'

'It's never simple. You must have seen what was happening in Italy and Germany to anyone who wasn't the right race or who disagreed. You're an intelligent man, how could you think it wouldn't be like that here too?' She sounded stronger now, a bit of Della's fierceness in her. Perhaps her father noticed.

He put his hand across the table again. 'There's not enough time for me to say much to you, to tell you how my views have changed. Visitor time is so short. The important thing is that I apologise to you. I struck you that evening after the rally. And I would probably have done it again in the Ritz that night in Paris, as you feared. It was very wrong of me. Do you think you can forgive me?' His fingers touched hers.

Lucia stared at the grime around the oozing bricks in the wall. She hadn't expected an apology. It pulled at emotions she'd bricked up inside herself for years. A yes or no wasn't possible. Not yet. There were more urgent matters for today's reunion. 'I came here to ask you something,' she said, removing her hand.

He looked down. 'Of course.'

'It was for help.'

'Anything.'

'Your contacts among German prisoners – there's someone I'm looking for.'

He looked up. 'What kind of German prisoner?' He gave a

wry smile. 'Other than my former cellmate, you'll appreciate many of the German Jews I've come across have treated me with caution. I can't blame them.'

'I don't think he's Jewish. A man named Ulrich Ketterer. He lived in Chelsea with his wife and daughter and was arrested at some point in the last month or two. The wife seems to have vanished in an air-raid. The seven-year-old daughter has no other family.'

'Poor child, all alone.' His face softened. He'd always been good at looking sympathetic, though. Ask those veterans of the trenches who'd found Sir Cassian so good at listening. 'Ketterer. I'll ask around.'

She passed her father the piece of paper on which she'd written everything she knew about the Ketterer family, the addresses of both places they'd rented in Chelsea and Miss Goodley's details. 'Could he be at one of the racecourses, like the men Della was visiting?'

'There's a chance. But he might be released fairly quickly. You said he'd already been picked up, earlier on in the war, and they'd let him go?' Papa was scanning the paper. 'He can't be considered very dangerous, in that case.'

'I need to get in touch with him urgently, but it seems so difficult.'

'Don't despair, it's surprising how well information can spread among internees. And some of those in charge of the camps are humane, reasonable people.' He pursed his lips. 'You should talk to Ketterer's local MP in Chelsea too. I seem to remember he was decent.'

The lock rattled on the door. The guard was coming back in. 'Will I see you again?' he asked quickly. 'Forgive me, I sound so greedy when you've already given up your time to come here.'

She didn't know what to say. 'When is the tribunal?'

'Could be the end of this week. It's not like a trial, where you get a set date. Sometimes people only have a day or so's notice. Or it could be postponed for a month or more.'

She frowned. 'It doesn't sound... I don't know, quite legal.' She still wasn't sure what she felt about her father being released, but all the same, the fact that decisions to imprison people or let them go were made behind closed doors, without notice, it seemed worryingly like what was happening across the Channel in Occupied Europe.

'There's no such thing as legal when war starts. Ordinary standards of justice vanish. It's one of the huge mistakes I made: not realising that so many of the things I valued in life – order and decency – were privileges of democratic peacetime.' He looked away. 'There were bigger mistakes in my family life, as you and I well know, Lucia.'

'I hope the tribunal goes well for you.' It was as much as she could offer him. Part of her still wanted him to be punished, but a more rational part asked what good imprisonment was doing? Surely there was some way in which he could help the country?

'I'm still strong, though I've lost condition in here. I could work on the farm at Claybourne, producing food for the nation.'

Mama and Della would be happy if he was freed too. The two of them mattered more to Lucia than the country.

'Thank you for coming here, Lucia, darling.' He patted the piece of paper on the table. 'I will put word out about your Herr Ketterer.' She noticed a bruise on his hand.

'What's that?'

'Nothing.' He grimaced at her raised eyebrow. 'My cellmate hates the air-raids. They drive him to hysterics. The guard came in and tried to calm him down and I got in the way and was thumped by mistake.'

'There's no shelter?'

He laughed. 'They say the cells are very safe. Usually they are.'

With a last nod, she was out into the corridor again, curious eyes on her as she walked past a group of men being escorted somewhere. She hadn't told him she'd forgiven him. It would take some time before she'd know if that was possible.

It was only when she found herself out in the street again, the prison locked up behind her, that she felt herself breathe deeply again.

He hadn't asked her the questions she'd been dreading, about France, about what had detained her there.

It was raining again. The wind blasted against her cheeks. Papa mightn't have asked where she'd been all those years, but she couldn't stop thinking about it now.

Absentmindedly, she fastened her coat. She wasn't here in Wandsworth. She was hundreds of miles away, looking at trees and hills, not the forbidding grey mass of the prison.

PART SIX

TWENTY-EIGHT

JANUARY, 2000

'Papa didn't ask you why you'd stayed away so long because he blamed himself for you running away from the Ritz.' Della sounded sad, not at all as she ought to be, celebrating the start of the new millennium. What had Effie done, bringing down that chest, causing all the old family unhappiness to seep out?

Lucia was gazing at nothing. Her expression wasn't sad. Her lips formed a little smile. 'I was wrong not to tell you I was safe and well. I'm sorry. I wanted to. I meant to.'

'And yet you didn't?' Della sounded resigned and sad rather than accusatory. 'For years I thought something appalling must have happened to you in France and you were shielding us from it because of the war, and Papa's imprisonment.'

Lucia turned white. 'Something appalling? That I was a victim of some kind of... attack, or rape? Oh, Della, I'm so sorry you thought that.' Her voice shook. 'I put you through that. I... I can't excuse myself.'

'The young French archaeologist? Sebastien?' Effie asked. Lucia's face glowed at the mention of his name.

'Sebastien, yes. He became more than a friend. He was everything to me. The two of us, it was more than just a summer holiday relationship. It... When I saw Papa, I saw someone else too. I...' She put her hands over her eyes.

'You don't have to tell us anything you don't want to,' Effie said, placing a hand on Lucia's.

'No. I want to. All of it. How it happened, how it all became more and more complicated. Not appalling, not in the way you feared, Della.' Lucia lifted her head. 'It was complicated. And wonderful. Then terrible.'

Sainte-Claire, Summer 1937

It was as though Sebastien and Lucia had fallen out of time. The world had shrunk to just the two of them, alone in the hills – so harsh, but beautiful. In the summer, they were a feast for the senses, with the aromas, the breezes rippling leaves and grass, and the long views.

They were lying on one of the huge ancient rocks they'd found after a swim. The water had taken Lucia's breath away and the rock was blissfully warm. Every cell of her body relaxed. Even the saggy swimming costume she'd bought second-hand from the weekly market was no longer an embarrassment now. Sebastien had given her a look that seemed admiring as she'd stepped out from behind the rock where she'd changed for the swim.

'This is pre-lapsarian,' Sebastien said.

When she looked puzzled he added: 'We've fallen into an earlier, simpler form of life.'

'Adam and Eve,' she said, without thinking. She blushed. 'Oh, I didn't mean you and I, I wasn't assuming...'

'Lucie.' He turned to her, his face very close to hers. 'I don't mind you assuming.'

Once upon a time she'd been very good at exchanges with young men, light flirting, keeping them a little distant, then letting them close, just a bit. She could have parried, gently let him down. But she didn't want to. 'We're both assuming the same thing, then?'

'I believe so.' He moved his arm under her head, lifting it gently, watching her. She kept her eyes on his. 'I know... I know you're a single woman, here by yourself. I don't want you to think I'm taking advantage, I—'

'We should stop talking,' she said, feeling his breath, smelling of the cherries he'd brought in the market and carried here for them to share.

He put a finger on her lips, traced their shape and smiled at her. 'Tell me when you want to start talking again.'

She closed her eyes. 'I'll tell you.'

His lips weren't the first male lips she'd felt pressed against hers. There'd been a ski instructor in Switzerland, just a quick embrace and a lingering kiss, that she had ended before it had gone anywhere. And a friend's brother in London, days before the Mosley rally... She'd enjoyed kissing him but that was all. Those two instances felt nothing like this. There were kisses and kisses, she now knew. Above them, when she opened her eyes, she could see the leaves on an old chestnut tree, quivering in the light, evening breeze.

Sebastien sighed and released her. 'Do you want to talk now?'

She shook her head. 'Not yet.' What was there to say? Everything had become so simple.

When they did start to talk, *really* talk, released by the kiss into a desire to confide, words fell out of Lucia. '*Désolée,* weeks of silence, I'm just catching up. Tell me if you've had enough.'

Sebastien laughed. 'I'm delighted that the enigmatic Mademoiselle Lucie Black is opening up to me.'

'Enigmatic? Me?'

'The beautiful young *anglaise* who looks so sad at times, and yet so inquiring, so bright. All of us have been mesmerised by you. I don't know why you've allowed me to come close.'

They were walking slowly back to town, arm in arm.

'I wasn't expecting this to happen.'

The walls of the town came into view. She let go of his arm. He nodded. 'Yes, best to be discreet, we don't want the whole town gossiping. But before I let you go, will you meet me tomorrow, Lucie? Same time? Same place?'

'If you have more cherries, *oui*.'

The weeks went on and on. Lucia continued to help at the site and the camp. If the other boys knew what was happening between the two of them, they were discreet, limiting comment to an occasional wink at Sebastien when they thought she wouldn't notice. The relationship hadn't progressed beyond increasingly passionate kisses, tentative stroking of legs and arms and backs.

The first of the late-summer storms changed that. Lucia and Sebastien took shelter in a cave as rivulets of water ran down the track they'd just walked up. Above them lightening flashed. Sebastien watched her. 'You're not frightened? My sister hates it.'

'My sister doesn't like it much, either.' The mention of Della sent a pang through her. She'd pushed her longing for her sister so deep inside her that when it emerged, it shocked her.

'You never talk much about your family.'

She shook her head. Thunder rumbled overhead.

'Have you heard from them at all?'

Lucia said nothing. His mouth opened as though he was going to ask another question. She pounced on him, pushing herself against his body, running her hands up and down his back, around his chest, anywhere, everywhere, to stop him asking questions and making her think about her family.

They slid slowly onto the floor of the cave, indifferent to the roughness of the surface, littered with shards of bark and small stones. 'Don't talk,' she said. 'Please.'

He hadn't touched her everywhere before; he'd been respectful, if passionate. A hand went under her blouse, to the silk brassière she'd worn the night of her escape from the Ritz. 'Lucie?' he asked.

She nodded.

'You're sure.' Her answer was to unbutton her blouse.

When they were naked the air felt cool against their skin. Splashes of rain blew in but they didn't notice, didn't stop. She knew enough to know she was smashing the old etiquette of chastity, for girls, until marriage, but in this cave it didn't matter. Who would ever know apart from the two of them? And if anyone here did find out, why would it matter? This wasn't Belgravia, with its clicking society tongues.

TWENTY-NINE

JANUARY, 2000

'It seemed impossible that the summer would ever end.'

Lucia spoke as though she was still hundreds of miles away, in a remote Cévennes region.

'I can see it was distracting,' Della said, in a tone that indicated she was trying to understand the long silence from her sister. 'A new relationship starting. Probably the first true love affair of your life. I understand how consuming it must have been.'

'But it was just because of Sebastien that you kept away? You thought Mama and Papa would force you apart?' Della asked.

'No.'

'Something else happened, didn't it?' Effie put the question so softly she wasn't even sure that Lucia had heard. She didn't answer at first, but then she nodded and the words started falling out of her.

France, August 1937

When it was time for the boys to return to Paris, there wasn't room for everyone to fit into the truck with all the crates. Lucia drove the truck, with Guy and Pierre, the others going on by train. She and Sebastien were still clinging to the pretence of nothing more than friendship existing between them.

The journey took them three days. Nights were spent in youth hostels. The other boys were meticulous about giving Lucia privacy. She'd feared they might tease her with questions about Sebastien, or, worse, treat her with contemptuous silence as a girl who'd surrendered herself. Yet either he'd kept the details of the relationship quiet, or they were naturally gentlemanly.

The drive seemed to go on for eternity, but Lucia's attention was given over to identifying rocks and bushes that would provide her with privacy.

'You need to drink less water,' Guy said, when, with a muttered excuse, she pulled off the road yet again and made a dash for a clump of trees.

'I'm not drinking that much. But I do have a slight headache.'

'You would like to stop? We could spend another night on the road, let you recover if you've picked up something?'

'I don't feel ill, just...' She didn't know how to explain. It was as though she was watching the world from a distance. This truck, the three boys with their talk of the semester to come, the summer camp they'd just finished, their plans for the autumn – it felt unreal. She shrugged. 'Perhaps it's change of altitude or something.'

In the rearview mirror she caught a glimpse of her face, tanned from the weeks in the hills and fuller from the food, although she couldn't recall ever eating more than usual, and she'd walked and walked. Perhaps she was settling into a more adult version of herself.

Sebastien had already rented an apartment for her and when the truck was returned to the university tutor who'd lent it to the group, she shook hands with the boys and took the metro to the quiet side street in the 17th arrondisement, on the right bank of the Seine, but a good two miles out from the Ritz. The concierge handed her the key and she found herself in a small set of rooms high up, with views across the city to the Eiffel Tower in the distance. She pictured herself during the autumn, sitting out in crisp weather while she studied. She had plans to improve herself, to acquire some kind of qualification.

He came to see her within an hour of her return, clutching a bunch of flowers and a baguette, folding her in his arms. 'I hope the others were good to you on the drive?'

'Perfect gentlemen.' She laughed. 'Even though I must have exasperated them, needing so many stops.'

'Stops?'

'I drink too much water, that's all. Makes travel complicated.'

'Ah.' He was looking at her, seeming puzzled.

She found herself puzzled by herself too, as days went on. Already she'd found work teaching English, the Spanish families in the Cévennes having provided testimonials to her ability. The fees almost covered the cost of the apartment and food, and Sebastien's generous parental allowance made up the difference. Lucia began to toy with the idea of a telegram home. Time to let her family know she was well, very well, in fact. Her hair was thick and glossy. She slept well.

'I should tell my parents where I am.'

Sebastien nodded. 'They're not going to drag you back to England though?' He frowned.

'I won't let them. Studying for some kind of qualification here sounds like a respectable undertaking, anyway.'

'I'll keep to the background if they ever come out to see you.'

She bought writing pad and envelopes. A telegram would be too curt. A letter would allow her to say more. Sitting at her little desk one evening, the pad open in front of her, she took off the lid of her pen. The autumn night was unusually mild and the room probably was a little stuffy. She yawned and stretched, thinking of how to start.

A button pinged off her blouse. She made a note to have a word with the laundry, who must have shrunk it. But then her skirt waistband was tighter too, she recalled. Had she been over-eating? She cast her mind over the last week's meals and exercise. Her budget didn't run to rich food and she mainly ate cheap pieces of meat and fish, with salads and fruit and a slice or two of bread. She walked everywhere.

Something else struck her too. Leaning back in the chair she counted back in weeks. Travel had always upset her monthly cycle. The drive back from the Cévennes might account for one missed period. Back in spring, Mama had promised a conversation about honeymoons and planning a family, *making sure the babies don't appear too frequently, darling*, to be held in between dress-fittings in the weeks before the Season and she'd groaned at the prospect. Obviously that conversation had never happened. Sebastien had always been careful, though.

Not careful enough.

She replaced the lid on her fountain pen and stared at the blank page. How on earth could she write to her family now?

'What are we going to do?' She dropped her head into her hands. 'I mean, what am I going to do?'

She felt sick to her stomach and she didn't think it was pregnancy hormones, just sheer terror. 'Can we find a doctor or something to... you know?'

He was shaking her head. 'It's too risky. They're butchers. Is it really what you want? To end the pregnancy?'

'No.' From her very core the message came back strongly. 'I want to keep the baby, but how...' She looked around the apartment. 'I can barely manage as it is.'

'We can manage. I can tutor in the evenings. There are enough pupils struggling with baccalaureate. There's always a demand for tutors.'

'But your own work? You are doing so well on your thesis. You said it might make a chapter in a book at some stage soon, or you'd turn it into an article for a journal. If you're worn out by tutoring and... me, a baby... how can you continue?'

'I will continue. Don't you worry.' He grimaced. Her heart fell. He must be hating the situation, hating her?

'We should be married,' he said. 'But we are too young to do it without parents giving permission. And then...' His sigh was a long one.

And then, the madness would start. His parents were strict Catholics, living in a conclave of wealthy but discreet professionals. A pregnant Protestant, a runaway English girl as a daughter-in-law?

'I don't think I could face telling my parents,' she said. 'Not when I already feel so overwhelmed.'

He was thinking, a small frown appearing on his forehead. 'If we can just hold on until we're both of age, parental permission becomes irrelevant. We just do as we please. You're twenty-one in July... 1940. I'm twenty-one in February 1939. Less than three years. The time will pass.' He took her hand. 'We're young, we can manage. I'll work so hard, study so hard.'

What was the alternative? A return to England? Lucia had heard whispers of what happened to girls like her. If it was too late for an appointment at some whispered-about doctor's, confinements happened far from home in maternity clinics in

Belgium or Switzerland. The babies were discretely adopted, possibly overseas.

Papa wouldn't let her marry a would-be Catholic academic and raise his child. She would never see Sebastien or their child again. She'd be forced to marry anyone who'd have her. No, this was no solution. Yet she'd had no experience of looking after babies – wives in her circle who'd given birth handed them over to the nanny and the work of looking after them was largely carried out in a distant nursery. She'd have to buy books to teach herself the basics of infant care.

Sebastien purchased an old wedding ring in the market. Madame Black's husband was a travelling salesman. The concierge must have suspected they weren't married but didn't seem to object to the arrangement. Lucia was a quiet tenant, who kept her apartment clean and tidy. The rooms below her were occupied by a deaf elderly man, who wouldn't be disturbed when the infant was born.

Every night, Sebastien appeared with food for her to reheat in the small stove. 'Your family cook must think you're permanently ravenous,' she said. 'I certainly am.'

She was still carrying on English conversation classes, though the embarrassed expression in some of her pupils' faces told her it wouldn't be viable for much longer. The winter and spring were cold in the apartment, so she spent free afternoons in the libraries and galleries, keeping away from the Ritz, the Rue St Honoré and the Place Vendôme. Not that the smarter parts of Paris were for Lucia Blake these days. Her clothes were few and becoming shabbier by the week. Yet there was enough to see and do that was free and perhaps it was the pregnancy, but she felt calm and content. Sebastien looked at the pile of napkins on her bed. 'You're practising?'

'I fold them round the end of the bolster and pin them in place.' She grimaced. 'Probably doing it all wrong, but how am I going to learn otherwise?'

'You seem to be studying hard for motherhood?' He picked up the book on the top. '*La Mère et l'Enfant*. Shouldn't we pay for someone to come in and help?'

'We can't afford it. Anyway, I can manage.' Her words must have sounded confident as Sebastien looked relieved.

Adèle was born in the middle of May, 1938. Lucia had suggested asking the local doctor for a midwife recommendation, but Sebastien had sold a silver clock, given to him at his christening, and paid for the confinement to take place in a maternity hospital. She'd wept when he'd told her. 'You shouldn't have done that.'

'Why not? You've given up enough for me. And given me more than I could have dreamed of.'

Her labour went smoothly, unusually so for a first-time mother, they told her. It hurt – a lot, more than she could have imagined. She screamed and when the pain passed she felt ashamed of making an exhibition of herself. Then another contraction gripped her and she didn't care who heard how much noise she made.

The midwife brought in a mask and canister and whatever was in it took the edge off. When Adèle was wrapped in a blanket and put in her arms, the memory of the pain subsided quickly. Everything, the weeks in the warm hills, the thunderstorm while they'd sheltered in the cave, the return to Paris and the emotional upheaval of knowing she was pregnant, all of it had led to this one, perfect, new person, looking solemnly up at her through her navy-blue eyes.

Sebastien, when allowed in, was instantly and equally

smitten with his daughter. 'Nothing matters apart from the three of us,' he said. 'No matter what I have to do, I will look after you both. We are a family now.'

She reached across the white sheet and grasped his hand.

THIRTY

FRANCE, 1938–39

On fine Saturday afternoons or Sundays that first summer of Adèle's life, the three of them would take the train out of the city and go somewhere Sebastien wouldn't be recognised for a picnic and walk. They'd bought a good-quality second-hand perambulator for Adèle and walked for miles around the Bois de Boulogne, where Lucia could almost imagine herself in the countryside. Adèle was doing well. Every week there was a change in her. Even feeding her, which Lucia had felt such nervousness about, hadn't been as difficult as she'd feared, after the first month. Sebastien had paid for an elderly woman to come in every morning to tidy the apartment and buy any shopping Lucia needed. She'd offered cheerful, non-judgmental advice on feeding and caring for a baby. For the first few months, Sebastien appeared every evening, sometimes telling his parents he was staying with a friend, so that he could hold Adèle for long enough to allow Lucia to eat a meal. Adèle seemed to need more attention just at the time when Lucia needed to sit down and feed herself. The books told her this wasn't uncommon for babies.

At least the fretfulness was confined to evenings. If Adèle

had been a less easy baby during the day, she would have struggled in those rooms, by herself, Lucia knew. But the summer and early months seemed to pass in a haze of bearable fatigue broken up with walks in parks, playing with Adèle. Sebastien visiting them in the evenings, or at lunchtime, when he could make excuses to his parents, who still expected him at home for the midday meal.

The winter was harder. The apartment needed to be kept warm for the baby. Lucia hated to ask Sebastien for money for more fuel. The concierge agreed to watch Adèle for a few hours each afternoon so that Lucia could resume conversational classes. Even then, the francs seemed to run out before all the essentials could be bought. Sebastien carried out more private tutoring. He looked pale over the winter. His parents thought he was studying too hard and threatened him with a ski trip to Austria after Christmas, which he managed to avoid.

'It will be easier in spring,' Lucia said. 'We just have to keep going for a little longer. And Adèle is well.'

The child had only ever had a few colds and a single mild ear infection, requiring a visit to the doctor's. Her evening fretfulness had eased and Lucia could normally put her down to sleep and eat a meal undisturbed, sometimes even read a book.

'You're so thin, Lucie,' Sebastien said, looking at her. 'You're not feeding Adèle any more and you should have regained your weight.'

'Fashionably slim. My mother would be most impressed.' She bit her tongue. She didn't often speak about her family because Sebastien worried that she should be in touch with them.

Lucia increased her conversational hours and the money situation eased a little as spring approached. In the background, the talk of war was growing louder again. In March, Hitler invaded the part of Czechoslovakia he'd promised to leave alone and Mussolini occupied Albania. Words of Papa's echoed in her head, claiming the dictators only wanted to reunite their own native peoples. Albanians weren't Italians and the Slav Czechs weren't Germans, were they? How was Papa reconciling these facts? She was relieved to be far away from Newton Terrace, concentrating on her pupils and planning excursions for their little family in their free time.

'If there's a war, they'll cover the beaches with barbed wire,' Sebastien said. It was August. Paris was occupied only by tourists, it seemed. Lucia found the boulevards made her feel depressed, the shutters pulled down over closed cafés. 'And ban non-essential travel.'

'It mightn't come to that.' Lucia smiled at Adèle, who'd discovered the empty box that had contained the groceries and laundry soap Sebastien had brought to the apartment. The toddler tipped herself over the side and sat, crowing with pleasure, inside.

'She's an archaeologist in the making, look at her,' Sebastien said. 'She wants to be in a pit, having a good look.'

'I wish you could see her every day like I do. She learns new things all the time.'

'So, a week's holiday on the coast makes perfect sense, doesn't it? I can spend all my time with her and you.' He put his arms around her waist.

'Aren't you worried someone might recognise you?'

'Le Crotoy isn't a fashionable resort like Le Touquet, but the beach goes on and on. We can set ourselves up at one end and barely see a soul. This little one can play with sand and water. And you can swim and sunbathe, Lucie. You know you're longing for time away from the city too.'

Lucia released herself gently and went to stand at the open window, longing for a breeze. Even now, with evening turning the sky pink, the air was oppressive. 'You're tempting me strongly. But I'm not sure we can afford it.'

'We can afford it. Guess who has just been given the job of tutor to a boy, a summer visitor to the seaside, who needs help with his mathematics?'

'Another tutoring job?'

'Two hours each morning for a week. That's all.' He shrugged. 'It's not a fortune, but it will go towards paying for a room at a modest hotel for us.'

'That's wonderful. But he's lucky to have you.' Lucia was still gazing out at the window, at the blush of approaching dusk. 'The last summer.'

'For now. Let's not be too pessimistic. I'm sure we'll plan other holidays in the future, when we're a respectable married couple with a child. Or children. But for now, we should grab this chance.'

'Why not? As you say, Adèle would love the beach.' Since she'd had the child Lucia had been astonished at how the world had changed, how she no longer examined it with a view to how it benefited Lucia Blake, but how it would accommodate Adèle, now fifteen months old.

They were so lucky, it seemed, that Adèle was a happy, healthy child. Other than sleep and their few francs, she claimed very little from her mother. Perhaps that would change as she grew up, but Lucia was content to live in this tiny set of rooms at the top of the apartment although now Adèle was walking, they'd probably have to find somewhere that didn't have windows leading onto the roof. Lucia knew she was paranoid, but she couldn't be in the room with Adèle without worrying about those windows being open. With Sebastien also present, she could relax and let in the fresh air. He could watch the child while she made coffee or Adèle's meals.

Sebastien was looking in the direction of the windows too. 'I know we'll have to find somewhere more suitable for her. But that's a task for after our little holiday.'

'*Oui*.' She went back to him and put her arms around him.

'We can be a family together, just as we should be all the time.'

Lucia didn't want to talk about their situation, as she and Sebastien termed it, this evening. She knew only too well how vulnerable she and Adèle were with no legal marriage. If something happened and Sebastien left them, or even worse... But she wasn't going to think about that.

Adèle called out from the cardboard box. 'She wants her elephant,' Lucia said. 'If he's out of sight for a moment, she's upset.' She released herself from Sebastien and located Adèle's toy elephant under the bed.

'I'll make all the arrangements,' he said. 'It's an interesting place. Jules Verne and Toulouse-Lautrec liked to spend time at Le Crotoy. Joan of Arc was imprisoned there.'

'Joan of Arc?' She smiled, remembering her brief stay in Rouen, where Joan had met her end.

She hadn't stepped foot on a beach for three years, Lucia estimated, on their first morning at Le Crotoy. The weather continued warm and settled, but the breeze off the sea made it so much more comfortable than the city. Adèle waved her arms and tried to throw off her sunbonnet. 'No, you don't.' Lucia made sure the bow was secure. 'No sunburn for you, mademoiselle.'

It was less relaxed than she'd hoped, taking a toddler onto a beach. Lucia had imagined herself reading the book she'd brought while Adèle played with her bucket and spade, but the child was drawn to the sea again and again, moving remarkably fast on her plump little legs. Eventually Lucia gave up on reading when she was alone with Adèle. When Sebastien turned up after his tutoring job, he would play with her and give her drinks and she could read in peace. She hadn't realised how much she'd missed being able to do things without part of her mind always tuned into Adèle. 'You're a wonderful mother,' Sebastien told her. 'A natural.'

'I'm surprised I enjoy it,' she admitted. 'I miss having my day to myself, but when she's older, Adèle won't be with me all the time.' More and more, Lucia was thinking of her own mother, who'd always seemed to enjoy being with her children, even if she had relied on Nanny for much of the day. And she'd been quick to surrender them to Nanny if Cassian required her presence or attention.

Sebastien was coming across the sand now, a Panama hat on his head, his linen trousers and rolled-sleeved shirt a relaxed counter to the clothes he wore in the city, an elegant and relaxed figure. Her heart skipped a beat at the sight of him. He beamed at the pair of them. 'Progress was made this morning,' he said. 'Algebra is less of a mystery to little Paul.'

'You'll have to give me algebra lessons. I was so dim at maths.'

'You are not dim and one day you'll realise this. Anyway, Paul's *maman* is pleased with how the lessons are going. The cook gave me these to thank me for lifting the black cloud over the household, as she put it.' He pulled out a linen cloth from his pocket and unwrapped it. 'Biscuits made with local butter.'

Adèle had already spotted them. 'Look at her move,' Sebastien marvelled. 'We have a future sprinter on our hands.' He broke a biscuit in half and gave it to the child.

'No more than that,' Lucia said, looking at her watch. 'It's getting on for lunch time and we mustn't spoil her appetite.' The hotel served a simple but ample meal. If Adèle ate well, she would sleep and her parents... well, they could remind themselves that they weren't just parents of a small child. The sight of Sebastien could still make her flush and the way he was looking at her in her swimming one-piece made her think the feeling was mutual.

Sebastien sat down on the towel she'd unfolded for him. 'You have your book? Good, I'll watch this one while you read, *chérie*.'

Her detective novel took her far away from the beach. Wanda would have scoffed and told her she could take the opportunity to read something more worthwhile, but her Simenon book was improving her French, if nothing else. Lucia was distantly aware of Sebastien digging in the sand, Adèle burbling to him. A small mound of dug-up sand formed behind the hole.

'You'll be a little archaeologist too, won't you? See those shells in there? Shall we pick up one for Maman?'

A chubby fist reached up and handed Lucia a shell. She admired it.

'Now you go in and see what you can find yourself.' Out of the corner of her eye she saw him lift Adèle into the shallow hole he'd dug. He laughed. 'She thinks you can't see her.'

'I can see you, it's not deep enough for you to hide from your *maman*,' Lucia told Adèle. Adèle chatted, her father responding with encouragement. Then he was saying something else, '...couple coming down the dunes, the tall woman in the black straw hat, I think they know my parents.'

She put down her book and looked over. 'Shall we walk down to the far end of the beach in case they come closer?'

'Perhaps a good idea.' He sounded resentful. 'I've had enough of this. We can't go on hiding away as if we're criminals.'

'In the meantime, let's not spoil our holiday. It's nearly lunchtime. Let's just pack up and walk back to the hotel along the road.' She put her book into the wicker basket and stood up.

'It's a shame, she's loving her excavation work.' Sebastien smiled at Adèle.

'We can come back here when we've had lunch, if they're gone.'

What happened next was silent. She could never pull any of the images in her memory into a single reel. Sebastien rolled up the towel. Lucia picked up the basket. As she slipped on her light summer jacket, the sleeve caught the tip of the parasol, which flicked up and loosened itself from the sand. The wind caught the parasol and she ran after it, laughing.

As she sprang after it, her sandalled foot must have caught the mound of sand at the edge of Adèle's hole. She didn't see it happen, only felt the warmth of the sand trickling and sliding through her toes towards the other two. She retrieved the parasol and heard Sebastien call out. As she turned around, he was lying on his chest, pulling Adèle out of the sand hole, dusting sand off her mouth and nose. He was staring at the child, talking to her in an urgent voice, shaking her.

'I don't think she's breathing.' He thumped the back of Adèle's chest. Lucia waited for her to take a breath. 'She wasn't even buried, she sort of tumbled backwards and some of the sand fell her over her face.'

'Blow into her mouth.' Lucia was speaking calmly because this could not be anything serious. Adèle had been playing in the sand on holiday, that was all.

The couple who knew Sebastien's parents were coming towards them now, puzzled looks turning to anxiety. The middle-aged man began to run, shouting at Sebastien. He'd reached them, was taking Adèle, was doing things to her small body, pulling her arms over her head, blowing into her mouth, patting her back to see if she would cough up sand, his wife was talking urgently to Sebastien. A young man who'd approached the group, wide eyed, was sent to fetch something or someone. It was all running in front of Lucia's eyes like an old silent film. None of it made sense.

And then the woman was taking her back to their hotel

room, telling her to lie down. Her husband would give her something to calm her. She kept saying that she needed Adèle, where was her baby? At the foot of Adèle's cot her toy elephant sat waiting for her to return.

The woman said something to the hotel owner, who'd bustled in, concern on her face. The two of them made Lucia lie down, bringing her a *tisane* and a glass of brandy and telling her she had to drink them. Sebastien had thought his parents' friends would be so judgmental when in fact the woman was so very, very kind, sitting with her, holding her hand until the husband came back, grave-faced, telling Lucia that he was so very sorry, and she needed to drink the medicine he'd brought her as she needed to sleep now.

PART SEVEN

'Oh my God.' Della had lost all the colour in her face. 'A child?'

'When I saw Papa in prison...' Lucia paused, seeming weighed down with the memories. 'I could see Adèle in him. And you, Della. But, of course, you're like our father too.'

Lucia reached into the chest and pulled out a silver-framed photograph of Sir Cassian, in his black tunic, dressed for a rally or address. 'That brow, that chin. I have a photograph of her somewhere at home, I'll show you.'

Della took the photograph without a word. 'And you named your baby after me? Adèle for Adela?'

'Of course.'

Effie had almost forgotten that Della had been christened Adela. She'd always been known as Della or Dell. 'Lucia,' she began, 'I don't know what to say... I feel...'

'Adèle,' Della said slowly. 'I had a niece, Adèle.' She seemed to need to say the child's name over and over. 'How is it possible we didn't know?'

Lucia shook her head. 'There was a moment when I was going to tell you, but then, well, things happened. There was never another right time. The war went on and on. So many had lost so much.'

'But a child?' Della's eyes were welling over.

'She'd be sixty-one now.' Lucia shook her head. 'I can't imagine it, even though there hasn't been a single day since she died that I haven't thought of her, haven't missed her. And when I saw Papa and he looked like her, it was a shock.'

'And the Westminster Bridge ritual? Each Tuesday at noon?' Della asked. 'That was to do with the little family you'd lost?'

'A kind of rite Sebastien and I had to keep us in touch. The war started soon after she died. I barely noticed. They didn't let me see her again and I kept dreaming that I'd just lost her, she was still on the beach.'

France, 1939

After Adèle's death, when the Germans invaded Poland, Sebastien had urged her to go home. 'Whatever happened between you and your father, this war changes everything. You're still his daughter.'

She'd flinched at the last word. Adèle had been to her what she had been to her father: his daughter – lost, taken from him?

'Once the fighting starts in France, you'll find it impossible to cross the Channel to England.'

'Perhaps Hitler will leave France alone? Or the Maginot Line will hold if he launches an offensive?' She said the words but barely knew what they meant: Hitler, Germany, war, they were all abstract. He'd wanted to take her to his parents' home, but she'd insisted on coming back to the apartment. Not that it made much difference where she stayed. She barely slept. Couldn't eat. All she could do was rerun Adèle's last moments through her mind over and over again. When she wasn't doing this, she wept, surprised at how many tears she could actually produce, how thirsty it made her. She'd never seen people really cry. Her sort didn't believe in openly expressing grief. But nobody could see Lucia weep, alone in this apartment. Occasionally it was briefly possible to carry out a normal human function. Wash. Make herself a cup of coffee, before another wave of grief hit her. She'd find herself curled up on the floor, the water boiling over on the stove.

He took her hand. 'We should plan for the worst. I'm not sure you even have the right papers to be here. If the situation worsens, the authorities will start checking up on people. Let me book you a rail ticket to London, *chérie*.'

She shook her head.

'*Bon, d'accord*. Move to my home? My parents can look after you.'

Adèle's toys were still in their basket, her favourite plush elephant, the ball she loved to push across the floor, the books she already loved Lucia to read to her. She shook her head.

Sebastien held her hand and fell silent, which was all he could do. His gaze went to the basket of toys and he blinked hard. 'If I'm called up, I might not see you again for a long time. I will write, but letters get held up in wartime. Remember our promise?'

She nodded.

'You will stand on Westminster Bridge on Tuesdays at noon and think of Adèle.'

Adèle had been buried at midday on a Tuesday. 'Wherever I am, I will do the same thing at noon on Tuesdays,' he went on. 'We will be together in our hearts then. And if you can come back to Paris or I can come to London, we will go to the other's Tuesday place and meet there.' He pressed her fingers urgently.

One day, the two of them would meet again. For the first time in days, she looked at him and knew that she would cling on to that.

. . .

Sebastien was right about the Germans invading. He was fighting them in the north-east of France when he received a final letter from Lucia. She'd written it weeks earlier, before the invasion, but the letter had taken that long to catch up with him.

You're right, mon cher. I have to return to England now, even if I can't face my family. I want to help the war effort and I badly need something to keep me busy. Perhaps helping other people, working for a greater good, will help me? I was a selfish person, but you and Adèle changed me, Sebastien.

I will be on Westminster Bridge at noon each Tuesday, and I will think of you and of our daughter. If you come back to Paris and go to her grave on Tuesdays at twelve noon, please place flowers there from me. Perhaps one day you will make your way to London and find me on Westminster Bridge at noon too.

I'm not going to tell anyone at home about you and her. You'll be like the treasures we dug up in the mountains, hidden away until the time is right.

January, 2000

'It all happened at once, you seeing your father for the first time in years, in prison, and then recognising Adèle's face in his,' Effie said.

'I wondered if he'd seen the surprise in my face.' Lucia brushed an invisible crumb off her skirt. 'Not that it should have surprised me that a child would look like her grandfather.'

'And even that didn't make you want to tell us, or at least Mama and me, about Adèle?'

'I still wasn't ready to open up about her, not yet. Silence, secrecy, had become habits that were hard to break.'

'So then?' Effie asked softly.

'Then the prison gates closed behind me and, unlike Papa, I was free to go wherever I wished. And it felt so strange leaving him behind, even though I still wasn't sure what I thought about him. So I just went home.'

Lucia took a deep breath of sooty, smoky South London air. It wasn't grass-scented and earthy, like the fields around Claybourne Manor, or herb-infused, like the hills of the Cévennes, but the air smelled better than anything she could imagine after the atmosphere inside that prison.

Her father would help her track down Effie's father. Whatever else he was, he had always kept his word. She was on duty at eight and needed to make herself supper and change into work clothes. The bicycle seemed to struggle against the northerly wind. Cycling across the Thames, it felt as though each turn of the pedals was a struggle. Seeing him had given her a jolt of recognition. That defined brow of his, the blue eyes – in a softer version she had seen them on both Della and on Adèle's infant face. He didn't know he'd had a granddaughter. Nor did Mama or Della. A bastard child, one to hide away they might have thought, Adèle's very existence a disgrace to them.

She'd managed to put her daughter in a kind of box of thoughts she didn't need to open. Living with Wanda, changing her name by deed poll, driving the ambulance, it had provided such a natural break with France that she had almost been able to forget in between the weekly vigils on Westminster Bridge.

But then Effie had appeared, years older than her daughter, but alone, lost, in need of help. Had Wanda not died in that warehouse fire, Lucia knew she would finally have opened up, explained what Effie had triggered within her. Wanda would have helped her make sense of them. *I'm so sorry*, Lucia cried silently out to her lost friend. *I should have told you everything when I first came home from France. I should have trusted you.*

Wanda was gone. Adèle was gone. Sebastien was gone. Della was wary of her. Lucia had reached the north side of the Thames and the flat was only a block away. She forced her mind back to the shift this evening. When everything else had gone, her work was all that was left. Mama had thought Lucia might have gone into the Wrens, the women's naval service. Perhaps she should consider the Wrens now. A complete change might be good for her, with more varied work and a chance to train in something new, possibly motorcycle courier work. Her driving experience would be a mark in her favour.

Yet she felt a sense of loyalty to Wanda to continue with the ambulances, to show that she really wasn't fancy or flighty at all, that she could stick with the work – dirty, emotionally draining and often either tedious or terrifying as it was. Potts might be pedantic and fussy. What Lucia saw on call-outs might haunt her dreams, but she wasn't going to stop now.

The Luftwaffe had decided to leave Chelsea alone tonight. The night's shift was broken only by a call-out to take an elderly man to the hospital for non-air-raid reasons. Lucia found the shift from working under ack-ack guns and the drone of bombers to ordinary blackout conditions disconcerting. Without the accompaniment of Dorners and Heinkels, it was harder to distract herself. Gardner was watching her, keeping an eye on her, perhaps worried about a delayed reaction to the death of Wanda. 'I am all right, you know,' she told her, when they were driving back to the station. 'I'm not going to dissolve into hysterics or anything.'

'I know, Black.' Gardner gave her a quick, warm smile. 'You're a champion.'

Was she a champion? Lucia felt it was more that she meandered, stunned, through the landscape of her own life. Other people's actions pushed her into her own. Papa's aggression had caused her to run away. Sebastien had captured her heart, Adèle had claimed it totally and kept her in France. When she'd lurched back home, too numb to think clearly, barely able to breathe, Wanda had guided her into this work. At some point, she was going to have to choose her own direction in life.

The following night brought a call-out for Lucia and Gardner, but the casualty was removed with a broken leg without difficulty from a house off the King's Road. 'It's worse south of the river,' Gardner said as they unloaded the stretcher at the hospital. 'Battersea and Wandsworth, they're being blasted tonight.' Lucia thought of her father in his cell.

The day after was completely clear for Lucia, no shifts at all. She decided to pack up what she could of Wanda's possessions and return the bicycle to Whitechapel. She could fasten Wanda's small suitcase to the bicycle rack and cycle the five or six miles east, returning to Chelsea on the Tube. If the shop was closed, or the Silbersteins away, one of the neighbours would probably take the bicycle and suitcase in for her. A cowardly thought struck her that it would be easier if she didn't have to speak to Wanda's parents and she felt ashamed and then resolute. She needed to admit her part in what had happened. She'd stopped running away from life. If the Silbersteins were hostile to her, it was no more than she deserved.

Lucia dismounted in the narrow street. Mrs Silberstein opened the shop door. She kissed Lucia, and then dabbed at a smudge on the window glass with the hem of her sleeve, looking guilty. 'We are only just out of shiva, the immediate mourning period. I probably shouldn't be doing this. Sidney's upstairs.' Her eyes were shadowed.

Lucia tried to recall what Wanda had told her about Jewish traditions after a death.

'He has lost all his energy. He was a boxer, you know, in his youth. The boxing halls were his kingdom.'

Her own father had been a keen boxer too, Lucia remembered. Strange how the two men, from such different backgrounds, mirrored one another in their aptitude for the sport.

'I wanted to pay my respects. And I thought I should bring Wanda's clothes. And this.' She pointed at the bicycle. 'You may be needing it.'

Mrs Silberstein forced a smile. 'Me on two wheels? You want to terrify the neighbourhood? You should keep the bicycle. Wanda would want you to have it. I'm so pleased to see you.' She opened the shop door and beckoned Lucia inside. It looked almost as it had that afternoon in 1936, unless you looked closely at the glass cabinets and saw how the displays had been spaced out.

'Let me bring you something to eat and drink.' Mrs Silberstein turned the open sign to closed. They walked through the studio. The backdrop with the Newfoundland dog on the lawn was on the top of the stack. Mrs Silberstein noticed Lucia looking at it. 'That one's been very popular during the war. Wanda always says – said – people associate dogs with loyalty and devotion.' She looked away. They went into the small parlour behind the counter.

'I must tell you something first,' Lucia blurted out as Mrs Silberstein brought in a tea tray. She couldn't let her show her such kindness under false pretences. 'You see, it was all my fault.'

'Your fault? What was?'

'That Wanda was on duty that night.' She wanted to run away, to dodge the confession. 'I made her swap.' She could hardly get the last words out.

Mrs Silberstein looked at her inquiringly. 'Made her?'

'Wanda wanted to go out dancing but there was something... I... something I needed to do, and I was the one on duty. She did me a favour. Wanda was always doing me favours.'

Mrs Silberstein looked down at the tea she was pouring. 'Did you do favours for Wanda, Lucia?'

'Not as many as Wanda did for me. I pushed her for just one more kindness. And it...' And it had killed her.

Mrs Silberstein was drinking her tea. 'Do you know how many family members Sidney and I have in eastern Europe, Lucia?'

It seemed an abrupt switch of subject. Lucia tried to remember what her friend had told her. 'Wanda mentioned five or six cousins in Russia and Poland.'

Mrs Silberstein's lips twitched slightly. 'That's right. And uncles and aunts. A lot of people. We haven't heard a word from any of them in Poland since Hitler and Stalin carved up the country. All this last year I've been telling myself how lucky I was that my daughter was here in London. I begged her to take on a less dangerous job. She might have found work in a ministry where they have deep underground shelters. Wanda was a clever girl. Women are going into all kinds of important jobs now.'

Lucia nodded.

'But she wanted the ambulance job because she said it would make her feel less helpless confronting the war like this. Over and over again we told her it was risky. She told us not to worry. She had researched the casualty statistics. Wanda always knew best.' She looked down into her teacup. 'But at night I blame myself. What kind of mother was I, not able to insist she kept herself safe?'

Lucia's cake seemed to catch in her throat. 'You can't keep them safe.' It came out like a sob. Mrs Silberstein looked at her, surprised. 'You can wrap them up warm, rub ointment on their chests and buy even more coal so the stove stays lit. You can put sun-bonnets on them to protect them from the sun.' Mrs Silberstein said nothing, still looking puzzled. 'But it only takes a second...' Her voice trembled. 'I'm sorry, this is inappropriate. I came to tell you I pushed Wanda into doing that shift in my place. I will always regret doing that and I will miss her terribly.'

'Wanda said you'd been looking after a child recently, a young girl?'

'Effie. She'd gone missing the night Wanda took my place. It was getting dark. I had to find her in case there was a raid.'

'Wanda thought it was strange, how keen you were to help the little girl. But she was touched by your response.' Mrs Silberstein's words echoed Gardner's. 'She would have wanted you to find that child. Anyone would. But the child you were describing just now, is that the child you were looking for? Is she still lost? You said she was destroyed?' Mrs Silberstein's eyes narrowed. 'It's not the same child, is it?'

'Effie is safe now. She isn't where she would wish to be, with her parents, but I hope we will find them again. The child I... that other child, was mine. My baby. She died. An accident...' Lucia heard her voice drop off.

'Your child died? Your little girl?'

'Yes.' Their eyes met. 'Adèle.' Adèle was finally acknowledged – her birth and her death, her name, finally spoken aloud for the first time since Lucia had come back to England. Lucia closed her eyes for an instant, overcome.

'I'm sorry,' Mrs Silberstein whispered. She was doubtless shocked, aware Lucia wore no wedding ring. When Lucia opened her eyes again, the older woman's face showed only shared grief.

'Forgive me, Mrs Silberstein. You have your own terrible loss to mourn.' She stood up. 'I should go home now.'

'You'll come and see us again?'

Lucia stared at her. 'You want me to?'

The ghost of a smile flittered over the woman's face. 'You bring something of Wanda with you. Talking about her with you is comforting. And you're mourning Adèle, just like I am Wanda. Now, off you go home, Lucia Blake, before you're cycling home in the dusk. The roads aren't safe at all. And I don't care for some of the types who take advantage of the dark to do goodness-knows-what.'

At the shop door, the two women held one another's hands for a moment. 'Remember, you have nothing to blame yourself for, Lucia.' Mrs Silberstein's shaky smile was like a blessing. 'Speak your daughter's name aloud often. Oh, and make things up with your family, if you haven't already.'

'Even my father?'

'I still loathe Sir Cassian for his politics, but as a parent, I want you to reconcile with him.'

Her cycle west towards the City passed in a blur. Lucia felt as though she'd been flayed, the tender parts inside her exposed to the world. She navigated closed roads, dismounting where the surfaces were too pocked with damage or debris, passing rows of smashed-up houses. By the time she reached St Paul's, she was in a landscape she wouldn't have recognised if it hadn't been for the cathedral itself, the survivor of the terrible air-raids in the City. The sun was dipping down and gave her a westward lead to bring her home, but instead she took an indirect route, finding herself cycling along the Strand, heading into Westminster and then Victoria, driven by an urge to be with her mother, to tell her everything, to say Adèle's name, to weep for her. Mama would know what to say, how to comfort her. She might be shocked but she would be gentle, too. She found herself in Belgravia, outside the family house. It was well and truly dusk now and the blackout had been pulled down on all the windows. She felt shut out from her home. Her *home*. That was how it felt now. The people living here were her flesh and blood, her family. She felt a need to be with them, to tell them about Adèle, to speak the child's name aloud again and again. She leant the bicycle against the railings and rang the front doorbell. Mama opened the door, looking astounded to see Lucia.

'But how did you know, darling? We barely had any notice ourselves.' She ushered her inside.

'Know what?'

'He's here. Your father's home. The tribunal concluded there was no good reason to keep him in prison.'

'What?' Lucia gripped the top of the console table where she was placing her gas mask and hat. 'He can't be?' How had it all happened so quickly?

'A wing of Wandsworth Prison was damaged in the raids last night. They had to relocate some of the prisoners and they've run out of space. The governor insisted some of us were released and that swayed the tribunal.'

Papa. He was smiling in the doorway, wearing a sports jacket and casual trousers, looking as if he'd just come downstairs from a hot bath, face glowing, already losing its prison whiteness. Within a month or so he'd regain his lost condition. Incarceration would be a thing of the past, to be referred to with jokes, a bad patch that was just history now. Or would it?

Was he expecting her to fall into his arms? 'They accepted the evidence from the internees at Kempton Racecourse?'

'Their affidavits that they had never spoken to me in the way alleged matched the sworn statements obtained from other third parties. I was not, in fact, organising a fifth column from West End barbers' and confectioners' shops.' He seemed to remember something. 'I made sure the message you gave me for Ulrich Ketterer was passed on to the racecourse and will go on to Douglas, if the poor man has been sent to the Isle of Man. The network will ensure he knows where his daughter is.'

'Herr Ketterer is Effie's father,' Lucia explained to her mother, who was ushering them both through into the drawing room.

'I still don't know how you knew your father was already home,' Mama said. 'But how wonderful that you came here to be with us.'

'I—' How could Lucia now explain the real reason she'd stopped at Newton Terrace? This was not the moment to tell them about Adèle. 'It was just a coincidence that I was passing the house,' she said.

'A piece of luck,' Papa said. 'I'm so pleased you're with us, darling.' She looked at him and saw Adèle in his features again. She couldn't talk about her child with him here, not yet. A door closed inside her.

'We all need a drink,' Mama said. 'I'll see what we still have. I haven't been bothering much while you were away, Cassian, and obviously Della's too young.'

'Too young for what?'

Della came in, dressed in her school gym tunic, looking younger than she had last time, more like the schoolgirl she still was. 'Oh,' she said. 'It's going to be like it was in the Ritz all those years ago when I wasn't allowed to have champagne but Lucia was.' The glance she shot her sister was amused but still chilly.

Mama returned, carrying a bottle of claret. 'Perhaps this should be drunk with a meal, but I can't find anything else without going down to the cellar.' Papa took the bottle from her. 'Champagne doesn't feel quite right,' Mama added.

'We'll save that for when we beat Hitler.'

Lucia looked at her father sharply.

'For God's sake,' Della said. 'Of course he wants to beat the Nazis.'

Papa didn't seem to be listening, his attention was on the bottle. 'I bought a case of this the year Lucia was born.'

'The prodigal daughter needs the best.' Della folded her arms. Papa poured four glasses.

'You were old enough to visit me in prison, Della. So quite mature enough for a glass of claret.'

Lucia took a polite sip of wine. Celebrating with her father, even in a muted way, didn't feel right. 'I should go. I'm not on duty, but I'd like to be close at hand in case they need me. We're short staffed at the moment.' As if in response, the siren started.

'Too late. Perhaps the cellar would have been a good idea, after all,' Mama said, trying to smile. 'It's not too uncomfortable. Della and I have spent quite a few nights down there. Probably not as safe as a public shelter, but more convenient.'

Lucia was considering a dash to the station, in case they needed extra hands, but already Newton Terrace was shaking. 'I think we should get downstairs immediately,' Mama said, sounding more decisive than she'd ever been in family situations. 'Things are hotting up rather quickly tonight.'

A gun opened up in Hyde Park, a good mile north. Della lost the colour in her face. 'Cellar it is,' Lucia said, trying to sound cool. She felt suddenly disconnected, almost dizzy, as if she'd already experienced this before, the four of them taking shelter. Part of her wanted to run away. Too much emotion on one day, talking about Adèle, coming here to tell Mama about her, seeing her father released, all being together in this house again. She followed the others into the entrance hall, pulling herself together, collecting her gas mask from the front table.

The first bomb fell close by before Mama had even unlocked the door down to the cellar from the hallway. Plaster dust trickled from the ceiling and the crystals in the chandelier tinkled. She pushed the door hard and turned on the light.

'Jacko,' Della said. 'He's in the kitchen.'

'I'll get him, you go on down.' Papa was already heading towards the door leading to the servants' quarters. Did the dog fear him because of how Papa had treated him those years ago, Lucia wondered?

Lucia followed her sister down the stairs. The space in the cellar was less cluttered than that in Effie's old home, but reminiscent of it, with the chairs arranged in a semi-circle and the oil lamp on the table in case of the power being cut. The air was damp and cool and she wished she'd put on her coat. They might be down here for hours. If so, she'd run upstairs to fetch it and perhaps something for her mother to wear too. Mama already looked cold. Was there a heater down here? Lucia looked around.

'Jacko must be hiding again,' Della said, looking anxious. 'He squeezes himself into the tiniest spaces behind furniture. Papa mightn't know where to look.'

Her words were lost in a thumping roar above them. The overhead light flickered and went out. 'Cassian.' Mama ran to the door and opened it up, calling up the stairs. 'Cassian!' A cloud of dust blew through. She retreated, coughing.

'Come back in,' Lucia told her. 'We can't do anything just now.' Her mind was flickering back over the dozens of call-outs she'd attended, assessing what was likely to have happened above them. Through the roar of planes overhead she heard the dog bark excitedly. Clearly her father had reached the kitchen. Was he still in there?

Della was sniffing. 'Fire.'

Lucia put an arm on her sister's shoulder. 'I'll go up and look. Stay here.' Della looked as if she was going to protest, but perhaps remembered Lucia had been trained in identifying hazards in bombed situations. Rubble was best left to the rescue crews to manage, as moving timbers or blocks might bring a wall down. Fire, gas or flooding meant you got out quickly and the

warden would know where to send you on to shelter. She
opened the door to the steps, closing it sharply behind her. 'Stay
there until I call for you. Don't let smoke get in.'

At the top of the stairs, the spaniel was trembling. 'All right,
Jacko,' she called. She put a hand out to him but he slunk away.
Lucia moved through the smoke towards the connecting door
leading to the servants' quarters and kitchen. 'Papa?' No
response. She felt a breeze from above and looked up. The roof
must have been blown open. Possibly an incendiary had then
fallen through into the exposed cavity and ignited. Time for
Mama and Della to leave the cellar. The warden would already
be summoning help. She ran back to the cellar door and called
down to them. 'Just get out of the front door now while I find
Papa.'

Returning to the door into the servants' quarters, she placed
a hand to the wood surface. Cool. No fire was going to burst
into her face. She opened the door. Her father was standing at
the kitchen entrance. 'I lost Jacko,' he said.

'He ran out when you opened the door. I've just seen him.'
The smoke was thicker now. Whatever was burning overhead
had taken hold. 'Come on, let's go.'

Della and Mama were already in the entrance hall, coughing. 'Where's Jacko?' Della asked.

'He was just there.' Lucia looked behind her. Black smoke
had filled the space. 'Come on, he'll make for the street.' She
was shouting now above the thunder of the bombers and the
increasingly loud whoosh of the fire above them. Mama opened
the door and pulled Della out, Papa and Lucia following.

'Where is he?' Della asked again, calling the dog's name.
The warden appeared, urging them to go into the public shelter
if they weren't hurt, checking names, his attention switching to
the fire engine pulling up.

'Nobody else inside,' Lucia said.

'Jacko's still there.' Della wriggled her hand out of her mother's and ran back up the stairs and through the open front door. The warden yelled at her to come back.

'She won't leave until she's got the dog,' Mama said.

Papa ran up the steps, surprisingly nimble for a man who'd been incarcerated until earlier in the day. 'Della!' He ran inside the house, vanishing into the smoke.

Della reappeared a moment later, Jacko at her side. 'Where's your father?' Mama shouted. Della put a hand to her head, looking dazed, bending to cough out smoke.

'Watch her,' Lucia called to Mama. 'Find some water for her. When the ambulance arrives, make sure they take her to the hospital for a check-up.'

She ran back into the house, shouting at the warden that she'd been trained, she was an ambulance driver, pulling a handkerchief around her mouth, ignoring the shouts. He wouldn't have returned to the kitchen. She tried the drawing-room but couldn't see him in the swirl of dark and acrid smoke. His study. She made her way along the entrance hall. The door was open. He was sitting at the desk, looking at the sofa and cushions Mama had brought in. 'It looks so different in here. I like what your mother did.'

'Papa, come on.'

'Jacko was under the desk,' he said. 'Did he get out safely?'

'Yes. Everyone's fine.'

'You need to go, Lucia.'

'Why aren't you moving? Come on.'

He smiled. 'It struck me this was the best thing I could do for you all.'

'What? You've only just been released from prison.'

'The shame will continue for my family.' He looked her squarely in the eyes. 'I know I was wrong. And I feel regret. I knew I was wrong the night you ran away. I saw how scared you were of me. And even now, you don't want to drink a glass of wine in my presence and I can't blame you, Lucia.'

Lucia put a hand over her mouth in an attempt to stop the smoke from choking her. 'But is that what you want for Della? Hasn't she had enough to deal with? Hasn't she done enough to help you? Come on.' Her words were gasped. There wasn't enough air to speak, barely enough to keep upright.

He stood up. 'I'm being selfish. I always have been.' Smoke was pouring down the hall towards the study now. He followed her out. Between them and the front door was blackness. Her lungs hurt. She couldn't see, couldn't think, couldn't move. It was too much. Lucia faltered. The world was spinning, her legs couldn't support her. She could just about make out the lighter rectangle of the open door but it was too far away.

Above them, brick, stone and timber shivered and groaned. The house was shaking, firemen shouting. Something was falling down towards her: dazzling white shards of glass clinking as they fell. The chandelier. She dashed forward but stumbled as it crashed down. She wasn't hurt and tried to get up, but something had wound itself around her leg – one of the chandelier chains. She tried to twist herself free. Her father was beside her. 'Go,' she shouted. 'The crew will sort me out.' Above them the house cracked and snapped with more intensity.

Papa shook his head, framed by the blaze all around them. Licks of fire caught his sleeves and trousers as he unwrapped her leg from the chain and freed her. 'You're going to be all right, sweetheart. Now run.'

She was a small girl again, fallen off her pony and he was scooping her up, telling her she was fine. He fell backwards, the fire and smoke claiming him.

'Quickly!' A fireman stood next to her, pulling her through the darkness as the walls trembled.

'Papa!' She and the firemen fell down the steps onto the pavement outside. Lucia turned to see the roof fall inwards, the upper storeys folding in turn.

'My father.' She could barely cry out single words because

her lungs were burning. She tugged herself free of the arms holding her and struggled towards the steps. Someone grabbed her and pulled her back. 'Papa.' She was a small girl again and she was calling out for him because he was the only person who could help when she was lost or hurt or scared.

In the hallway all she could see was rubble and chunks of plaster, smashed timbers and burning metal.

Effie

Mrs Barker let Effie play outside in the garden with her West Highland Terrier, Tansy, unless the rain was absolutely shocking, as she put it. Tansy liked chasing a tennis ball and jumping over the small stream that ran across the end of the garden. Both of them would appear at the kitchen door for refreshment to the accompaniment of Mrs Barker's gentle chiding.

The village school was a five-minute walk away. They told Effie she'd be starting in a week, once she'd had a chance to settle in and the village doctor had checked her over. In the meantime, the neighbour's son, Peter, a boy a year younger than her, ran eagerly round to play with Tansy and Effie in the garden. He didn't seem to notice her slight German accent. Mrs Barker was kind, a middle-aged naturalised German widow, whose English husband had died a few years earlier. Speaking German with her felt good.

The nights were hard. Effie felt exposed, as if she'd emerged into a world that was still dangerous, even if it was quiet out here in the country. In Lucia's bedroom, lying on her makeshift bed, squeezed into the small space just like a mouse, she hadn't felt like that. Her dreams now were filled with images of her parents boarding trains, their backs to Effie. She ran up the platform, shouting at them to turn round, to wait for her. But they always boarded the train and were whisked away.

Miss Goodley wrote to Effie, telling her Lucia had also been caught up in a bomb blast, which was why she hadn't been in touch.

A week passed. Mrs Barker found some old pieces of school uniform for Effie to wear on her first day, telling her she'd feel happier once she was back in a classroom again.

On the Sunday evening, she found a crumpet, something Effie had never eaten before, and toasted it for her, using precious butter and honey to make it more special. 'I'll save rations and bake a strudel for you next week.'

The butter on the crumpet ran down Effie's lips. 'Delicious,' she told Mrs Barker. Her face relaxed.

Someone rapped on the door. 'Who can that be?' Mrs Barker sighed as she went to answer it. 'If it's Peter, he can't come in. We need to check you have everything for school.'

A man's voice was saying something at the front door, followed by Mrs Barker's confused replies, a concession that, yes, he could come in. Effie finished the crumpet and guiltily licked butter off her fingers.

Mrs Barker and the visitor weren't speaking in English, she noted, just as the door to the kitchen opened. The man stood in front of her: thin, pale, shadows under his eyes.

The glass of milk she'd been raising to her mouth slipped slowly down through her fingers onto the table. She stood up. 'Papi?'

'Effie.'

Even then they didn't rush into one another's arms. Effie walked very carefully around the table.

He bent down to her. He smelled of old clothes and travel; not fresh, like the old Papi. 'It is you?' Effie said.

'Yes, *mäuschen.*' The sound of that nickname broke the spell. This was no dream. She fell into him, clinging to him, not sobbing, not saying much, hearing Mrs Barker in the distance, telling them to go into the sitting room, she'd light the fire and they could be alone.

Tansy ran in circles around them as they walked into the cold room, where Mrs Barker fiddled with kindling and wood, hardly noticed by the pair of them.

'Where is she? Where is Mami?' Effie sat beside him on the small sofa. 'Why didn't she come too?' Perhaps she was back in the mews house, getting it ready for their return, taking the boxes out of the cellar and unpacking them.

'*Mäuschen*, it is just me now. Just the two of us. Your mother...' He looked away. 'She died that same day your house was bombed.'

Effie stared at him, but his expression didn't change, watchful, grieving.

She still didn't cry. She didn't say anything but sat looking at the feebly burning logs in the grate. 'She died?' The words startled her as they were spoken, as though the sound was making it real: *her mother was dead.* Papi nodded. There was a little part of Effie that already knew it to be true, had picked up something from the controlled expressions on Lucia's and Miss Goodley's faces back in the rescue centre.

'Will I still go to school here tomorrow?' The immediate future pulled at her attention. What he'd told her about her mother dying was too much to think about for now.

'No. You and I are going back to London. We'll stay in a hostel while I find us somewhere to live.'

Mrs Barker, who must have been hovering somewhere, came back in. 'I am so sorry,' she said softly, in German. 'But you must stay here tonight, Herr Ketterer. I will make up a bed.'

She silently prepared an evening meal for the three of them. They ate without saying much. When she'd cleared the dishes, she looked at the green pinafore dress hanging up by the ironing board. '*Ach*, you won't be needing that tomorrow after all, Effie.'

'I am sorry that my letter didn't reach you, Frau Barker,' Papi said in German. 'You have been so kind to Effie, taken so much trouble.'

'Does this mean I can see Lucia again?' Effie asked. Lucia had not brought Mami back to her, but she had found Papi, just as she had promised.

'Of course. When she's recovered from her own loss. She was so kind to you, *mäuschen*.'

'And one other thing...'

'*Ja?*'

'I don't want to be a mouse anymore. Mice are scared and have to hide.'

He looked at her and didn't say anything for a while. Then he nodded. 'Yes, why would you want to be a mouse, a brave person like you?'

THIRTY-FOUR

MARCH, 1941

It was the first Tuesday Lucia had been back in London since the house in Newton Terrace had collapsed and her father had died inside it, pushing her clear of the falling beam.

Sir Cassian's contacts among German detainees had passed on the message. Ulrich Ketterer had been tracked to a camp in Douglas, on the Isle of Man, and had written to Miss Goodley to identify himself. His MP had already objected to Ulrich Ketterer's detention and Ulrich's employer had vouched for him. His name was suspiciously similar to that of one Udo Ketterer, a petty criminal already suspected of espionage. There was no reason for Mr Ulrich Ketterer to be kept behind bars, especially as he could play a useful role as a dental laboratory technician. People still needed dentures and bridgework, war or no war. He was sent home – except that Ulrich and his daughter no longer had a home.

Before he returned to work, Ulrich spent two weeks at Claybourne Manor, leaving only to attend Hanna Ketterer's funeral, her body finally identified thanks to the photograph Lucia had found in the basement. Hanna had died in the streets, probably attempting to run back to her daughter after the alert sounded. Her only form of identity, her ration card, had been lost – possibly stolen by the same person who had also stolen the basket of food she had just bought before the siren went off.

Mama, Della and Effie made Claybourne Manor their home. Mama had convinced Miss Goodley there was no better place for the child to stay for now, while her father resumed work in the dental laboratory. Claybourne Manor was already home to a number of refugees and evacuees and Lady Blake herself had formed a strong attachment to Effie.

The flat she'd shared with Wanda was Lucia's home once again. Her name was back on the roster board at the ambulance station. Gardner had sent a postcard to the flat, saying she was lobbying Potts to pair her with Lucia again. *You're the only person who knows how to drive that dratted ambulance so patients aren't shaken to bits. Clement says to tell you none of us appreciate his repartee like Black.*

The station crews knew she'd been injured in an air-raid and that her father had died. Lucia wasn't sure if they knew who exactly her father was. It didn't seem to matter now. Once she was back in the driving seat of the ambulance, she was just Black, who could coax a temperamental vehicle into gear and liked milk chocolate and a game of rummy on quiet shifts.

The prospect of being back at the station was both daunting and reassuring.

Returning to London alone made Lucia feel as she had at the time of Adèle's death, as if the intervening years hadn't really happened. She had looped back to being as lost and desolate as she had those last days in Paris. The thought of going back to Westminster Bridge once again to commemorate those she'd left in France had made her physically tremble. But the ritual couldn't be put off any longer.

A barge passed beneath her, pulled by the current, heading downstream towards the docks and the sea beyond. She felt herself pulled by a current too, one which was moving her back into life again, insisting that she did what was necessary, if painful, now. Part of her still wanted to resist, to say it was all too much, to return to Claybourne Manor and the days spent helping on the farm or teaching the children to ride old pony. And yet Claybourne wasn't where her destiny lay. She belonged in battered, grimy London.

The river was in constant flux yet always the same. At various points in her life, she'd thought of herself as different people, Lucia, then Lucie and now Lucia again. Debutante, runaway, lover, mother, ambulance driver, friend. All the time, she'd been the same person, and those had all just been different parts of her.

She cleared her mind and thought about Sebastien.

Where Sebastien was at this particular moment, she could only guess. He might even have found his way onto the opposing Vichy French forces – fighting on the other side of the war now alongside the Germans. Or he might be a prisoner of war in Germany. Or fighting for the Allies in North Africa. She'd imagined he might come here to London to rally to General de Gaulle. For a while she'd tried to pluck up courage to ask any French soldiers she came across if they knew of him. Something always stopped her, as if she'd somehow be working against fate. She'd lost Adèle and blamed herself. Separation from Sebastien was the price she'd pay.

As months in London rolled by, she'd realised disaster and sadness weren't a price or punishment. Nobody was keeping tally of human misdeeds and doling out chastisement to the guilty, otherwise why take James? Why Wanda? Why Effie's mother? Or Adèle? Why had her child died, an innocent who'd barely lived? Why had she been condemned to this pain, which seemed to be rising up from a place inside her she hadn't known existed? Her first sob came out as a gasp. A woman turned and looked at her, puzzled and then sympathetic. The next sobs were silent. She propped up the bike on the parapet and turned towards the river, not daring to lean over in case someone thought she was going to jump. Half of her wanted to plunge into the water, to let it all end now. Lucia shook with grief, not caring that she was shedding tears in a public place. Her eyes stung. Exhausted, she stared at the water, barely aware of where she was.

The clock had already struck twelve and she hadn't heard it. This Tuesday was a kind of farewell to Sebastien and the life they'd had in France, the promise that had been taken from them by Adèle's death and the coming of war. Lucia couldn't say goodbye to Adèle, because her daughter was always part of her, even if her remains lay hundreds of miles away, in Occupied Paris. She couldn't cut her out of her heart, even if she never spoke of her, not even to Mama or Della, who didn't need any further pain. Now that she'd wept for Adèle it felt as if her daughter was even more of a presence inside her, as if she'd expanded to fit inside Lucia.

Sebastien might be alive and well. She prayed this was so and wished him joy, imagining the wishes passing downstream and across oceans and seas to wherever he was now. The memory of warm Cévennes days and their walks up to the dig, his explanations of Roman roads, the nights around the camp-fire, these had rescued her from herself. And Adèle had completed the work.

Adèle meant everything, Lucia told the old grey river. *My daughter didn't live long but she mattered, her life counted for something.*

When she'd seen a plush toy elephant just like Adèle's in Effie's arms, it had felt like a sign. Lucia had almost wondered whether it was the same toy, though she knew she'd left it behind in Paris with the rest of Adèle's things. The toy elephants had been popular – sold across Europe, lots of children had them.

She should have explained to Wanda what was going through her head when she'd rescued an unknown child from a bombsite and brought her home, but she hadn't understood what she was doing.

The hand on the clock tower was moving forward.

Lucia wiped her eyes and remounted her bicycle.

She'd almost reached the flat when she slammed the brakes on. Crossing the street in front of her was a black, shambling figure, with long matted hair. 'Wait,' she called. 'Please wait.'

He swayed onto the pavement, removing his hat.

'I found Effie's father. Her mother died. You helped us that night.'

He gave a little bow.

'I wanted to thank you. Would you be offended if I...' She put her hand to her coat pocket.

'If you covered the expense of a bottle of brandy?' His voice was cultured. 'No, I'd thank you. Is she all right, the mouse?'

'She will be now.'

His smile, even though it showed blackened teeth that were beyond saving, gave her a glimpse of the man he'd have been before that earlier war had ground him up. She thought fleetingly of her father, how he'd been moved by the plight of returning soldiers like this man. Cassian had started by wanting to help, at least in the early years of his politics.

'It all ends,' the tramp said. 'Eventually.' With a cheerful wave, he went on his way with Lucia's ten-shilling note.

PART EIGHT

The three of them sat in silence for a moment when Lucia had finished talking. Effie's tabby pushed the door open, making them jump before he retreated behind the television.

'You'd had all those losses of your own. Your child. Your friend, your colleagues. You must have felt destroyed by it all.'

Lucia didn't deny it. 'But I wasn't the only one at that time walking around having suffered successive tragedies.'

'Even so, you came down to Claybourne Manor after Papa was killed, Lucia.' Della's voice was husky. 'You took care of Effie and you pretty well organised Papa's funeral single-handedly as well. We all leant on you, Loo, and all the time...' Della shook her head, her words choked up.

'Mama had just lost her husband. You had lost your father too. You'd both been far closer to him than I had,' Lucia said. 'I wasn't there for the two of you when he was imprisoned so it seemed obvious that I should be the one who stepped in then.' She rolled her eyes. 'I surprised myself. But perhaps it was good for me to talk to the vicar and put death notices in the newspapers. 'I remembered Mama making all those plans for my London Season, talking to caterers and florists and dressmakers.

All that effort and it never came to anything because I ran off. In a perverse way, it felt as though I was making some amends to her.'

Effie could remember what it had been like at Claybourne in the early days. She'd been grieving for her dead mother. Images from that time still ran disjointedly through her mind on occasions. She'd been so utterly lost. Crying out for her mother at night. Unable to eat. Her father had stayed down there for a few weeks and that had been a comfort. But then he'd had to return to his job in Ealing, which couldn't be held open any longer.

She'd been left with the Blake women. Martha Blake had been quietly sorrowful, not showing her emotion much publicly, but obviously distressed at the death of her husband. Della had been inconsolable. 'What was the point of Papa's release?' she wept. 'For a few hours' freedom before he died? It was cruel.'

At first Effie had found Della intimidating in her grief. That had changed one rainy afternoon when Della came across Effie crying silently in the paddock where the pony grazed, suddenly pierced with pain for her mother's loss. Della's arm had gone cautiously around Effie's shoulders. 'I know,' she said, starting to weep. They hadn't exchanged many more words. When their tears had dried up, Della had asked if Effie wanted to help bring the pony in from the paddock.

The next afternoon Della saddled the pony up, helped Effie mount him and led her up and down the drive. 'You might as well learn something useful while you're here,' Della said gruffly.

Martha Blake recovered too. The manor now housed ten people at any given time, not including those living in the estate cottages. Martha had formed them into a community, calming squabbles, and organising cooking and childcare schedules.

'I was only down at Claybourne for two weeks after Papa

died,' Lucia said. 'I felt bad about going back, but the ambulance station couldn't give me a longer leave of absence. Perhaps if I'd stayed with you all longer, the secret about Adèle would have come out.'

Perhaps, Effie thought. But she suspected Lucia had hidden the secret for everyone's sake, believing she was sparing her mother and sister when they were still fragile. Lucia had intervened in Effie's life because both had experienced tragedy, trauma. Yet it had been more than just a rescue; coming into one another's lives had been a gift.

Effie was reminded of something else. 'It's very old and tattered now and I should probably throw it away, but I wonder if you'd like to see it?'

'Eff,' Della said. 'What are you talking about?'

'This.' She rose and knelt down at the cupboard beside the fireplace, opening a drawer. 'There he is. I found him when I was sorting out a cupboard.' Some of the plush fur had rubbed off the elephant's back and trunk and one of its eyes was missing, but the toy had been well constructed in a German factory back in the 1930s and sold across the world, including Paris, where Adèle's parents had bought one for their new daughter. 'I daredn't let anyone know I still have him, it's ridiculous.'

Lucia took the elephant. 'Sebastien spotted Adèle's elephant in the toy department of the Galeries Lafayette. He barely had any money. It all went on our food and rent. But he had to have the elephant for Adèle.' She handed it back to Effie. 'I'm glad you kept yours. He feels like an old friend.'

'I can't bear to throw him out, even though he's so tatty, so he'll make the move with us.'

'But you won't want to take all this, Eff, so we do need to make some decisions.' Della was picking through the British Union of Fascist memorabilia. 'Dump it outside a museum at night perhaps?'

'No, we should say it belonged to our father.' Lucia sounded determined. 'Let them judge us by who we are, our own lives. God knows, Dell, you and I have lived long enough to show we're more than a Blackshirt's daughters. I'll take the chest back in my car and ring around museums when they open again. If nobody wants the stuff, I'll make a bonfire.'

'It doesn't seem as important anymore,' Effie said. The story had been more than just about Lucia and Della's father and his Blackshirt history. Cassian had provoked Lucia into running away, launching her eventually into the affair with Sebastien, and the birth and death of their child. Adèle's death in turn was linked to Lucia's reaction at finding Effie clutching a toy elephant. Looking after Effie had brought hope into Lucia's life again. Hope. The temporary name Lucia had given her was so appropriate.

'There was a whole other chapter to your story, Lucia,' she went on. 'I'm so glad you told us about it. And I'm glad you've spoken Adèle's name aloud.' She reached over to give Lucia a hug.

'Oh, it didn't end there,' Lucia said, smiling. They looked at her, curious. 'There was a coda.'

THIRTY-SIX

MAY, 1951

Michael and Paula had been left with their grandmother, Martha, in Lucia's Kensington house as Lucia couldn't imagine touring the Festival of Britain with two tiny children. Effie had been persuaded to abandon her schoolbooks for the afternoon. Really, Della said, they should have planned to be there earlier, instead of aiming to have lunch in one of the Festival restaurants. They mightn't have enough time to see everything in a single afternoon. Della's editor had allowed her to use the outing as research for an article about the economic renaissance of Britain after the war, its re-entry into the world as an innovative, modern country. She only had a short walk to the South Bank.

Effie was coming from Chelsea, where she now lived with her father again. Lucia had allowed too much time for the cross-London journey, she realised, giddy at having her mother on hand to look after Michael and Paula. She was going to arrive at the Festival entrance gate far too early. She changed her plans, alighting from the District Line at Westminster, intending to walk up the Victoria Embankment and then up the Strand towards Aldwych to call for Della at her office.

They could continue together to the South Bank via Waterloo Bridge.

It was only when she was actually halfway across the Thames that she realised that instead of heading along the Embankment, she'd instinctively turned right onto Westminster Bridge. She stopped, turning to look back at Big Ben. A minute to midday. If she hurried, she could almost be safely across and on the other side before it struck the first of its twelve chimes. She'd shunned this bridge for years, sometimes walking out of her way to cross the Thames elsewhere, recalling how she'd wept here on her return to London in March 1941.

Yet her feet seemed to be walking through sand and she couldn't move them quickly enough. A woman in front of her dropped a purse and stooped down to retrieve a handful of small coins. A group of schoolgirls coming the other way insisted on taking up all the pavement so she couldn't pass them.

The first bong sounded. Lucia stopped. She wasn't going to do this. She wasn't going to wait on the bridge as agreed nearly twelve years ago just before war broke out, at a time when her heart had been shattered.

Coming towards her was a small group: a man of about her age with a group of teenaged boys. They stopped too. The man, clearly their teacher, pointed towards the Palace of Westminster and the Abbey. Once his explanation was finished, he wandered on a little, his face thoughtful as he turned it towards the clock.

She looked at him. Her brain was whirring. It couldn't be...

'Lucie?' He looked at her. He took a step towards her. She shrank back. Was she seeing some kind of ghost? The bridge seemed to sway beneath her feet. She grabbed at the parapet.

She'd given up years ago. No word about Sebastien had ever reached her. She could have written to his parents, but once she'd met the man who would become her husband, she'd decided to leave the past in the past. Yet here Sebastien was, in front of her, older, just like she was, face slightly lined. Her mouth opened to say something but nothing came out. She was shaking.

'It can't be you, Lucie, can it?' he said, in English that was more fluent than she remembered. 'I'm sorry,' he added. 'I don't mean to startle you, but it is you, *non?*'

'It's the right place and the right time.' The words came out in a squeak. The world was still spinning.

He came closer. 'I realised what the time and day were as we stepped on to the bridge and wondered if I'd planned it subconsciously.'

'I wondered the same thing. Noon on a Tuesday on Westminster Bridge.'

'Lucie...' His hand was reaching towards her. She released one of hers and touched his. The clasp became tighter. 'Did you come to the bridge during the war? I always wondered.'

'For the first year and a half.' Her heart was still pounding but she was regaining control. 'And I looked for you every time I saw Free French soldiers on the streets or in nightclubs. Until I realised it was unlikely you'd come to London. Even if you did, what good would it have done?'

He nodded. 'The war would have taken me away again. There'd have been yet another parting, more grief.'

She couldn't have coped with parting from him again.

'Last time I heard you were still in northern France, trying to stop the Germans breaking through.'

'When it was obvious the north was falling I managed to get down to Bordeaux with a group from my unit. That was June, 1940. I made it onto one of the last boats out but never reached London. I docked at Portsmouth and was sent on to Canada just days after. I didn't know where to send a telegram to tell you.'

'Canada?'

He smiled. 'Someone thought I could help with the Free

French cause over there. It wasn't what I wanted, I wanted to find you. But then they sent me to the Middle East. After the war I married a Canadian nurse I'd met there.' He swallowed. 'That's where I live now. And you, Lucie?'

She told him about Max. 'I met him in the last months of the war when we were both feeling rather bored with life in the services. He was in the Navy. I was a Wren. He's a barrister.'

'You have children?' He looked stricken. 'Forgive me for asking, I just always hoped... You were such a good mother to our Adèle, and she brought us so much joy.'

'A boy and a girl.'

'I have one of each too.'

She wanted to ask their names and ages but knew it was best not to know details, to keep Sebastien in her past, rounded off, completed, with no regrets. Otherwise she'd be thinking of the child she and Sebastien had lost, the other children they might have gone on to have together. 'You're here for the Festival?'

He nodded. 'In my spare time I'm involved in a youth group. We were sponsored to come to London.' His group was becoming restless, staring at Sebastien and Lucia, nudging one another, muttering and grinning. Monsieur Durand would be the source of gossip in their hostel or dormitory tonight.

'Looks as if their patience is running thin.'

He rolled his eyes. 'They'll be up to mischief in a moment.'

'You should go.'

'I never forget Adèle,' he said, in a rush. 'Never. Every night I say a prayer for her.'

Lucia nodded. Nobody had spoken their daughter's name out loud for so long. 'She was wonderful, wasn't she, Adèle?' She had to speak the name again, roll it off her tongue, feel the softness of it dissolve into the rattle of a tram and the rumbling of a barge on the river below. 'Even if we didn't have her for very long. She looked like my father and my sister. I see it more and more now. I'm glad we named her after Dell.'

His hand on hers was tighter. He blinked. 'Thank God I've seen you, Lucie. And you're well. I never dreamed...'

'I'm glad too, Sebastien.' She released her hand. 'I am happy and I am well.'

'I should have tried to write to you from Canada. I didn't—'

She shook her head. 'We had our time together, with our daughter.'

'It was my fault she—'

She put out a hand. 'Nobody's fault. An accident, as much my doing as yours.'

He nodded, never taking his eyes off her face. She squeezed his hand. 'It seems we were both given second chances.' Her voice was cracking. 'Now take those boys somewhere before they jump off this bridge and cause you all kinds of problems.'

'We could write,' he started cautiously, stopping when she shook her head. 'Perhaps you're right.' He smiled and looked like the boy he'd been in the Cévennes when they'd first met. '*Au revoir*, Lucie.'

With a last glance at him, Lucia walked across the Thames. She didn't look back, reaching the bank before the quarter hour could chime.

A LETTER FROM THE AUTHOR

Dear reader,

Thank you for reading *The Weight of Goodbye*. I hope you were caught up in Lucia's story. If you want to join other readers in hearing all about my new releases, you can sign up here:

www.stormpublishing.co/eliza-graham

And if you would like to sign up for my regular newsletter, please sign up here:

www.elizagrahamauthor.com/newsletter

If you enjoyed this book and could spare a few moments to leave a review, that would be hugely appreciated. Even a short review can make all the difference in encouraging a reader to discover my books for the first time. Thank you so much!

I hope you'll stay in touch – I have so many more stories for you to read.

Eliza

facebook.com/ElizaGrahamUK

instagram.com/elizagraham1

ACKNOWLEDGEMENTS

This book was written with the illness and death of my mother cutting through the process. The theme of mothers and daughters is actually at the heart of the book: Lucia can't cut herself off from the memory of her infant daughter. Her sister and mother have formed a close unit of two in her absence, which she perhaps envies. And Effie is desperate to know what has happened to her missing mother, caught up in an air-raid.

During a series of ambulance trips to A&E departments this year, I've seen Lucia's successors, the paramedics, at work and have been overwhelmed by their professionalism and kindness. Modern paramedics are trained in more skills and technology than Lucia ever was, even if they're not usually going out during air-raids, but share the same resilience and compassion.

The same people's names come up again and again in my personal acknowledgements, showing just how lucky I am to have such a loyal group around me: my husband, Johnnie, my children, Mungo and Eloise, and my brother, Matthew Day, who shouldered a lot of 'sadmin', meaning I could crack on with the edits. Thanks also to my dear and longstanding critique partner, the talented novelist Kristina Riggle, and my fellow authors at the Macmillan New Authors group we formed about seventeen years ago. We're not so new now, but we have not lost our enthusiasm for writing.

Storm Publishing have been so supportive to me over the last year and a bit. My thanks again to Kathryn Taussig and

Kate Smith, and to Emma Beswetherick for seeing what I wanted to do with *The Weight of Goodbye* and helping me do it. My gratitude also to Liz Hurst for her sharp-eyed catches on the manuscript, saving me from myself many times, and to Maddy Newquist for that final, so important, look at the text. Marketing is always the lifeblood of a book launch and I owe much to Elke Desanghere and Anna McKerrow.

Covers are the first opportunity to grab a reader's attention. This one, by Sarah Whittaker, does that perfectly.

Audio is becoming an increasingly important and exciting part of a book's life, and I'd like to thank Naomi Frederick and the audio team for bringing *The Weight of Goodbye* to life for listeners.

A final thank you to Alexandra Holmes for her smooth project management of all the versions of *The Weight of Goodbye*.

BIBLIOGRAPHY

The following books and websites were useful references for me while writing this book.

The Blitz in general

The Blitz
Juliet Gardiner

Wartime Britain
1939–45
Juliet Gardiner

The Myth of the Blitz
Angus Calder

London at War
Philip Ziegler

East End My Cradle
Willy Goldman

An Underground at War
Donald Thomas

Auxiliary Ambulance Drivers

An account of her experiences by Edith Myra Taylor (Messenger).
www.bbc.co.uk/history/ww2peopleswar

Under Fire
The Blitz Diaries of a Volunteer Ambulance Driver
Naomi Clifford

Blackshirts and imprisonment in Wandsworth Prison

Diana Mosley

Anne de Courcy

Feminine Fascism
Julie V Gottlieb

I found a fascinating talk on YouTube, organised by Wandsworth Prison Museum's Curator Stewart McLaughlin:
www.youtube.com/watch?v=KZGTJtFgiJQ&t=930s

Printed in Great Britain
by Amazon

53457044R00189